King of Calamity

BRAD ALLIS

To my mother and father who first inspired me to read and put great books in my hands. To my Aunt Linda, who showed me it could be done.

"I'll be the king of calamity from my high volt throne / I'll hold my court over everyone / All I see is all that I own"
     -The Deadlights, *Falling Down*

1. The Tribunal

T he University of Arizona is essentially a 3/4 square mile, self-contained city. It has its own government, police force, and power plant. The only thing it is lacking from being totally autonomous is its own water supply. Between the hours of 8:00 a.m. and 3:00 p.m. it has a population of nearly 45,000 people, which would make it the fifth largest city in Arizona. Of those 45,000, 33,000 live within 3 miles of the campus. 8,000 of those actually live on the campus itself.

I am one of those 8,000. The name on my driver's license reads Eric Langston Slade. So does the name on the University police report. You can just call me Eric.

Unlike normal society, the University doesn't have a trial by jury system. No defense attorney, no prosecutors, no bailiffs, or judges, or juries. Three-disinterested faculty members mete out Justice at the University of Arizona. These three administrators, who hold my fate and future in their hands, don't want to be here. Somehow they got roped into conducting this hearing. Usually, they hear minor cases, marijuana busts, academic fraud, or fraternity parties out of control. This case was a little more serious and definitely higher priority.

The three inquisitors, two professors, and the vice president of student affairs would conduct this case as they would any case. They would read the report, listen to witnesses, and ask a few questions. After all of this, they will hand out a decision, not based on justice, a strict code of conduct (even though there is one), or even a set of written laws. No, their decision is usually based on what they deem best for the University, which actually means what is best in the eyes of the rich alumni who contribute heavily to the University.

This little theater act, posing as institutional justice, is performed on the fourth floor of the administration building. I imagined my fate would be decided in a dark, dank room, by robe-clad judges. Their faces clouded in shadows. Instead, I walked into a well-lit, nicely furnished meeting room. No water stained brick walls. No torches. Fluorescent bulbs instead illuminated the room.

My three inquisitors sat wearing casual dress, behind two fold-out tables. Their jeans and polo shirts made me feel overdressed. The rest of us sat in metal chairs lined up in front of my judges.

I was sitting next to my father. He had made the two-hour drive from Phoenix to lend some moral support. After all, his little boy was facing expulsion from this esteemed institution. He was wearing one of his many gray suits, which made me feel underdressed. I was clad in brown corduroy pants, a plaid collar shirt, and an understated black tie. I was just casual enough to feel cool and just dressed up enough to look sincere.

I shifted nervously in my seat and surveyed the room. My mother was here as well. My peril leading her to visit Arizona for the first time in four years. Several campus police officers stood joking in the back of the room. The Senator and his daughter sat behind us. Several people I had never seen before, or at least never met, sat scattered around the room.

A reporter for the campus newspaper nodded at me from behind his notebook. Tomorrow I would be on the front page, if there was a front page any more. The Arizona Daily Wildcat went all digital several years ago.

Normally a hearing of this nature goes unnoticed, but today reporters from the state's two biggest newspapers were on hand, as were all the local Television stations. Typically, these inquiries involve drug usage, selling, or distribution. The odd DUI, assault, or fraternity hazing case comes before the board. I'd be willing to bet that this was the first time they heard a case involving a Senator's daughter, kidnapping, and firearm's possession.

The room continued to fill as we waited. I ran my hands through my hair, as I am apt to do when I am stressed or nervous. It was crispy from the extra hair gel I had to use to keep it back. It's a little on the long side, and I usually let it fall around my ears, sweeping it back when necessary. Today I wanted to look more respectable. I shaved, tucked in my shirt, and slicked my hair back. My look was somewhat less than Wall Street but more kept than the guitarist for a garage band.

My judges finally sat down to begin the proceedings. I only recognized one of them. One was the vice president of student affairs who became very unpopular when he suggested canceling several programs, including the much needed Central American Art History Program and Physical Education. Now I like playing softball for credit, as much as the next guy, but if it's the difference between softball and fire extinguishers in the student union, I'll take fire safety. Needless to say, I was enrolled in Softball 101 last fall, and the student union was still a firetrap.

Another woman, apparently an astronomy professor, called the proceedings to order. She went through some official jargon, which I pretty much ignored. The charges against me were read, and then it was my turn.

"As you know Mr. Slade," the gray-haired administrator addressed me. "This is not a criminal hearing, in fact, I believe most of the criminal charges against you have been dropped."

She paused and sipped a cup of water.

"This matter is purely academic," she continued. "We are here to decide your future at this university."

I knew all eyes were on me. I squirmed a bit in my seat. "Um," I started brilliantly. "I'm not sure where to start?"

"Start at the beginning son," she instructed. "Start at the beginning.

2. Big Ed

Then-December

I t was a few days before Christmas. I was back home for the holidays. Final exams had wiped me out, and the prospect of rising before noon was not particularly appealing. However, my father is not one who I wish to argue with, so when he informed me of a 9 a.m. appointment with Senator Ed McCauley I merely shrugged, said "okay", and went off to sulk, and possibly nap.

My father is a hotshot CPA, as are both of my brothers. Needless to say, when I declared criminal justice as my intended major the family was less than pleased. I smoothed things over by saying that criminal justice was a good major for getting into law school. Being a lawyer was a suitable alternative to being an accountant. I wasn't as convincing when I changed my major to history. And we won't even talk about my stint as a creative writing major.

Anyway, my father Alan J. Slade (the J. is for Jameson) made his reputation in finding loopholes in tax reform. I won't even attempt to explain it, but it had something to do with charities, and businesses losing money or something. After garnering fame (or as much fame as a CPA can garner) he moved on to campaign finance. After being on the winning side of countless state and local races, he moved on to the big time. This is where he met and befriended Edwin "Big Ed" McCauley.

"Big Ed", like my father, is a business-first Republican. Much to Dad's dismay, I tend to lean ever so slightly to the left. Considering my differing political opinion, I was somewhat surprised that the senator wanted to speak with me regarding an employment opportunity.

The senator lives in a relatively modest (as modest as one can live in a country club) four-bedroom townhouse, just off of the fifteenth green. It was modeled in southwest design, extra wood, and faux adobe walls. The matching southwestern landscape subsisted of brown volcanic rock and assorted species of cacti.

I got there just a few minutes past 9:00. I rang the bell and was quickly escorted by a plump Hispanic woman to see the senator.

I was deposited into a room that would be traditionally called a study. In this case, it was more like the "Big Ed" McCauley hall of fame. The small office's walls were filled with framed photographs and newspaper clippings. I'm sure if I had taken the time I could have traced his entire political career. The walls seemed to record every famous person he had ever met, every good deed he'd ever done, and every award he'd ever received. I wondered to myself if he bought the frames in bulk quantities.

"Big Ed" really isn't that big at all. He stands about 6'2", but does not have a particularly robust build. I'm about 5'11" and probably outweigh him by 15 pounds.

He was sitting in a high-backed leather chair in the middle of the room, sipping on an orange juice. On a small table was a decanter of juice and two glasses. On the couch next to the senator was a man I did not recognize. He wasn't drinking juice.

The senator was decked out in Arizona winter golf gear, khaki pants, turquoise polo shirt, and a lightweight white sweater vest. He was already wearing his trademarked grin that helped get him elected but looked to me like he was secretly laughing at you just a little bit.

The man on the couch seemed overdressed compared to the senator and myself. He wore a charcoal gray suit and newly shined shoes. The suit looked like a nice one, but didn't seem to fit him right, or else he didn't fit the suit right. It seemed a tad tight in some places but baggy in others. Although it did not fit, it was impeccably pressed. In fact, everything about him was perfectly coiffed, it slightly out of touch with modern styles. His shirt was starched, he wore a shiny, if not gaudy watch, and his thinning hair was slicked back, his mustache trimmed and neat. The only thing the defied the exterior he was trying to present was his hands. They were rough and calloused. They were hands that had known work. He wore the trappings of office life, but he knew another life.

He seemed relaxed enough, his feet stretched out, arms wide on the back of the couch. He was clearly at home in front of the senator.

"Big Ed" stood up and extended his hand. He shook my hand and gave me a wide smile, the one seen on countless campaign stops.

"Eric, I'm so glad you could make it. Juice?" He pointed to the table.

"Thanks," I said helping myself to a glass.

He instructed me to have a seat and I did. I sat down in the other high-backed chair, directly across from "Big Ed". The plush leather seemed to melt around me. I could get used to this.

"So how's hockey going?" the senator asked.

"Still out with the knee injury," I lied. "Probably won't be back until nationals."

"That's too bad," he sympathized.

Until three weeks ago I played hockey for the University. Contrary to popular, or at least widespread belief, Arizona has a pretty decent hockey team. Granted they play less than stellar competition. West Coast teams, club teams from the Midwest and lesser Division 1 programs. They do win more than they lose and draw quite well doing it. A weekend series could easily draw 6,000 drunken, rowdy fans.

I was a prized recruit for the program. An in-state player, who had goaltended in the junior leagues up in the Midwest. My much-ballyhooed signing was a real feather in the cap of the program. I had garnered a decent reputation playing in Iowa and when I turned down a chance to toil in the low minors for a chance to play for a relatively unknown college program, the team got some much-desired publicity.

There was only one small problem--my performance. There was only a small amount of concern my freshmen year when I was unable to beat out the incumbent senior goaltender, despite his less than stellar play the previous year. The grumbling became a little louder when the next season I split time with a junior college transfer and was benched just before the national tournament.

This season I once again was given every opportunity to win the starting role. After two poor performances, I was relegated to platoon status with Kevin Duffy, the aforementioned junior college transfer. By the middle of November, I was clearly second string, though still playing. I was teetering on the edge of slipping to third string when I sprained my knee in practice. To rehab my injury I decided to get drunk with the coach's seventeen-year-old niece. Needless to say, when the coach found out he wasn't happy and did not believe nothing physical happened. Instead of taking my life, he kicked me off the team, at least for the season.

He was kind enough to tell the media that I was injured, that my little ol knee sprain was severe ligament damage, and that "through hard work, and a little luck, we'll have him back for the nationals."

The best I could hope for was to come back next season. The only way I'd see the ice this season is if the coach died or every goalie in town was suddenly out of commission. More than likely I'd never compete on the collegiate level again.

I sipped my juice and made some more small talk. He asked about my classes and the dorms. He said he played golf with my father last Friday. It was all quite trivial, and I was quite bored. I was hoping that he'd get to the point. Now I kind of wish he never had.

"You remember my daughter Caitlin?" he asked. I nodded in affirmation. "Well as you may or may not know, she's a freshman at the university this year."

I did know. I had seen her a few times on campus and told him as much.

He leaned forward and a grave expression overcame the senator's face. "I trust your father with my life, and more importantly with my money," the man on the couch laughed. The senator and I did not. "I'm hoping I can have the same trust in you."

I assured him he could. He turned to the man on the couch, who in turn reeled in his legs and sat up.

"This is Martin Harris," the senator said. "I'll let him explain why you're here."

Harris shook my hand. He had a hard, firm grip. A confident handshake. While shaking his hand I took my first good look at him. Up until then, my attention had been focused on "Big Ed" and his myriad of press clippings.

He was stocky, had a powerful build. He wasn't a bodybuilder, just strong. More like a longshoreman than a weightlifter. With him sitting down, I wasn't sure, but I pegged him at about 5'8". He had dark thinning hair, which he meticulously styled, He had a thin, well-kept mustache and dark eyes. He looked like a cross between a Mafioso and a beat cop. A pinstripe suit or a donut would have tipped the scale in either direction.

"I'm a private investigator," Harris informed me. "Senator McCauley has retained my services over the years. Usually doing background checks on potential employees and opponents."

I read between the lines pretty well. Mr. Harris served two purposes: dig up dirt, and make sure employees were squeaky clean, or at least appeared so.

"All of the jobs I've done have been routine stuff, until now," Harris paused, consciously or unconsciously to add a dramatic effect.

He reached down to the floor and came up with an envelope. He reached into the envelope and pulled out a printed digital photo.

"This was e-mailed about three weeks ago," Harris handed me the photo. It was a picture of the senator's daughter asleep in what I assumed was her dorm room.

"No note, just the photo attached," Harris continued. He reached into the envelope and pulled out some letters.

"Every couple of day's we'd get a new mail, and then they started sending physical letters in the mail." He looked down at the letters and shuffled the papers. "Each a variation of the same theme, 'we know who she is', 'we know where she lives', 'do you love your daughter?' 'How much is your daughter worth to you?'"

I was puzzled. Why were they telling me all of this?

"Each correspondence was postmarked at a post office within three miles of campus," Harris informed. I looked over at the senator. He stared at the stack of letters in the detective's hands. A pained, worried looked came over his face.

"Excuse me," I interrupted Harris as he described how several different printers were used to print the letters. "What does this have to do with me?"

Harris and the senator glanced at each other in a moment of indecision. Finally, the senator picked up the reigns.

"I want you to keep an eye on her," he said. "She's unaware that these threats have been sent and I want to keep it that way."

He took a long swallow of his juice.

"She knows Martin and his presence would raise suspicions."

"Why me?" I asked. "Why not hire a local private eye?"

"Because he'd be noticed," it was Martin this time. "There aren't many college-age P.I.'s floating around Tucson."

"Plus she knows you," the senator added. "If I'm not mistaken you live in the dorm across the street from hers. I realize you're not exactly friends, but I don't think she'd be suspicious if you dropped by to say 'hi'." I could see "Big Ed's" gears turning. "Maybe you could slowly integrate yourself into her circle of friends."

"I'd still need an excuse to drop by," I said, doubting the feasibility of what he was asking.

"We're throwing a New Year's Eve party. Your father is already coming. Why don't you stop by? I'll make sure Caitlin will be there. She'll be thrilled to see someone her own age."

I could tell the senator was thinking hard on this one. I wondered if he spent as much time thinking about legislation, or did he just pick the side that pleased his campaign contributors.

"You'll chat. Find something in common. And presto, you'll have a reason to stop by."

Somehow I doubted I'd find anything in common with the senator's daughter. I bit my tongue and agreed with the plan. What the senator wasn't aware of was that our respected kinds didn't mesh. I'm a beer swilling jock who listens to heavy metal, gambles on sports and enjoys action movies short on plot and long on explosions. Caitlin on the other hand, is a high-grade pot smoking, tree hugging, neo-hippy, Coachella-chick who listens to the Grateful Dead and world music.

An agreement was made on my fee. I was thanked enthusiastically by the senator. He was back in campaign mode, all smiles and handshakes. Martin Harris gave me his card and told me to call anytime, even though he'd call in periodically to check in.

I shook both men's hands again and told the senator I'd see him at the party.

As I drove back home I started to wonder what the hell had I gotten myself in to

3. How I Spent My Christmas Vacation

December/January

I've got to admit the thought of playing private eye excited me. I had read a few mysteries in my time (and you thought I was an illiterate jock). The logical side of me realized I'd just be following Caitlin, taking a few notes. In general, spying on the poor girl. But part of me, my fanciful side, pictured me saving the day. Rescuing Caitlin from the clutches of some fiendish, perverted, would be rapist/kidnapper.

I had visions of me busting through the door of some run-down warehouse. Guns blazing. I'd flip and roll. Never reloading as I fire off a hundred rounds. Blasting away at hordes of marauding evildoers. After defeating the enemy, I'd untie Caitlin and she'd give me a deep long kiss, with the promise of more as my reward.

Just because we run in different circles doesn't mean I don't find Caitlin McCauley attractive. I may not necessarily be in tune with her lifestyle, but there is no denying that the girl is hot.

Caitlin left home, came to college, and discovered marijuana, Birkenstocks, obscure political causes, and minority boys. I came to school and learned the joys of beer, bookies, and girls who play sports.

Before she came to college Caitlin was every parent's dream. Cheerleader, prom queen, Little Miss Popularity. About the only thing she lacked were the grades to get into an Ivy League School, which wasn't a big deal because "Big Ed" was adamant about his little girl attending college "in the great state of Arizona". Well, at least that's how he spun it for the press.

Now she resembles stock footage from Woodstock. Her once colored, overly styled hair, was now long, straight, and its natural color somewhere between blonde and brown. Gone too are the manicured nails and designer clothes. The last time I saw her she wore a homemade sundress and was walking barefoot to class.

She threw away the make-up kit, but in reality, didn't need it. She was good looking any way you spun it. She made a pretty cheerleader and she made a good looking hippy. Her mom was a nice looking older woman, the perfect complement to "Big Ed's" million-watt smile, and it was obvious that Caitlin got the best of her mom's genes.

I saw her briefly at her father's party. It was a swank affair. With many of the Valley's wealthiest dressed to the Arizona nines, which is somewhere along the lines of the East Coast's sevens. Arizonans are notoriously casual. Events that the rest of the country would take for granted as being black tie, are specifically mentioned as such in an Arizona invitation. Hell, I wore high top basketball shoes to my senior prom and didn't have the worst footwear.

I was struggling to find comfort in my sport coat and tie when I spotted Caitlin. I hadn't been at the party long, just long enough to scarf down several hors-d'oeuvres, and half a flute of champagne.

Caitlin looked lovely if less than happy. She was wearing a stylish, yet slightly ill-fitting gown. I realized that she had put on a few pounds since she had gone to school. Unlike most college students, she wore her "freshmen fifteen" fairly well. Unfortunately, from my guesstimation, the dress was purchased before her recent matriculation. It fit a little more snugly than she probably would have liked. Even more surprising than the gown, was that she was wearing shoes. High heeled shoes at that.

As I mentioned before, she looked great. She looked miserable.

We exchanged a few words. Small talk really. After the requisite "How are classes?", "How's the dorm?" etc., etc. After that she politely excused herself, and I didn't see her the rest of the night. Apparently, and I learned this a few days later, she snuck off with one of the caterer's busboys. He got fired, she got a stern talking to, and I was without an excuse to drop by her dorm room.

Some detective I was shaping up to be. Jim Rockford would shake his head in shame. What? I know who Jim Rockford is, I am an avid consumer of old television shows, even if I do watch them on my laptop, downloaded from some sketchy Russian website.

I put my assignment on the back burner for a few days. I had more important things to worry about--New Year's Day bowl games, the NFL playoffs, and exchanging the hideous sweater my aunt Roxanne bought me for Christmas.

When it was all said and done I'd watched seventeen football games, lost $25 on said games, and exchanged the sweater for a home white Phoenix Coyotes Hockey jersey (I already owned a red road jersey). During this whole time, I gave Caitlin McCauley nary a thought.

That was until Martin Harris called.

I was in my room, firmly entrenched in my beanbag chair, watching the Flyers pound the Cannucks when the phone rang. The detective identified himself, made a weak attempt at small talk, something about the Cardinals game this weekend. Then he got to the point.

"I hear the party idea didn't work so good."

"No, not really," I said, ignoring his poor grammar. "She wasn't in a very good mood, not real talkative."

"Hm," was his only reply. Harris stayed silent for a few moments, and I didn't add anything to the conversation. I was more interested in the highlights of the Maple Leafs-Canadians game that was currently on my television screen. Finally, he broke the silence.

"I've got an idea," he said. "You'll enroll in one of her classes. That way you have an excuse to drop by. You can study together or something."

I was already signed up for fifteen units, a full course load, but the thought of dropping an upper-division English-Literature class did not bother me at all. I wasn't sure the plan would work, but if I could avoid reading the complete works of Chaucer for another semester, then dammit, I'd make the sacrifice.

Harris gave me the run-down of her schedule, and we settled on Sociology 101. It was a freshman class. One in which I had already met the requirement, but the time was right, and I figured it would be easy enough. Lord knew my grade point average could use the boost.

I logged onto the school website and within moments I had dropped English 375-Chaucer and added Sociology 101-Introduction to Sociology.

The rest of my vacation was rather uneventful. I went out with some old high school buddies who attend college out of state. I spent some "quality" time with the family. By that, I mean that I was grilled about my career plans (or lack thereof), my love life (or lack thereof), and my collegiate hockey career (or-you guessed it, the lack thereof). Needless to say, by the time January 6th arrived I was more than ready to go back to school.

And that is where the real fun began.

4. SOCIAL SCIENCES 100

My roommate once told me that you could spot a freshman by the clothes that they are wearing on the first day of class. If they have brand new clothes on--freshman. If it was fall semester, then they would be sporting their new school clothes that mommy and daddy bought. If it were spring semester, which it currently was, then they'd be clad in their new Christmas clothes. If his reasoning was correct, and I had no reason to doubt that it wasn't, then I had to estimate that almost five hundred of my classmates, roughly ninety- percent, were first-year students.

I, of course, was in that 10 percent that was not a first-year student, and in reality, as a junior, I had no business being in this class.

The Social Sciences building is not one of the newest buildings on campus, nor is it one of the oldest. The building was constructed in the sixties, and it is stuck there. Fifty-year-old fixtures and furniture are still present. It's old enough that it shows its age, but not old enough where you fear for your safety.

It continues on with the campus' original fascination with red brick, but adds concrete flourishes, especially at the doorways, which are quite ornate. The oldest buildings are all brick, with columns and ivy, which makes no sense in the desert. The newer buildings are concrete, steel, and glass. This one and many of the others built in the 60's and 70's construction boom are somewhere in between.

It's a four-story building that houses numerous offices, classrooms, and on the first floor an auditorium. The notorious Social Sciences 100.

It's a cavernous room. It must seat upwards of 800 students. Professors are forced to use microphones just to communicate with the students. The acoustics are horrible, causing the instructors' voices to echo from the P.A. system. Many times the professors sound more like Darth Vader than a Ph.D.

Most of the freshman "weed out" classes are held here. History 101, Psychology 101, Biology 101, and in this case, Sociology 101.

My freshman year I took three classes in this monstrosity. I remember being in awe of the size as I took my seat. Only twice had I played hockey in front of a crowd this big. Somehow I was expected to learn the intricacies of Psychology here.

The guy next to me, who grew up on the Apache reservation, was in even worse shape. His eyes were wide, and his jaw was even wider. He looked at me and shook his head.

"My hometown doesn't have this many people."

By now auditorium learning was old hat. It was a pleasant surprise when a class had less than one hundred students in it. I feel downright vulnerable in a class of less than fifty.

I took my customary back row, corner seat. Instead of my usual intention, to stay out of the instructor's view for optimal napping. This time I sat in back so that I could scan the entire room. In less than a minute, I spotted her. She looked incredibly bored, resting her head on one hand. She was writing or doodling. I couldn't tell which.

The instructor was droning on about her expectations for the course. Several teaching assistants we busy handing out the syllabus, which was a rarity these days, most just post them online. The professor was in her early forties. She had her curly dark hair pulled up haphazardly so that the curly strands frazzled out and up. She was wearing an unflattering brown dress that looked Middle Eastern or something.

I had heard the first day, introduction to class speech at least twenty-five times in my short college career. So I ignored the instructor and did an inventory of my classmates instead.

This is where I confirmed, using my roommate's clothing hypothesis, that I was in the minority of students who had already survived their freshman year.

The professor was now talking about the University honor code, and how it applied to this class. I had heard it all before and continued to survey the class.

Joining me in the back were several football players. All gigantic, muscled men. Black or white, they all had shaved heads. They all wore Athletic Department issued sweatshirts, some gray, others navy. I recognized one as a preseason All-American linebacker. Another, the smallest of the bunch, was a second-string cornerback who I met at a keg party. He nodded to me in recognition, and I nodded back.

Next, I noticed the packs of sorority clones, err, I mean girls. In one corner were the gals from Sigma Delta Tau. Wealthy East coast Jewish girls with a little too much make up, and a lot overdressed. In the middle of the room, I noticed several Tri-Delts. Tall and athletic, they all seemed to wear nice sweaters and jeans. Finally, near the front were my personal favorites, the women of Kappa Kappa Gamma. They all seemed to be blonde, tan, with nice shapely legs. It seemed as if they all wore gray sorority sweatshirts and had their hair pulled through the back of their baseball caps.

Since there were sorority girls, there were fraternity guys. They seemed to come in two varieties: thin and preppy, or short and slobbish. They tended to be the loudest people in the hall, not needing to pay attention because daddy would get them a job after graduation. Okay, I am sure there are plenty of studious frat boys, but I am biased, both of my brothers were frat boys, and my father got them their jobs.

Of course, I'm being a hypocrite, because my dad would probably get me a job after graduation as well.

Class finally ended and I waited until Caitlin passed to leave. She was with a bunch of her friends. A motley collection of unkempt hair, sandals, and hemp jewelry, she seemed to be heading back to the dorm. I deemed her safe, and headed in the opposite direction, to the student union.

I grabbed a couple slices of pizza and a large coke and sat down to read the sports page. While it was just as easy to read the paper online, I still enjoyed the experience of reading the newspaper. My father still read the paper every morning and I picked up the habit. He would read the front page and finance section, while I would read the sports page and comics. We would hardly say a word to each other, but it was as close as we got to bonding for most of my childhood.

Pretty soon I was more engulfed in the point spreads of the weekend's football games than some hippie senator's daughter.

I took one last swallow of soda, dumped my trash, and headed to one of my "real" classes. As I left the student union my thoughts were on Ellison's "Invisible Man" and not on Caitlin McCauley

5. Clear Cut Case of Serendipity

I t's funny how things work out. As bad as things were going in my attempts to infiltrate Caitlin's life, it was ridiculously simple in how I ran into my first suspect. Actually, it took no special effort on my part. Really it was fate or at least a clear-cut case of serendipity.

The problem was my "brilliant" plan didn't pan out as expected. It should have worked. In theory, it was sound. By enrolling in Caitlin's Sociology class it should have been easy to keep tabs on her. It should have been easy to drop by to compare notes, and slowly infiltrate her life.

One small problem, Caitlin didn't go to class.

I went to the next three classes. Caitlin however, didn't show. Each day I'd take my accustomed rear, left seat, and would wait. Each class a different hippie friend would show up and take notes.

I was stumped. I thought about calling Harris for help, but that would mean admitting defeat, and I hate to lose. Even more, than losing, I hate asking for assistance. I'd rather do a job horribly wrong, or not at all than to ask for help. My mom says that stubbornness is a common trait in the Slade men.

I clearly come from the old school of thought where men don't ask for directions. Heck, I don't even admit I'm lost. I'd rather drive around for four hours than stop and admit I need help. Some may call it stupidity, I call it pride.

So I ruled out calling Harris. If he called me, great. I might even ask him for suggestions. Until then I'd work it out on my own.

The biggest problem I was having was the fact that I had no plausible reason to try to meet up with Caitlin. Although she had the same class as me, she never went to class. We had no common friends anymore and an attempt to start hanging out with her friends would just not work out. They'd spot me as an interloper at best and a narc at worst.

That did not mean I did not get a bit lucky. Although I did not get any closer to Caitlin, I suddenly had someone who I could consider a suspect of sorts.

I'm not even sure why I kept the class. I almost dropped it on a number of occasions. It was a Political Science class that didn't really accomplish anything academically. I had already taken a class that filled this particular requirement.

The class just seemed to me that it would be interesting, and because of my aimless ways, I kept Poli Sci 220: European Political Systems. It was a good thing I did, at least at first.

It would be almost a week before I would discover the benefits of keeping the class. The class was held on Tuesdays and Thursdays at 11:00. Unbeknownst to any of the students, the professor was attending a conference in Belfast the first week of the Semester. Of course, no one informed me, and I wouldn't learn this somewhat important fact until I hauled myself to class.

I had rushed across campus in an effort to be on time. I bypassed the student union, skipping breakfast and the paper, and scrambled to find the classroom, and when I finally did get to the room I noticed a small gathering of students milling around the door. Several talked amongst themselves, while one student tried to open the door, which was appeared locked.

Taped on the door was a single piece of notebook paper with the following message scrawled in magic marker: "No class until next week, read chapters 1,2,3."

I stood and stared at the door for a moment slowly processing the information. Another student tried to open the locked door. I resisted the temptation, as I knew I had no special door-opening powers and went to lunch.

Class finally convened the next Tuesday. I was a week into the semester and already falling behind. The prospect of adding another class load of work was not particularly inviting.

I glumly trudged into class, plopped down into my standard back row seat, and began ignoring class, reading the school newspaper instead.

The professor came to the front of the room and took his place firmly entrenched behind a wooden podium. He looked vaguely familiar, but I couldn't remember ever meeting him. He was in his fifties, wearing wrinkled khakis and a golf shirt.

Although it was still an auditorium-style room, there were only sixty or so students, and at the back of the room I was still only fifty feet from the professor's podium,

I decided to be uncharacteristically polite, so I put down the paper and gave him my less than rapt attention.

The class started out the same as almost any first-day class. His name was Professor Volpe. We would have two midterms and a final. We had to write two papers. Cheating was prohibited, etc., etc.

At some point during the first-day routine, a syllabus wound up in front of me. I was absently staring at the list of requirements when Professor Volpe revealed as my first suspect.

"Many of you are probably wondering what my qualifications are," he said. "For a lot of you my doctorate holds little credibility, and that's understandable."

The professor finally emerged from behind the podium for the first time in 20 minutes.

"I have been teaching political science for over twenty years," he continued. "More importantly I assisted with the first free election in Eastern Europe. I served three terms in the state legislature. And possibly most impressive to you, I ran for, and narrowly lost, the state Senate seat two years ago to a free-spending, well-to-do, conservative Republican from up north."

With those words, I was hit with the proverbial ton of bricks. The venom was easily apparent on Volpe's lips, even if the truth wasn't. I don't remember much of that particular election, even if it was only two years ago. I do, however, remember that "Big Ed" crushed the esteemed professor, garnering 64% of the vote. So much for "narrowly" losing.

McCauley was everything Volpe wasn't. McCauley looked more like a tennis pro, tall, tan, fit, with a fifty-dollar haircut and a manicure. Volpe was also tall, but he was very thin, with a pot belly. He had unruly, curly hair, a big nose, and a bushy mustache.

McCauley was always well dressed, even in his leisure time he wore a crisp shirt and pressed pants. Here was professor Volpe, apparently trying to make a good impression on the first day, donning an old golf shirt and wrinkled Dockers.

"I will refer from time to time to my experiences, both in Europe and here in Arizona," he continued. "And I will try to give you an unbiased view of these experiences, although especially with my prior political career that may prove difficult." http://www.perimeterbicycling.com/el-tour-de-tucson/

He rambled on a bit, but I paid little notice. My mind was racing. Here was a former political rival of "Big Ed", who had publicly expressed his disdain for my employer. Things were going well. I had my first suspect. He wouldn't be my last.

6. Instant Inspiration

B y day that area surrounding the student union is a madhouse. Thousands, if not tens of thousands of people, converge on the area. The grass area in front of the union can become a sea of activity, and there is plenty to look at. So much so it can be a bit overstimulating.

At night it becomes almost peaceful. The campus can become quiet and serene, and it is a nice place to do some thinking. I was taking advantage of that peace and quiet on my way to the union to eat.

My plan was to grab a quick dinner, do some light studying, and then try to figure out my next move in my attempt to save Caitlin. Chuck was off playing chess, and so I decided to grab a sandwich from the student union and go back to the dorm.

I ran into some guys from the dorm and we talked about basketball while we ate. They invited me to a movie, but I declined. I was still puzzling over the Caitlin dilemma.

How could I enjoy a movie when I was shirking my responsibility as a detective?

Well actually it would have been easy, but I decided not to go anyways. Plus it was some second run movie that I had already seen four times and probably owned on DVD somewhere.

I grabbed my dinner, plus a late night snack, and headed off back to the dorm.

Despite being a desert, nights can get cold in Arizona, especially in January. It wasn't frigid or anything, but the night did require me donning a nice, thick Nike sweatshirt. I am partial to the hooded ones, but it wasn't so cold that to pull the hood up. Then again it never is, sometimes fashion has to take precedence over comfort.

When you step out of the Student Union, you find yourself on the mall. Think mall as in Washington D.C., not outlet stores and Cinnabons. The mall is a long patch of grass that extends from Old Main, the first building on campus, to the eastern edge of campus. About half a mile, although a road runs on either side of the grass, half of it is not accessible by cars and is a great place to jog, ride a bike or skate.

During the day the mall is one of the biggest centers of congregating on campus. On a nice day, and most days in Tucson are nice, you will find plenty of students (and some faculty) tossing a Frisbee or football, or playing hacky sack. Other sit and read or eat a meal. It is also where you will find various clubs and student organizations looking for signatures or members. It is where you can get your first credit card, return books at the end of the semester, and heckle a street preacher or a conspiracy theorist.

At night it is less busy, but you can still find an intramural football team practicing and see a jogger or 20. Had I not been pretending I was hurt, I would have considered a run myself, especially since I had put on a few pounds since being kicked off the team.

The area is illuminated by orange street lights that reduce the amount of light pollution for the astronomy department but also gives the campus an eerie glow and almost give the area the appearance of a haze. Since they are designed to give off less glow, they also create huge pools of shadows.

I came up with my next idea In between wondering how I could exercise in secret, and how they keep the grass on the mall relatively green. Nowhere else in town, save for the golf resorts, had anything other than brown straw posing as turf. Even the football stadium abandoned their award-winning sod several years ago to install the fake stuff. While they said it was to give the players a competitive advantage with speed, I could not help but wonder if it cut costs to get rid of grass which required a full team of specialists to maintain.

One of the biggest shocks for people from other parts of the country when the move to Arizona is the lack of grass. Most homes have rock or gravel in their yards. You are more likely to see cacti than grass in a person's yard.

I had not been walking long. Just long enough to get a nice glance of a jogger, who was wearing those short silk shorts that joggers seem required to wear. Don't get me wrong, I love it when the ladies wear them, I just want to tell male runners that long, baggy shorts are better, at least for my eyes.

In this case, the young lady wore the shorts well and I let my eyes linger just a little bit longer after she passed me.

Maybe it was the cool night air, maybe it was the hot jogger, or maybe it was my own brilliance, but it hit me, just like that. It was sudden and instant inspiration. Without warning, it came to me. If Caitlin was not in class, she wouldn't know if I was there either. For all, she knew I was just as truant as she was. Suddenly, I had my excuse to drop by. I could just act like I missed class and ask if I could borrow her notes. Of course, she'd explain that she too had missed class, but that maybe one of her friends had the notes. Since I knew one of her friends was at each class, there should be no reason she would not have the notes.

She would probably ask me to come back a little later and pick up the notes. I had my 'in.'

Suddenly, I was back in business. Thoughts of me and Tom Selleck solving cases danced in my head as I continued my short trek home. What? I already told you that I watched a lot of old cop shows when I was a kid and may or may not avoid studying by watching re-runs.

All I was missing was my Detroit Tigers baseball cap, a shiny, red Ferrari and, of course, a sweet, bushy 1980's mustache.

Maybe I wasn't Thomas Magnum, but I had a plan. I would soon learn that my plans were more than a little dangerous.

7. Exhibition In Stark Contrast

My roommate Chuck and I have come to a compromise. I don't play video games when he's home, and he doesn't listen to opera when I'm around. The beeps and whistles drive him crazy, and I'm not too fond of fat European people reaching high enough octaves to shatter glass.

Compromise has been the key to our survival as roommates. Everything about our room is a compromise. His maps and European flags harmoniously share wall space with my hockey posters. Action shots of goalies sit comfortably next to a map of Scandinavia and the Union Jack. The only mutually agreed upon wall hanging was the Raquel Welch poster from One Million Year B.C. which was made famous in the Shawshank Redemption. We, of course, loved the movie, but we're also fans of the timeless beauty in her cave girl costume.

His opera and electronic dance music alternate on the speakers with my heavy metal and hip-hop. The aroma from his espresso machine almost overpowers the stench of my hockey equipment…almost.

We have successfully coexisted for two and a half years because we are both willing to compromise.

Chuck was much better at cleaning than I was, so I let him do it. That's not to say he was a neat freak, far from it. Like me, he is sort of a slob. But unlike me, he would clean up the room. His messes were new messes. Mine were continuous messes. I had piles that were about to attract the archaeology department.

Since Chuck cleaned, I handled home repairs. It was I who built the shelving unit, fixed his bike and pirated cable from our neighbors. I am quite handy with a hammer, drill and duct tape, especially duct tape.

There were fewer repairs and construction projects than messes, so I also did the cooking. One night a week I'd cook dinner for the two of us. I also prepare meals when he decides to bring a date home for a romantic dinner. Luckily that didn't happen too often. I'm a pretty fair chef. Nothing spectacular, but I can hold my own in the kitchen.

If mine and Chuck's room was a study in compromise, then Caitlin and her roommate's room was an exhibition in stark contrast.

Caitlin's half of the room was a disheveled mess. If Chuck and I were considered messy, then Caitlin's space could be declared a disaster area. Clothes were strewn about everywhere, on her bed, on her chair, on her desk and of course on the floor.

Interspersed with the clothing were food wrappers and aluminum cans. Empty bags of Doritos and pretzels along with almost a case worth of empty Diet Coke cans were scattered all over her side of the room.

Ironically enough her wastebasket was nearly empty and quite possibly the cleanest part of the room.

Her walls were covered haphazardly with assorted torn and faded posters. There was the blue and red Grateful Dead skull logo, a poster of Jimi Hendrix and a big tie-dyed bed sheet. And of course, no neo-hippy's décor would be complete without the close-up, black and white photo of Bob Marley smoking a big, fat joint.

Conversely, her roommate's side was immaculate. No clothes, no foodstuff, only a solitary pizza box sat poking out of her trash can.

Her bed was made, a nice, fluffy comforter covering the barracks-style bed that is standard in the dorms. She even had a plant. A real live, thriving plant sat on her desk.

Her posters were framed, evenly spaced and as best as my eyes could tell, perfectly hung. She had a Monet print, a black and white photo of Audrey Hepburn in "Breakfast at Tiffany's", as well as movie posters from "Gone With the Wind" and "Titanic."

The door was slightly ajar when I arrived there, so I simultaneously knocked and entered. The roommate was sitting at her desk apparently studying. She informed me that Caitlin wasn't around and that she had no idea when she'd be back.

"In fact, I haven't seen here since yesterday afternoon."

"Just tell her that Eric Slade from her Soc class dropped by."

With that, I turned and limped away. My quick 15-second appraisal of the roommate was "cute". She was sitting down, but I guessed that she was short, maybe 5'2", with shoulder length wavy brown hair, that was pulled into a haphazard mini ponytail to keep it out of her face, with little regard for how it would look. Function over form. She was young, most likely a freshman. I thought I picked up an East Coast accent, New York most likely, but it could have been New Jersey.

She was cute, I would even go so far as to deem her pretty, but she was a step or two shy of stunning. She was clearly in study mode, with little or no make-up and baggy sweats. She was a pleasant and pleasing looking girl, and I determined she would likely clean up well, so I thought of her as reasonably dateable.

Two days later I returned and was once again informed that Caitlin was not around. Like the previous trip over there, the roommate had no idea where she was or when she would be back. These two were obviously not the best of friends.

Chatting with her this time I noticed that she had really big, brown eyes. They were so dark they bordered on black. I thought they looked cool, very mysterious like she was always hiding something. This time her hair was down, she was wearing jeans and a t-shirt that fit her better than the baggy attire from the last visit.

I started to leave. I hit the door as my previous analysis of "reasonably dateable" echoed in my brain. Although I was now prepared to upgrade her in the appearance department, that was it. The roommate! If I couldn't keep tabs on Caitlin, then her roommate was the next best thing.

My mouth and body were two steps ahead of my brain. Before I knew what was happening I was already turned around and talking.

"There's this really cool party Friday night," I said. "Would you like to go?"

She looked up from her book looking a tad bit startled. To be honest, I was more surprised than she was. The words were out of my mouth before I had time to think or be nervous.

I do alright with women, but I rarely ask them out like this. Not without provocation, not out of the blue, at least not with a few beers in my system. My romantic entanglements are usually more organic with several bouts of flirting, or several bouts of drinking, spurring it on.

She took a few seconds to appraise me. After determining I wasn't a psycho or more importantly a total loser, she answered.

"I'd like to, but I already have plans," she answered.

Well, so much for my latest and greatest scheme. She was politely blowing me off. Strangely my ego was not nearly as bruised as I was crushed because I was running out of ways to keep tabs of Caitlin.

"But I am free on Saturday if you want to hang out or something," she added with just a touch of sheepishness in her voice.

Bingo! A plan was finally coming together. Maybe I was cut out for this whole detective thing after all.

8. Memories Remain

I was in a good mood. My plan was back on track. My knee felt reasonably good and now I had a date.

Rachel, that was the roommate's name, didn't have any hold on me, I really did not know her at all, but she seemed nice. She was cute, maybe not stunning, but very cute, and certainly someone you could safely bring in front of your friends.

To be honest I was more excited with the concept of a date. It had been months since my last official date and a year and a half since I'd had anything resembling a girlfriend. Oddly enough, I was quite pleased with that. I had done the long-term girlfriend in high school and was enjoying my freedom in college. Unfortunately for my plan to continue my bachelorhood was in jeopardy. Even stranger, I wasn't overly concerned with a potential loss of freedom.

I don't really date much. I prefer to drink beers and watch sports instead of going to the movies or doing the boyfriend routine. Luckily, I seem to be reasonably attractive, or so I've been told. Apparently, I have that 'rugged jock thing' going on. Instead of dating, I usually just settle for the occasional hook up. Most of the time it's just some drunken fumblings with a girl I hardly know. Maybe not the most wholesome activity, but it works for me.

My last "real" date was a disaster. I agreed to go to some sorority formal with a friend of a friend. The girl was really good looking, your typical thin, blonde sorority girl. Definitely a very pretty girl. She asked me to the formal and I enthusiastically agreed. She was fit, tan and apparently had a lot of daddy's money. Combine that with an invitation to an event with an open bar and I was sold.

That was the end of things going well. Before the formal, we went to a nice dinner with several of her sorority sisters and their dates. Apparently, I was the only one not to have Greek letters attached to my identity and was lost for most of the conversation which revolved around parties, fraternity fundraisers and which frats and sororities should lose their charters.

I like to drink. I mean, I'm a college student and a hockey player. Those two things make it a law that I have to overindulge, but it is not necessarily my favorite topic of conversation. By about the fifth story that began with "I was so wasted," I just tried to lose myself in my steak. Occasionally I'd look up and feign interest or laugh when the others laughed, but mostly I tried to shut them out.

I hoped the formal would be better. I hoped that she was a different person alone than she was with the rest of the flock. Sadly, I'd never know. She spent the rest of the night going from group of friends to group of friends. I, of course, got dragged along, having to go through the same introductions over and over.

Despite what 1980's college movies might tell you, sorority girls are not named Buffy and Muffy. Now they have names that sound like strippers. I think I met four Tiffanies and a handful of Amethysts and Jades. I even met not one, but two Mercedes.

I eventually slinked away to a quiet corner and met up with a former teammate of mine. He filled me in on the latest team gossip but seemed to be happier at the party than I was.

After another failed attempt at striking up a conversation with my date, I slipped out of the party. I'm not sure she even noticed. When I ran into her a few weeks later she thanked me for helping her home and that she was so embarrassed that she passed out.

Apparently she never even missed me.

My last girlfriend, my first and only love really, was the girl I dated while playing junior hockey in Iowa. Her name was Maggie. We met my second week there and dated until I left for college. We actually tried the long distance thing, but inevitably it fizzled out. We parted on good terms and still speak frequently.

We met playing racquetball. A coach suggested I take up the game to further improve my reflexes, so me and the team's other goalie, Byron, headed to the local health club for a game. He had played before and I hadn't, so the results were not pretty. While taking a break he spotted a pair of girls playing and decided that challenging them to a game would be a great way to break the ice. Before I could protest, he was off striking up a conversation. Suddenly we had a game.

As we strolled over to the court he whispered to me, "I get the brunette."

There was no doubt why he was interested in her. She was short, pretty and had a huge chest. She wore a sports bra that showed off those assets. She had her makeup perfectly done and had long, painted nails that were not well suited to racquetball. She obviously was used to getting attention and seemed to relish in Byron's advances.

I really didn't notice much about the other girl at first. She was tall and thin, but understated. While the friend had the tight top and the short shorts, she was wearing a baggy t-shirt and long basketball shorts. The friend had her dark hair styled and sprayed, while she had her blonde hair pulled back into a ponytail. It wasn't until we started playing that I took notice.

Jessica, the friend, did not play well and didn't care. She swung haphazardly and squealed when the ball came too close. Maggie did not. She wasn't a great player, but she moved with grace and athleticism. She was obviously an athlete. As she chased down the little blue ball I could tell that she was really fit and had nice legs.

Byron managed to talk the girls into hanging out with us after the game. He was really busy working on Jessica while Maggie and I were sort of forced to watch. Byron and Jessica dominated the conversation during dinner and it wasn't until afterwards that we really got to talk.

While she did not worry about appearances when she was playing racquetball, she did not take the same indifference when we met up later. She was never one to go heavy on the make-up or stray too far from her comfort zone in the way she dressed, but she knew how to dress for her athletic body, and when she was not sweating and trying to kick my ass in racquetball, she was very pretty.

Somehow Byron got them to agree to go to a park, despite the cold temperatures and lack of adequate lighting. It was pretty obvious what his intentions were and did my best to be his wingman and not make Maggie uncomfortable. While their flirtations intensified, we were able to really start talking. She was a high school basketball player at another high school in town. She was really impressed that I played junior hockey as she went to a ton of games with her father and sister.

Byron and Jessica went off for a "walk" and we were left alone. We had this long amazing talk and it was obvious that something was there. Before the disheveled couple returned Maggie and I shared a quick, soft kiss. Nothing intense, nothing overtly sexual, but just sensual enough to cap a really cool evening.

After that we were inseparable…

My spirits were running high when I got back to my domicile. I could hear classical music emanating before I even opened the door.

Chuck was home.

He was engrossed in his studies and tried not to disturb him. Of course the quieter I tried to be, the louder I was. I clipped the table, lost my balance and hit the fridge, knocking over the orange juice bottle. I wound up falling into the side of the trash can, denting it ever so slightly.

Chuck looked up from his book, removed his glasses and said, "Eric, so nice of you to drop in."

I just shrugged my shoulders. One thing I like so much about Chuck is that he rarely loses his cool. I knew he was pissed at me for disrupting his studies, but he kept his cool, which made me feel even worse.

Chuck's mother is French and his father is black. Chuck is the curious combination of both. He has light skin, but his father's African features. He has curly, light brown hair, which juts out at the sides. It's not quite an afro, but it has some height.

His sense of style is flamboyant as well. Lots of colorful shirts and vests. He has a disdain for long pants and usually wears shorts year round. His collection of shoes is both vast and eclectic. He must have at least 50 pairs, some in colors that you only see in a box of crayons.

I plopped down on the couch and picked up a school book. After twenty minutes I was reading a novel on my phone. I was ignoring my academics and focusing on the adventures of a southern lawyer.

After about an hour of reading, I had had enough of the written word.

"Chuck," I began, tossing my tablet aside.

He looked up, just slightly agitated and waited for me to continue.

"You have a choice," I continued. "You can either get a beer with me or I play video games."

Chuck put down his book and glared at me.

"First round's on you."

9. Fight for Your Right to Party

The rest of the week went by in a blur. I saw Caitlin hanging out around the campus, talking with her usual assortment of hippy friends. I called Harris with what I had seen, disappointed that I didn't have better news, but he seemed pleased.

I got ready for the party in my usual manner. A two-minute shower, a little gel in the hair, deodorant and a dash of cologne that would go unnoticed with all of the smoke in the air at the party. I wanted a look that was nice, but not obviously nice. I wanted to look good, but not like I went out of my way to look good.

I settled on a dress shirt, which would go untucked. I threw on jeans and was done getting ready in less than 30 minutes. I was on the couch and ready to go when Chuck emerged from the bathroom. Seeing this I knew we wouldn't get on the road for at least 45 minutes, so I turned my attention to video games.

To his credit, Chuck was ready earlier than I thought he'd be. I timed him at 37 minutes.

We met up with some other friends in the lobby of the dorm and I soon realized what a motley group we were.

Mike Gillen was the dorm's resident guitarist. He was the guy who was always playing guitar but was never in a band. He could play about 2/3 of any song, but I'm not sure if he knew more than five complete songs.

He wasn't a huge pothead but sure seemed like it. He always looked half asleep and spoke very slowly. The only way to tell if he'd been imbibing was to look at his eyes. If they were glassy and bloodshot he was stoned, just bloodshot and he was merely Mike.

I liked having Mike along because we could talk music. His tastes were even more extensive than mine, but we had a mutual love for loud, aggressive music. The kind Chuck rarely let me listen to when he was around.

He wore what he always wore, tattered jeans, flip flops, a dirty t-shirt, and a backwards baseball cap. The only question would be whether his long hair would be worn down or in a long ponytail.

He wore it down.

"Little" Mark was a freshman who attached himself to us. He was this tiny Asian-American kid who was a kind of a geek. He was maybe 5'0" and weighed less than 100 pounds.

Occasionally we'd get drunk and play catch with him. We'd literally toss him back and forth across the room.

We hoped that after four months in college he'd tone down the obsessed sports fan look but it had only gotten worse. Tonight he wore a tent-like baseball jersey that made him look even smaller.

In addition to loving sports Mark was kind of our resident computer geek. The only thing he liked more than sports was computers. He was the kind of guy who loved Star Trek and role-playing games, but his true passion was sports. He was a lot to take in one sitting, but he knew his stuff. I often picked his brain before placing a bet.

The best, and worst, aspect of Mark's personality was his incessant need to please. Sure it was cool when he'd go down to the vending machines to grab you a soda, but cooking us dinner was going overboard.

We entered the party. Some of the guys wanted to do a lap to scope out the girls, as well as the competition, but I insisted we make a beeline for the keg.

With beers in hand, or hands as I was double fisting, we staked out a corner in which to survey the room.

The space in the apartment was fairly limited with all of the bedroom doors closed. The party was now contained to three rooms, the television room, a small dining room, and the kitchen. The furniture was pushed to the sided of the room to make more room for party goers. The place was already filling up and top-40 music was blaring from tiny speakers.

"Whose party is this?" Mike asked, his first beer half finished.

"A girl from French class," Chuck informed. Chuck had dual citizenship from both France and the U.S. but was a French major. He already spoke fluent French but wanted a good undergrad GPA to boost his chances at Grad school.

Chuck getting a degree in French would be like me getting a degree in eating sandwiches.

At that moment Chuck spotted the hostess and went over to say hello. They exchanged quick pecks on the cheek and started conversing in French. Knowing Chuck's love for anyone who'd speak with him in French, it was clear he was lost for the evening.

I assessed my situation. On my left was Mike, who would be well on his way to intoxication before I knew it. Mike was normally a quiet fellow, but I knew he'd get feisty from the beer. He'd start ranting and raving about this band or that band. By my count, we had argued at the last seven straight parties over the merits of David Lee Roth vs. Sammy Hagar as lead singer of Van Halen. Mike preferred Diamond Dave, I preferred Sammy. No one else at the party knew who we were talking about.

Mike headed to get more beer. I turned to Little Mark. I knew invariably our conversation would turn to video games. Normally I'd try to turn the conversation to something else. Women, sports, movies, hell, anything other than his video game exploits.

Mark was still droning on and on about the new NBA game when Mike came back. I was doing my best to ignore the video Nets highlights. Occasionally I'd nod my head or say "oh really?"

I sipped one of my beers and scanned the room. I recognized a face or two, but most of the people here were strangers.

Mark had moved on to a description of some racing game, Mike was getting drunker and I was soon out of beer. I excused myself and went back to the keg. If I was smart, I would have brought a 44-ounce convenience store fountain soda cup and filled it with beer. It would have saved me several trips to the keg. As it was, I was filling up two cups and making due with cutting my trips down by half.

I was topping off the second cup, the first delicately clinched in my teeth. I was trying not to make any sudden moves so I would not spill the first beer all over my shirt when I heard the squeaky voice.

"Eric, how's the knee?" she asked.

"She", was Wendy Zink, sophomore soccer sensation. A 5'6", 105-pound dynamo on the soccer pitch. For such a small person she was amazingly aggressive and tough when playing the game. She was also incredibly attractive. She had these stunning blue eyes and like most soccer players, a near perfect body. She also had recent knee surgery.

I transferred the beer from my mouth to my hand and looked down at her a bit dumbfounded. The knee sprain had all but healed, and occasionally I forgot that I was supposed to be suffering from cartilage damage.

"Oh, it's not too bad. I may actually be back for nationals." Not unless every other goalie in the state came down with the plague I thought to myself.

"How's rehab? I haven't seen you with any of the trainers."

Again I was forced to lie "I'm doing it on my own, away from the athletic program. My dad hired some hotshot rehab guy that he thinks will speed up the progress."

She smiled, gave me a little pat on the arm and left me to my beers. I stared intently as she left the room.

I started to head back to my compatriots when Mark intercepted me.

"You know that 17-year old hottie that got you kicked off the hockey team? She's here."

I don't know what surprised me more. The fact that she was here, or that Little Mark knew the truth about my dismissal from the team. As far as I knew only Chuck knew. He must have got drunk on rum and told Mark. Chuck can't hold his rum and is prone to ramblings and a lot of puking when he drinks the stuff.

After I reminded myself to kill Chuck I let Mark's warning run through my head, along with Coach Kovalev's warning: "If I ever catch you within five miles of my niece again I'll kill you."

As I understood it, Anna Kovalev had been a fixture around the hockey program since the age of eight. She first served as a stick girl and later moved to the promotions side of the program. At the age of 12, she began selling souvenirs and programs.

Around the age of 13, she discovered boys and beer, and more specifically, hockey players. She was barely fifteen when I joined the squad and was already a fixture at team keggers. There were always rumors that she was sleeping with a number of players. No one would admit it, but there was always a hearty debate about who was scoring with Anna.

Sometime around my sophomore year, she started showing an interest in me. It was flattering, Anna hardly looked 17, more like a 23-year-old stripper. But with me being a law-abiding citizen, and also having my scholarship depend on her uncle, I kept my distance. We flirted a little bit, but I was able to keep my distance, but only to a point.

In addition to being a stick girl, she was also very responsible for the marketing and promotion of the team. She helped manage the team's social media accounts and helped the team transition from just a regular terrestrial radio presence to doing a variety of online shows and interviews.

Once she took over the social media accounts, they transformed from a standard, straightforward dispensing of information, to a more playful, yet incisive platform. She found a balance between being entertaining, and informative, and utilized her own personality (and looks) to expand the reach.

She interviewed me for a video segment or two, but other than that and a few brief "hellos", I said I kept my distance.

That was until December.

It was relatively innocent. Really, it was. It was right after I hurt my knee. At that time it had not been diagnosed as a sprain and there was still some concern that it was a torn ligament. I was sitting in my room, three beers into a bender, an ice pack on my knee, watching TV. There was a knock on the door and Anna slinks in, a six pack in each hand.

She was a dichotomy of hotness. Not overly tall, but leggy. Not big breasted, but you could not miss them. She knew how to pick her shirts, or bras, or both. She did not wear a ton of makeup but still remained sultry. She was simultaneously the girl next door, yet slutty-hot.

I put up a mild protest, but the throbbing in my knee told me to drink up. We put way the six packs and put a huge dent into a bottle of tequila. Although she was looking good, dare I say great, and more than willing, I didn't touch her, I mean it. She gave me a long, deep kiss as she left, but that was it.

Soon word got back to her uncle, except the story seemed to have switched to me providing the beer and trying to get into her pants. With that my hockey career was in all likelihood over.

Since then I'd done my best to avoid her, as per the coach's demands. Part of me wanted to stick it to her just to spite him, but he was good enough to allow me the dignity of the cover story and I abided by his wishes. So far I had been rather successful in avoiding her.

Tonight, however, my luck would more than likely run out.

I tried to slip out of the party unnoticed. Anna was busy talking to a bunch of her friends and taking pictures with her phone. I was halfway home when a heavyset girl in her entourage pointed in my direction. Anna swung around and saw me. A sly smile spread over her face. Defeated, I stopped walking to the door as she headed over.

She was about a head shorter than me. She was wearing a little sweater, cut to show off her midriff. It also showed off her breasts. As I mentioned she knew how to pick her bras and shirts. I couldn't help but notice.

"You've been avoiding me," she accused, giving me her sexy little smile, she pulled the phone back out and snapped a selfie of her and I. I was startled and probably had a dumber look on my face than normal.

"What? No," I denied. "I just haven't seen you since the injury. I'm not around the rink that much."

She leaned in closer, I could smell her perfume. "We both know it was just a knee sprain."

I was not sure what to say, so I stayed silent and stared down at her.

"So what are you going to do with all your free time," she said in a way that was both inquisitive and suggestive at the same time.

I made my best attempt at sounding both cool and interesting but probably failed at both.

"Play video games, drink, and read," I said.

Her demeanor changed, and she got visibly excited.

"I read the best book over Christmas break," she exclaimed.

She looked down at her phone, touched the screen a few times, and then looked back up at me. At that moment my phone buzzed, announcing a text message.

She had sent me the link to a novel about a small town whose very identity is shaped by the local junior hockey team and how the community reacts when one of the star players fails to live up to the adulation that the community bestows upon him.

It sounded interesting, like something I should have read, but I have to admit I hadn't even heard of it. I considered myself an avid reader. On road trips, I would have an e-book loaded on my phone and pack a second paperback in case we were going to be on a bus or in a van for an extended period of time that would cause the battery to die on my phone.

My teammates called me a "bookworm" but I was hardly reading great literature. Although I have taken several lit classes in my time in college, if given my choice to read for pleasure I gravitate towards, ironically enough, mysteries, as well as spy novels and legal thrillers. If I am feeling particularly highbrow I might choose the biography of a musician or athlete.

"It sounds good," I said. "I may need to check it out when I am done with my current book."

I did not tell her it was a very popular legal thriller that had been made into a mediocre movie and sold millions of copies.

"Right now I am reading a book on female journalists," she added. "I am hoping to utilize some of their techniques in my interviews with the team, but it is hard to find time to read it with classes starting up again."

"I just ignore my school work and read paperbacks instead," I said truthfully but hoping she thought I was kidding.

Whether she thought I was kidding or serious, she did not let on. Our moment of serious conversation disappeared and she got flirty again. She gave me a devilish smile and texted something else. I was already looking at my phone when the text came through. It was a book written by a porn star about spicing up your sex life.

While staring at my phone screen, she moved in even closer. I could feel her breath on my neck. "I could talk to Uncle Vic and get you back on the team."

She tiptoed and whispered in my ear. "All you'd have to do is finish off what we started."

She pulled away, turned on her heel and walked back to the group. She looked over her shoulder and said, "you have my number."

*   *   *

"How did you not hit that?" Mike asked incredulously.

The night had gotten a lot colder, but we were too drunk to care. We were staggering home from the party, passing a small bottle of vodka we bought at a convenience store. We did not stay much longer after my encounter with Anna.

"She's still in high school," I answered.

"Yeah but she's a senior," Mike countered.

"She's seventeen," I shot back.

"So?" Mike and Mark replied.

I turned to Chuck for help.

"C'mon, you see where I am coming from?"

"Nah, she's freaking hot," he answered. "You should have gotten with her."

I can neither confirm nor deny that when I went home I looked Anna Kovalev up on social media. If I had, I would tell you that I was quite impressed with the pictures of Anna in a half shirt and cut off jean shorts. Oddly enough, I was also impressed with her video interview with the team's freshman right winger Steve Terry, and how he has made the adjustment from prep school hockey to college. I can neither confirm nor deny which I found sexier.

10. A Lazy Saturday

I found myself getting more and more excited for the date. I didn't think I would, but I was looking forward to it. I kept telling myself that I was just doing my job, going out with Rachel to keep tabs of Caitlin, but that wasn't the whole truth. I wanted to go out with her.

I thought about it and I realize maybe I just needed some female companionship. In high school, Lacey and I were always together. Here I was always hanging out with guys, whether they were my teammates or the guys in the dorm. Sure I was occasionally hooking up and scratching that itch, but part of me was craving more. Maybe I just needed a female's touch on my life.

I woke up on Saturday a little bit after 11. I didn't drink enough to be hung over, but I did have enough beer that I got a nice long, sound sleep.

Chuck was gone when I awoke, but that was natural. Even on weekends, he was up early and off doing something academic. I should have done the same. Instead, I poured a bowl of cereal and watched the end of the Saint Louis/Marquette game. I didn't have money on this one, but the next few hours would have a number games that I had some action on. Basically, I was going to waste the early part of my day watching college basketball.

Miami upset Duke and Kansas crushed Oklahoma, but Kentucky covered the spread against Vanderbilt, so all in all I won was $50. Not too shabby for a lazy Saturday, but not nearly as much as I could have made had the stupid Commodores hit their free throws down the stretch and at least made the game close.

I'm not a compulsive gambler, but I do it frequently enough. As an athlete, I wasn't allowed to work and needed to supplement my income. At least that is how I excused it. My father sends me money, a generous amount at that, but his checks were usually accompanied by a lecture. In addition to his "words of wisdom," I was also required to turn in my receipts and an expense report. Yup, I had to files my expenses like I was a salesman.

It's kind of hard to get beer money when you have to provide a receipt. You can't lie and say you needed to buy "another book". I guess that's the downfall of having a CPA father.

My foray into gambling started as soon as I moved into the dorms. I was dropping $5 a week on a football pool. After winning the pool three of the first six weeks I was approached by my first bookie. Pretty soon I was dropping $10 a football game. I ended up winning $100 on the World Series and for a lack of a better word I was hooked.

My current bookie is a 350-pound Texan by the name of Ike. Obviously, he usually is referred to as "Big Ike". At one time one of his clients tried to dub him "Tiny" but that didn't take and the guy was rewarded with a busted jaw the first time he tried out the new nickname.

Ike rarely leaves the house and I don't think I have ever seen him without his faded Texas A&M ball cap. It used to be a dark maroon, but now it is more of a sweat-stained pink.

Ike has lived in the same house for as long as I have been in school and apparently many years before that. He's still in school, at least technically, but I don't think he has any real desire to finish that double major in mathematics and computer science.

His place is a little one-bedroom about a stone's throw from campus. A realtor would probably tell you that the hardwood floors would make the resale value high on the place, but Ike is not concerned with the value of the house. Almost every square inch is devoted to his bookmaking. He has about seven televisions in the house and I've never not seen them all on. Usually, they are tuned to sporting events, but occasionally he'll have a cable news network playing if there aren't enough sports for each screen.

The walls of his house are all covered with dry erase boards. The latest lines are posted and updated hourly. If you are a client, you can walk in uninvited to see what odds are being given. He subscribes to three newspapers, five sports magazines, and no fewer than 10 betting magazines. All of these can be seen scattered around the house, a virtual sea of newsprint and glossy magazine pages.

One side of the room has two desktop computer stations set up and everyone there has a laptop open, buzzing the internet on a wireless connection. While the computers were high tech enough to be an ultimate gaming or multi-media the latest rumors or injury information could be found. machine, their sole purpose was to be logged onto the offshore betting houses and sports websites where

Ike had four full-time employees. Two Indian guys did most of the legwork around the house. One was named Sanjay and the other Kip. As bad as it sounds, I didn't know which was which. They were brothers from Mumbai who were in the computer science program (or was it mathematics?) with Ike but slowed up their academic pursuits for a $30,000 a year job helping to run the book.

Ike's brother Rod served as his right-hand man. He was always hovering around Ike when he wasn't out collecting money or finding new clients. It was Rod who enlisted me into Ike's services. Rod is as skinny as Ike is fat. He's tall, with a hook nose. He's a redneck version of Ichabod Crane, though I'd never tell him that to his face. He may be skinny, but he's tough as shit. If Ike didn't have an enforcer, Rod was mean and tough enough for the job.

No, Ike had a better man of the job of enforcement. Omar Sanders used to play defensive end for the school. He wasn't a particularly talented player, but he was tough. He played at 245 then, but was probably over 260 now, all of it pure muscle. By looking at him I could guess that they don't test for steroids when you work for a bookmaker.

Omar had a shaved head and was covered in tattoos. He was working on getting a sleeve on his right arm, in essence covering every inch of skin from his wrist to his shoulder. He was light enough skinned that you could see the work and it was quality work. Most of the tats were of a dark variety. A lot of demons and dragons, plenty of skulls and monsters.

He had a reputation as a cheap shot artist when he was playing. He always worked hard but was known for his toughness and for being a bit dirty. He picked up his share of late hit flags. If he was on your team he was the player you loved because his motor was always running. If you had to play against him he was a player you hated because there was a good chance you'd have one of your players get hurt.

Ike rarely left his house, but when he did he took three cell phones with him. You rarely saw him without one of his phones on his ear and often he was passing a second to Rod. He also had a couple of tablets that displayed nothing but scores and lines, or the latest game off the internet. It was not uncommon to see one of the tablets showing a cricket or jai alai match.

My wagers now rarely drop below $25 a game and usually push $50. Quite frequently I get a good feel on a game and I lay down $100. I win more than I lose, but just barely.

I knocked on Ike's door and walked in. I was well enough known that I didn't need to be invited in, but they liked a little warning. One of the Gupta brothers was on a laptop in the kitchen, which was separated from the main room by a counter but was essentially part of the room. The other was changing lines on one of the dry erase boards.

Ike was sitting on a couch, cradling a phone on his ear, watching the final moments of the Houston/Dallas NBA game. He was jotting things down in a notebook and had a half-eaten hamburger in front of him.

Omar was sitting off to the side playing a game on his phone.

Ike motioned for me to sit down by him and I did so. After a moment he hung up the phone and I told him I wanted to cash out my winnings.

"Sure, Sanjay double check what we owe him and get him his money," Ike ordered. The brother behind the kitchen counter typed a few things into the laptop and then headed to the back bedroom.

"What's the line on the Carolina game tomorrow?" I asked, trying to find it on one of the numerous boards.

"Right now it's the Heels giving four and a half," he answered, not even looking.

"If it drops to three, give me a call." He agreed and we chatted for just a moment.

"By the way," he added at the end of our conversation. "There's some rumors out of So Cal that one of the smaller schools may have a guy or two shaving points. I'm still looking into it but I'm taking them off the board. One of them is a former high school teammate of a guy on the hoops team, so if you hear anything fishy let me know."

"How do you hear this stuff?" I asked, remembering that he had known about several unreported football injuries last fall.

"I always have my ear to the ground," he answered. "I gotta keep informed with everything. All it takes is one cheating girlfriend and suddenly you have an unstable kicker or an ineffective pitcher. Sick parent? Stay away from that guy. Anything and everything can make a difference."

Sanjay gave me my money and I excused myself as Ike went to answer another call.

In keeping with my theme of not trying too hard, I went fairly casual for the date. I put on a plain black t-shirt and tucked it into a pair of jeans. I debated whether to stick with sneakers, but settled on a pair of casual boots. I did actually wear a wristwatch. I usually don't wear a watch, relying on my cell phone for the time. I also spritzed on just a touch of cologne. Honestly, the only way she'd know that I had on any was to get close. I didn't foresee that happening, but a guy can hope. I capped it off with a weathered leather jacket that probably isn't as cool as it sounds.

Rachel answered the door more dressed up than I was. She wore a tight fitting sweater, a skirt, and heels. She looked nice enough to let me know she was trying, but not so much that she looked too anxious. I had to wonder if she was playing a game herself or if this is what she just felt would be nice to wear.

As she stood at the door I realized I had never seen her standing up. Every time I came over she was sitting at her desk. Seeing her standing up I realized she had a better body than I had thought. She was thin and firm. I guessed maybe she ran or at least tackled a stair master from time to time.

She was not quite ready so she invited me in. She looked good to me, but I learned a long time ago that you don't hurry a woman getting ready to go out.

As she returned to her mirror I was surprised to discover that Caitlin was actually home. She was laying on her cluttered bed next to someone I soon recognized as a local celebrity.

Tariq de la Roca was a University legend in the making. He was an outspoken activist with numerous causes under his belt. You could hardly go a week without seeing his name in the student newspaper. If there wasn't a story about him then there was a letter to the editor from him.

His causes were well known, as were a number of rumors about him.

It is said that his father is from Mexico and has some Aztec (or is it Mayan, I always confuse those two) blood coursing through his veins. His mother is African-American according to those same rumors. By looking at his features I assumed this to be true although he could have also had some Asian in him as well.

He had nappy, out of control hair that lingered somewhere between an afro and dreadlocks. His features leaned more towards his African heritage, but his complexion was more a product of his Spanish/Indian blood.

From my understanding, he fancies himself a bit of an Aztec (or is it Mayan?) warrior, instead of bloodshed his fight was the fight of social injustice. He had been here as long as I had and from what I heard he was in his sixth year and apparently he had no intention of going anywhere.

He tried to be a champion of many causes. He fought to establish a Mexican heritage department. He protested telescope construction on Indian land. He led a boycott of the athletic department because they signed a sponsorship agreement with a shoe company that farms out most of their factory work to Southeast Asia.

His current cause was fighting for the rights of the city's homeless population. Just last November he led 50 homeless people into the student union where he bought them Thanksgiving dinner and invited them to spend the weekend inside the building. I have to admit that it was a nice gesture, but the University administration and University police did not agree.

Even though he was leading people to trespass, it was the school that looked bad. He smartly had the television cameras on hand as police officers asked the people, many families with small children, to leave the premises. He was good. He knew how to use the media and he knew how to promote himself.

They were all over each other, sharing a can of BBQ Pringles. They were laughing and giggling, oblivious to my entrance and indeed, my very presence.

Rachel had moved from the mirror to a small jewelry box, looking for what I could only assume was jewelry. See, it was obvious that I was a natural detective with my power of detecting the obvious. While her search went on I ventured over to her desk and noticed she had her music collection on the screen.

I'm a CD and vinyl record junky. I know most kid's music collections are completely digital, and I myself have a cell phone full of songs, but I like the tactile experience of putting on a record or popping in a CD. I probably own well over 500 discs of the compact or vinyl variety. I'm oddly drawn to them like a bug to a light. I can spend hours in a record store without a dime in my pocket. When I enter a new room, invariably I find myself looking to see if someone has a music collection. If they do, I can spend a long time sifting through rows of plastic cases. This makes the digital mp3 age so frustrating. While no one minds you browsing their CD collection, grabbing their iPod, or worse, logging onto their computer can really annoy them.

She looked over and I pointed to the screen, and she gathered that I was asking permission. She nodded affirmative and I began judging her musical tastes.

I was somewhat impressed. I was prepared for the worst. I expected a lot of bad pop music or modern country. She had the pop, but she also had some classic rock and a few alternative albums that I held in some regard. She also had a ton of film scores. Not just soundtracks with songs, but classical scores.

I debated whether or not to say something to Caitlin. I wanted to establish a relationship but didn't want to come off as a dork by forcing something. Caitlin opened the door for me.

"I know you," Caitlin said pointing and giggling. "You're Eric, you know my dad or something."

"Yeah, we used to have some friends in common," I noted.

Tariq gave me the once-over and then turned to Caitlin.

"Another spoiled rich kid I assume."

"I think so, his dad worked for my dad I think," Caitlin said, a bit confused.

"I assume that your father is not the gardener or chef," he said, nearly spitting out the words.

"No, he's an accountant," I said, regretting my words as they escaped my lips.

"Finding tax loopholes no doubt," he said, his contempt obvious. "Helping the rich stay richer. Making the poor pay for a system that rarely benefits them."

"I wouldn't know," I weakly added.

"Of course not," he said. "You just cash daddy's checks and assume he is a good guy. Your kind never looks closely where the money comes from, as long as it comes."

I knew I should have avoided a confrontation, but I couldn't help it. Rachel tried to diffuse the situation by announcing that she was ready, but I held her off.

"I'm not going to pretend I come from some deprived situation. I'm not going to pretend I am dialed into the woes of the world like you are. But I am here because of my hard work. I'm in school on a scholarship that I earned with my hard work. I don't know what my dad does, because I hardly know him. I left home at 14 to pursue my sport. I lived with host families in two countries in an effort to improve myself."

He interrupted me.

"Oh, you're some kind of jock. The only thing worse than some rich kid is a jock rich kid."

Rachel ushered me out of the room before any more trouble could ensue. It was obvious that I was losing my temper and she was smart enough to curb the confrontation before it escalated.

"I'm sorry," I said once we were outside.

"That's okay. He is so pretentious. He is always putting me down. He's subtle, it's almost as if he thinks I don't understand what he is saying. He thinks he is so smart."

We left the building and headed to my jeep.

"The problem is that he is smart," I noted. "That's the problem. He may be a pretentious fuck, but he's a smart pretentious fuck.

11. Deception as Truth

n my attempt to impress by not impressing, I chose a fairly seedy restaurant for dinner. Leo's has outrageously good food, but the place is a hole in the wall situated between an indoor gun range and a strip club. From the outside, it looks like it should be a bail bondsman's office, not the place with some of the best Mexican food in town.

The look on Rachel's face when we pulled into the parking lot and she caught a glimpse of the strip club's neon sign was classic. Any first date between relative strangers can be awkward, but add an unconventional soundtrack in the car, and a less than scenic drive to a hidden gem of a restaurant, and you can imagine the unsure look on her face as we pulled into the parking lot.

Tucson is known for their Mexican food. From upscale restaurants in the foothills to small family places on the Southside, to food trucks and small taco stands, there is good Mexican food all over town. Some of the oldest restaurants in the west are local Mexican restaurants, and there are places in the Hispanic neighborhoods that are world famous, attracting famous actors, musicians, and even a U.S. President.

This restaurant was midtown, in an area known more for antique stores and dive bars, rather than world-class Mexican food. A convenience store made most of the small strip shopping center invisible from the main street, and the gaudy neon of the strip club is what attracted the eye.

You pretty much had to know the restaurant was there because it was nondescript from the outside and hard to see from the street.

The inside is not much better. Every expense was spared on the décor. There were some cheap, faded crepe paper streamers that look like the came from a Cinco De Mayo celebration from the 80's. There are a few sombreros and maracas thrown up for good measure, almost as if someone informed the owner that there was a county code that said that every Mexican eatery had to have them displayed in the wall. Other than that there are a few neon beer signs and a faded Mexican soccer poster.

The tables are plain and the chairs have an orange faux leather that has not been used in mass production since the early seventies.

The lighting probably makes things dingier than they really are. The weak neon bulbs give off a jaundiced light that makes everyone look just a tad sickly. Half the time you get a couple of bulbs fluttering which can give certain corners a strobe effect.

The scenery outside is bad as well. The place actually sits behind a convenience store. As ugly as they are from the front, they are worse from the rear. Nothing like a view of a dumpster and piles of old boxes while you eat. Sometimes you get lucky and some of the neighborhood kids will tag the store. Sometimes their vandalism borders on art, but mostly it consists of misspelled curse words and not-so-clever nicknames.

The strip club takes up most of the view. The parking lot is always full and there is some great people-watching as the patrons go in and out. Most of the guys look normal. Just college kids out having fun, or construction workers letting off a little steam. There are always a ton of businessmen in their suits handing out singles. Once in a while, you get the weird guys. Most seem harmless. Awkward guys for whom the club is the only way they'd get to see a naked woman up close. Sometimes the guys are just a little strange. There is that something that you cannot quite place. They look like the kind of guy who would be a stalker or even worse. In reality, they are probably the nicest guys in the world, but at first glance, they give me the creeps. I can only imagine what it must be like to have to dance for them.

Occasionally you can see one of the dancers leaving the building and that is always kind of fun. Most fail to change out of their skimpy clothes. Nothing like a girl walking to her car in six-inch heeled go-go boots and a shorter than short mini skirt.

Other times it is just the opposite. You see these fairly attractive girls leaving the club with dingy sweats. Nothing like spoiling the illusion ladies.

The ride over was pleasant, but first date awkward. I played a mix of unusual music, my guess it was nothing she had heard, in an attempt to seem cool. The playlist stared with mid-tempo blues, then some quirky rock songs, with some odd world music and even some hip-hop to keep her guessing. Nothing too slow that it seemed that I was getting ready to put the moves on, but nothing so rocking that we could not talk.

Walking to the car I noticed she smelled good. All too often, girls my age smell like candy. I am not sure if it is their perfume, lotion, or body wash, but they smell like fake fruit, fake vanilla, or some other kinds of baked goods. If they don't smell like a Starburst or a bad candle, then they buy expensive perfume and wear too much of it.

Whatever Rachel was wearing was subtle. She obviously not only knew how to pick a pleasant scent, but knew how much, or how little of it to wear. I could only notice it when we were standing next to each other, or when we were in the car. I did not have to worry about staying upwind from her to avoid having cheap perfume inundate me.

The restaurant is about four and a half miles from campus, a straight shot down Speedway Blvd. In the 1970's some Life Magazine called it the ugliest street in America, but near campus, it looks like everywhere else. For the first two miles, it is just a collection of turn of the century strip malls and uninspiring office plazas with a lot of glass and palm trees.

Save for a car wash that was built in the 70's, and a dive bar, the stretch of road could be in half a dozen western cities. About a mile from the restaurant things take a drastic turn for the worse. While buildings close to campus have been renovated or demolished and rebuilt, that type of care has not been taken as we neared our destination. These were buildings that saw little care or upkeep. They were not in disrepair, but this area went from being upper middle-class neighborhoods 30 years ago, to being typical inner-city fare.

The population in Tucson moved to the suburbs and left this part of Speedway behind. It was home to strip clubs, adult bookstores, and blue-collar businesses.

During the drive, we chatted about school and our families mostly. Nothing too exciting. I found out that she was a business major and I told her all about my knee injury.

I pulled into the parking lot and her face soured when she saw the strip club. I could tell she was doubting me, the dinner, and this date. The look was a mix of doubt, displeasure, and a touch of fear. I figured she thought I was a moron, a pervert, or possibly a serial killer. Maybe a combination of all three.

I hopped out of the Jeep but could not get to her side to open the door in time. She instantly took a defensive posture but softened just a bit when she saw we were headed to the seedy Mexican restaurant and not the even seedier topless bar.

We were soon seated and opened our menus.

"Interesting place," she said, still a bit unsure.

"What it lacks in decor and upscale surroundings it makes up for with amazing enchiladas," I replied.

I soon had her sold on Leo's signature cheesy sour cream enchiladas. Despite not having ID I was able to secure her a margarita while I ordered a Pacifico with a wedge of lime. I learned this little trick where you put your thumb over the bottle and tilt it upside down allowing the lime to mix in with more of the beer. If done correctly the beer tastes even better. If you allow too much air to build up inside the moment you pull your thumb away beer jets out in a quick stream. Luckily I deftly tilted the beer without making a mess.

Before our food arrived we talked some more. After a bit of chit chat, she started fishing a bit.

"So you knew Caitlin from high school?"

"Actually, our fathers know each other," I answered. "If I had gone to school in Phoenix we would have gone to the same school, but I was off in Iowa playing hockey."

I continued to explain about my time playing junior hockey, leaving out references to the ex-girlfriend. After a few minutes, she steered the conversation back to Caitlin.

"So you guys know each other fairly well?" she asked, obviously trying to figure out just how well we knew each other.

"Nah, we had some mutual friends," I answered eating a tortilla chip dunked in salsa. "She went out with some friends of mine but we didn't really hang out."

She seemed a bit relieved.

"So you aren't her stalker," she affirmed.

"Her stalker?" my interest was piqued, to say the least.

"About once a week we get a call that just hangs up," she continued. "I thought it was just some stupid crank caller, but she thought it could be an old boyfriend."

I racked my brain. There were not many of her boyfriends that I knew that seemed jilted. Most either broke up with her or just drifted apart. I would have to make some calls later on, but this was an interesting development. Could there be an ex-boyfriend that was the potential kidnapper?

Although I was having fun on the date and actually liked her company, in the back of my mind I was focused on these phone calls and whether or not an ex-boyfriend was behind all of this and not some politically motivated kidnapper.

Our food came soon after and whatever reservations she had about the restaurant disappeared with her first taste of the enchilada.

"Wow, this is really good," she said, her mouth still full of food. "When you first pulled in I thought you were either the ballsiest boy I have ever met or the stupidest."

"And now?"

"The jury is still out," she said smiling.

She could dish it out. I liked that, it was a definite point in her favor. I did not like timid girls and the fact that she seemed comfortable busting my chops was a plus.

We continued to make small talk, nothing too interesting but I'd like to think that I was charming, funny and keeping her entertained. She laughed at my attempts at humor which I hoped was a genuine reaction and not her just placating my male ego.

"So you are from the East Coast I gather?"

"My accent gives it away huh?" she laughed.

"Just a little bit," I chuckled as well.

"I am from New Jersey," she added.

"How'd you wind up here?"

"My grandparents live down in Green Valley," she explained, referencing the retirement community about 45 minutes south of Tucson. "I used to visit every summer and I love Arizona. It also helps that I can use their address to get in-state tuition."

The difference between in-state and out-of-state tuition is nearly $20,000 a year. The Arizona colleges' tuition is very low. Even out of state is more affordable than many states' in-state rates. That is why you get so many students from California, New York, and Connecticut. It is cheaper with tuition and expenses to ship off your kids to Arizona than it is to keep them close to home.

Leo's has an amazing flan, but I opted to skip it and instead go get some ice cream. I am not a big sweets eater, but I thought it would be a good chance for Rachel and me to talk. I love to go to the movies, and would soon find out she was a huge film buff, but I don't think it makes a very good date since you can't talk.

We went to one of those upscale ice cream parlors where they mix in all sorts of toppings on a marble slab. We took our ice cream and went back on campus to walk around.

She ordered frozen yogurt with strawberries, while I opted for vanilla with a chopped up Snickers bar and extra caramel for good measure.

We were walking, enjoying the cool night. Brick buildings modeled after schools back east shared the land with 50-foot palm trees that were decidedly western. Add in the occasional cactus and you had something distinctly Arizona. We were near the planetarium, one-part telescope with a large metal dome, and one-part museum, when she turned to me.

"So why did you ask me out? It was kind of random don't you think?"

"My horoscope said that I should ask out the first pretty, dark-haired woman from the east coast that I meet," I took a bite of my ice cream and tried not to laugh.

She sized me up and as soon as it sunk in that I was joking around she gave me a light-hearted little punch in the shoulder.

"No, really, what made you just ask me out like that?"

I pondered the question a moment, knowing I could not tell her that I was using her to keep tabs of her roommate whose father was being extorted with a threat to her safety.

"I don't know," I stalled. "I just got a vibe."

"I gave off a vibe?"

"Not you, not really," I was scrambling a bit. "It was just a gut feeling. I just had this feeling that I needed to get to know you."

She smiled.

"Don't get me wrong, I thought you were very pretty, but I just had this little voice inside my head that told me we needed to hang out. I thought about how to make that happen and before I knew it I was asking you out."

This answer seemed to please her quite a bit. She stood there and stared up at me with a big smile on her face and a certain look in her eyes. I could tell I said something right. Normally that look is an opening for a kiss. In most instances, I would have swooped in and given her my best performance.

This time I didn't.

Oddly, I felt guilty. I was having fun and truth be told, I was kind of digging her. Had the situation been different I would have been way into the moment. I was feeling guilty. The only reason I asked her out was to keep an eye on Caitlin. The fact that I actually liked her only clouded things. Instead of a kiss, I offered her a bite of my ice cream.

The moment was over.

We continued to walk and talk. We found out we both loved movies but had a thing for older movies. She was a fan of classics from the 50's and 60's, while I was more a fan of action movies and dramas from the 70's and 80's. We had several we liked in common, but for the most part are tastes were a little different.

We both agreed that remakes were an affront to cinema.

I was extolling the virtues of the original "Manchurian Candidate" when we realized we were in front of her dorm. It was pushing midnight, not exactly early, but not late enough that the date couldn't conceivably continue.

"Can I see you again," I threw out there.

"Did you really have to ask?" she threw right back.

"Well I didn't want to be too presumptuous," was my reply. "And we already established earlier in the evening that I might be stupid."

"You could come up and watch a movie or something," she invited.

I gave the offer serious consideration. I didn't really want the date to end, but at the same time, I knew temptation lay ahead if I went upstairs. I did not know how far she'd want things to go, but there would be next to no chance that there would be no contact. The only place to watch the television was her bed or an uncomfortable desk chair.

I opted out.

"I want to, but I can't," I searched for a lie. "My dad is coming down and we are supposed to have an early brunch."

She seemed to accept my deception as truth and flashed me a huge smile. She said goodbye and awkwardly gave me a hug. She turned to go inside and I realized I needed a better end to the evening.

"Wait," she turned and I took her hands. "I want you to know that I had a blast."

She smiled and I pulled her closer. Normally I'd go in for the kill, but in this case, I gave her a small peck on the side of the mouth. She lingered waiting for more, but it was not forthcoming.

She unlocked the door and went inside. I strolled back to my car and considered what was and what could have been.

12. Serendipity Again

A chance encounter and a fortunate phone call gave me another suspect. Dating Rachel allowed me to keep tabs on Caitlin, but other than making sure she was safe, the only thing it as doing was helping my love life.

It had been a little over a week now and Rachel, it seemed, was falling for me hook line and sinker. I liked her a lot as well. My goal was to be able to keep an emotional distance of sorts, but I was failing.

Our second date saw us forgo my plans of a nice Italian dinner, and instead, we introduced each other to one of our favorite movies. She showed me "Some Like It Hot", while I introduced her to the "Godfather." We may or may not have been interrupted a few times during the movies by making out.

I learned that she had been in school plays in high school and had considered studying theater in college, but her dad would not allow it. Her father wanted her to pursue a degree that would actually lead to a career. She was into the actors and their performances, while I was interested in plot and storytelling.

She had considered joining a local improv group but so far had not worked up the courage to actually try.

When Chuck asked me about her, I described her as a "sweetheart" and she proved me right by bringing me a batch of cookies that she baked. We hung out and ate the cookies together.

"She might be a keeper," Chuck said to me, a mouthful of cookie.

"Assuming I want to be kept," she shot back. "Maybe I want to upgrade to his better-looking roommate."

She maintained a stone face for just a moment longer, before breaking into laughter.

We had fun together. In many ways, this was good for me. In the past, if I wasn't smitten on the first or second date I split. I rarely showed patience with a relationship. If I wasn't ga-ga, I was gone.

In this case, I had to ignore the things I didn't like, or at least focus on the good. I had to continue the relationship or I lost my ability to follow Caitlin.

Really the only problem was that things were going too well, too fast. We were now hanging out all the time, which was good for my keeping tabs on her roommate, but also meant things were escalating. The night before we hung out. Nothing special, just a quick taco run. We were up in her room and found ourselves alone. We were watching another movie and she laid her head on my chest and I gave her a little kiss on the forehead. She looked up and gave me such a look that I could not resist. I went in for the kill and despite my reservations, had no intention of stopping.

For the first time in my life, I was happy to be interrupted by the roommate. Caitlin staggered in and we immediately peeled off of each other.

"Sorry to interrupt," she said.

I stood up and gathered myself. "No that's okay."

I turned to Rachel, "I really should get going."

She followed me downstairs and offered to come over to my place, but I told her Chuck was around.

"We'll pick this up later," I promised.

"Not too much later," she said.

"No, definitely not too much later," I said.

While a small part of me felt guilty for the false pretenses under which I asked her out, in reality, I was really starting to like her and realized that I wanted to date her regardless of whether she was rooming with Caitlin or not. While I artificially had to keep the relationship going, I had no reason to not want it to continue.

Other than the possibility of finally sleeping with Rachel, I was also thinking about the case. I was still racking my brain about who the possible stalker could be. I asked Harris if he knew of any bad break-ups and he said he'd look into it. I did not know Caitlin well enough to remember every boyfriend, but that was now kind of my job.

I'd have an answer sooner than I expected.

Had one of my classes not ended 10 minutes early I would not have been limping in front of the student when I was. Despite having my earbuds in a stranger was waving excitedly at me. I turned off my music to figure out what was going on.

"Eric, buddy," the stranger said. "Man, it's been forever."

I was a tad confused. The face seemed familiar, but I couldn't quite place it. His hair was slicked back and he was sporting a gray SAE fraternity sweatshirt. I knew that I knew him, but I didn't know who it was standing there.

"Dude," he bellowed. "It sucks about your knee."

"Yeah," I replied trying to disguise my confusion.

"I don't think I've seen you since last Easter at the country club."

That is when it clicked. I mentally dropped twenty pounds, added three inches of hair and exchanged the sweatshirt for a loud golf shirt. Using my great investigative powers, I quickly surmised that the sweatshirt indicated that Devon Bloom had gone the frat route. It shouldn't have been a surprise since he always thrived in the country club scene. He was much more like my brothers in that sense (my brothers were also fraternity men).

Devon had added at least 20 pounds on the standard college barley and hops diet. He had also abandoned his relatively fastidious appearance for the Greek slob sheik. I was used to seeing him cleaned and pressed and ready for 18 holes. Now he was rumpled and wrinkled and a little hung over.

I know he originally wanted to walk on the golf team but also knew that he hadn't. I didn't ask him why, but he brought up the subject of golf anyway.

He blathered on for a few minutes about an intra-fraternity council tournament and his new golf clubs. He added a story about an upcoming road trip and the course he was going to play. None of this interested me, but since I am such a polite fellow I just nodded and inserted a few random "wows" and the occasional "uh-huh, you don't say".

Now, I like golf just fine. I play a few times a year and usually have fun. I really like any sport you can play while drinking beer. I am not a bad player but much to my father's chagrin, I am not as good as I could be if I really worked on my game. I'll watch occasional major on television, maybe lay some money down, but that's it. I don't obsess over it. I certainly don't brag about it and I definitely don't want to hear someone else talk about it.

I was ready to get out of the conversation when it took an interesting turn. I'm usually not one for gossip, but what he said next had a great deal of impact on me and my investigation.

"Dude," he began, again. "Did you hear about Murphy?"

"Murphy" referred to Patrick Murphy, another country club kid and the son of one of my father's circle of friends. Murphy went to high school with Devon and was an All-State golfer. He was set to try out for the golf team but a wrist injury had sidelined him.

"Murphy went all granola and shit," he continued.

If Devon had been a preppy, then Murphy was his king. Murphy and Caitlin had dated for over a year but had broken up over the summer. Once Caitlin embraced her retro hippie lifestyle, Murph quit his fraternity, sold his BMW and was last seen sitting out in front of the student union wearing soiled, tattered clothes, playing hacky sack and sporting long, matted hair.

At one time Patrick Murphy was something of a legend. Tales of his exploits were famous throughout Brophy College Prep and Paradise Valley Country Club. Whether the stories were true or not I didn't know, but they were bordering on mythical in my circle of friends.

Murphy or "The Murph" as he preferred to be called, seemed to succeed at everything he tried. He was a scratch golfer, state runner-up in the 100 Meter Butterfly and was one hell of a tennis player.

As numerous as his athletic achievements, his drinking exploits and his sexcapades were even more renown.

According to the legend, the "Murph" lost his virginity at age 12 to a high school junior in her father's Jaguar. There's video proof of his threesome with two cheerleaders from a rival high school, which sadly I saw a few seconds of and cannot erase that image from my mind.

Popular rumor has it that he was carrying out a three-month affair with a hot 40-year old divorcee, while simultaneously banging her 15-year old daughter.

Not being particularly close to Murphy, I was unaware that he gave up his tomcat ways (if he indeed did) to settle down with Caitlin McCauley. I knew they hooked up from time to time, but I had no idea they were a couple. Anyone who had heard the rumors or met the Murph would have been shocked to learn that he had a steady girlfriend. And no one would believe that he'd become so emotionally invested in a girl that he'd abandon his whole persona in an attempt to win her back.

I hadn't seen Murphy in a couple of years. It was summer after my freshman year at the University. Murph was still in high school, during the time he was reportedly nailing mother and daughter. I had decided to go to a high school party for cheap beer and bad conversation.

I had met up with two of my neighbors, the Metzger twins. It was their idea to check out Dawn Tyler's annual "My parents are in Tahoe for the Fourth of July bash". The older Metzger (Jay by seven minutes) wanted to go hit on a girl who was headed to Notre Dame in the fall and figured Dawn's party was his last chance to make a move.

We waded through a sea of underage drinkers, trying our best to avoid lit cigarettes and haphazardly held keg cups. Bass heavy hip-hop blared through speakers more used to the gentle crooning of Frank Sinatra or Tony Bennett.

Jay spotted his target and left Brian and me to search for the beer. We avoided a pile of vomit, a broken lamp, and two overturned houseplants to find three ice-filled coolers filled with various brands of bargain basement beer.

We rummaged through the coolers trying to find the least offensive brew. We were college sophomores-to-be and fancied ourselves sophisticated beer drinkers, although to us Bud Light was a highbrow ale. Brian settled on a Keystone. I "lucked out" and discovered a lone Coors Lite.

We took our beers and made a beeline to the back patio where the smoke and noise would be considerably lessened.

We exited into the reasonably cool Arizona night, which in early July meant it was still 95 degrees. The crowd in the backyard was relatively sparse, but it was there that the Murph was holding court. He was drinking what appeared to be a scotch on the rocks while regaling a small crowd of drunken teenage boys with various tales of his sure to be exaggerated exploits.

Brian and I started discussing the merits of the movies we had seen this summer, both agreeing that one of the big budget blockbusters was actually very good and worth owning.

"Slade!" Murph bellowed when he saw me. "Get your hockey playing ass over here."

I strolled over and his small cadre of admirers parted. They looked upon me with some kind of reverence due to my having been personally addressed by their hero.

He touted me to the group as the "best hockey player in Arizona" and a "sure-fire NHL player". My reputation with the seven 15-year olds in his midst was cemented.

Our brief conversation was nothing more than small talk. I received the same general questions I'd been getting since I went off to college. "How's school?" "How's hockey?" "What's your major?" The only main difference is that he seemed to linger on the subject of "college girls" a lot longer than most.

I made my way back to Brian who was now chatting up a nubile high school junior who wore only a bikini top and cut-offs. Needless to say, I really wasn't missed. Murphy returned to the adoring glow of his admirers. He really seemed to be eating it up. I was, and still am, surprised that he gave up his role as super, stud boy, sex god, idol to dozens, king of the country club set, for Caitlin.

The good news was that I knew where to find Murphy. The bad news is that I had no logical reason for approaching him. With Caitlin, I had to stoop to dating and deceiving her roommate. Somehow I didn't think that ploy would work twice. Besides, for all I knew Murphy's roommate was another long-haired, bearded hippie. Not exactly my type.

Since I was with the Metzger twins the last time I saw Murph, I decided to give them a call.

After high school, the Metzger twins went their separate ways. Brian headed west and went to Stanford for a future in medicine. Jay went East to the Cornell hotel school, to pursue a career running resort hotels.

With the time difference, it would be after 5:30 in Ithaca, NY. I hoped to get a hold of Jay before he left for dinner. Two quick rings and I had his roommate. Thirty seconds later and my old next door neighbor was chatting me up over 3,000 miles away. After a few minutes of small talk, I brought up my recent conversation with Devon and the changes in The Murph.

"Yeah, I heard that already," Jay said.

We both expressed our mild surprise and dismay at the dramatic transformation.

"I heard he's amassed this incredible collection of 'Dead bootlegs," Jay let me know.

"Like the Grateful Dead?" I asked.

"Yeah, them and any number of jam bands," he said. "He went all out and has been just buying up anything he could get his hands on, but mostly the Dead. He's got several hundred bootlegs now. Brian is all into the Dead now and he and Murph have been trading stuff back and forth."

Bingo! I quickly ended the call, some excuse about not putting too many minutes on my calling card.

I had my in. I could now approach the Murph.

The Grateful Dead are the band that will never die. They were never a hit with the mainstream, but have lived on with generation after generation of people who don't want the 60's to die. Known for their live shows and improvisational jams, they found a cult following with those who like to expand their minds with a variety of chemical substances. For generations their bootlegs were a hit with collectors and even in the digital age, having physical copies of their concerts are still prized possessions.

If Jay was right, then that is what Murphy had. Murphy, in an effort to be embraced by those he wished to become, used his wealth and connections to buy up as many hard to find bootlegs as he could. He was becoming a Dead dealer.

I tried to find out as much as I could about the Grateful Dead as I could. I spent a few hours on the Internet that night. I learned enough, as you gather from the report above so that I could ask for something real when I approached the Murph.

It was another nice Tucson day. I finished a morning class and headed to the front of the Union. For the first time, something worked out as Murph was there smoking a hand-rolled cigarette and chatting with a couple of guys who looked more like homeless people than students. He was entrenched amongst the smokers, jugglers and Frisbee players I passed every day with little or no notice

I approached slowly, knowing full well I was out of place.

"Murph," I said, wondering how they'd feel with an outsider in their midst.

I could see the confusion on his face, but he quickly realized who I was, even if he didn't know why I was there. He smelled of patchouli, tobacco and just a hint of marijuana. I guess the Murph liked to wake and bake.

"Eric, it's been a long time man," he said slowly, and emphasis on the word 'man' that would make Cheech and Chong proud.

It was strange. I had known him for over five years and he never once referred to me by my first name. I was almost always 'Slade", occasionally, mostly when he was drunk, I would be referred to as "E", "E-Dogg" or "Easy-E".

He walked over, leaving his friends behind.

"What's going on?"

"I was talking to Brian Metzger last night, he told me you had this amazing collection of Dead bootlegs," I said. "I was seeing if maybe we could do some trading."

"You're into the Dead?" he asked, not believing me.

"Yeah, I got into them last summer," I lied, I was getting better and better at it. "I am looking for bootlegs or any other similar bands."

"That's cool, I know some really cool websites where you can grab all kinds of shit."

There was a hole in my plan and he exposed it. Of course, I could just download the music. The whole Internet/Mp3 movement had radically altered tape trading. Once hard to find bootlegs are now just a mouse click away. Especially a band that was as bootleg friendly as the Grateful Dead.

I had to scramble.

"Yeah, I know a lot of them, but I keep getting viruses," I was getting good. "I like to know where my source is and I know you're a diehard."

I figured playing to his ego was a good move. I was right.

"Yeah, I can understand," he said, slowly. "That's cool, we can work something out. Either trades or maybe you can burn some stuff if you have a laptop. Why don't you swing by my place sometime and we can look and see what you might want."

"That'd be cool," I replied. "Can we meet up this week?"

"Yeah, give me a call." He scribbled down a phone number and I pocketed it. I would enter it into my cell phone as soon as I could.

I had made another small step of progress in my investigation.

13. Carne Asada and Machaca Burritos

I was feeling good. I had an in with Murph, an in to Caitlin's room, and so far nothing bad happened to her. I needed to explore Volpe some more and maybe explore some other potential suspects.

Then my phone rang.

I grabbed the cell phone out of my pocket before the ringtone could annoy anyone next to me. Is there anything worse than a cell phone ringing with some little song? All it takes is a bad pop song getting stuck in your head to ruin a day. And, of course, I have a little song programmed, so I am guilty myself. (For the record it is the theme song from Hockey Night in Canada, so 70's with its brass section and driving bass line).

I looked at the display, it was Harris.

"I'm in town, we need to talk," he said.

"What's up?" I said, concerned.

"Not on the phone," he cut in. "We need to meet."

This had my curiosity piqued. Why could he not talk on the phone? What was so important? All sort of conspiracy theories would soon run through my head. While I would normally be annoyed to be taken out of my daily routine, I was one part excited, one part concerned.

Twenty minutes later I was standing in front of a burrito stand. Tucson is full of small, kiosk style burrito stands. They serve decent Mexican food for cheap.

Harris was waiting, another odd fitting yet perfectly ironed suit. This one was a lighter grey. His shoes were polished and he had a gold watch that was even looked big on his meaty arm. It was just cool enough that he could keep his jacket on. He saw me and hopped off the bench.

"Let's get some food."

It was more of an order than a request, but I was hungry.

He went carne asada, with guacamole, basically, a marinated steak burrito slathered with the green stuff. I went with machaca, dried, seasoned beef and skipped the avocado based condiment. We both got a soda and sat down.

He placed two cell phones on the table. An iPhone and an old flip phone. He saw me looking at the two phones.

"Senator McCauley got me the smartphone," he said, an ounce of disdain in his voice as if McCauley saddled him with an incompetent partner. Then I realized maybe he saw me that way.

"I don't like it, too many buttons and I always hit things with my face when I am cradling it on my shoulder," he continued. "I prefer the old phone, plus I like slamming the lid shut when someone pisses me off."

He tore into his food before starting with why he called me here.

"We hadn't received any correspondence from the stalker in weeks," he said between bites. "But last night another package arrived."

He slid over a manila envelope. I opened it up. Inside was a color photocopy of another Polaroid. It was a picture of Caitlin sleeping. This time the photo was taken inside the room.

"The bastard has access to her room," Harris noted. "All of the other photos were taken outside. A lot less intimate. Now he can get in."

I don't know what shocked me more, the fact that he had access to the room or that he had access to a Polaroid. I said as much.

"I know," he said. "Who the fuck uses a Polaroid anymore?"

He took a long pull off his soda straw. He held the paper cup in his meaty hands by the top, the straw resting between his spread thumb and forefinger.

We ate in silence a few minutes before he asked me to fill him in on what I had been doing. I told him in more detail about the Murph and Volpe. I also let him know about my infiltration into Caitlin's life through Rachel.

"Could she be involved?" he asked.

"Who, Rachael?"

"Yeah, bear with me, I am just thinking out loud," he dropped the burrito. "Do they get along? Does she need money, is she on scholarship or anything?"

"They are not best friends," I seriously doubted Rachel was involved but I guess I had to consider the possibility. "I think her family is doing well enough."

"It's probably not her, but look into it a little bit."

I said I would.

I looked back down at the picture. It sure looked like the inside of her dorm room. Suddenly it occurred to me that it was also the inside of the girl I was dating's dorm room. I was suddenly getting angry and that surprised me.

I ate in silence a moment and considered the photo. Dorm rooms by nature are not the most secure. My dorm had a rash of laptop robberies last semester, but they are not that easy to get into. I tried to think of all the people I had seen in the room and I realized the most frequent visitors were myself and de la Roca.

"Have you looked into her boyfriend?" I asked, thinking out loud.

"That de la Roca guy?" he asked, pronouncing Rocha Rock-Ah. "Are they that serious?"

"I don't know if they are serious, but he is there quite a bit," I said. "He has stayed over and could have snapped a photo."

He picked the photo back up and studied it a bit.

"I did look into his background and nothing jumped out," Harris explained. "His family is not rich, but they are not poor, guy seems to pay his bills."

In the back of my mind, I laughed. While he did not come from the abject poverty he was fighting to abolish, the thought of the school's wannabe revolutionary growing up in middle-class suburbia cracked me up.

I imagined him mowing the lawn, with a solitary fist raised in protest.

We turned out attention to the other facts I dug up and he wanted me to look more into Professor Volpe.

"I took a long look into that guy when he was running against Senator McCauley," Harris said. "He's clean, as far as moral conditions. His politics are screwy and he can't stay married, but nothing out-of-line. See if you can't find anything out."

I left our meeting with my mind racing. Someone was in Caitlin's room, which meant that someone was in Rachel's room. Unless of course, it was Rachel. No, it couldn't be. I could not let Harris' suspicions get to me. He was paid to play every angle and I just didn't see Rachel being involved.

How well did I know her? Maybe I just didn't want it to be her.

I debated inside my head most of the drive home and finally decided that while it was doubtful, I couldn't rule out her involvement entirely. I would look for clues that implicated her, but I would not go out of my way to fit a piece of evidence to damn her.

Volpe was another story. I had to feel him out. I needed to go into his office hours and get him talking. I made a mental note to get an appointment with my Political Science teacher as soon as I could.

I was feeling guilty about suspecting Rachel so I decided to drop by. I wanted to surprise her, but you can't get into the dorm without a key or an escort. I had neither, so I needed good timing. I waited by one of the side doors and as soon as a resident emerged I pounced. Luckily for me, the guy was holding a guitar so he couldn't slam the door shut. I deftly slid in behind him and made my way into the dorm.

I knocked on the door and Rachel told me to come in. She seemed a little surprised to see me but smiled as I strolled in.

She was sitting at her desk with a book cracked open, but she stood up to greet me. Caitlin was laying on the bed with an oversized pair of earphones on her head. She was zoned out and didn't notice me come in.

"What are you doing here?" she asked

"I just wanted to see you," I said, leaving out the whole guilt I was feeling in suspecting her. She gave me a quick kiss and then sat back down at the desk.

At that moment Caitlin sat up. She stripped off the earphones.

"Hey Eric, what are you doing here? I haven't been to that class in weeks, so I don't have the notes."

"Uh, I have them, if you need them, let me know," I informed. "I'm actually here to see Rachel."

She had a puzzled look on her face, somehow she forgot seeing the two of us on the bed watching a movie a few weeks back. I guess the dim light and her pot induced haze made it hard to recognize me.

"You guys have a class together too?"

"Actually, we're kind of dating," Rachel interjected. She shot me a look, I surmised it was to see what my reaction would be. Some guys freak out when a girl puts a label on things. I don't.

"Oh, good for you," Caitlin said, no surprise on her face. "Eric's a cool guy."

She sounded less convinced on the 'cool guy' part. Maybe it was just my insecurities, but I swear she paused before "cool" as if to figure out the right word.

She got up and excused herself. As she left I walked over to Rachel at her desk. I gave her shoulders a little rub.

"You want to do something tonight?" I asked.

"I can't," she said, disappointment in her voice. "I have a big test tomorrow. I really need to study. I can't let my grades slip, I have to keep a 3.0 to keep my scholarship."

Suddenly Harris' suspicions crept into my head.

"I didn't know you were on scholarship," I pried.

"It's just a little partial scholarship, but every bit helps," she said. "With both, my sister and I in school things are a bit lean."

I was stunned, just a bit. It did not mean anything, but there was just an ounce of doubt in my head. I really didn't think Rachel was behind the threats, but there was just enough suspicion that I had to keep an even closer eye on her.

At least she was better to look at than Volpe, the Murph, and de la Roca.

"What are you doing later?" she asked.

I admitted I had no plans now that she had blown me off to concentrate on her studies.

"My friends think I am making you up," she said. "We were all going to meet up for a late night study break, you should come."

Meeting her friends would make it seem more real, but I really had no reservations about it. Our relationship was still in its infancy, but the way things were going I could envision us dating long after Caitlin was safe.

After making plans I gave her a kiss and wished her good luck on her studying and made my exit. My guilt about suspecting her did not diminish and now I had to pay attention to the girl I was dating. I tried to tell myself that I was using her to solve the case anyways, but that didn't help me feel any better.

14. The Dish

I headed outside and there was Caitlin, talking to a couple of smokers. She wasn't smoking herself, but she was chatting with a few guys by the ash can.

She saw me emerge from the side door and started over to me.

"So how long have you been banging my roommate?"

"Who said I was banging her?" I followed her question with one of my own.

"Oh Eric, I've heard about you," Caitlin said coyly, with just a hint of mischief in her voice.

"Really," I shot back. "I'm not sure your info is that accurate. I'm a good boy."

"Whatever you say," she returned. "I know you had that girlfriend in Indiana or whatever. But after the break up you started to sleep with anything that moved."

She had some details that were wrong, but the general gist was accurate. After Maggie, I gave up on relationships. It wouldn't be inaccurate to say that I had more than a few notches on my headboard. Probably less than she was insinuating, but more than a lot of my friends.

"I don't get it?" she continued. "She seems like a nice girl, I guess, but why the attraction?"

"She's cool," I said, less than descriptive. "I mean she's no revolutionary, but she's a very sweet girl. We have fun."

She gave me a dirty look after the dig at Tariq.

"But what do you have in common?" she queried. "You're a rich jock from Scottsdale and she's the daughter of a plumber from New Jersey."

With that comment, I realized I didn't know that much about her. I had no idea what her parents did or what background she came from. Since she was from the East Coast I just assumed her family had some money. Not many blue-collar families could afford to send their kids across the country for school. Her comment about in-state tuition on our first date started to make more sense.

"We have fun," I was on the defensive. "She's easy to talk to. It's comfortable."

She gave me a funny look.

"Comfortable? Isn't that like a girl calling a boy 'nice'?"

She had a point.

"Why are you so interested? It's not like we've ever talked much."

"I figured if you were going to be around so much I might as well get the dish," she replied. "I may have distanced myself from my high school friends, but I still enjoy the gossip from home."

"That's cool, I guess."

I found it interesting that she was aware of her transformation. She did not pretend that she has always been this little counterculture queen.

"We may not be friends or anything, but she's a nice girl. I just don't want you to fuck her and drop her. I can't deal with more relationship drama from her."

I did not expect that. I was unaware of any other guys. She picked up on it.

"You didn't know about Vince." It wasn't a question.

"I didn't ask."

"Ooh, I hold all of the cards on this one," she was enjoying it. For a moment she seemed like the old Caitlin. "Do you want to know?"

I did, but I didn't want to let on. I had my share of secrets, it was only fair that Rachel did as well.

"Not really," I said.

"You know you do," she had me, but I tried to play cool. "Rachel dated this guy Vince last semester. He was a musician or something. Always brought his guitar around, so I guess he was in a band. They went out a few months and then he dropped her cold. She was devastated and cried for an entire weekend."

I felt a twinge of jealousy and that shocked me.

"Just be good to her," she added. "I don't need any more drama."

I almost laughed. Here was a girl who had a stalker and a potential kidnapper trailing her. Her father had secretly hired me to keep an eye on her and I was slowly infiltrating her life. All of that and she was worried about a crying roommate.

"Don't worry, I kind of dig her."

With that, she seemed satisfied and our conversation ended. I headed home, puzzled by my dislike of this Vince character.

I spent a few hours pretending to study before meeting up with Rachel and her friends. They were making a late night taco run at an area Mexican restaurant that had delicious tortillas and a lax policy of checking IDs.

The girls had already staked out tables in the dining room, which had garage-style doors, that turned it into a patio when the weather was warmer. I ordered a beer and joined them at their table. A few jokes were made about me really existing and then after a few questions, I settled in as more an observer than an active participant.

They seemed nice enough, but I was clearly an outsider to their little realm. I did not know the jokes or the stories and mostly focused on Rachel.

Her friends are what I call "first-year" friends, that is a mismatched set of friends who come together the first semester not based on mutual interest or compatibility, but because they live on the same floor.

What starts as a big group slowly thins out over freshman year as people find real friends in various classes, clubs, and extracurricular activities.

In most cases, if you are still close with two "first-year" friends your sophomore year you are lucky.

Other than teammates, Chuck is my lone "first-year" friend I still see and he isn't even a real "first-year" friend as we met second semester. My first roommate, a defenseman from Chicago, got homesick and never returned from Thanksgiving break. Chuck's first roommate found an out clause in his dorm contract and bolted for his frat house, leaving us both looking for a roommate.

It was a rough start with our clash of styles, but once we figured out a compromise it was great symmetry and a pretty decent friendship. The rest of our little motley group just sort of latched onto us over the next few years, as real friend usually do.

From my limited interaction, I couldn't really tell which of Rachel's "first-year" friends would last.

There was Maura, the band geek. Truth be told, she was pretty good looking for a girl in the band, but she was a band geek all the same. She had been dating the same guy since her freshman year. He was older, but stayed in their hometown to be close to her, then was rocked when she decided to move away to school. They were still dating, but she was making more and more excuses to avoid weekend trips home and I got the impression that she may have been straying from the relationship more and more.

Also joining us on both outings was Tracey, who I judged to be the most likely candidate to remain friends with. Tracey, like Rachel, was from out of state and they had that in common. While, Rachel was from the East Coast, Tracey as from the Midwest and had dreams of being a cable news channel producer. It was obvious that they had bonded more than the others and I got the distinct impression that if I screwed over Rachel that I would invoke Tracey's wrath. Considering she took two different self-defense classes, her wrath is not something I wanted to face.

And yes, I referred to her as "Kung Fu" Tracey in my head, even though she made it clear on several occasions that she studied Krav Maga and Tai Kwon Do.

The others were less memorable. Nice girls, but since I was on the outside looking into their group and had no interest in anyone other than Rachel. I paid little attention to them.

There was Jade, who seemed to be the group flirt. Okay, she portrayed herself as more than just a flirt. She did not flat out brag about her sexploits, in fact, she seemed to downplay them to the other girls, but I could tell the truth.

Jade had attitude. I got the impression that she got just enough attention from the guys that she garnered an inflated impression of herself. While she thought they were into her for her "rare combination of brains and beauty", my guess was that they really knew a sure thing when they saw it.

Still, she was confident and busted my balls about being a junior and still living in the dorm. I laughed it off, but she was trying to cut me off at the knee in front of my girlfriend and that annoyed me.

Needless to say, I did not have a great impression of Jade.

Dana was the introvert. She was a little on the chubby side and seemed to have little self-esteem, and as such, said little. I got the impression that she was quite bright but was afraid to open her mouth and let anyone know. I think she could have been cute if she got the hair out of her face and made eye contact, but the two times I saw her she failed to do either and maybe said five words total.

After the study break/interrogation, we walked back to her dorm. Her friends quickly dispersed, leaving us alone in front of the building.

"So when do I get to meet your friends," she asked. "Or are you ashamed of me?"

"No, but I might be ashamed of them," I joked. "I want you to still like and respect me."

"Who said I respected you?" she was quick with the comeback.

We laughed and that led to a lengthy kiss.

"Tell you what," I said. "How about we get everyone together on Friday and then you and I spend some alone time together on Saturday?"

I had purposely kept her away from my friends because I figured they might spoil my illusion I was trying to build. While things were going great, I needed them to continue to go great The last thing I needed was "Little Mark" embarrassing me or even worse, Chuck drinking rum and spilling the beans on my true intentions.

15. Peering Into Dark Corners

Professor Volpe's office was disappointing, even by university standards. One of the biggest surprises for me, when I came to campus, was at how unimpressive the faculty's offices were. Sure, some of the more prominent professors had lavish offices, but most were just small cramped spaces.

Volpe's was no different. He was a full professor, which meant that he had an office to himself, but that was his only luxury. The back of the office was filled with a number of rickety bookshelves. They were filled with various volumes stuffed wherever he could find the space. He had numerous books stacked sideways, on top of other books that were not as tall as the space provided. Papers and magazines jutted out every direction.

If there was a filing system, I could not fathom it.

He sat at an old metal desk that was probably not new in the 80's. The body painted a sort of greenish blue, with plenty of scratches and dents. The top of the desk was covered in more books, more papers and all sorts of office supplies.

He had a small radio on his desk as well, and it sounded as if he was listening to conservative talk radio. This surprised me as he was a noted liberal.

There was barely room for the one metal chair for students to sit on. He gestured me in and indicated that I should take a sit.

"Mr. Slade is it?" he said, eying an appointment calendar. "How can I help you today."

Volpe himself was also less than impressive. He had curly hair that wasn't quite an afro, but it was far too long to be stylish. His graying curls were out of control. He had a bushy mustache, the hair slightly stained from cigarette smoke.

He had a sharp nose and blue eyes that rarely seemed to blink. He routinely wore short-sleeved dress shirts that had their share of stains, most of them sweat stains, but other appeared to be food and coffee. He liked to wear a tweed sport coat, although every once in a while he'd pop on a blue blazer.

The room was cooled, efficiently I must add, by a rather noisy air conditioning unit.

I really had a firm grasp of the class, but wanted to get a feel for Volpe. We had a paper coming up and I acted as if I could not settle on a topic. In reality, I was going to compare the health care system in Sweden to the system in the United States, but I feigned as if I could not decide between two topics.

After a few minutes of discussion Volpe "convinced" me that I should choose the healthcare paper and I readily agreed. I then turned the topic of the conversation to a more personal nature.

"How does someone who ran for Senator teach a class on European politics?" I asked, trying to get the ball rolling.

"I have interests in a lot of different political aspects," he began. "I have always been fascinated with European governments, especially socialist countries. I helped oversee the first democratic elections in Romania and Bulgaria and have done a lot of other philanthropic work over there."

I knew some of that already from his lectures in class, but I acted as if it was the most interesting topic I had ever heard. He told a few quick stories about working on the elections and while they were of some interest, they were not as enthralling as I made them seem.

Twice during our conversation, he paused to yell at the radio. He vehemently disagreed with the talk show host. Apparently, he listened to the conservative shows to disagree with them. I surmised that he was studying the enemy in some manner.

I needed to get him to really like me, so I started to weave my little web of deceit.

"I feel that socialism is a flawed system, but I really like how socialist countries provide for their citizens, especially the underprivileged," I counted on this winning him over.

He cocked an eyebrow. He wasn't prepared for that statement.

"You sound like a true liberal," he was smiling. "I would have pegged you for a Republican."

"No, much to my father's dismay I really lean to the left." That was mostly true, though in reality I can't stand either party and take topics one at a time to form an opinion. "He hates the fact that I voted Democrat in the last election."

Truth was, I have never voted, but he didn't need to know that. He seemed intrigued with the thought of a liberal rebelling against his conservative upbringing.

"Are you politically-active?" he asked.

"Not really. I vote and study the issues, but there has never really been a candidate that I felt strongly about that I would give up my free time to help elect," I paused, here came the line that would win him over. "When I was 16 my dad made me help volunteer for a friend of his who was running for election. I had to stuff envelopes and make phone calls for Ed McCauley."

"You worked on his campaign?" his voice lost just a touch of its bluster.

"Yeah, why do you think I'm a Democrat?" I laughed. "He was so phony and so fake. All he cared about was winning. He would tell everyone what they wanted to hear. I'm not sure he even has a real platform."

This is exactly what Volpe wanted to hear. I had struck a nerve.

"You saw right through him." He sounded proud. "I don't see why anyone else couldn't. He had no convictions other than promoting big business and wanting to close the borders. He was so anti-immigrant, yet over 40% of Hispanic voters supported him."

He was just getting started.

"He has been terrible in supporting education, the environment, and healthcare. If it is good for developers or large corporations he is all about it, otherwise he couldn't care less."

Volpe was getting fired up.

"Did you know that he had the third worst attendance record in the Senate? He never missed a photo op, but sure did miss a lot of votes. What kind of representative is that?"

I shrugged my shoulders as if I had no idea. Truth be told I really didn't. I knew "Big Ed" the country club member, not Senator McCauley the politician. Truth be told I had spoken to him and he was always nice to me, a little fake, but nice.

"He's all smiles and flash, no substance. Pretty wife, handsome kids, hell even his dogs were picture perfect. In this day of the media's glare, there was no way a divorced college professor could unseat a made for television candidate like McCauley. I spent so much time and energy trying to beat him and I came so close"

He was never in the race, but I said nothing.

"It cost me two years of my life, a relationship and a chance for advancement in my teaching career."

He calmed down a bit.

"I'm sorry, it just makes me so angry. A man with so few convictions but a ton of connections gets elected."

He looked at me, and I could see an idea formulate in his mind.

"I am not sure if I am running against him or not, but I will be backing whoever the Democrats send against him. I know at least three of the potential opponents and all three are great people. I'd like you to meet some of them. Hear our ideas. If you become inspired by one of us, maybe you'd like to work on the campaign."

I told him that I would indeed like that if the right person was out there.

"I don't want to make you uncomfortable or put you in an awkward situation, so tell me if I cross the line, but I think you could be very valuable to the campaign due to your father's ties to McCauley."

"Huh?" I said, less than intelligently. Did he know about my father?

"Well, I take it you are the son of Alan Slade," he said, sizing me up. "I didn't put two and two at first but the name 'Slade' kept bugging me."

"Yeah, that's me," I said, still unsure of what was going on. "I am surprised that you know of my dad."

"Oh, after the loss I looked into every aspect of his campaign and his life," Volpe said. "I know your father was a finance whiz who was key in McCauley being able to outspend me."

It was weird hearing my father being described as a finance whiz, I just thought he was an accountant. One of those guys with the green, plastic, see-through visors and adding machines with the big handle.

"I have done a lot of research, a lot of peering into dark corners and finding things he doesn't want anyone to know," Volpe added.

"I figured you might hear things from time to time," Volpe continued. "I don't want you to be a spy or anything, but maybe you'll hear some things that may be of use."

I said I would consider it if the candidate was right. He claimed he didn't want me to be a spy, but that is precisely what he wanted me to be. The man of conviction wanted me to conceal my political leanings from my family to aid his political party.

I realized that I was now a secret employee of both Senator McCauley and a man who wanted to unseat him. I was hired to spy on his daughter and now I was being recruited to spy on the Senator himself.

There was no doubt in my mind that Volpe had the venom in relation to McCauley, but did he have enough venom to harm Caitlin? I would have to get politically motivated to find out.

16. Search Engineer

I was on a roll. Over the past few days, I had discovered two new suspects and had a perfect way to keep tabs on Caitlin thanks to my burgeoning relationship with Rachel. After a slow start, I finally felt like I was contributing to this case.

Inspired I took my laptop to an area bar, ordered a beer, and decided to do some more research on Volpe and McCauley. One hour and two beers later I realized that there was not much more I could learn about Volpe's past that I did not already know.

With a third beer on the way, I decided to do a more general search on the Senator. I typed in "Ed McCauley Senator" and let the search engine do its magic. In less than a second, I had nearly 70,000 links to look at. I knew there would be a lot, but here I was overwhelmed.

I skipped over the links that were from government-provided websites. I didn't want propaganda, I wanted criticisms. I needed people who didn't just dislike McCauley, I was looking for people who hated McCauley.

At first, I was looking for Democrats other than Volpe who might be involved. It was obvious that liberals did not like him, but was anyone going to kidnap his daughter over tax reform or welfare benefits? I just didn't see it.

Two hours and numerous websites later I found something very interesting. The article in question read: Appeal thrown out, Senator in the clear

PHOENIX – A multi-million dollar lawsuit has been thrown out by the state appeals court. Developer and Arizona State Senator Ed McCauley was cleared of any wrongdoing after being sued by a former business partner for $27 million dollars.

The suit by builder Landon Richmond II stated that McCauley duped him into selling off his portion of a business just before the firm landed a multi-million dollar contract from the state. The court of appeals upheld a decision by the lower courts.

"I am just so relieved," said McCauley. "I can now focus 100 percent on representing the great state of Arizona."

The two were partners in the early stages of McCauley/Richmond builders. Their fledgling company never got off the ground and Richmond sold off his share to McCauley for an estimated $50,000. Four months later McCauley Inc. merged with The Vasquez Group to form McCauley/Vasquez and they were awarded a lucrative contract to build student housing at Arizona State University.

In his suit, Richmond contends that McCauley bought him out in an effort to make more money from the merger and the impending contracts from the University. The court felt that McCauley was clear of any wrongdoing.

"I am very disappointed," Richmond said after the verdict. "I felt that we were done wrong, but the courts did not see it that way."

That was interesting. I scanned a few more links but could not shake the thought of Richmond. I quickly Googled his name and found another interesting story, this one from six months ago.

Businessman's death deemed a suicide

PHOENIX – Prominent Phoenix businessman Landon Richmond II's death was ruled a suicide by the Maricopa County Medical examiner.

The developer was reported missing last Saturday and on Friday Richmond's car was found in the desert near Fountain Hills. His body was found in the car with a single gunshot wound to the head.

Richmond's personal and professional life had been in disarray the past few years. He and his wife of 27 years were divorced six months ago and he recently filed for bankruptcy. Richmond's company lost a reported $11 million dollars when their proposed Rio Salado Center failed to acquire backing from city planners.

He is survived by his daughter Jenny, 24 and son Landon, 21.

I didn't remember much about this, but it seemed interesting. The poor guy loses a huge lawsuit, gets divorced and has a huge business deal fall through.

I was new to this whole investigating thing, but I had a gut feeling about him. Here was a guy whose whole life went downhill after dealing with McCauley.

The problem was that I didn't know any more about Richmond than what I read on the net. I did know one person who would know about Landon Richmond II, but I didn't want to talk to him.

I really didn't want to call my father.

It's not that I don't like my dad, I love him. He just scares the crap out of me. We couldn't be less alike. My older brothers are virtual clones of him, but I am somehow the black sheep.

My father is about as proper as it gets. I'm not sure I've ever seen him in a casual moment. He is always dressed nice, even when he's relaxing. Casual to him means that he's wearing chinos and loafers instead of a suit. I'm not sure he owns a pair of jeans, and if he does I'm sure he has them pressed and starched.

Everything with him is formal. He comes down to breakfast fully dressed, even on weekends. I can't recall him taking me or my brothers out for pizza or McDonald's. Mom handled that stuff. In fact, mom handled us most of the time.

Maybe that is why she split.

Dad was the disciplinarian. Dad doled out the chores and handed out the allowance. Occasionally he'd take us out on weekends, but usually, it was to buy new clothes or get a pair of dress shoes.

As I got older I could feel that I disappointed him. I did not like the country club set. Mom got me into hockey very young and I never grew out of it. No one counted on me getting so good at it. I played golf and tennis to hang out with him and my brothers, but I never embraced the games like they did.

I was not a rebellious kid, but I wasn't the little "yes" men my brothers were. They liked buying clothes, I wanted to go to the sporting goods store. They loved the country club, I'd rather go to the mall.

My father never looks happy. He has these small, squinty eyes that always seem to be glaring at you, even when he's reading the paper. When he sits in his chair, nursing a scotch and watching television he looks angry. Even when he watches a sitcom he rarely laughs, although he'll turn to you and tell you who he thinks is funny.

In many ways, I think my father has always been old. He's had the same grey, short cropped hair as long as I can remember. I have never seen any pictures of him when he was young where he does not look exactly like he does now. Only younger and less angry.

Some of it I understand. He grew up in a blue-collar family and was himself the black sheep because he wanted to go to college. With no emotional or financial support, he put himself through college by working numerous odd jobs and basically having no social life. That carried on after graduation when he devoted his life to his career. He took a low-level accounting job and within five years ran the department. He had gone into business for himself a few years later and was 33 when he met and married my mother who was a decade younger.

I was born in Chicago and we lived there until I was seven. When he saw the growth potential in Phoenix he moved the family there and built his business even more. He quickly befriended a number of developers who were putting up housing communities in every inch of spare desert the Valley of the Sun had. He went from having money in Illinois to being wealthy in Arizona.

I talk to my dad about every two weeks. I talked to him about five days ago so this would be a surprise.

He answered after three rings.

"Eric, I wasn't expecting you to call," he said, not exactly thrilled. "Is there something wrong?"

I knew what he was getting at, he assumed I needed money.

"No, I am doing pretty good actually."

His tone changed a bit, not happy, but the caution was gone from his voice.

"So, Ed McCauley is pleased with the work you've been doing."

As far as my dad knew I was keeping tabs on Caitlin to ensure she wasn't doing anything to embarrass the campaign and if she was, no one would be surprised.

"That's good, I'm trying."

"It's good to see you enthusiastic about something other than hockey." He had to go there. "Maybe politics is something you'd like to get into. I have a lot of contacts."

I didn't want to fight so I was vague.

"You never know," I skirted. "I figured I'd just see how all of this goes and see if it is something I like. I don't want you to start making phone calls or lining things up if this is something I hate."

"You have to find some direction, Eric."

"I know," this was a conversation we've had many times before. "Speaking of connections, I actually called to see if you knew much about Landon Richmond."

"Richmond? Why do you want to know about him?"

I had to think quick.

"I was doing some online research for class and read about his suicide," I hoped I was convincing enough. I wasn't too far from the truth, but not honest either. "The name sounded familiar and I was wondering if I knew him."

"I'm sure you've met him," my father started. "I wasn't friends with him, but we were in the same circles."

"I read that he lost a lot of money on a failed project."

"Ah, yes," he was involved now. "He tried to build an entertainment complex in Tempe, near Arizona State.

He explained that the project was going to have a 15,000 seat arena for the concerts and hockey, plus a mall, movie theaters and even museums. He sunk all of the money he had into the project but the city never got behind it and he was ruined.

"In doing research on his voting record I stumbled upon an article about a lawsuit by Richmond and that led to the suicide story."

"I forgot about the lawsuit," my father admitted. "I guess that was the beginning of the end if you think about it. He always hated McCauley. Felt he swindled him. Of course, his feelings were way off base."

Of course, to my father, Big Ed could do no wrong. Richmond hated McCauley, but he was dead. I was not sure what to make of this.

"Do you know his family at all?" I was grasping at straws now.

"His ex-wife married Bill Brammington a few years ago," my dad said as if I had to know who Bill Brammington was. "I don't know his kids, although I think his son is your age."

Within a few moments, our conversation was over. I was intrigued by the Richmond family but had nowhere to really go. I did an online search on Brammington, but nothing interesting came up.

Next, I moved onto the kids. I found two phone listings for a J. Richmond, but no Jenny or Jennifer, so I had no idea if it was her. There was no listing in the Phoenix area for a Landon Richmond.

He also did not have much of a social media presence, just a Facebook page that had not been updated in a few years, save for the odd birthday greetings from friends.

This was just too juicy to ignore, but I had no idea how to proceed. I would call Harris in the morning, but my mind was racing. I tried video games, but that didn't work. There was no way studying would happen.

I called Rachel but she wasn't home.

In the end, I resorted to nerf basketball. We, and by 'we' I mean I, hung a nerf basketball hoop over our door. Occasionally I shoot on it when Chuck is not home and I am procrastinating. I used to use the lightweight foam ball that comes with the hoop, but I don't like how it really doesn't bounce. Invariably I buy a heavier foam ball that bounces but does more damage when it ricochets off the wall.

I always start shooting sitting down but wind up trying out my best post moves. Although there are no defenders, I always assume that if I was only seven-feet tall I'd be an NBA superstar.

I threw up a fadeaway jumper over my desk and missed badly. The ball caromed off the wall and landed on Chick's desk, scattering books and papers. As usual.

This is why Chuck hates me playing when he is home.

I went over to pick everything up and there it was. I don't know what possessed me to flip through it, but I did. Lying open was the student directory. Essentially a phonebook of all of the students on campus. While I was looking for Landon Richmond in Phoenix and on social media, I never thought to look to see if he was on campus.

I opened to Richmond and there he was. Listed as a junior was Landon Richmond III.

He was a student here, as was the daughter of the man who his father hated. Somehow I needed to talk to him. Could he blame McCauley for his father's downfall? Certainly, the death of your father and the loss of the family fortune would be a reason for revenge.

17. Technical Difficulties

I hadn't heard from Harris in days. I called him a few times and left messages but nothing. No call, no text, nothing. I was starting to feel like I had done something wrong.

I was walking across campus when my cell phone rang. Finally, it was Harris and he was almost apologetic.

"Fucking cell phones," he blurted. "I had the damn thing on silent for three days. I don't even know how to turn it on silent mode, but apparently, you can do it by dropping the damn thing."

He kept venting about his cell phone, complaining about the fact you can hardly find a payphone anymore and how that it has made staking out people tougher as you can't camp out by a phone booth.

I was getting a pretty clear picture that McCauley's super sleuth was a bit of a technophobe.

His rant continued to his teenage daughter who apparently never removed her earbuds, though I am 75% sure he called them "ear butts."

Again, I did not share his views as I was listening to music on my phone just moments before his call.

Soon our conversation turned to the case and I filled him in best I could, though I left out the details of my meeting with Volpe and he let me know that he looked more into De La Roca and turned up little that would make him move him to the top of the list.

Soon the conversation turned to the Richmond family. Harris was very aware of them and had been looking at them from the start.

"The ex-wife checks out," Harris explained. "She's living in Hawaii with her new husband now and trying to make the world forget her first marriage."

The daughter, he explained was living in Chicago, working for an advertising agency and really did not look like she had any involvement. Landon also checked out, or so he thought.

"The kid had a very strained relationship with his father all through high school," Harris said. He went on to explain that the son rebelled and wound up on an East Coast boarding school and spent his senior year studying abroad in Belgium.

"In fact, he's studying abroad again," Harris added. "He's in South America as we speak."

"I'm not sure about that," I countered. "I found his name in the current student directory. I have an address."

Harris found the news very interesting and said he'd look into it.

I hung up with Harris, turned my music back on, and became one of those "punk-ass kids" as Harris so eloquently put it.

I continued my trek across campus when I got a text from Rachel seeing if I wanted to eat lunch.

She wanted Chinese, and there was a passable place with a decent Mongolian Beef about 500 yards from her dorm, so we agreed to meet at her place.

Two and a half songs later I was sneaking through a side door as someone was coming out. They gave me a dirty look, but I still had the music playing and acted as if I did not notice.

I reached her room and had the unpleasant opportunity to run into Tariq. I was prepared to ignore him, as I ignored dirty look girl at the door, but he was not going to give me the choice.

"Katya," apparently Caitlin was now Russian. "Did you know that the athletic department spends $53 million dollars a year on non-academic pursuits that could go to fund other, more important programs at the school and that two of the coaches are among the top-5 highest paid state employees."

I should have let it rest, but I could not. I may be a jock, you could even argue a dumb jock, but I was not stupid.

"Rachel," two could play at this passive aggressiveness. "Did you know that the athletic department is self-sustaining and does not receive a single dime from the state or University?"

I did not give Tariq the satisfaction of looking at him, but Rachel was giving me a glare as she was finishing packing her book bag for the class she had after lunch.

"Did you know the football stadium uses more electricity on a game night than the entire dorm system does in two weeks?"

My turn.

"Rach, did you know that every home football game employs over 300 people and that every year the athletic department gives nearly $4 million dollars to the University general fund, four million dollars the school could not otherwise raise"

I ignored his predictable comments on the sweatshops that one of the major athletic apparel sponsors of the school uses and launched into my final salvo.

"Did you know that of the 370 scholarship athletes, over 65% of them are minorities and that 55% of them come from low economic backgrounds, providing one of the best opportunities for impoverished youths to attend college with all expenses paid?"

And with that, we walked out the door.

I did not mention that the sport I play, er played, hockey, had exactly zero minorities on scholarship, unless you count white, male, Midwesterners as minorities.

Super China Garden a two-minute walk from her dorm. Our food had just been delivered when she got a phone call and mouthed to me that she was going to step outside.

I chose to be a gentleman and not eat in her absence, though I knew my food would be getting cold.

I alternated between watching her through the window, easy to do considering the entire face of the restaurant was glass and checking point spreads on my phone. I found a few games I wanted to bet on later (Pitt was getting points at home!) and then noticed that Rachel was very animated on the phone.

She finally came back in but appeared upset. She silently started picking at her lunch and it was clear I was going to have to spearhead the conversation if I wanted the info.

"Is everything okay?" I asked, finally breaking the silence.

She continued looking at her plate of food before answering.

"It will be," she finally said. "My dad needed to buy a new truck for his company and things are tight right now. I was supposed to get some money from them but it is going to have to wait a few weeks. It's not that big a deal, but I just have to be careful not to spend much money."

She seemed to perk up just a bit and I let it dropped. But the fact that her family could be having money issues really bugged me. While it seemed far-fetched that she could try to extort money from her rich roommate's father, it was a possibility.

We finished up and headed outside.

"We probably need to cancel Friday night," she said. "I just shouldn't spend the money right now."

While I was nervous at first for her to meet my friends, I was now looking forward to it. So far my friends and my, er, girlfriend (did I just say that?) have been mostly separate entities and a little crossover would be a good thing.

"You know it is really too late to cancel," I tried to say coolly. "I mean Chuck canceled a chance to play speed chess with three French speaking international students. He would kill both of us if we did not show up."

I grabbed her around the waist.

"I got you tomorrow night," I said. "Just don't drink too much."

She laughed.

"You're the first guy I ever met who didn't want to get a girl drunk."

She then gave me a lingering kiss, pulled away and gave me a sexy look I had not seen from her before.

Then she turned around and left. I watched as she descended down the stairs before I popped my earphones into my ears and headed off back to my dorm before my last class.

I was left with quite an image and I have to admit, I was now looking really forward to what was going to happen on Saturday night. My guilt was subsiding, it was still there, but other emotions were pushing it to the back of my brain.

An hour later I headed for my afternoon class. I felt my cell phone buzz and looked down and had a text. I was stunned to see that it was from Harris.

"1724 n tinedahl lundon adrus"

It took me a while to figure it out, but then it made sense, "1724 N. Tyndall, Landon's address".

Harris may be a lousy texter, but he got some good information. We now seemed to have an address, now for me to figure out if he was our guy.

18. Officer McHotty

I was going to feel that in the morning. Who am I kidding? I was feeling it right now.

I have played hockey since I was five years old, but as a goalie I was used to dishing out contact, not taking it. It was rare that I got hit, much less plowed over by another man. And certainly, I have not been run over by someone who was not wearing skates

There was a first time for everything.

The hallways of Rachel's dorm are cramped enough for people walking side by side. Add a third person walking the other directions and adjustments have to be made. Usually, it means I either slow my pace and slip behind Rachel, or I turn my torso to the side and let the person slide by me.

We had just finished a combination dinner and study session. Rachel had an English paper due and had some reading to do for Volpe's class, so we decided to get a few slices of pizza and do our work on the patio of a nearby pizza place. We ate a little, studied a lot, and called it an evening around 8:00.

Her dorm was not far away from where we ate, and instead of dropping her off outside, I walked her up to her room. The cramped corridors were nothing new, so I thought nothing of it as I had to turn to allow a few different people slide by. The first was a short girl wearing a robe and carrying her things to the shower. The second was a guy I knew lived down the hall for Rachel. Heath always wore slacks and a collared shirt, regardless of the weather. Rachel was pretty sure he did not own a pair of shorts, but claims to have seen him wearing jeans, once.

When we passed the third person, I barely registered anything about him, save for the fact that he wore a sweatshirt with the hood on his head. While it was clearly sweatshirt weather, I did think to myself has stupid he looked with the hood up and both straps on his backpack slung over his shoulders.

As he passed I gave him wide berth, but he never wavered and clipped me with his shoulder.

"Excuse you," I said with some agitation to my voice.

He did not bother to turn around and kept heading towards the stairway. We rounded the corner and although it took a moment to process what I was seeing, I quickly realized Rachel's door was open.

I have to admit I had a nervous feeling in my stomach, but if she was concerned Rachel did not notice it.

"Caitlin, keep the door...closed," she said as we entered.

The problem was, Caitlin was not there.

It was then that I fully realized someone had been in the room. I turned around and hurried down the hall. I had no proof that the guy in the hoodie had been in the room, but I was damned if I was not going to try and find out.

Working on a lot of assumptions, the first being that he was the person that had been in the room, and the second was that he did not live here in the dorm, I headed down the stairs. After weeks of pretending my knee was a lot worse than it was, I did not worry about witnesses and appearances, and flew down the stairs, taking two at a time.

I nearly fell twice trying to navigate the narrow staircase, but was able to keep my feet and hit the door out of the building at a great rate of speed. I rounded the building and looked to the right, towards my dorm and saw plenty of people, but no one in a gray hoodie.

I looked left and there he was, Mr. Hoodie walking at a casual, but brisk pace away from the building.

I took off in pursuit. After several strides, he must have heard the pounding of my feet and he started running himself. At the edge of the building, he went left, and I lost sight of him. A few seconds later I rounded the same corner and he was not there. There were several areas where he could have ducked into, and I kept jogging that way.

I approached the alleyway behind the dorm and slowed to look into the darkness for him. I could not miss him as I saw a gray flash before he exploded out of the alleyway and barreled into me. He lowered a shoulder and threw his forearm into me, sending me to the ground.

The air rushed out of me, and my whole torso hurt, but I was able to grab his backpack. My desperate maneuver slowed him up for just a moment. I tried to stagger to my feet, while simultaneously maintaining my grip on the backpack.

I got to a knee and kept the grip, but backpack unzipped, sending three laptops spilling out. The cascading computers caused me to lose my grip and allowed him to sprint off. I struggled to my feet and chased after him as he ducked into the parking garage. I gave chase, but once I entered the parking structure I couldn't see him. I looked behind cars for a few moments, but it was clear he had slipped away.

I went back, gathered up the laptops and called Rachel to let me into the building.

We arrived at her hallway to find a lot of commotion. It seemed as if the entire floor was out and about. Rachel's resident advisor was on the phone, and within a few seconds, it was clear that he was speaking with the police. A second person, who I later learned the resident advisor from another floor, was dealing with several residents. Some looked scared, while others were mad.

Caitlin emerged from her and Rachel's room, apparently, she had gotten back while I was wrestling with Mr. Hoodie.

"Nothing is missing that I can tell," she said, an annoyed tone to her voice. "I guess it was a good thing I left my computer buried under my laundry."

Rachel had her computer with her, so if the intruder's intent was to steal laptops from their room, he failed. If he had other nefarious intentions, then I might have to do more digging.

I entered the hall with an armful of computers and all eyes were on me. For a split second, I got the feeling that they thought I had stolen them.

"He got away," I said. "But I grabbed these."

One of the girls recognized her computer and hurried over, reaching for a laptop covered in stickers. One of the bystanders recognized their roommate's computer, leaving me just one final computer to return to its owner.

The resident advisor hung up the phone and informed me that the police would be by shortly and wanted to speak to me.

Rachel and I entered the room and noticed that Tariq was there as well as Caitlin.

"What's up hero boy?" Tariq said, giving me a mocking air clap.

"He got people their computers back," Rachel said defending me.

"That was pretty brave," Caitlin added.

Tariq shot her a dirty look at her defense of me, but she either did not notice or did not care. Less than 10 minutes later there was a knock on the partially open door and a uniformed, University Police officer entered.

He got a brief statement from Caitlin and Rachel, then asked me to join him in the hallway. I quickly recapped my brief encounter with the thief. I left out any mention of Caitlin's predicament or my role in investigating it. I had no idea if this person was involved, and since the Senator had not gotten involved, I thought it best that I didn't either.

"That was pretty stupid," said the young officer who was probably just a few years older than me. "First of all, you had no idea if he was the guy. If he wasn't I might be here arresting you for assault."

It was tough getting scolded by someone who was probably a senior in high school when I was a freshman. I knew he was right, I hadn't given any of my actions a second thought before I started running, but I was still bristling from being admonished by a 25-year old.

"More importantly, that was really dangerous," he said. "You had no idea if he was armed, or strung out, or just a badass."

I realized at that moment I was rotating my arm and wincing from where Mr. Hoodie ran me over. Again, the officer was not wrong, which hurt my pride more than getting run over hurt my body.

"The good news is you did recover the three laptops," he added. "It looks like he may have gotten a few phones as well, but I guess he had those in a different pocket or bag."

So I was only a partial hero, but I could take some pride that I helped three people.

"One girl was more freaked out about her term paper than she was having her room broken into," the cop said chuckling.

He now turned his questioning to the suspect. He asked me for a description and I was pretty confident about his height and weight, but then he asked me "what did he look like?"

At that point, I realized I had not seen his face, at least not his features. I knew he was light-skinned, but in reality, he could have been white, Hispanic or Asian, and I would not have known. The dorm hallways were dark, and outside the orange lighting so prevalent on campus gave me a distorted memory of his skin.

Worse, I never fought to look at his face. He had the hoodie on, and during the skirmish, I was behind him and on the ground. Even if the hood had slipped, I was never in a good position to see his face. Whether he was just a two-bit thief, or he was the stalker, I had failed to identify him.

Some detective I was.

He wrapped up with a few more things, then handed me his card in case I thought of anything else. I walked back into the room, realizing that I was going to be very sore in the morning.

"What's this," Rachel asked, grabbing the business card from my fingers. "Oooh, you got me Officer McHotty's phone number."

"He wasn't that good looking," I said sitting down.

Rachel sat down next to me.

"No, he wasn't that good-looking," she said, in a soothing tone. "Unless you're into a chiseled jaw, big muscles, and a tight-fitting uniform."

She perked back up, the sympathy was gone.

"Oh, wait, I am into all of those things," she said, laughing.

I glanced over at Caitlin and she was nodding in agreement. Tariq was enjoying Rachel busting my chops and actually smiled for maybe the third time since I met him.

Rachel looked down at the card, flicking it a few times with her finger.

"Maybe it is time for me to upgrade," she said, a mocking wistfulness in her voice.

With that Tariq stood up, still laughing.

"I don't like the guy, but that's harsh," he said, extending a hand to Caitlin and pulling her up to leave.

Once they left, Rachel planted a big, wet, exaggerated kiss on my lips.

"I'm sorry, I don't want to trade you in for Officer McHotty," she cooed.

19. Behind the Music

It took a few days but I finally settled on a time to meet Murphy at his house to do a potential Grateful Dead music swap. I could care less about the music, in fact, most of it bored me to tears, no wonder most of those who love it are under the influence of something.

No, all I wanted was to have an excuse to get closer to Murph to see what was up.

I planned ahead, which would make my father proud, and had Brian Metzger FedEx me some CD-R's of Grateful Dead Bootlegs so I had something to show Murph. I converted most to MP3 and loaded them on my laptop but kept a few of the CD-R's for show as well. Either way, I hoped I'd be prepared.

I listened to a few songs, but they did nothing for me. I was going to have to act a little bit on this one.

I was supposed to meet Murph at his place around 4:00 but got there early on purpose. It is very rare that I am early for anything. It is part procrastination, part a total aversion to the uncomfortableness about sitting around and having to wait for things or people.

I once had an appointment with a trainer when I was playing high school hockey, and since it was a new gym I left early to make sure I would be on time. I got there early. A rational person would have gone in and waited but not me. Nope, I drove around the area, ended up getting stuck in traffic, and wound up being five minutes late.

Murph's house betrayed his rich roots, despite his best efforts to stay true to his new ideals. The house was actually a townhouse. It was one of 20 built in the last 10 years all in a row about a mile from campus. Each one had a two car garage with the bulk of the home on the second floor.

Murph's home looked identical to the other 19 on the street, pink stucco with brown painted wrought iron and a matching garage door. The only difference was the tie-dyed Bob Marley flag on one side of the balcony and a Jamaican flag on the other.

I was early on purpose but Murph's disheveled roommate did not seem to notice. He had wannabe dreads and, despite it being almost 3:30 in the afternoon, was still in a ratty blue, terrycloth bathrobe.

The house had a faint reek of pot smoke that I guessed was a fairly permanent fixture.

The rest of the home was a clash of Murph's old and new ideals. Everything was expensive and fairly new, but nothing was in good shape. A leather sofa that had to cost more than most people's cars, was now scuffed, stained and had a number of tears and burn marks.

Murph had a stereo I would kill for, but it was covered in melted candle wax. Similarly, a Blu-Ray player appeared to be sitting in a puddle of bongwater.

In fact, I counted no fewer than three bongs in the family room and that number was matched once I ventured into Murph's room.

His roommate made his way back to the couch and gave a grunt in my general direction when I told him I was heading to Murph's room.

The room was a lot like the rest of the house, very nice, expensive stuff blended with hippy accoutrements. By now I was starting to wonder if Murph wasn't purposely damaging his stuff so that his new friends would not take the same attitude towards him that Tariq had recently taken to me.

Apparently, it was okay to come from wealth, you just could not like it. Somewhere I imagine there are about 50 million Americans who'd gladly take some of Murph's money, or at least one of his three flat-screen televisions.

I casually scanned the room. At first, there was nothing out of the ordinary. Clothes and CDs were strewn everywhere. I started moving around the room. I started at a chest and drawers, opening a few and glancing in while the eyes of the Grateful Dead looked down upon me disapprovingly.

On his desk was a nice computer that now had Marijuana leaf and Free Leonard Peltier stickers. I opened a drawer and found the first thing that would make me have a quick pause. Peeking out from under a few notebooks was a Polaroid camera.

I quickly remembered the photos Big Ed and Harris showed me that first day the living room.

I closed the drawer and worked my way over to his CD collection. They were in cases that looked like old vegetable crates, but I knew were actually from Ikea. Gone was the hip-hop and top-40 music I knew him to listen to in high school. Now the crates were filled with some classic rock, reggae, and jam bands, mostly the Grateful Dead, but the occasional Phish or Rusted Root CD were housed in there for good measure.

I had to admire that he still had CDs, even if he was, at worst, a crazy stalker, and at best, a phony.

Above the CDs was a cork board. The board was mostly covered in photos and postcards, but I noticed two things. One was a card that was unmistakably a University schedule. Next to it was an index card with hastily scribbled notes.

The schedule was Murph's. He was taking 15 units, of which I'd be shocked if he passed nine. I noticed he had a music appreciation class mixed in with the normal slate of Math, English, Psychology, and Spanish.

The index card also appeared to have a class schedule written on it. Half of it was obscured by a photo of Murph and some black guy glassy-eyed and smiling. It was actually a very good photo, save for the large amount of smoke obscuring half the photo.

The card was attached to the cork board by a single thumbtack, so I was able to rotate it from underneath the photo without removing it. I only had to read it once to know exactly what it was…Caitlin's class schedule! I had received the exact same list of classes from Harris just over a month ago.

The door opened to the room and Murph walked in. I thought I was dead to rights but was able to take the photo off the board. It appeared as Murph bought my ruse.

"Dude, we were so baked in that photo," Murph said with a giggle.

Murph proceeded to tell me a not so interesting story of the night the photo was taken. It began "we were so wasted" and ended "man that was some good Denny's breakfast."

I had heard some variation of this story a hundred times. The only difference is that in high school he was drinking Grey Goose and trying to nail a sophomore. In this variation, he was smoking some "kind bud" and did not mention women at all.

We started swapping music. I was very interested in a bootleg of a European festival performance from 1976 and he took a real interest in a soundboard recording of a sound check from a show in Pennsylvania.

We each found two more concerts we wanted when Murph retrieved a small box from a nightstand drawer. He pulled out a small bag of weed and some rolling papers. He quickly rolled a joint and held it up to inspect it.

"You want some?" he asked.

"I can't," I said. "The team still drug tests me."

That is actually not true. On the college level only football players and track athletes are drug tested, and then only for performance-enhancing drugs. If they did drug test the hockey team, we'd likely lose 40% of the roster.

Of course, if they tested for alcohol, only reserve defenseman David Hosier would remain. Hosier was the son of an alcoholic and just did not touch the stuff. Normally a guy who was not much of a drinker would get hazed, but we found out that Hosier's old man was a violent drunk who nearly killed his mom during a fight. With that piece of news, we did not pressure the guy to drink at all. Besides, we always had a designated driver.

Murphy did not need to know I just didn't like the stuff. I have been an athlete for most of my life and the thought of ingesting smoke of any kind just seems kind of counterproductive. I did try it when I was 16, but did not feel much other than very drowsy and figured there were cheaper ways to be tired.

Murph did not seem to worry that secondhand smoke might affect my fictional drug test and lit up the joint.

Midway through he had a coughing fit and after he recovered he looked my way through bloodshot eyes.

"I hear you're dating Caitlin McCauley's roommate," he asked.

I was a little surprised. We no longer ran in the same circles, how would he know that?

"Uh, yeah, how'd you know?"

"Uh, what's his face told me."

Good old what's his face.

Frankly, there was really no one Murph would talk to that should know who I am dating. I rarely speak to anyone we went to high school with that is still in the state of Arizona. Even if he saw me on campus with Rachel, he shouldn't know she was Caitlin's roommate. Unless of course, he was breaking in her room.

"Was it Kenny Morris?" I asked.

"Uh, that might be it," he started coughing again.

Kenny Morris was a guy we used to know. He was in my graduating class and was at Arizona for a semester. He dropped out, moved back home and last I heard he was in school somewhere in the Midwest. I had not seen or spoken to Kenny in nearly two years.

"It was either Kenny or Devon Bloom," Murphy corrected.

Devon Bloom and I had spoken, just a few days ago, actually. He was the one who tipped me off on the Murph's lifestyle change. That was more plausible, but I could not remember if I told him I was dating anyone, much less Caitlin's roommate.

Some detective I was.

We traded a few more discs, ripping the songs to our laptop hard drives. Within 48 hours most would be erased from the computer. Other than to keep tabs on the Murph I had no interest in them.

I turned off my computer and slipped it into my backpack. Murph got up off the bed and escorted me to the door.

As I walked out of the room I noticed the picture of Murph and the black guy was back on the cork board, but the index card with Caitlin's class schedule on it was no longer there.

20. Surprisingly Bright Flash

Friday was progressing nicely. One of my classes was cut short and the other was actually very interesting.

I was looking forward to the evening. I thought it would be fun to hang out with Rachel and my friends. As embarrassing as "Little Mark" and the rest of my friends could be, they are in reality very good people and a lot of fun.

No matter what my original intentions were, the fact was I really did like Rachel. Having her meet my friends would make it real. Maybe when this was all over we would have a future after all.

The plan was to grab a quick dinner then head out to the bars. Rachel's friends wanted to go to a trendy place. Bad music, expensive drinks and lots of people who wanted to see and be seen. We, and by we I mean me and Chuck, were more adamant about a low key place. We preferred the Shanty. It was hardly a dive bar, but it was not slick and modern either. It was older, lots of wood and brass. Ugly faded paintings and paint that was stained yellow from years when smoking was legal in bars.

The bar was a good place to hang out and actually converse. It was not a meat market, though you'd get a handful of good looking girls who were more interested in a stiff drink and a game of pool, than trolling for frat boys.

There were new pool tables and a patio where you could hear the jukebox, but still, have a good chat. The bartenders had a heavy pour and the doormen did not scrutinize well-made fake I.D.'s.

I was awkwardly eating and walking when the cell phone went off.

It was Martin.

The last time we spoke he gave me good news and Landon Richmond's address. This time the news was not as good.

"We got another picture," Martin said.

"You got another Polaroid?" I asked.

"No, this time it is digital," he explained. "Looks like it was from a cell phone camera. Another photo of Caitlin sleeping."

Apparently, the photo was sent from a blocked number. They were trying to figure out who owned the phone but so far no luck.

"If it was me, I would have used a prepaid phone," I said. Amazingly, Harris actually knew what a prepaid cell phone was. I guess he was not completely technologically inept.

I told him about Murphy, the missing class schedule and the Polaroid camera.

"Maybe, he knows you saw the camera and switched to his phone," Harris said, after a brief moment.

We chatted a few minutes more. I told him I'd check out Landon over the weekend and he told me that he'd keep me up to date if anything else happened.

It was a chilly night, so I went with a solid black sweater that looked like something a British commando might don. It had black, vertical ribs on the torso, but the arms and shoulders had a different knitting, while the elbows had patches of solid material. It was nice but just quirky enough to make it look like I was not trying too hard.

To complete my look, I donned some well-worn jeans and some boot, that had the look of work boots without the functionality. The hair was purposely messy, a look that actually took me 20 minutes to perfect, and to top it off I slipped on a stainless steel watch that was a gift from my mother.

By now you must have noticed I rarely talk about my mom. She left my dad shortly after I moved away from home for junior hockey. I assumed she was waiting for me to graduate high school, but once I left home at 15, she got three years removed from her sentence.

While I am not happy my parents split up, and even less thrilled that my mom essentially bailed on me and my brothers, I cannot really blame her. I think I was only 12 when I realized my mom was unhappy. I did not understand the specifics, but I could tell she and my dad were not right for each other.

My mom was a free spirit, who was into art and writing and poetry. She took numerous art classes when I was a kid. She tried to learn watercolors, pottery making and even took a weekend class on batik.

My dad is rigid. He hardly has time for the arts. While he has an appreciation for classical music and some jazz, I almost think he feels he has to like it, rather than truly enjoys it.

He did not understand that being his wife was not enough for my mom. She didn't seem to have a problem being on his arm for social events, but she wanted more. She didn't want to belong to charities because it looked good. She didn't want to conform to the rigid standards of behavior that their social circle called for.

My mom got me, which was nice. While my two older brothers were in lockstep with my father, my mother realized that I was just not like them. She never got my love of sports, but she never tried to make me conform like my father tried with us all.

The watch was a perfect symbolism of this understanding. It was a birthday gift three years ago. Frankly, my brothers did not like it. They liked more traditionally fancy watches. Big name brands, gold or even platinum timepieces. This watch was a flat gray. It was stainless steel, not a precious metal. It was some obscure European company, not one you see in the pages of Esquire. Despite lacking flash, it was still elegant just different than what most were accustomed to. And that is why I liked it so much.

The fact that my mom and I clicked so much made her departure all the more painful. Although I was no longer living at home during the season, when I did go back home I was in my father's care. I love my dad, but it can be tense. We were frequently at odds over everything from my sleeping habits to how I read the paper. Even though the paper was destined for the recycling bin, he still wanted it put back together like I found it.

Of course, the fact that I was usually the last one to read it and did not place it in the recycling bin did not help my cause.

I took a final look in the mirror and liked what I saw. Chuck emerged soon after. He decided on a much flashier sweater, full of vibrant colors, with a white dress shirt poking out of the collar and bottom of the shirt. He wore black cords and had his lucky purple shoes on.

In the lobby "Little Mark" and Mike were waiting. Marcus apparently could not be bothered, but unbeknownst to me, Chuck recruited this guy named Geovany to come out with us.

I did not know Geovany well. He was a big guy but tried to hide it. He was not muscular big or even fat big, just a large guy. If pressed, most people would have trouble describing his build other than he was "big".

Maybe "forgettably big" would be the best description.

He wasn't intimidating big, nor was he cuddly big. I guess in the right situation you might be afraid of him, but I guess he was the kind of guy who got challenged frequently because he was big enough that the challenger would not look weak for picking on him, but not so big and tough that he posed any kind of a threat.

He tried to hide his size. He wore a lot of baggy clothes and sported a few different trench coats.

I wondered what he might wear when things got hotter in the spring.

I had not hung out with Geovany very much, but Chuck had a habit of adopting a few wayward freshmen, "Little Mark" being another, and Geovany would pop in and out of the group from time to time.

I worried about him being a buzzkill tonight, but maybe hanging out with a bunch of women might cheer him up.

Of course, I was not sure. The skull earring and spiked rings were not exactly welcoming to the female species, but what did I know? Maybe under all of that armor was just a sad, sensitive guy.

Mike had gotten the memo that women would be involved in the evening He sore untucked, dark red dress shirt on, it was not completely buttoned and he had a black t-shirt on underneath. I recognized it to be a Metallica t-shirt, but he hid it well.

He also had his hair pulled back into a ponytail, a look he rarely, if ever sported. I would say for maybe the third time I knew him that he seemed to actually care about his appearance.

The five of us headed out. The plan was for the guys and girls to eat separately then meet at the bar around 9:00. While many bar-goers prefer to not even think about getting to a bar until 10, sometimes even 11, I did not subscribe to that theory. Why would I want to miss valuable drinking time? 9:00 was actually late in my book, but the girls wanted to go somewhere "nice".

Us guys settled for wings, NBA basketball on the big screen and even two pitchers of beer to get things started.

We beat them to the bar and had to wait outside because it would be easier for them to get in with us here. The doorman was a former football player who I knew from my days on the hockey team and Chuck actually tutored in French last year, helping him stay eligible. The bar was normally lax anyways on fake IDs, but with our boy watching the gate, we were sure to get our cadre of characters in.

The girls sauntered up just a few minutes later. The first thing I noticed was that Rachel had vamped it up more than usual. She went just a little heavier with the make-up, especially the eye makeup and was wearing a tight, low-cut t-shirt that I had never seen before and would later find out she bought just for this occasion. To complete the look she sported big hoop earrings, pigtails and a skirt that was not ridiculously short but not modestly long either. Frankly, I got the best look at her legs in the few weeks we had been dating. I got the feeling that she was letting me know what I had been missing out on and what I had to look forward to.

In the end, I knew the slight alteration in look was for my benefit, but I also got the distinct impression it was also for my friends' benefit or her friends' benefit. She was making me the star of the evening.

"Dude, she's dating you?" Mike said, a tad incredulously.

The rest of her friends each took different approaches to the look of the evening.

Jade could not let Rachel be the complete center of seductive attention. She went with a ridiculously short denim skirt and a sweater that would have been described as too tight.

Maura, the band girl, went with the high school short-shorts and her baggy Arizona sweatshirt. Kung-Fu Tracey went simple jeans and t-shirt that worked probably more than she expected.

Dana, the introvert, went with a big sweater and slacks. Like every other time I saw her, she was seemingly hiding her shape. The sweater was a tad too big, as were the slacks and she remained quiet the whole evening. She was one who was used to blending into the background and this night was no different.

Before we could even get the first round of drinks back to the table Jade was all over Chuck. She was oozing sex and it was no secret to either Chuck or myself that he could get whatever he wanted from her.

I gave him a knowing smile, and he just rolled his eyes. We both knew that he would have no interest in Jade. It was too easy. Chuck liked a challenge and there was no challenge to Jade. Physically Maura was more his type, though Kung-Fu Tracey was more his style in terms of conversation. I actually put Dana as the dark horse, if she'd actually talk.

After half a beer I made Maura the favorite if Chuck was thinking below the waist and Tracey the favorite if he was thinking above the neck.

After the second round of drinks, we were shooting pool, more than that we were shooting the shit. My group of friends has enough trouble holding a conversation that can include every person. Add four women to the mix and it was impossible.

I was eyeing a shot, trying to ignore Rachel, who was purposely trying to distract me by getting into my line of site. I did not know if it was the alcohol, the outfit or what was on the horizon, but she was acting more carefree and flirty than ever.

Frankly, I liked it.

If I was not distracted enough by Rachel. I had Mark talking my ear off. He was discussing last week's Penguin/Devils game, not knowing that I did not see it and did not care. As odd as it may sound, if I am not playing in it, or betting on it, I don't really follow hockey.

We were several rounds into the evening when my cell phone rang. It was my father. He routinely called when he knew I might be misbehaving. Never mind that I have seen photos of my father's old fraternity days and he almost always had a scotch in his hand, apparently, my brothers and I were only at college to learn and possibly meet a spouse.

The only difference between my brothers and myself is that they were better at hiding their college misbehaving from my father than I was. While I was not about to flaunt my partying to my father, I did not go out of my way to hide it either.

I debated whether or not I was going to answer the phone, but I knew if I didn't he'd just call back repeatedly.

I stepped out to the back patio and answered my phone. Although there were a handful of tables out there and still some music playing, it lacked the clamor of the bar's inside.

"Where are you?" my father asked after a few pleasantries.

"Out to dinner, with a friend," I said, avoiding the truth.

I paced a bit by a wrought iron fence that's separated the patio from the apartment building next door.

He started to grill me on who I was with and I decided not to dodge his questions.

"It's a date dad," I snapped at him. "I am on a date."

He cheered up a bit. While the thought of me out carousing was not to his liking, apparently having a love life was alright.

I quickly broke down that he did not know her or her family, that she was from out east and her father was an entrepreneur. I did not mention he was a plumber and he actually seemed to accept my vague answers. It was a minor miracle.

He then asked the million-dollar question.

"So is she just a fling or is she special?"

I paused for a second, then gave him the only honest answer of our conversation.

"Yeah, she's kind of special."

That pretty much ended the call as he hung up to let me get back to my date.

I shut off the phone, turned around and saw Rachel standing there. She had her arms behind her back and looked up at me with this coy look on her face.

"Special huh?" she asked, already knowing the answer. "You talking about me I hope?"

I reached around her waist and pulled her closer. She tiptoed up to get close to my face.

"No, I was talking about Chuck."

My answer caught her off guard, but after a split second she got the joke and gave me a playful slap to the chest with the back of her fist.

"Of course I meant you," I said and leaned in.

It was one of those really good kisses. Even though I loathe public displays of affection, I did not care that there were four tables of people watching. It was a longing kiss, with perfect rhythm. Had we been alone it would not have stopped until we were quite naked and quite sweaty, but here, on the back patio of a bar, we had to stop.

"You left me with a lot to think about until tomorrow night," I said, just a tad light headed.

"I know," she said and promptly spun on her heel and walked back inside.

I admired the view as Chuck walked out. He took a glance himself.

He carried two beers and handed me one.

"You have an admirer," I said, smirking.

"Yeah, maybe a few," he shot back.

"You going for the sure thing or a dark horse?" I asked, before taking a big gulp of the Rolling Rock.

At that moment my phone buzzed. I was dreading that it was my dad again but looked down to see it was a picture mail from a blocked number. Perplexed, I opened up the file to see that it was a photo of the girls in the bar, apparently taken by Rachel, whose arm was stretching off to the side as she tried to hold the camera phone far enough away to get all of them in the shot.

I was puzzled. Rachel's cell phone had a broken camera, yet here was a picture.

I walked back into the bar and before I could take two steps Rachel was up taking my picture with a metallic pink phone I had not seen before.

"Where'd you get that?" I asked, trying to sound light-hearted.

"I borrowed it from a friend," she answered vaguely before swinging to my side, pressing our heads together and taking another picture. The tiny camera had a bright flash that caught me off guard.

She showed me the picture and I indeed had a look on my face that had more than a trace of confusion and worry on it.

"Not a great pic, but I think you are cute anyways," she said, then gave me a kiss on the cheek and headed back to the table.

I sat down with the group and was promptly handed a shot. I gave the tiny drink a cursory glance and downed it. I normally do not like shots, but hey, this one was a gift. Apparently a gift of Tequila.

I scanned our quirky table. Little Mark and Mike were doing their best to get the attention of Jade, but she was too busy hitting on Chuck. Conversely, Chuck was chatting up both Maura and Tracey, and the looks on their faces said he was being his normal charming self.

The surprise was Geovany and Dana. They were not talking but were writing or drawing in pen on each other's hands.

Another round of shots hit the table, Jägermeister this time, and after it hit my gut I turned to Rachel.

"Why'd you send me the picture on a blocked number?"

"I did?" she replied, laying her head on my shoulder. "I guess I just never turned the block off since the last time I used it."

Suddenly my head was cloudy with more than too many drinks, though that was there. Suddenly my girlfriend had a new "borrowed" phone, which was set to make blocked calls.

I pulled my phone out and texted Harrison, asking him to forward me the latest picture of Shannon sleeping. I knew it was a longshot to see if he could actually figure it out, but I had to try.

The night wore on, more alcohol was consumed and as the bar closed we decided to leave vehicles behind and walk home.

It had gotten chilly, so Rachel snuggled in and as the two of us walked entangled, we dropped behind the rest of the group. Soon the same dynamics at the table were apparent on the street.

Chuck was still regaling the girls with his stories and Maura and Tracey still looked enamored, but Jade had a scowl on her face since she was being ignored by him. That did not prevent Mark from still trying to talk to her. Mike was on the fringe of the Chuck/Maura/Tracey trio. He was involved, not pathetic like Mark, but not entirely behind the ropes.

By the time we reached the girls' dorm, it was pretty apparent that Chuck had chosen Tracey and I wondered if they might both retire upstairs. Jade glared at the two, and while ignoring Mark, seemed to be flirting with Mike who had turned his attention from Maura to her.

By that time Geovany and Dana were gone. I am not sure what happened to them, but we saw very little of them the rest of the semester.

I gave Rachel another kiss, and she excused herself and went inside with Maura. I looked at Chuck, Mark, and Mike to see if they were ready to go. Chuck gave me the nod in the direction of our home, indicating I should go on without him. Mike looked at me with a questioning look on his face, essentially asking me if he was making the headway he thought he was. I tried to look non-committal, but walked over and pulled Mark away. I wasn't sure Mike was making headway with Jade, but Mark wasn't and was a potential cock block.

Mark and I left the foursome behind us and walked the short distance to our dorm.

"I think she was into me," Mark boasted.

"Sure she was," I said, the sarcasm dripping off my words, but unnoticed by him.

I was too tired to debate and as he told me his plans for wooing her, I walked in silence. I was in the room, all but ready for bed when my phone buzzed. I assumed it was Rachel with a good night text, maybe I'd even get a memorable photo from her.

I did indeed get a memorable photo, but not from her. It was from Harris. It was the latest photo of Caitlin from the stalker. It was clearly her, in her dorm room. It was clear because the picture was illuminated with a surprisingly bright flash.

21. The Sure Thing

For only the second time in my life, I woke up knowing that I was going to have sex that night. Needless to say, that put a little extra hop in my step.

The only other time I absolutely knew that sex was on the agenda was the time me and Maggie planned a weekend getaway. She had access to a cabin and we both knew that there was a good chance it would be our final weekend together. Three weeks later I was back in Arizona and she was off to school on the East Coast.

My plan was to make the evening as romantic as possible so the first move was to make a few bets. I did well the night before and decided to get some of the money owed to me and risk a little bit more of my winnings on some NBA games.

On my way out of the door "Little Mark" corralled me.

"Want to get breakfast?" he asked eagerly, a baggy L.A. Clippers jersey drooping all the way to mid-thigh.

"I already ate," I lied.

He asked where I was headed and I vaguely mentioned my errands. He was looking for something to do and I was having trouble dissuading him from wanting to tag along.

"Look, I am going somewhere and they don't take kindly to uninvited strangers dropping by," I spat.

He looked at me wide-eyed.

"You're going to buy drugs?" he asked, stammering.

I started to laugh. The look on his face was a combination of disappointment, fear, and excitement. I forget sometimes that Mark was a pretty sheltered kid who learned a lot about the world from afternoon specials and the movies they show in health class.

"No, I am not going to buy drugs," I looked around, making sure no one was listening. "You can't tell anyone, but I do a little gambling from time to time. I am going off to see my bookie."

Gambling was a big no-no if you are an athlete. If my career wasn't already over, it sure would be if anyone knew I was gambling. It did not matter if I didn't gamble on my own games or any of the sports at the school, gambling was the ultimate sin. Criminals, drug addicts, and cheaters usually got a second chance, but not gamblers.

"I want to go," Mark said.

"These guys'll freak out if I bring you," I said.

"What if I gamble?" he asked. "I've got money."

He proceeded to pull out his wallet and flash a few hundred dollars.

I called Ike's house, Rod answered. I explained the situation and I could hear Rod confer with his brother.

"How much does he want to bet?" Rod finally asked.

I cupped the phone and turned to Mark.

"How much you want to bet?"

He frowned a moment, deep in thought. I think he was silently doing calculations in his head. Finally, he looked up at me.

"Two hundred, maybe two fifty?"

I relayed the number to Rod and confirmed that Mark had the cash in hand.

"Shit, bring the boy over," Rod said.

We hopped into my jeep, blaring some tunes, I picked a playlist of extreme heavy metal in an effort to freak Mark out, but it did not seem to work. After a brief stop to get Mark a bagel, we were at Ike's place. The front door was open, only the screen door was latched. I gave it a quick knock and walked in.

All five inhabitants were there and if five people could be bustling, these five certainly were. Well, four were, Omar was on a chair doing what appeared to be lounging. I knew he was keeping watch and would be on either of us if we stepped out of line.

Surprisingly, Ike was not on one of his cell phones but was doing some serious damage to an oversized iced cinnamon roll.

"Slade, come here," Ike beckoned. He turned to Rod, "Get the little man a drink."

Mark bristled at the comment, but I did not care. Ike looked at a notebook, then looked up at me. He ripped off a hunk of sweet roll and devoured it. He licked the icing off his fingers in a loud, thorough way, sucking on the top of each to get the last bit of icing. It was not something I needed to see.

"You're on a bit of a win streak," he said, matter of factly. "That concerned me. Normally when someone connected to the athletic department wins as much as you have I get suspicious. However, Rod tells me you have had next to no contact with any athletes. He says you spend all your time with your new girlfriend. Unless she has some hidden contacts we don't know about, I'd say you're just lucky."

After being cleared of any wrongdoing, we settled into the plan of action. I took $50 cash and played the rest of my winnings on the night's NBA games. I needed the Suns and Celtics to play well, and the Warriors and T-Wolves to forget how to play defense.

Next, our conversation turned to Mark. He was sitting on a bar stool taking in the whole impressive scene. His face had a look that was one part scared shitless and one part impressed with the whole set-up.

"So what's the deal with your boy there?" Ike poked another piece of sweet roll in Mark's direction.

"He's kind of like a mascot, just sort of tags along," I tried to explain. "He's a rabid sports fan and expressed interest in betting some games."

"He new to it?"

"I think so," I responded, pretty unsure of my answer.

"You should know your friend's better," Ike said. "He's dropped some money, not much mind you, with an offshore betting house. He also plays a lot of online poker."

I stared blankly at him.

"How'd you…" I finally managed to stammer before he cut me off.

"Any time an athlete comes in here I need to do a lot of checking," Ike explained. "There are a lot of risks associated with you guys. I keep a lot of tabs on you. I know about all your friends, I know about your new little girlfriend, I even know that knee of yours is not nearly as hurt as you make it out to be."

I kept staring. I wanted to be cool, but it was tough. Ike was suddenly more intimidating than ever.

"But your boy is cool, I'll deal with him," Ike said as he turned his attention to Mark. "Little man, get over here."

I traded places with Mark. He sat down in front of the massive bookie and his sweat-stained Texas A&M hat. They had a brief, but intense discussion and not five minutes later Mark was walking away with a betting slip.

It was a big sandwich for lunch followed by a serious nap, then a trip off to the grocery store. I decided that my red hot spaghetti might not be the best choice and although I make some pretty good BBQ ribs, their messiness is not great for a romantic evening.

I settled on Lasagna. It tends to be a dish that anyone who is not lactose intolerant seems to enjoy. It is not the toughest thing to make, but it just difficult enough that it tends to impress if it comes off right.

I strolled through the aisles picking up what I'd need: noodles, sauce, ricotta and mozzarella cheese, ground beef, eggs, and some herbs. I also nabbed a bag of salad and the makings for some garlic bread.

I was stumped for dessert, mainly because I was thinking of a dessert that had nothing to with food. I settled on strawberry shortcake. Although I despise strawberries, I know girls tend to dig them and I figured if we actually got that far I could just have a little poundcake and whip cream.

I picked up a few more necessities and then headed to the checkout.

The checker was a middleaged woman I recognized but I did not see the same recognition in her face. I got the feeling that she was once quite pretty. She was not necessarily unattractive now but just looked perpetually tired and beaten down by life.

She started scanning my items one by one. As she was scanning the lasagna noodles she said, "making dinner tonight?"

"Yup," I said, not offering anything extra.

She scanned the rose I grabbed in the floral department.

"Oh, a romantic dinner?" she added.

She next picked up a box of condoms to scan.

"Ah-ha," she said with a knowing, leering smile. I could only shrug, pay and be on my merry way.

A lot of guys are embarrassed to buy condoms, but I never understood it. I mean, the purchase in and of itself means that you are probably going to have sex and that means you are at least cool in someone's eyes. The funny thing is while I am not embarrassed by the purchase, I also don't like to buy them alone. Even if it is just a pack of gum, something about having at least one other item along with the condoms makes it seem less seedy.

It wasn't long before I had the lasagna built and in the oven down in the dorm basement. While the microwave and stove top get frequent use, the oven gets next to no use unless a guy's girlfriend was over and decided to bake cookies.

Soon I was showered, shaved and smelling pretty good thanks to some cologne that was a Christmas gift from one of my brothers. While we rarely see eye-to-eye on anything, they do have expensive taste and the cologne was high quality.

I had the lasagna and garlic bread resting under foil, mixed up a salad and after 20 minutes of deliberation, settled on 20 song playlist that I thought was sultry, but not trying too hard. Even though it was a sure thing, I did not want it to feel cheesy or even rehearsed. The intent was to make Rachel feel special.

I was giving in the playlist its first run through when there was a knock at the door.

I opened it to a beaming, if not slightly bashful, Rachel. No one buzzed me from the front desk, so she had snuck in which was for the best as I was well-known enough that if a good looking girl in a nice dress came to my dorm room, and did not leave it would raise attention.

And she did look great. She wore a black dress. It was not skin tight, but it sure clung in all the right places. It was probably too short for church, but too long for most nightclubs. It was sexy, without being too obvious.

We shared a long kiss and I escorted her over to the couch, which doubled as our dining room. An old steamer trunk served as our coffee table, but I placed a tablecloth over it, had candles burning and made the most of what I could from a dorm room.

"You really cooked me dinner?" she asked as if she was unsure whether I was sincere about making her dinner.

"I did not want tonight to be tawdry," I defended myself. "Sultry, sure, but surely not tawdry."

To be perfectly honest, we rushed through dinner. We did not scarf the food down, but we ate with a purpose, drank the wine quickly and about 17 minutes after that I was leading her to the bedroom.

While I made every attempt at making things romantic, in the end, we were in a dorm room. My room was a double, so we had a separate bedroom, but it was still two twin beds, that had been bunk beds, in a room less than 12 feet across. It was hardly a suite at the Ritz Carlton.

That being said, I had candles burning, washed my sheets and had a brand new comforter on the bed. While leading her to the bed II turned on a Bluetooth speaker and the playlist I had on in the other room, was now beaming into the bedroom. As I began kissing her and lowering her to the bed, the room filled with the sounds of an old Etta James song that I figured she probably did not know, but certainly enhanced the mood.

This was hardly my first rodeo, though it had been several months since I was in this situation. I had a two-week fling with a cross-country runner in early September and wound up in a bathroom at a Halloween party with a slutty nurse (I went as a hockey player naturally). But since that midnight fumbling on some poor guy's bathroom counter, nothing.

I'd love to tell I guided her to the bedroom and proceeded to blow her mind with the most awesome sex two people ever had, but that would be a lie. It was our first time together and while we certainly had our moments, we also went through some of the awkwardness most new couples have.

We bumped heads not once, but twice. She yelped once when I inadvertently pulled her hair when I rested my forearm on it. It took a minute or two to really get into a rhythm once we actually started.

But there were plenty of good moments too. Despite the awkwardness, I was able to showcase my abilities. We kissed for a good long while before slowly undressing each other and taking things to a hotter level. I am pretty sure Marvin Gay was on the stereo at that point. Marvin had always been good to me and tonight was no exception.

The kissing gave way to more as I slid down and gave her plenty of attention before finally completing the task. Leave it to me to make sex sound like a home improvement project.

It was sometime later and we were in each other's arms. We didn't talk too much afterwards, just relished in the moment. Despite the lusty nature of what occurred, there was still a sweetness to the moment.

I kissed her on the forehead and she looked up at me beaming.

"I love you," she said.

Oh shit, I thought.

22. Quintessential Greasy Spoon.

The words hung there for a second.

I wanted to pretend that I did not hear them. I was pretty sure I could almost talk myself into believing she had not said them, but that was not fair. She had already given me her body, and now she was doing something almost, if not more vulnerable.

For only the second time in my life, a woman told me she loved me.

The first time I was actually the one who said it first. Maggie and I were cuddled on the couch watching a hockey game. After a particularly bad offsides call, she called the referee a "blind piece of shit," which caused me to laugh hysterically. She soon joined me in laughter.

Somewhere between a laugh and me trying to catch my breath, I blurted out "I love you."

She stopped laughing and stared at me.

"Do you mean you 'love me' cause I am a cool girlfriend who knows that the linesman made a shitty call or are you telling me that you are in love with me," she demanded.

It was only then that I really realized what I had said. There was a tension between us and I had to consider what did I really mean.

"Both," I finally answered. "I did not mean to say it this way, but I am really, truly in love with you."

She remained silent for a moment, her gaze never left my face. Finally, she turned back to the television and said confidently, "I know."

I did not know what that meant. A strange terror swept over me for a split second, as she kept her eyes on the hockey game. Did that mean she did not love me? Did I just make a huge tactical error in our relationship? I felt like an idiot.

I almost missed that she was looking at me out of the corner of her eye. I noticed when she began to smile. Soon she pounced on me and gave me a big kiss.

"Of course I love you too," she giggled.

I remembered that brief moment of terror when I did not know how Maggie felt and I did not want Rachel to feel that same discomfort.

Fortunately, I did not have to. Before I could figure out what to say, Rachel started laughing maniacally.

"You should see the look on your face," she said, nearly crying as she laughed. "I mean I really like you, and you better think highly of me after what we just did, but telling you that 'I love you' after just a few weeks is crazy."

I have to admit; I was a little disappointed. Don't get me wrong, I was relieved because I had no idea how I would have responded to her proclamation of love, but the fact it was so easy for her to make light of it left me off balanced.

It was not the first time she had "gotten me." We were watching "Heat" and she started crying during the big shootout at the bank. I thought she was completely moved by the performances.

"She I told you it was good," I gloated. "You are moved to tears."

She instantly quit "crying" and stuck out her tongue at me.

"I was bored to tears," she said laughing.

I looked at her slack-jawed.

"I told you I was a good actress," she said, now quite proud of herself.

Now as we lay in bed, she had that same pleased look on her face.

"That was uncool," I said, pretending to be madder than I was.

"No, that was funny," she said. "You were taking everything so seriously."

"Well, next time I will just throw you down on the bed and ravish you with hardly a word."
And I did.

We fell asleep in each other's arms, which, to be honest, is the only way two adults can sleep together in a twin sized bed.

We woke up and did it again. This time it was a little smoother, a tad less awkward. When we were done I insisted we go to breakfast and gave her little option of saying "no."

For most, the logical conclusion to a romantic Saturday evening would be a nice brunch or breakfast at a quaint café. For me, it is Bobo's. Bobo's is the quintessential greasy spoon.

I do not know who or what Bobo is, but his or her or their place is awesome. It is nothing to look at. It is a small, cramped hot brick building about 10 minutes from campus. It is about six tables, a counter, and an open kitchen. Nothing to hide in back except storage. It is so small that if two people wait for a table inside, they create a logjam for those trying to pay or trying to leave their name on the list for a table. It is one of those places that everyone who eats there loves, regardless of the lack of décor or ambiance.

I am not sure how people learn about Bobo's, they just go and become devotees. There is always a wait, with a diverse grouping of people, yet you never seem to wait too long.

This Sunday we waited in for our table with another motley crew. There was the aging biker with the bandana and graying beard and his heavyset biker babe with a too tight top that showed off her ample chest. There was a young couple and their two young kids who were dressed as if they were coming from or going to church. Plenty of plaid and khakis for father and son, and sundresses and ribbons for mother and daughter. There were also four hungover college students who either dragged themselves out of bed to eat or had not yet been to sleep.

The inside is crammed with old tables pushed together and nearly every seat is full. The only thing separating us from two Asian exchange students was napkin holders, sugar packets and four laminated menus jammed between the napkin holders. I recognized one of the regulars in a booth. He was in his early 50s, with a graying braided ponytail and wire-rimmed glasses that made him look on- part shaman and one-part professor. Arturo and I had sat next to each other waiting for a table on more than one occasion, and bonded over sports and a couple of local bands.

People I bring here either have a look of complete mistrust or complete joy. Rachel's was the latter.

"This is totally the type of place my dad likes to eat," she said.

They prepare food in one of three ways at Bobo's. They can toast it, deep fry it or cook it on the flat top. That's it. Sometimes you get a combination of all three, which is ideal.

I insisted that Rachel get the apple pancakes. In my experience, all girls love the apple pancakes. I got the biscuits and gravy because I am a total health nut and nothing says healthy like country gravy.

The two Asian exchange students were also eating the biscuits and gravy. They spoke to each other in their native language. What that was I am not sure, but when my order came one of them gave me a knowing nod when he saw we were getting the same thing. Our homelands may be 6,000 miles apart, but for this one moment, we could share a mutual admiration for Southern comfort food.

About midway through our breakfast, they finished and left. They were replaced by a couple who looked and smelled like they were still stoned.

"A little wake and bake I assume," I said nodding in their direction.

Rachel ignored me. "These pancakes are so good," she said with a mouthful.

"So do you think those two Asian guys will move back to Japan or China and continue to eat biscuits and gravy?" I asked. "Or is it an indulgence that they have while in America and when they go back home they will forgo this quintessential American dish."

She paused eating for the first time since the waitress brought our order.

"How the crap do you think of this stuff?" she asked, before diving back into the pancakes, a huge smile on her face.

23. A Motley Mix

The Sonoran Dog is quite possibly one of the greatest inventions known to mankind. Although Hermosillo, Mexico claims to have invented this wonderful concoction, my adopted hometown of Tucson, Arizona is where they came to popularity.

In essence, the Sonoran Dog is a bacon-wrapped hot dog, but it is so much more. The dog is placed in a steamed, sweet bun and then covered in pinto beans, onions, tomato, salsa verde, mustard, and, for most, mayonnaise.

While Midwesterners may be partial to the Chicago Dog, give me the Sonoran any day.

Harris was already on the second of four when we began discussing the case again.

"We also got an e-mail from him," Harris said between bites. "We are trying to trace the IP but it looks like it came off an on-campus machine."

Every computer that communicates over the Internet is assigned an IP address. The address uniquely identifies the device and distinguishes it from other computers on the Internet. It's essentially a very long number that tells us what computer sent the e-mail.

Sadly, it does not tell who sent it.

He was wearing a very expensive light gray suit. Like most of his suits it was a little too tight through his beefy shoulders, and a tad too baggy through his thick midsection. Though he was tearing through his hotdog, he had his tie draped over his shoulder and leaned far forward so as to not get any of the drippings on his clothes. His mustache and chin were not so fortunate.

"I am trying to find out where it came from, that might be very helpful," he added. "I am guessing it is a public use computer. Maybe a library or an internet café."

"It could be one of the computer labs," I added, taking the first big bite of my second dog. He looked a bit confused.

"There are still a couple computer labs on campus," I continued. "Most of them are specialty labs for particular majors, like landscape architecture or graphic design, but there are still one or two general use labs. All you need is an ID and sign in."

His face brightened.

"That would be a huge break," his mind was racing. "If it was a lab maybe our guy was dumb enough to sign in and then we'd have him."

He let me know that the e-mail was another thinly veiled threat and that money was again a subject, though no specifics were mentioned.

He took a long drink of soda and then began hot dog no. 3.

We sat in silence for a few moments. One television showed Mexican music videos, while another showed a telenovela, but the sound was not up for either. A motley mix of students and blue-collar workers occupied the tables. I looked over at a table full of house painters and envied the tacos they were eating. I decided I should have gotten at least one taco to accompany my hotdogs.

Yeah, I admit it, I had taco envy.

"So what is his endgame?" I asked.

He looked almost startled at the query. He took a minute to consider his answer.

"I am not entirely sure," said Harris eventually. "He definitely wants to us to know that he can get close to her. There is a power element there. He is trying to show that he is in control."

If this was the case, then this was less about money and more about making McCauley scared. I thought of Landon and Volpe, they were made to feel less than powerful by "Big Ed", so a power exchange made sense.

"If that is the case, then he may be content to just keep scaring us until he gets bored," Harris added. He did not seem convinced by his own answer.

"I heard about some similar cases where the would-be kidnapper eventually extorts money from the families in exchange for not kidnapping his target," Harris said. "In most of the cases, they get the initial payoff and disappear, though a few kept extorting money until they were caught."

I thought about it and it made some sense. Why tip your hand? How did they know McCauley would not have just pulled Caitlyn out of school at the first sign of trouble? Did they have an idea that McCauley might be stubborn enough to keep her in school? Would a political rival like Volpe know that? Would Murphy have figured that out from his time dating Caitlyn?

"Of course, he may have every intention of kidnapping her," Harris continued.

"Why would he tip his hand?" I asked.

"Could be a few reasons," Harris replied. "Could be he is trying to get a feel for how much money to extort. Could be he is trying to figure it out as he goes along, that each time he contacts us he is trying to learn."

He paused, this time he had a grave look on his face.

"We also have to consider that he is just a psycho, and that money is not a factor."

I left the meeting feeling like I had a lot more answers, but those answers just led to a bunch of brand new questions. His last scenario caused me to worry the most. I had been operating as if my job was to save McCauley some money and possibly save Caitlin some discomfort. Now I realized there was a chance that I was actually trying to save her life.

24. Haphazard Tequila Concoction

I wanted to keep tabs on Volpe and after making me his spy, I was suddenly his prized pupil. After class, he stopped me in the hallway and invited me to what he dubbed an informal meeting of Democrats who "get it."

"The party leadership in town and in the state is shortsighted," he explained. "I have been meeting with a number of the true visionaries in the party on a semi-regular basis and think it would be interesting for you to meet them."

Translation: I want to show you off and get you working for us.

So instead of watching Syracuse/UConn with the guys, I was heading to discuss politics and get recruited. At least when I was being recruited for hockey they took me to keg parties and introduced me to recruiting hostesses and former All-Americans.

I set a time to meet Rachel for coffee at 10, that would give me a convenient excuse to leave the party in case it was a total waste of time. I had the text message as evidence, in case I needed to provide proof of my plans.

I had no idea what to expect. Would food be provided? Would there be drinks? Did they sit around and just complain about the state's conservative legislature or was there something at least a bit interesting going on? I was far more interested in whether or not UConn's guards could penetrate the Syracuse match-up zone than I was whether the Democrats could penetrate the Republican stranglehold in the legislature.

I pulled up to the house, or more accurately, pulled up near the house about 20 minutes after six. There were a number of cars in the modest driveway and lined up and down the midtown street.

The house itself was quirky, a multi-story affair hidden behind a bright maroon stucco wall and several Mesquite Trees. The house was stucco as well, painted with several bright hues including purple. Both the house and wall had a lot of stained glass.

I started to knock on the door but it was ajar and I let myself in. Instantly I heard voices talking as I walked in. First I was faced with a small entryway and right up ahead was a small dining room and behind it a kitchen.

A quick scan revealed no one that I knew.

There were several small groups having their own private conversations, but no one paid me any attention. I did not see Volpe, but I did see that people held drinks so as soon as I spotted a makeshift bar in the kitchen I made a beeline for it.

The kitchen was bigger than it looked from the dining room. Again there were a couple of small groups talking and I instantly heard they were talking one form of politics or another. I heard one snippet about "downtown revitalization" and another lambasting the elimination of ethnic studies classes.

I really did not know much about either. I assumed "ethnic studies" did not refer to checking out Hispanic girls in front of the student union.

I looked at my alcohol choices. There was no beer. There was a lot of wine. There was a halfway decent bottle of scotch. There was a bottle of tequila, a bowl of limes and a few bottles of soda.

I played mad scientist and made a concoction of tequila, Sprite, and a lot of lime juice. It was not very good, but I figured I needed a buzz to get through the evening. I put a wedge of lime on the edge of the glass to make it more "classy." I might be able to fool someone taking a quick glance, but inside I knew it was a mess.

I took a huge slug and felt the heat of the alcohol slide down. Two more big sips and I needed to top it off. I knew within minutes I'd be feeling something.

I started to re-enter the party when Volpe found me.

"Eric, so glad you could make it," Volpe said, practically beaming. "I have some people for you to meet."

He guided me right to the family room, at least I think it was the family room. Maybe it was the living room. There was no television, but there was a really nice stereo and two bookcases full of books. There was also a lot of art on the walls and several plants. In addition to a couch and chairs, there was a small desk by a window. So, in theory, it could have been a study.

If this was a normal party and not a reconnaissance mission, I would have spent quite a bit of time checking out the voluminous vinyl record collection and the books, but alas, I had a job to do.

There was a small group of people talking. Three who appeared to be in their forties and fifties, and a fourth who stood out and could not be missed.

She was significantly younger than the bulk of the party goers, though probably a tad older than me. The first thing I noticed was a deep tan, then her beaming smile. She was pretty, but not made up. Maybe it was the tan or the lack of make-up, or maybe it was the more obvious khaki shorts and hiking boots, but I took her for the outdoors type. I am a detective of sorts after all.

She had long, wavy hair that was not styled but still looked good. She was likely the type who looked ready to go whether she was just getting out of bed or just finishing a hike. The shorts revealed great, tanned legs that I probably looked at a little too long. I'd like to blame the haphazard tequila concoction going to my head, but I'd probably be staring stone cold sober.

She saw Volpe and immediately excused herself from the group and came over to us. Before Volpe could say a word the woman spoke.

"You must be Eric, so glad you could come."

I recognized her for what she was at once, a recruiting hostess.

Before agreeing to play hockey at Arizona I made three other recruiting visits. All of them were the same variation of the same trip. You fly in, meet the coaches, get assigned a player to show you around, get assigned a recruiting hostess to show you around and then spend the next 48 hours hearing sales pitches, taking tours and going to some of the craziest parties you've ever attended.

Hockey trips were crazy, but they are nothing like the trips basketball and football players get. For those high profile sports, no expense is spared. My freshman year they arranged for a small forward to have a lingerie show and then he disappeared with two of the "models".

It wasn't quite like that on my trips and every school has different theories on recruiting hostesses. At some schools, they are glorified tour guides. They will show you around, get you everywhere you need to go and make sure you have a good time. At other schools, they are little more than prostitutes. If they are not willing to have sex with a prospect, they certainly know someone who will.

That is the way it works at nearly every recruiting visit. If a player wants to get drunk, they go to a party with booze. If they want to get high, they get matched up with players who get high. If they want to get laid, they get laid.

The better schools know before a recruit gets on campus what he is interested in. If he is religious, they match him up with a current player who is religious and they avoid the wild parties.

Some schools are not that good at it. One of my teammates is a devout Christian, but within three hours of landing for his visit to a school in Ohio, he was sitting in a strip club. On his next trip, he was taken to a bar, where they ignored the fact that he was just 17 years old.

He was actually not very interested in Arizona but was hosted by one of his former teammates. They spent the first night of the visit watching movies and playing video games. The second night they raced go-carts and were at church before a breakfast meeting with Coach Kovalev.

Two years later he's an All-American.

My visits were not full-on debauchery, but they were hardly innocent. At Ohio State, I got so drunk that I almost missed my plane home. At Michigan State, they snuck me into a bar where we ran into Michigan football players and nearly got into a brawl.

I had a girlfriend for those two visits, so I never worried about whether or not I could get laid.

Maggie and I had a fight and temporarily broke up before my visit to Boston College. I am ashamed to admit that I made out a little with my recruiting hostess the first night I was there. I didn't let it go further, and truthfully I am not sure she would have either.

The second night I was at a wild party and fooled around with a pre-med student from Harvard who had just broken up with her boyfriend. We did not have sex, but it went further than it had the night before. I blame the three kegs at the party. Well, that and the tight sweater she was wearing.

So I was able to recognize that Karen was essentially a recruiting hostess, minus the polo shirt with the logo and the khaki skirt. All schools seemed to have the same uniform for their recruiting hostess.

She was drinking wine, but took a hold of my glass and took a sniff.

"What have we here," she said suspiciously.

"It's a Gretzky," I said in jest, naming my horrible concoction after the greatest hockey player of all time. It was not a fitting tribute, but suddenly I felt the need to impress her. She missed the reference and handed me back my glass.

"Unique," she said with a mixture of disgust and amusement. Quite often that is the reaction I get from beautiful women.

Karen grabbed me by the arm and dragged me off to "meet important people." I met three lawyers, a city councilman, a political radio host, and three other professors. Nearly all of them seemed to have at least some inkling who I was. It was getting a little weird.

Volpe rejoined us after the first tour of the party. I was bored, but had refilled my drink again and had already downed another half a glass. I was feeling really good by the time I was introduced to the guest of honor.

Jesse Griffin had not announced that she was going to run against McCauley, but most at the party seemed to hope that she would. She was a pretty woman in her mid 40's. She had hair of wild brown curls and wore unflattering red glasses, that somehow worked. She wore a light sweater and some khakis but had a bright beaded belt and long, dangly earrings with the same color scheme.

I learned that she was an engineer who gave it up to become a teacher. She was elected to the local school board at 32 and then moved onto city council. For the last six years, she had been a state senator.

Her husband was tall, angular. He had salt and pepper hair, a little long in back. He wore a tan sport coat with blue jeans. He looked distinguished, but not stuffy. I later learned that he was a literature professor.

They were one of those couples that just seemed to fit. Although they were just beginning to hit the first few years of middle age, it was clear that they were aging well. Both were fit and trim and wore their years well. She had a sexiness and confidence about her.

Karen continued to engage the couple and after a minute I sort of slinked back towards the doorway. My glass was nearing empty and I could feel my thoughts thickening.

I hardly noticed the face next to me. He was peering into the room from the edge of the doorway.

"Isn't she amazing," he said.

I turned to look at this new person. He was so close that I had trouble taking in the details. The tequila did not help, either. I followed his lovesick gaze and saw that he was either talking about Mrs. Griffin or Karen.

I assumed he meant Karen.

"She seems to be," I answered.

It looked as if he was now eyeing me suspiciously.

"She's the kind of women my girlfriend would hate," I added.

With the mention of "girlfriend", he seemed to soften. He came around the corner and stood next to me.

"Eric," I said, extending my hand.

"I know," he said shaking my hand. "Professor Volpe told me who you were."

"There's been a lot of that tonight," I said. "It's a little disconcerting."

"Yeah, I know, he did the same thing to me last semester," he said. "By the way, I'm Landon."

I am not sure how fast my head turned, but it felt like I broke the sound barrier. I knew I was on my way to drunkenness, but I was pretty sure he said Landon and how many Landon's could there be?

"Are you okay?" he asked. He was eyeing me suspiciously again.

"I knew you looked familiar," I lied. "You're Landon Richmond, from Phoenix."

His suspicion was replaced with confusion. I was about to sink or swim depending on how well I lied.

"We've met a few times, I can't remember exactly when, but it was one of those stupid parties my dad dragged me to," I added. "He always made me come and then stuck me with my older brothers, who'd invariably ditch me."

"Yeah, I've been to my fair share of those parties," he answered. "I'm sorry, but I don't remember meeting you."

"I don't doubt it," I was still trying to think on my feet. "I bet we talked for less than two minutes. I just remembered your name, 'Landon', it's close to my middle name, 'Langston'.

"Stupid, huh," I concluded.

"No, not really," he replied. "But it is a tiny bit weird."

We both laughed. Karen looked over, smiled and gave a wave. I am not sure who it was for, but Landon thought it was for him and waved back.

"I've had a little too much to drink," I asked. "Is there a place to get some coffee close by?"

10 minutes later we were sitting at a booth at a Denny's. I hate coffee but nursed a cup. Landon sat across from me, adding a boatload of cream and sugar to his.

I guessed he was about my age, maybe a little older. He was a few inches taller, but I had him by 30 pounds. He was not scrawny but was certainly in the neighborhood of painfully thin. I guess he was a decent enough looking guy, but awkward. His hair was a little messy. He attempted to part it, but it was a little too thick and curly to really work.

"So is Karen your girlfriend?" I asked.

"No, I mean we've gone out a few times, but it's not serious yet," he answered.

"But you'd like it to be," I stated.

"Yeah, I guess so," He blushed. "She's a great girl."

I took a sip of my coffee and had to fight from making a face from the bitterness. I couldn't fathom how people drank so much of this stuff. Landon turned away for a second and I added more sugar to my coffee. It did not help.

"She seems like it," I answered. I could tell he was wary of my questions. It was obvious he was really into Karen and wanted to make sure I was not a threat. "She's a lot more outgoing than my girlfriend."

I figured if I mentioned my girlfriend enough he'd back off.

"Are you two serious?" he asked.

"Very," I replied, not really sure if I told a lie.

He seemed far more comfortable at that prospect. We swapped small talk for several minutes, he got a refill on his coffee. I did not really need one, but the waitress topped off my cup, which meant my attempts to soften the bitterness with sugar would need to be amplified.

"So Volpe sees you as some secret weapon," Landon said.

"I think he wants me to spy on McCauley's campaign," I added. "Thinks my dad will spill some secrets or something."

"Volpe will never flat out ask you to do that, but he will hint at it and try to make it seem as if it is your idea," he said matter of factly.

"So what do you do for Volpe?" I asked.

"Nothing really, my interest is in the campaign."

"Diehard democrat, huh?"

"Not at all," he answered. I pretended to look more surprised than I was. "I actually identify more with the Republican platform. I'm fairly conservative. I just want to do anything I can do to defeat Ed McCauley."

"Isn't he a conservative?" I asked, playing along.

"He's a crook," Landon shot back, full of venom. "He swindled a lot of people out of a lot of money, including my family. He ruined my dad."

We sat in silence for a bit. Just as I suspected, Landon Richmond III hated McCauley and was willing to do things against his beliefs to hurt him. Now I had to determine how far he'd go.

"Volpe needs you," Landon said. "He has been sort of relegated to the fringes of the state Democratic party. Heck, after his loss he is not even a big player in the county party. When he started telling people about you, suddenly he was back in the inner circle."

He took another sip of coffee.

"Of course I am not supposed to know this and neither are you."

"So why are you telling me?"

"Because, I believe in being upfront and honest," Landon answered. "If you decided to help the campaign, you should do so because you really want to help, not because you get manipulated into it.

"There is no way some college student who is still in the recruitment phase should have been invited to that party tonight," he added. "Volpe was trying to impress you, and hoping you'd impress the party bigwigs."

"Let me guess," I cut in. "You and Karen were there to make me feel at home and even do some recruiting."

"If worst came to worst I was supposed to start talking hockey with you," Landon said.

He drove me back to my car. I actually kind of liked the guy but had to keep tabs on him. Like all the others I'd need an excuse to get back in contact. Although we bonded over coffee, I did not know if we were exactly best friends.

I purposely slipped a few credit cards out of my wallet and dropped them onto the floor. As carefully as I could I slid them under the seat with my heel so he wouldn't see them right away.

Two missing credit cards. Now I had a reason to call him back.

25. The Cacophony That I Listen To

I did not have Landon's phone number, but I figured I could get it from Volpe.

What I did not expect was that I could get it from Karen when she called at 9:30 the next morning. I was up, but barely. I was on my way to the shower, naked with a towel wrapped around my waist.

"You disappeared last night," she said after the obligatory answering of the phone and identification. "We really didn't get a chance to talk."

"Landon and I ran out for coffee," I informed.

"You should have invited me; it would have been fun." She was very bubbly. It was too early for me to deal with bubbly. I knew that in the next few years I would most likely be working at a job where 9:30 a.m. was already an hour and a half into the work day, but as a red-blooded, All-American college student it was too early. I studied my course guide too hard to avoid early morning classes. I made a mental note to pursue a career that did not require me to be alert this early in the morning and realized I probably doomed myself to just that.

Before I knew it we had a plan for lunch and I was in the shower. With the hot water trickling over my head it occurred to me that this was a little unusual. Was she still recruiting me? Did Volpe need me this badly? Did he or Landon have anything to do with Caitlin McCauley, or was this really about politics?

My head hurt and it was not from the night before's tequila.

I went to my early class, that stupid sociology class that was going to do me no good, especially since Caitlin never went. I went to every class and had not seen her since the second week. The good news was that as a freshman level class I was destined to get an A, well at least a B, I was starting to convince myself that Professor Friedman was oddly sexy.

I killed an hour at the bookstore before it was time for my lunch with Karen. We had agreed to meet at a pub just adjacent to the West entrance of campus.

Even though I knew Rachel had class, I decided to shoot her a text just in case someone saw me eating with Karen. Enough of her friends could be in the area, so I did not want the gossip circle to start.

"Having lunch at Frog U should swing by if dun early" I typed in broken English, shortening the name of the pub from the Frog and Firkin.

The Frog and Firkin is modeled after an English Pub. It actually sits in an old house that is in a row of old houses that have been converted to businesses. All are small and locally owned, quite the contrast from the stores across the street which are all new buildings, filled with national chains.

The best part of "The Frog" is the fact that it has a very large patio area in front. In fact, most of the seats are outside. Inside it is very cramped, with tables jammed in several small rooms. Outside was also jammed with tables, but there was some room to stretch out and breathe.

Karen already had a table. A small two-top next to the railing out front. Apparently, we were not expecting visitors.

I took a seat across from her.

"I hope I am not late," I said, removing the messenger bag I used in place of a backpack.

I have to admit, she looked great. She was a little more casual than she was the night before. She wore a t-shirt, with frilly sleeves that elevated it from a regular t-shirt. I noticed she was also wearing jean shorts, although it was the middle of February, it was a relatively warm day. She did have a sweatshirt with her but did not need it.

I was certainly not dressed to impress, sporting a grey "Property of Arizona Hockey" t-shirt and a pair of jeans that had seen better days. To make matters worse, I wore flip-flops. Yes, I am that guy. I had no qualms about mismatching sandals and jeans. In fact, there are few clothing items that are taboo save for socks and sandals, and fanny packs. Fanny packs are totally out.

She ordered a salad and an iced tea, I opted for a slice of deep dish pizza and a soda. For good measure, I added a side salad so I did not look like a total lout.

After a moment of small talk, I finally spoke up.

"Look, I appreciate the invitations, but you guys don't need to recruit me anymore, I am going to help with the campaign."

"Is that what you think this is?" she asked a bit surprised.

"Isn't it?"

She took a moment to consider her answer. "Sure Professor Volpe wanted Landon and I to make you feel at ease last night, but it isn't like I was going to put on the hard sell.

"He wanted me to feel you out last night and frankly, I wanted to see what you were all about," she continued. "I take this campaign very seriously and you don't necessarily fit the type of student who volunteers to help Volpe."

I did not know if she meant beer swilling athletes with a penchant for gambling or sons of Republican Senator's campaign finance chairs.

"So what's your deal?" she asked bluntly.

"I wrecked my knee playing hockey and now feel like I don't belong," I said, the half-truths already flying, though in this case, they might be closer to ¾ truths. "The people my dad deals with pretty much suck and I was really taken by Volpe's passion."

I paused as the waitress brought us our drinks.

"I guess I am looking for some answers," hey, finally a truthful statement. "And I want to see if this campaign has them."

She seemed to accept that. Was it a good thing that I was getting good at lying?

"So how about you?" It was my turn to ask. "How'd you get involved?"

"Well, I am one of Professor Volpe's TA's," she answered. "I come from a long line of practicing Democrats. I worked on some campaigns when I was at UVA and now I am getting involved here."

"So are you from back East?" I asked in reference to her mention of the University of Virginia.

"No I am from Phoenix, I actually went to Xavier Prep," she answered. "I went to high school with McCauley's daughter. I hated that little bitch back then, so beating her father would be sweet in more ways than one."

What? I did not see that one coming. She not only knows Caitlin but has an overt dislike for her. Did I just stumble into another potential enemy? How many people hated members of this family? Could they possibly be working together? The headache was returning.

"I know Caitlin a little bit," I said. "We had some mutual friends in high school and I am friends with one of her roommates."

I realized that I was vague about my relationship with Rachel. I never claimed to be a good guy. While I have never been one to cheat, I have consistently had a bad habit of downplaying my relationship statuses around other women. I would tell myself later it was because I did not want to close a door if I determined that she really was a suspect, but I knew it was more likely that I was attracted to her.

Like I said, I am not a good guy.

Karen expanded on the story. She had gone to high school for a year with Caitlin, before graduating and heading back east to attend Virginia. She was not thrilled with the winters and graduated in three and a half years before getting into accepted into grad school here.

She was now in her third semester at Arizona.

Our food came and the conversation got more casual. Talk of classes and movies mainly.

"So what do you do for fun?" she asked.

"Gamble heavily, play amateur detective and play far too many video games," I said, truthfully, knowing she would not believe me.

"No really," she said, sounding annoyed, but smiling as if she found my answer amusing.

"Nothing exciting really," I answered. "Until a few months ago every waking moment was devoted to hockey. Since my injury, I have more time for my friends, I date occasionally and I actually get some time to myself on weekends."

For the second time, I was purposely vague about Rachel. I told myself again it was because I might need an opening in case I needed to investigate Karen for the McCauley stalking, but I had to admit that part of it was because she was really attractive and I do stupid things in the presence of attractive women.

We both finished our meals and kept talking. This time about classes, television and what I deemed her shitty taste in music, but I can guarantee you that she would hate mine. Few people like the cacophony that I listen to.

"We should hang out some more," she said after we paid our bill.

"On the campaign or in real life?" I asked.

"A little of both," she said.

We started to leave the pub. I slung my bag over my shoulder and she put on her sweatshirt.

"What's the deal with you and Landon?" I asked. "I got the impression from him that you guys were seeing each other."

"We've gone out a few times," she admitted. "He's a nice guy, but right now it is very casual. Nothing serious."

I may have mentioned this, but I have a hard time reading women. I got the feeling that she was interested, but I could not tell if the interest was genuine or part of her keeping me interested in the campaign. She did not overtly flirt, or really say anything suggestive, but there were enough smiles and hints to make me wonder.

We parted and she said she hoped to see me at another campaign meeting.

I started to walk back to the dorm. If she was interested, I risked treading thin ice because of Rachel. I not only cared about Rachel but had to keep tabs on her and use her to keep tabs on Caitlin.

I also could not rule out Karen, or Landon for that matter. If I attempted to get closer to Karen, I risked alienating Landon, who obviously had a thing for her.

I was halfway up the front steps to my dorm. In a perfect world, I'd become friends with Landon, and he'd be dating Karen. Well, actually, in a perfect world I'd be dating both Rachel and Karen, and they'd be into each other, but that was not realistic.

I dialed the number for Landon that Karen gave me.

"Landon, it's Eric from Volpe's party," I said. He recognized me. "A few things. One I think I left my credit card in your car. Second, I need to talk to you about Karen."

Three hours later we were having beers, ironically enough at the Frog and Firkin. He gave me back my card and I went into sales pitch mode.

"So you had lunch with Karen?" he asked suspiciously.

"Yeah, she was still trying to sell me on the campaign," I said. "I told her I was in and I did not need the hard sell.

"Let me be honest," I went on, changing the subject. "I get the impression you are really into her. She had good things to say about you, but I am not sure she is quite sold. I think I can help."

He eyed me suspiciously.

"You are straddling dangerously close to being 'too nice'," I went on. "Nice is good, but 'too nice' is not. Believe me, 'too nice' does not get the girl."

"So I should be a dick?" he asked.

"Sometimes," I said. "You need to keep her guessing. Be nice, but not all the time. Be interested, but only some of the time. Girls don't like jerks, but they always drift to a sense of mystery and the unpredictable."

I acted like I really knew what I was saying. I did up to a point, but I was winging it a bit.

"I think we just need to make some subtle changes," and as if almost on cue, Rachel walked up to the table.

"You must be Landon, I hear we are giving you a makeover," Rachel said, literally clapping with excitement.

26. Intermission

Now

I took another drink of water and realized how quiet the room was. I am not sure how long I had been talking but realized I had polished off two and a half bottles of water.

The grayhaired administrator looked quickly at his watch.

"Why don't we take a 15-minute break?"

And with that, all three of my judges stood up and walked out of the room.

I turned around and realized the crowd had grown quite a bit. There were several reporters and two television stations on hand. They could not have their cameras running, nor could they report on specifics of my standing at the University, but they were given permission to be on hand and were allowed to discuss the incident as a whole.

I walked out to the hallway with my father.

"You are doing well so far, Eric," he said. "You are coming off as likable, prepared, yet not rehearsed. You are sticking to the facts, yet shedding enough light on things to avoid too many questions."

"The hard part lays ahead," I said. "I am going to have to delve into some stuff that could hurt people."

"Right now, the only thing I am worried about is keeping you in school, clearing your name with the college and letting the world know what happened."

I went outside to let the warm Arizona sun hit me. I really wanted to just walk away. Just walk away and leave everything behind me. Leave this meeting, this school, heck, even this family.

A few minutes later I walked back into the room. I soon realized that, in addition to the senator and his daughter, and of course my father, I knew several of the other people watching the proceedings. Several of them were intimately involved in what I was going to be talking about.

I also knew that if I continued they would not like what I had to say.

Just a few minutes later everyone was finally settled. The Astronomy professor then looked at me.

"Please continue Mr. Slade, and don't leave any pertinent information out."

27. Who is Brian Stabler?

February

I was on my way to visit Rachel at her place. My idea was to just sneak in like usually do. I was waiting for someone to come out a side entrance so I could dash in, but an unexpected appearance changed those plans.

The side entrance burst open and Murphy came out in a hurry. He nearly ran me over storming out the door.

"Watch it there, chief," I said.

He nearly jumped when he noticed me.

"Slade, what are you doing here?"

"My girlfriend lives here," I answered. "What brings you here?"

He gave me a blank stare, for a second, then answered.

"Dropping off some homework to a friend of mine," he said.

"Anyone, I know?"

"What? No, I doubt it," he said. I thought I noticed some hesitation in his voice, but I was in the business of being suspicious. "Just this guy from my astronomy class, Brian Stabler."

We exchanged goodbyes and I headed in the side entrance. I was up a flight of stairs when I kept coming back to Murphy. He was obviously on my suspect list and here he was coming out of Caitlin's dorm, the exact same entrance that I used.

I stopped and went out the way I came. I walked into the main lobby and headed over to the front desk. Sitting behind the desk was a slightly plump, yet moderately cute girl with a mess of curly brown hair. She was wearing a baggy Arizona sweatshirt with plaid lettering over standard sweatshirt grey.

Because of privacy laws, a dorm cannot give out information on who does or does not live there. If this was going to work, I was going to have to finesse this a bit.

She greeted me with a big smile. She was cute, in a girl next door kind of way.

"Can you call room 334, ask for Brian?" Room 334 was down the hall from Rachel's room and I knew guys named Steve and Yoshi lived there.

She dialed the room and asked for Brian. Predictably, he was not there.

"Shoot, maybe it is room 336 then," I said, knowing that 336 was actually the RA's room and his name was Keith.

She got the machine but informed me I had the wrong room.

"Geeze I am so sorry," I apologized and began digging through my pockets, pulling out receipts and change. "I know I have his room number written somewhere."

I put my backpack on the counter in front of her and started rummaging through it. Pulling out notebooks and folders. I was making a mess.

"He's my lab partner and we have a big lab due tomorrow." I lied. "I was supposed to meet him here 20 minutes ago, but got off work late."

She finally got fed up with the mess I was making as I was not pulling individual pieces of paper out of the folder and turning books upside down and thumbing the pages so any loose pieces of paper would fall out. Twice I dropped the book I was holding, just to make it more annoying.

"I'll just look it up," she said exasperated. "Just give me his last name and start cleaning all this up."

"Stabler, Brian Stabler," I informed her.

As I put everything back in my backpack she flipped through the Rolodex three times. She even asked me for the spelling before going back through a fourth time.

"I'm sorry, no one by that name lives here," she finally broke the news to me.

I tried to look as upset as I could.

"Are you serious?" I whined. "But he told me he lived here. He told me specifically that he lived at Manzi-Mo," I added, using the nickname for the Manzanita-Mohave residence hall, a dorm about half a mile up the street.

She looked at me like I was the biggest moron ever.

"This is Kaibab-Huachuca," she told me as if it was common knowledge. "Manzi-Mo is down the street."

"What?" I asked, staring at her as dumbfounded as I could muster.

"You're in the wrong dorm. The one you want is down the street."

I sheepishly walked out of the lobby and waited back at the side entrance. 90 seconds later the door opened and I snuck through. This time I made it to Rachel's room without turning around.

She greeted me with a kiss. She was alone, and there was a good chance we'd be naked in a few minutes. I noticed her backpack was on the bed, zipped up.

"Good timing, I just got here a few minutes ago," she told me. "My study group ran late."

Had Murphy been around this hallway, Rachel would not have been around to notice.

"Do you have a student directory?"

She grabbed one off her desk, she had a whole slew of books organized. As best I could tell the student directory was sandwiched between an abbreviated version of the white pages and the schedule of classes.

I flipped it open and quickly found Brian Stabler. He did exist. He was a junior, but the address listed was for an off-campus apartment.

I had to ask myself again, what was Murphy doing here?

I did not have long to think about it as Rachel plopped down on my lap, wrapped her arms around my neck and gave me another long kiss.

"Caitlin won't be back for a few hours."

"Really?" I asked, trying to sound as if I was into the thought of a few hours alone when in reality I was really puzzled. Caitlin did not have class right now.

"Yup, she at a meeting about a trip to Mexico for her marine biology class," Rachel told me.

With the potential for no interruptions, we resumed kissing. Since we had taken the next step a few weeks ago, we struggled for "alone time." Chuck was good about clearing out if I needed the room, but he had his own need for privacy now that he was sleeping with Tracey and neither of us wanted to impose too often.

Conceivably Rachel and I could be alone in the bedroom, while Chuck studied in the main room. Such is the advantage of the two-room double, but neither Rachel nor I were comfortable with the situation. Somehow it was alright in my mind that Chuck knew what I was doing, as long as he was not within 20 feet of the activity.

It was worse in Rachel's room. She did not have a suite and she and Caitlin did not get along well enough to request the other to leave.

We were lying side by side, still kissing, shoes now off and hands exploring over and under clothing when we heard the click of the door lock opening. We pulled away quickly, but it was obvious what was going on.

Tariq walked in. He had a key. He was not supposed to have a key, each resident had just one and they were not supposed to be copied, but he had a key.

He gave us a brief disgusted look but said nothing about what was happening seconds before.

"Where's Caitlin?" he asked, possibly the most civil tone he had ever taken with us.

Rachel explained where Caitlin was. I had assumed that he'd just leave, but instead, he plopped down on her bed and pulled out a well-worn book from his bag and started reading. It was like he owned the place.

Apparently mine and Rachel's plans were now null and void.

We gathered up our stuff and headed out to my place. Chuck was there, but when he saw us I gave him a knowing nod and a questioning look as if to say "is this alright."

So as to not be too obvious, he returned to his homework as we went to the sofa. Two minutes later he looked up at the clock. "I am meeting some French students for dinner over at the Ethiopian place, you guys want to come?"

It was smooth and believable.

"I don't really like Ethiopian," I said. I had never had Ethiopian. To continue the charade I looked over at Rachel with a questioning look.

"I'm not really hungry," she added.

Chuck packed up his backpack and left. Later I found out he just went to the common room to watch television.

Seven minutes after he left we were going at it. While having sex with my girlfriend I kept coming back to the fact that Tariq has a key, he has full access to the room.

While I should have been in the throes of passion, I also kept asking myself what was Murph really doing there?

Apparently, my absentmindedness during the act was beneficial to my performance. Rachel seemed quite pleased.

"Wow, that was intense," she said, sweating and just a bit out of breath.
Apparently, dwelling on two potential kidnappers is good for one's sex life.

28. Single Malt Sermon

know had a fairly lengthy checklist of things I had to do. I had to give Landon his makeover and help earn his trust by trying to improve his chances with Karen. At the same time, I had to keep Karen interested in recruiting me to the cause, while trying to find out just why she hated Shannon McCauley so much and could that hate turn violent.

At the same time, I still needed to learn more about Volpe and figure out if he was motivated enough to go after McCauley.

Add to that I still did not know what the Murph's role in all of this was and could not completely rule out my own girlfriend.

While I had all of that still on my plate, I still had school, a relationship and the sham of a fake knee injury to worry about. If that was not enough, a very important mid-afternoon nap was ruined by a phone call.

It was my father. It was less a conversation than a list of instructions. He was coming into town and demanded that we have dinner. He also demanded that I bring Rachel. Just what I needed, my overbearing father meeting my girlfriend, who I only began dating because I was trying to determine who was threatening to kidnap her roommate. What could go wrong?

Plenty. He knew that I was working for Senator McCauley. Rachel did not.

I ran through a list of scenarios through my head. I tried to find the best excuse for him not to ask about my work with McCauley. I chose the least likely, the truth.

"Dad, I need a favor tonight," I said, hesitantly. "You can't mention the work I am doing with Senator McCauley."

"And why not?"

"Well, she is Caitlin McCauley's roommate," I started. I then explained in a little more detail what my role was for McCauley. Before I got too in-depth he stopped me and let me know McCauley informed him of my role and the potential kidnapper, just in case he had to liquidate some funds to pay a ransom.

"I originally asked her out as an excuse to keep tabs on Caitlin…"

"And now you have feelings for her," my father interrupted.

I paused a moment, I was shocked he did not go right to the more pragmatic answer, that I did not want to blow my cover.

"Yeah, I do," I replied, completely comfortable with my answer.

"Fine, I will make sure not to mention the McCauley's," he confirmed. "But I cannot promise that I will not critique the way you are dressed."

I almost laughed.

"I would be disappointed if you didn't sir."

I dressed more for my father than for my girlfriend. That included pressed Khakis, and yes, Chuck ironed them. I also grabbed a golf shirt and actual dress shoes.

Rachel tried to play it safe as well, sporting a fairly conservative dress that came just below the knee. She added a light white sweater and even a little headband at the top of her head. She looked ready for a church social. So was it wrong I was kind of turned on?

We met my father at a nice steakhouse, one we had eaten at before. While I always dreaded spending time with my father at least we eat very well. I was also counting on him being fairly well behaved, at least in front of Rachel. While he might embarrass me a tad, he would not be rude or a poor host. My old man had manners.

My father can be intimidating, but he is courteous. We walked into the restaurant and found him sitting at the bar, nursing a scotch. He got up off the stool and warmly greeted Rachel. A few moments later we were at our seats. My father ordered a bottle of wine for the table, even though Rachel could not drink. I am not a huge wine fan so I could not tell you if it was worth the hefty price, but free booze is free booze.

It was mostly small talk at dinner. My father quizzing Rachel on her life's details and grilling me on school. The tone was probably more civil that it would have been had we been alone, but my grades were good, I hadn't embarrassed the family and I had a job of sorts.

We all had a steak. Rachel, at my father's urging, opted for a filet, I went the ribeye route and my father, as he almost always does, enjoyed a particularly pink piece of prime rib. We added dessert and he enjoyed a post-meal cocktail.

As we headed out to the parking lot my father turned to us.

"I hate to interfere with any plans you might have, but I was hoping you could drop Rachel off and then meet me for a drink at my hotel." It was a request, but one I took as an order.

I dropped Rachel off, a little depressed I would not get a chance to sully her church social attire, but she admitted she still had a lot of homework. I was disappointed to leave, both because I wanted to spend time with Rachel and because I had trepidations about dealing with my father.

Twenty minutes later I ventured into the hotel bar and quickly spotted my father sitting at a table, two-thirds of the way into a glass of scotch. While I have been in many bars, I have not been in many hotel bars, especially high-end resort bars. The place was in sharp contrast with itself. It was dark, both dark wood and dark lighting, yet it had huge glass windows that showed off the lights from the city below. During the day there would be plenty of sunlight and early evening would provide a gorgeous view of Tucson's patented multi-hued sunsets.

I made my way to the table and sat down, scooping up a handful of peanuts as I did. My father signaled to the waitress and ordered two glass of Macallan 12.

"I know you are partial to beer, but we are going to drink like gentlemen tonight," my father said.

He was right, I preferred beer. If I was going to drink hard liquor, I generally chose tequila or possibly vodka. I had only tasted scotch on one occasion and I am guessing the bottle we swiped from Kevin McKinley's father's stash probably cost less per bottle than this scotch cost per glass.

The waitress was a good looking woman of 40 who I caught my dad looking as she walked off, seemingly admiring how she filled out her dark gray pencil skirt.

He picked up his glass while sliding mine towards me. He admired the gold liquid for a moment. He nodded in my direction, encouraging me to pick up my glass.

"This is a Macallan 12, which means it has been aged for 12 years," my father began his lesson. "This is considered a very good scotch."

He moved the glass under his nose and I did the same.

"Take a sniff," he commanded and I obeyed. To me, it smelled like booze, though I faintly recognized it as my father has been a scotch drinker for as long as I can remember. "You should get a whiff of vanilla with a hint of ginger."

I admit that I did not get any of that, but I did not let him know that and simply nodded.

He took a small sip, and again I followed.

"It is a very smooth scotch, you may get a bit of dried fruit, and of course the smoke," he added.

While I could see why he described it as smooth, it pretty much tasted like fire. It burned going down the way that hard liquor does, but I had to admit it was better than the cheap box store vodka that I occasionally swilled.

He ended his single malt sermon.

"Rachel seems very nice," he said, catching me off guard. "She was very charming, I can see why you have taken a fancy to her."

I was taken aback. I am used to my father being very critical of, well, just about everything. This was high praise from him.

"If she was intimidated meeting me, she did not show it, she was able to contribute to the conversation." Again, that was high praise from my father. "Kyle is dating a woman from his firm who is an absolute bore. She is apparently a very gifted accountant, but apparently has no interests save for work gossip."

My father was eviscerating my brother's girlfriend, and I wonder what he'd say about my oldest brother Jeff's wife. I had always had the inkling that, while she was from a "good family," my father was not a fan.

The conversation remained civil. He asked me a little bit more about Rachel, then asked about my classes. He asked if I was still interested in going to law school and I told him that I really did not know.

"Well Senator McCauley is pleased with you, so maybe something in politics would suit you," he said, less to me and more to himself. "Maybe there is a something you could pursue with him."

He drained his drink and I was not far behind. He ordered another round and I hurriedly finished my scotch before the waitress returned. Apparently, we were now drinking Glenfiddich 15. It was darker, redder than the last drink.

My father said something about it smelling of heather honey and vanilla fudge, but again, it just smelled like scotch. It was smooth like the last one and when he told me I should be tasting marzipan, cinnamon, and ginger, I still tasted fire, but I could swear there was a hint of cinnamon in that flame.

"McCauley let me know what you are doing for him," he said. "Care to fill me in on what you have discovered?"

I spent the next few minutes filling him in on what I had been doing, though I edited out any suspicions I had about Rachel.

"I know Volpe and I always assumed he was a decent man, but having three people who all seemingly have an axe to grind with either Ed or Caitlin seems suspicious," my dad chimed in. "The Murphy boy has always struck me as a buffoon, much like his old man, so if he is behind it, then I would expect him to mess up and implicate himself sooner rather than later."

He took another long swallow and I wondered if he was going to order a third. I was lagging behind, but the scotch was already going to my head.

"What about the boyfriend?" he asked. "He seems like an unpleasant fellow."

I took a deep sip before answering.

"I thought of Tariq because he has access, but Harrison says he checks out," I answered, more enthusiastically than I thought I would.

My father looked at his empty glass and tried to get the waitresses attention.

"My guess is that if Harrison was actually good at his job he would not need your assistance on this," my father said dryly.

"He has opportunity, but he seems to have no interest in material things, so what is his motive?" I asked.

The waitress came by and another order was placed. I had a feeling this was not going to end well.

"He has to fund the revolution somehow," again, he said it more to the universe than to himself. "As someone who knows a little something about money, I would be on the lookout for something that would tie him to this. Figure out if there is a debt or a need for a cash infusion."

It made sense, but only to an extent.

"Like if he is planning a protest or something," I asked.

"I really would not know, that is for you to determine, after all, you are the amateur Sherlock Holmes."

Two more drinks came.

We sat in silence for a few moments, sipping the drinks. Then he hit me with a question from out of nowhere.

"Have you spoken with your mother recently?"

When I have gone to visit my mother, or have talked to her on the phone when at home, my father would always politely ask after her, but I could not remember him asking me out of the blue.

The fact was, and it just occurred to me when he asked, that I had not talked to her in months. I spent a few days with her right after finals but only spoke to her twice over the Holidays. I had been so busy with school, Rachel, and of course the Caitlin incident, that I had not called her. Of course, she had not called me.

Even after she left my dad, my mother and I would talk several times a week. She made a trip out to Iowa to meet Maggie. Slowly as I got older we spoke less and less. It seems strange that I did not think to call her for advice on my investigation.

I informed my father that I had not spoken to her in a few months.

"That is too bad," my father said. "I always thought that it was a good thing you two were so close."

He drained his glass and looked wistful for a moment.

"It was obvious early on that she never fully bonded with your brothers," he continued. "Although she spent far more time with them, they were always Daddy's boys. It did not take long to realize that you two had a bond."

"Is that why you resent me?" I blurted out my question without thought to the ramifications. I looked down and realized my glass was almost empty.

"Resent you? Why would you say that?"

He looked a bit hurt. I had never seen that look from him.

"We've never been close," I said. "You've always been hard on me."

I quickly took another drink. My glass was empty.

"I am hard on everyone," he shot back. "I demand excellence, just as my father demanded excellence. I am hard on my employees. I am hard on your brothers and I am hard on you. Like your brothers, you are smart and talented. Unlike your brothers, you lack focus. If I was not there to steer the ship, I fear you'd venture down an aimless path."

I was not sure if he was complimenting me or insulting me. It seemed like a lot of both.

"You are a lot like your mother," he went on. "She flitted from one interest to another. She would try one new hobby, adopt one new cause, discover a new philosophy every other month. She did not know what she wanted, only she did not want me."

"Us," I corrected.

He nodded as if to agree with my point.

"Maybe so."

I looked down, somehow two new drinks were on the table. I realized I could focus on one thing at a time, and since I was focused on my father, the rest of the world was little more than a peripheral mist. We both took another slug.

I could see he was sad. I knew my father was not an easy man for my mom to live with, but I suddenly realized he had loved her, and probably still did. She had been gone nearly seven years and he had barely dated. I just assumed he was asexual, more interested in accounting and status, but maybe he was truly wounded by my mother.

I wanted to probe deeper, but knew at this time nothing good could come of it. I switched gears.

If I was full of single malt courage, I might as well go full bore therapy session.

"But you have to admit you like my brothers more," I said.

"I will concede no such thing," he shot back.

I noticed he was no longer enjoying the scotch, he was drinking it with a purpose. I tried to keep pace.

"Bullshit," I said. "You always liked Kyle and Jeffrey better."

"No," he looked angry now. "Yes, I was closer with them, but it was not a matter of liking them more. Your brothers gravitated toward me and that wounded your mother greatly. When you and her got along better, I realized my only chance to make her happy was to stay out of the way and give you both space. On a few occasions, she accused me of stealing your brothers away from her and I was not going to provide another obstacle to her happiness."

We both picked up our glasses and took twin swallows. Lesser men might have died consuming this much scotch, in this short of time. We Slade men are made of heartier stock. Of course, I was not sure I could still stand, and I wondered if I could speak coherently and was pretty sure I was so numb a punch to the face would not hurt.

"In the end, I could not make her happy," he added.

"We could not make her happy," I corrected.

29. Catharsis and Alcohol Poisoning

Catharsis and alcohol poisoning make strange bedfellows. I woke up on a couch. More specifically I woke up in a pool of drool on a couch. Shockingly, I did not have much of a headache. Sure, every other part of my body hurt, including my toenails, my eyeballs, and my hair, but I was less hungover, and more the victim of sleeping on a hard couch, upside down, in my dinner clothes.

I looked over and saw not one, but two glasses with water in them and a crushed water bottle I assumed was from the minibar. I had to figure I was smart enough to slam down some water before passing out, but I did not recall any of it.

Usually, when I have a long evening of drinking planned, I prepare for my hangover prevention ahead of time by placing a bottle of water and an aspirin or two by my bedside. In this case, I had neither planned on drinking nor was I anywhere close to my bed.

I did not recall much of anything. I had a clear memory of finishing the scotch and had a fuzzy memory of drinking at least one more. My unreliable recollection seemed to indicate I may also have had a beer…or two, but that seemed like something out of a dream. Almost as if I was watching a movie of myself drinking beer. A very hazy, distorted movie.

I may or may not have an accurate recollection of stumbling to the elevator. After that, absolutely nothing.

I managed to sit up. The room was spinning a bit, but at least my stomach was not. No headache, no puking, I was ahead of the game. I looked up and there was my father, tying his tie. He looked like a man who went to bed at 9:00, not someone who had six scotches in 90 minutes (and who knows how many he had before I arrived.) He was tying his tie and looked ready for the office.

I assumed I looked like a denizen of Skid Row.

"I have to admit, you hold your liquor far better than your brothers," my father said. "and I am almost positive they would not have been my wingmen with the waitress."

I prayed he was kidding but was pretty sure I helped my dad hit on the pencil-skirted waitress. I hope he got her number but was not going to ask.

As he put on his sport coat, he made it clear that I needed to clean myself up and, if I did so I would be getting a free breakfast. This was a bit surprising as my father never ate breakfast on weekdays. For as long as I could remember he drank coffee for breakfast every weekday. Saturday's were 50-50 on whether he ate breakfast.

My dad never made dinner, and almost never made lunch, but he not only made breakfast every Sunday but had a wide repertoire. He was good for eggs in several different styles, with a penchant for Eggs Benedict. Before my mom left he frequently made her Juevos Rancheros, but after she left that dish was abandoned. He could make a fluffy pancake and liked his bacon extra crispy.

As we got older we also learned he made a mean Bloody Mary (though I like his mimosas better) and getting a little tipsy on a Sunday morning has been a bright spot of staying with my father.

We ventured down to one of the hotel restaurants. He ordered a black coffee and some fruit, I went the opposite direction with a big omelet filled with several types of meat and cheeses and added a side of hash browns. I firmly believe that grease is the best way to combat an evening of heavy drinking.

"Senator McCauley really does seem pleased with you," my father said.

"That's good, I guess."

My father picked up on the somewhat puzzled tone and shot me a look as if I should continue with my point.

"I don't really speak with him," I added. "I just report to Harris and I assume he is filling in McCauley. I guess he is saying good things about me.

"To be honest, I wonder why they need me other than to personally keep an eye on Caitlin," I added.

"My guess is that Harris is covering all his bases," he said. "From time to time he has enlisted outside help and worked well with others, so it is not unusual."

He told me that Harris had been military and transitioned to police work after his service. He occasionally worked security during his days off and earned the trust of McCauley. Eventually, he left the police force to work full-time for the senator.

"His methods were always very effective, but he has not adjusted his methods over time," my father said.

He explained that Harris was tasked with doing a background check on a potential staffer. She came highly recommended and Harris subjected her to the usual FBI background check, verified references, and even did a Google search.

"As far as everything was concerned she was squeaky clean," said my father.

It turned out she had an old social media account she no longer used and failed to scrub. Apparently, she used to like to get drunk and make out with her female friends. One of the interns found it and passed it on to Harris, who was able to get her job offer rescinded before she joined the staff.

"Could you imagine those pictures getting out in connection to a Republican Senator with a very conservative base?"

I chuckled to myself. I debated whether to ask, but I had to.

"You still have those pictures?"

My father shot me a look of disgust.

"Of course I don't," he said before pausing. "Anymore."

We shared a brief laugh. This was weird. Last night he showed vulnerability and today a sense of humor.

"Just be careful and be prepared to fight for yourself if need be," my father continued. "Makes sure you properly note your contributions and if it goes poorly, do not let him pin the blame on you."

That left an impression. For about the 1,364th time I wondered what I had gotten myself into.

Alas, our father/son bonding had to come to an end. After paying the bill, we left the hotel together and before we parted he took a few shots at my clothes, my shoes, and my intelligence.

"Make sure you get to class," he said. "I dare say with your grades you cannot afford to miss any more lectures."

That was the Jefferson Slade I was used to. Our Bromance was no more.

I made it back to campus, and probably had enough time to get to class if I hurried. Instead, I rationalized that I did not want to risk coming in late and 5 minutes after returning to my dorm room, I was face down on my bed.

30. Elegance to the Violence

T homas Hearns was a boxer from Detroit whose Hall of Fame career that lasted nearly 30 years.

He was known as both "The Hitman", and the "Motor City Cobra." Why is this important? On this day I was wearing a Motor City Cobra T-shirt and it was the gateway for Tariq and I to have an almost civil conversation.

I was sporting the red shirt emblazoned with a black cobra and did not think much about it when I went over to Rachel's. I had a pretty extensive collection of T-shirts, a mix of bands, sporting events, and comic book characters. I also liked obscure shirts that kept people guessing.

The Motor City Cobra was one such shirt.

Unless you watched a lot of ESPN Classic, people my age had no idea who the Motor City Cobra was. Tariq, I soon learned, was quite the boxing fan and for one brief moment, he actually resembled a decent human being, although it took several minutes of his pretentious bullshit to get there.

After lunch, Rachel and I ventured to her place for a movie and maybe more. Sadly, we opened the door to find Caitlin and Tariq in the early stages of their own "maybe more." They were only kissing, but it still burned an image into my brain that I did not really care for. Caitlin almost looked embarrassed, as she wiped her mouth with her sleeve and left her arm there. Tariq just looked mad, and I could not blame him, though I had no pity for him either.

He noticed my shirt sneered as Rachel and I strolled to her side of the room.

"Do you even know who the Motor City Cobra is?"

"No, I have no idea who Thomas 'The Hitman' Hearns is," I said, the sarcasm dripping.

I could see he was a little surprised by my answer.

"I assume you are wearing the shirt ironically," he shot back.

"I don't wear anything ironically," I answered, staring him down the whole time. "If I wear a Marvin the Martian Shirt, it is because I think Marvin the Martian is funny as shit. If I wear a Johnny Cash shirt, it is because I think Folsom County Prison Blues is the greatest live album of all time. And if I wear a Motor City Cobra shirt it is because I thought Tommy Hearns was a badass."

He moved to the edge of Caitlyn's bed and actually made normal, non-judgmental eye contact with me.

"So you're a fan?"

"Yeah, though I must admit I was more partial to Marvin Hagler," I said.

"Hagler was a bad man," Tariq said, basically agreeing with me.

Oddly enough my father is a huge boxing fan, though he much preferred the fighters of the 70's and 80's. He and my brothers and I would have periodic fight nights where he would put on classic fights and tell us all about the fighters. While he was a bigger fan of the heavyweights, he loved Larry Holmes for some reason, the lighter weights appealed more to me.

My father was also a big fan of Sugar Ray Leonard, so in my normal state of rebellion, I tended to root for whoever Leonard was fighting, be it Hearns, Hagler or Roberto Duran. Although Hagler, with his bald head and constant scowl scared me, he also enthralled me and I became a huge fan.

Tariq and I spent a few minutes talking about some classic fights. I told him I was a bit surprised he liked boxing, and he actually did not take offense.

"It is one of the few enterprises where a man of color can dominate the market based upon his own ability, and not the whims of a white patriarch," he countered. "Men of color, even those without education or even those with less than stellar backgrounds, can call the shots. Boxers control their brand and there is room for promoters of all colors.

"Plus it is the most honest competition," He continued. "It is just two men, pitted against each other with just their strength, speed, and wits. Unlike MMA or street fights, it is an art. There is an elegance to their violence."

He said something about the Aztecs, or was it the Mayans, I always get them confused, and I started to lose interest.

The conversation turned to modern boxing and I became re-engaged in the conversation. I had to admit I did not watch nearly as much of the modern fight game. This seemed to turn him against me again.

"You probably like to watch MMA with your bros, while you pound Budweisers, energy drinks and make plans to go to the gun show this weekend," he said in a mocking "white guy" voice. I would have found it funny if it was not being used to make fun of me.

"They don't punch enough in MMA and I don't like seeing two guys roll around with each other in a cage," I began my retort. "I prefer microbrews, get enough caffeine from soda and wouldn't know where to find a gun show even if I wanted to go, which I do not."

I'd like to tell you from that moment we became friends, but we didn't. We may have had something in common, aside from dating roommates, but we hardly became friends, though we did have a few more civil conversations over the next few weeks.

My snotty retort seemed to end the conversation abruptly. Realizing we were not getting the room to ourselves, Rachel and I headed out.

"Even when he's nice, he's an ass," I said as we left the dorm and emerged into the Arizona sunshine.

"For a second there I thought you thawed the ice," Rachel said.

"I am not sure he would allow himself to let that ice thaw. It would ruin the façade."

After a quick bite to eat, I texted Chuck and learned he was not going to be home for most of the afternoon. Suddenly Rachel and I knew how we'd spend the next hour or so.

31. Emotional Betrayal

decided to be efficient and spend more time with Volpe, Landon, and Karen. All three had an axe to grind with McCauley and/or Caitlin and I figured being in the room with three of them was the best way to obtain evidence.

I volunteered to spend a few days a week helping out with a potential Jesse Griffin run for McCauley's seat. I had visions of late-night strategy sessions and crafting her platform, but mostly I was charged with calling potential donors and looking at polling data.

The dislike for McCauley was apparent, but verbal criticism was mostly levied at policy and the 1 percent that McCauley seemed to best represent. Whatever overwhelming evidence I hoped that they would let slip just was not there, or they were being careful with their words.

I found out that first night that promptly at 9 p.m. the phones stopped and the beers came out. As Volpe handed out some German bottled beer, I thought that I could get used to this.

To my disappointment, if not my surprise, beer drinking was secondary to clerical duties. Phone lists were prepared for the next night, filing was done, and at one point I was tasked with taking out the trash to the dumpster behind the building.

Night two saw a bigger group of people gather and once again the beers came out right at 9:00. This time Volpe and Langdon, plus a few other volunteers left to go get pizzas. This left me alone with Karen. Well, not alone, as there were two other volunteers there, but alone as in I did not have the distraction of Volpe and Langdon there.

Several of us sat talking about current events, though I admit I knew very little of what they were talking about since it did not involve college basketball or the NHL. My mind started wandering during the conversation and Karen seemed to notice. She flashed me a smiled and raised her eyebrows at me.

Eventually, she ventured over my way with a fresh beer and we started a side conversation.

"So why are you here?" It took me a second to realize that she was referring to my lack of interest in the political discussions and not my true intentions. "These kids could talk all night about politics and you got bored after five minutes."

I took a swig of the beer and tried to figure out where to cast my gaze. While I wanted to maintain eye contact, I did not want it to seem as if I was staring. I am not intimidated by beautiful women, but I have trouble knowing how to act.

Karen was the type of woman who dominated a room. You could not miss her and all eyes were usually on her. I made a conscious effort to note my attraction to her and not let it cloud my judgment in trying to discern if she was involved or not.

"Nothing they say matters," I finally answered. "They can talk and talk and not much matters. It does not matter what they think of gun control, or healthcare, very little of what we want matters with the way the system is rigged."

I chose my words carefully but realized I was telling the truth.

"Plus, my beliefs don't conform with a party platform," I continued. "I believe in the second amendment, but also believe in gun control. I do not feel like they are mutually exclusive. I am personally against abortion, but do not believe it is my place to tell a woman what she can and cannot do with her body."

Back to the beer and I found myself sitting down on the corner of a desk.

"I believe it is up to the government to help those who cannot help themselves and I do not see McCauley helping anyone who is not in his same tax bracket," I added.

She was digging what I was saying and I thought in other circumstances I might have a shot with her.

"So McCauley is really a bad guy huh?"

"No, he is very nice," I said, shocking her a bit. "I have never seen him treat anyone poorly, from his biggest donors to the people catering his parties, he treats them with nothing but respect and courtesy."

She looked at me if I was crazy. Shortly, I would look at her the same way.

"The problem is that he has had chances to do the right thing and continuously fails to do so," I said. "He cut education funding at every turn as a state senator. He always votes for tax plans that do little or nothing to benefit the middle class. He courts the religious right, yet has not been to church in decades. He is a nice guy, who may not be a good guy."

Suddenly I sounded more like a suspect than my actual suspects.

I knew the pizza would be back soon, so I was running out of one-on-one time with Karen. I had to turn the conversation from myself to Caitlin and her father.

"I get why you don't like 'Big Ed' but it sounds like you hate the whole family."

I knew full well she had never mentioned McCauley's wife or younger son in our prior conversations, but I did not want to be too obvious in my attempts to distill information from her.

"The Senator is a scumbag, but at least he is upfront about it," Karen said. "Caitlin is a two-faced bitch who committed the ultimate act of betrayal."

She went from being completely serene when I was speaking to completely enraged in mere seconds. This was not a mere dislike, this was contempt.

"Even though I was a few years older, we actually hung out quite a bit in high school," Karen continued. "She dated a few different guys my age and we became quite friendly, even if I was more dedicated to my studies and less dedicated to partying."

I was not sure where this was going, but I leaned in to let her know I was interested. I noticed she smelled great, so that was a plus.

"In the middle of my senior year, I started dating Donovan…"

This was over a guy? Her commitment to the campaign and hatred over the McCauley's was over a high school boy?

You might be surprised to find out that I have never been a teenage girl. Most guys can feud over a girl and eventually mend fences. Guys can literally spill each other's blood and eventually become good friends.

When I played high school hockey I literally got into a brawl with a player from another team. Although he denies it, to this day I believe Jimmy Quinn gave me a cheap shot. He says hitting me in the jaw with the butt in of his stick was an accident. Our disagreement led to a fracas. We dropped gloves, punched each other half a dozen times and got ejected from the game. After leaving the ice I looked for him and he looked for me and we eventually continued our melee in the parking lot. He split my eyebrow open, I still have a cool scar and broke my nose. At some point, he broke his hand, probably on my head, and I added a black eye so swollen he couldn't see out of it for two weeks.

Later that summer we wound up on the same all-star travel team. We nearly came to blows a few times during the first practice, but other than a few really hard, yet legal checks, we avoided conflict. We ended up at the same house party and came face to face at a beer cooler. He handed me a can of some shitty domestic swill.

"I don't know what is harder, your skull or your right hook."

I laughed, he laughed and we became friends. For the rest of the time I lived in Phoenix we were good friends. He's playing college hockey out east and we talk a few times a year during the season and then hang out a lot during the summers. He's engaged and I have been told I am on the list for consideration to be a groomsman, though I figure I will probably just miss the cut.

Girls are rarely that forgiving, at least in my experience. Even the smallest perceived slight can lead to a lengthy, healthy hatred. Even the most level-headed woman can hold a grudge against a former friend for an eternity.

Of course, the opposite seems to be true when it comes to the opposite sex. Guys seem to hold onto resentment towards exes far longer than women, who seem willing for forgive far easier. Guys will hold an irrational hate for an ex, even if she did nothing wrong to lead to the break-up, while women seem to actually look for the positives in their ex-boyfriends, no matter how dastardly their actions were to lead to the dissolution of the relationships. (This does not hold true for marriages, where it seems like both the ex-husband or the ex-wife goes from soul mate to scumbag loser with one stroke of a pen.)

It was clear from Karen's story that no one was going to be forgiven anytime soon. She dated Donovan for several months, and just when things got very serious things went sour.

"I could not get ahold of him," Karen said. "I try to call but no answer. The next day I still don't hear from him and decided to go to a party with my friends. I am there a few minutes when Donovan and Caitlin walk in together and they are all over each other."

I could see the humiliation in her eyes.

"They not only make it clear to me that they are together, but they let the whole party know," she said. "She not only stole my boyfriend, at my most emotionally vulnerable to do so."

At this point, I was sorry I was prying. I needed to know if she could be behind the threats to McCauley, but I did not want to make her feel like shit doing so.

"I thought that was the end of it but she then kept posting photos of us together and then them together online," Karen continued. "She would privately send me pictures. First, it was pictures of his room and his car. Soon she was sending me photos of them kissing, or holding hands. There were also pictures of us from when Donovan and I were dating."

And then it hit me. I realized I knew Karen, or more specifically, I knew of Karen. While I did not know Donovan well, he was a peripheral member of my circle of friends, I had heard about this. It happened when I was playing hockey in Iowa. If the rumors were to be believed, not only did Donovan dump Karen for Caitlin, but he did it the day after taking Karen's virginity.

To make matters worse, he had tried to film it. Fortunately for Karen, it was too dark to see anything on the recording, but a grainy photo of a girl in her underwear was passed around. I never saw the actual photo, but heard about it and know it got passed around.

While it was not the most severe case of cyberbullying, it was a terrible thing to do. Those bullied online have been known to take their own lives, is it really that big of a stretch that Karen would wish ill-will on Caitlin?

"It wasn't so much the actual transgression, I could get over the heartbreak, but it was the emotional betrayal. The cold, calculating plan to try to befriend me to take my boyfriend.

"And of course a few weeks later she dumped him," she added. "He actually had the gall to try and get back together with me."

While I thought she was carrying a little too much hatred for something that happened four years ago, I was reminded of the old adage of "hell hath no fury…"

"So what did you do?" I asked.

"I slashed her tires and keyed her car," Karen said. "I tried to poison Donovan but apparently untraceable poisons are not easy to order online."

My face must have betrayed my shock because she just started laughing.

"I didn't try to poison Donovan," she said while cracking up.

Then her face got very serious.

"Untraceable poison is really hard to buy," she said stone-faced.

32. The Universal Hot/Crazy Matrix

Both of my brothers are jerks. I am not saying that in an affectionate way. They just aren't very nice people. Well, that may be harsh, but they are not people I would ever associate with. If they were not family, I cannot fathom spending any time with them. They were never overtly mean or cruel, but they were closer in age to each other than to me, and it was clear even at an early age that we were very different. I was more drawn to experiences; they were more drawn to stuff. They wanted the latest video games and coolest toys, and I was drawn to sports and trying to go on adventures.

For the most part, they ignored me. They were very close and I was always a third wheel who never felt left out. I did not idolize my brothers, instead, I had an uncle on my mom's side who I thought was the coolest. It was my Uncle Steve who introduced me to hockey and heavy metal, and, on my 18th birthday, dive bars (thank you fake ID)

That is not to say that my brothers occasionally did not try. As I entered my teens, my brother Kyle felt it was his part to "educate me" about women. His advice ranged from worthless to misogynistic, so I took it with a grain of salt.

He swore by the Universal Hot/Crazy Matrix and bestowed its virtue whenever he took the time to "teach me" about girls. He stole his philosophy from a YouTube video, which essentially said that the hotter the girl, the more likely to be crazy. While the video was primarily a comedy routine, my brother took it as gospel.

Kyle uses this flawed premise as his mantra in dealing with women even today, I took it to mean simply, the better looking she is, the more annoying habits a guy is willing to put up with. I am sure the same is true for women dealing with good-looking guys, but I have no empirical knowledge of that to say it is 100% true.

While I wouldn't brand Karen as "crazy", she certainly had justification for being hurt and angry. I just had to figure out how deep that anger and resentment went. Was she hurt enough to threaten Caitlin? Was she crazy enough to hurt Caitlin?

I didn't want it to be Karen, just like I didn't want it to be Rachel. The question was who did I want it to be? I guess I wanted to be some nameless, faceless ghoul. Some obvious monster with no redeeming values, but that wasn't the case, was it?

It wasn't going to be some green-faced creature in a Victorian-era trench coat and top-hat. It wasn't going to be some demon dwelling in a desert cave. It was going to be some real person. It was likely going to be someone with a family and feelings, someone who was risking repercussions to extract revenge of some sort.

The McCauleys were no angels, but they didn't deserve this. I was just worried I was going to think the same of whoever was behind the threats. I could almost sympathize with someone who was cyberbullied. Or someone lovesick. Or someone whose life was turned upside down by tragedy. Or even someone who was struggling to stay in school.

I wanted a monster but was probably getting a person. Maybe a person I even liked.

Rachel had a test she had to study for. I had a relatively easy week so while she was hitting the books, I decided to hit the bars and we were destined for Fourth Avenue.

I once again assembled my motley crew, Mike, Chuck and "Little" Mark and somehow "Little" Mark got to pick the bar, so instead of some quiet dive bar with character, we wound up at a corporate bar with an Irish Pub name, but none of the Irish Pub charm. Sure it had a lot of wood and faux leather, but it also had loud, soulless top-40 music, too much neon, and drinks that each ran about $2 too much. While the scenery was good, a lot of tipsy sorority girls in skimpy outfits, there were twice as many lunk head fraternity guys, in tight t-shirts and pristine ball caps of teams they don't really root for.

While I like to look at sorority girls as much as the next guy, I like good conversation and cheap drinks more. This bar had neither.

The bar was an anomaly on Fourth Avenue, but probably not for much longer. Fourth Ave is a half-mile stretch of road between the University and Downtown. Most of the storefronts are older buildings hosting locally owned businesses. There are diverse bars, 70-year old restaurants and a variety of niche businesses from feminist bookstores to army surplus stores to art galleries. Recently developers have been buying up some of the adjacent neighborhoods and demolishing the classic homes to build luxury, high rise student housing.

It was only a matter of time before some of the great dive bars and sandwich shops were replaced by apartments that cost more per month than my dorm room costs a semester.

I tried to make the most of it, and after two beers I was only mildly annoyed, as opposed to majorly annoyed. I tried to have a conversation with Mike about a new band he discovered, but only make out every third word. The only positive was that I could not hear about whatever video game Mark was talking about.

I decided it was a push, but that a third beer might further improve my mood. I made my way to the bar and began the scrum to get noticed by a bartender. I knew with all the sorority skin I had no chance of getting a drink from a male bartender, so my only hope was that one of the female bartenders found me less douchey than the other guys.

That apparently was not the case as after five minutes I still did not have a beer. After getting passed over for the third time by the same cute bartender with a nose ring and cool skull tattoo, I dropped my head in frustration and muttered a curse word under my breath.

At that very moment, I felt a huge hand clamp my shoulder, which scared the hell out of me. I assumed it was a bouncer and I wondered what I did wrong.

"Slade!" exclaimed a booming voice.

I looked back and saw the smiling face of Omar, Ike's bodyguard. It was weird seeing the heavily muscled Omar away from Ike's house, but after he caught the attention of a bartender and bought me a beer, I decided I could get used to running into him.

He had a silly grin on his face and it was not hard to deduce that he was a few more drinks into the evening than I was.

He began steering me to the opposite end of the bar than my friends and I was pretty much powerless to do anything against the former college football player, even though he had two drinks in his left hand (and had shoved a third into my empty fist).

"This is perfect," Omar boomed. "I need a wingman. I am working on this pretty little girl, and need you to sweet talk the friend while I work my magic."

Normally when I have been asked to be a wingman, it is because the friend is unattractive. This was not the case. The friend I was presumably running interference for was tall and skinny, but not in a bad way. She had long dirty blonde hair and glasses, that really made her eyes look nice. Her face was prettier than Omar's "little girl."

All that said, I could see why Omar was into his girl. She was a head shorter than the friend, and probably the same weight. She was very curvy, with a huge chest and an outfit that showcased all of her curves top to ample bottom. While I thought the taller friend was prettier, Omar's girl was still a cutie.

I handed the taller girl her drink and introduced myself.

"Please tell me he did not drag some stranger over here to distract me while he hits on Jenna," the taller friend said. Because I am a detective I deduced that the shorter, bustier friend was Jenna.

"No, we've known each other for a few years," I said. "Although I was apparently at the right place at the right time to get drafted into wingman duty."

I looked over and Omar seemed to be charming Jenna, so I was going to be here a few minutes.

"Let's make this easy. I am Olivia, I am a junior English major and I just broke up with someone and I am not looking for a boyfriend or a rebound fling," she said, and I suddenly realized the music was not quite as loud in this corner, though we were standing and were close enough to the bathroom that we had a steady stream of people walking by us.

"I am Eric, I am a junior who may or may not still be a history major, and I have a girlfriend I have no intention of cheating on," I said, mimicking her.

A lot of the tension seemed to leave her.

"So now that I know you are not going to hit on me I will lay out the ground rules," she said, and I had to admit her sassiness was fun. "My friend will not be going home with him no matter how much she likes him."

I nodded in agreement.

"If she likes him, I will allow him to give her his number and will ensure that she calls him tomorrow afternoon," she added. "Tonight there will be no kissing, no hugs, and if I get any bad vibes from him I will drag her off with no explanation."

I gave her a side head nod to confirm that her demands seemed reasonable, but could not let her have the last word.

"I accept your terms, with one caveat," I said, trying to sound just as tough as she did. "If you do get a bad vibe, you will do your best to explain what rubbed you the wrong way so that I may coach my friend for the next time."

She held out her hand to accept my counter offer, then said: "now tell me something interesting."

"I might be the biggest disappointment in the history of Arizona hockey…"

Thirty minutes later I was double fisting bottles of beer courtesy of Omar. Jenna had his number and practically had to be dragged away by Olivia before the no kissing pledge had to be amended.

"Man, you are alright Slade," Omar said handing me the two beers. "We should do this again sometime."

While I did not want to play wingman for him again, getting on the good side of my bookie's hired muscle had to be a good thing.

He started to walk off but turned around to say a final word.

"I owe you one."

I returned to my friends three free beers richer and it was obvious that I had not been missed. We soon left the bar top find a quieter establishment. Little did I know I now held a very valuable chip.

33. Blind Date

Thanks to three bottles of water and my normal post-drinking aspirin chaser, I woke up feeling fine on Friday despite what ended up being about a nine-beer Thursday night. I made my classes just fine, mostly paid attention, and was well into my Friday afternoon routine of music and movie shopping when I got a phone call from an unfamiliar number.

With the McCauley case and all of these new people coming into my life, I felt it important to answer.

It was neither a sales pitch or a suspect. Instead, it was Omar. Just 18 hours before he was a guy I had only seen at Ike's house and now I had served as his wingman and was getting a surprise phone call. After some initial pleasantries, he got to the point.

"I need your help tonight," Omar said in his deep rumbling voice. "I am supposed to go out with Jenna, but that chick with the glasses insisted you and your girlfriend make it a double date. I guess she still does not trust me."

I said I would run it by Rachel and get back to him.

When Rachel was out of her final class I texted her to give me a call. A few minutes later the phone rang and filled her in on the request.

"So you want me to go on a double date with someone I have never met and someone you only kind of know, all because some girl, who you had to run interference on, insisted?"

"That sounds about right," I said, figuring the ideas was already dead in the water.

"Sure," she said, her voiced changing from skeptical to pleasant.

Around 7:30 I was at Rachel's place and she was almost ready. Tariq and Caitlin were on the bed talking. I pulled out the chair from Rachel's desk and sat in it backwards, resting my arms on the back. The move served two purposes, it allowed me to look cool and casual (at least in my own mind) and I could turn my back to the other couple in the room. Invariably Tariq would say something vaguely insulting, and my plan was to just ignore him.

Rachel was putting in earrings and doing what I perceived to be a final check of hair, makeup and outfit in a full-length mirror hung on her closet door.

"So who is this friend of yours?" she asked, fastening an earring.

"Omar," I replied, not able to further explain because of a large amount of giggling from Tariq.

I had told myself I was not going to let Tariq bother me, but that did not last more than two minutes. His condescending laughter was perfectly pushing my buttons.

"What's so funny?" I asked, turning around to glare at Tariq.

"Nothing," he said between giggles. "Just did not expect the rich white hockey player to have any friends of color, assuming this 'Omar' is indeed a person of color and not just a nickname masking as cultural appropriation."

"What? The white hockey player can't have minority friends?" I asked, full of anger. "For someone who demands everyone else be open-minded, you sure have a limited worldview."

He just stared at me with a look that was part glare, part surprise, but all contempt. He was not used to people his own age standing up to him.

"I may play a sport with a lack of diversity, but that does not mean my life is also devoid of diversity," I said.

Now it was Tariq's turn to sit up and square up to me.

"Let me guess 'some of your best friends are black'," he said in a mocking tone, using air quotes.

"Not some," I said. "My roommate and best friend in this world is as black as you are."

He pulled his head back started laughing at me.

"I am only half African American," he said, still mocking.

I remained calm, never taking my eyes off him.

"I know," I shot back. "And so is he. He is African American on his father's side. Most likely his family is from what is now Ghana, though it is hard to really say since his ancestors were brought over as slaves, most likely in the early 1800's."

I am sure I had a look of satisfaction on my face. Chuck had researched his genealogy for a project last year and I helped him with the project.

Tariq was silenced for a second and I did not let him recover. I continued my verbal parrying.

"If you must know, and I owe you no explanations, two of my other closest friends are also minorities. But that does not really matter to me," I said. "It seems to me you are the one separating everyone by their differences, instead of looking for commonalities."

And with that, I grabbed Rachel's hand and we stormed out the door. We got halfway down the hall before I stopped.

"I hope you were ready to go," I said, getting a smile out of her.

I have been on a number of first dates and group dates in my time. Back in Iowa Maggie and I were one of the few constant couples, so my teammates and her group of friends were constantly hooking up and more often than not we were the once accompanying these burgeoning couples on their initial dates.

While I did not mind group dates per se, they could be strange experiences. You are either awkwardly on someone else's first date, or when it was a pair of established couples, you are invariably comparing the relative strength of the two couples and wondering how your relationship stacks up.

We met up with Omar and Jenna at a local pizza place. It had a wood-burning brick oven as the centerpiece and was known for their great cheesecake and decent wine and beer list. Rachel and I got there just as Omar and Jenna were being seated.

We joined them at a small corner table and made the introductions. After majors and hometowns, the small talk turned to what we were going to eat, and then we hit the inevitable conversational lull. Omar turned to Karina to talk to his date and so that left Rachel and I chatting to ourselves.

"I can't believe what a jerk Tariq was to you," Rachel said.

"Technically he was being a jerk to both of us," I replied. "I was not much better. I should have let it go, but he just pushes my buttons."

Omar overheard our conversation.

"You talking about that guy Tariq who leads all those protests?"

I nodded in affirmation.

"You know he is at Ike's all the time," Omar said, leaving the statement vague. When you work for a bookie you don't exactly make your boss' true volition public.

I wanted to ask more but did not want to let Rachel know about my little money making habit and I was pretty sure Omar did not want Jenna to know what he did.

"Who is Ike?" Rachel asked.

"He's a mutual friend of ours," I said nodding in Omar's direction. "We go there to watch games sometimes."

Omar seemed content by how I walked that tightrope and Rachel did not pry.

"Tariq loves to watch the fights," Omar added. I inferred that Tariq was betting on boxing and MMA, but had to ask.

"He chip into the kitty?" I asked, hoping that Omar understood what I was asking.

"Yeah, in fact, he has put a lot into the kitty of late," Omar said, giving me a look that confirmed that Tariq was not only a client of Ike's but had been losing a lot lately.

The rest of dinner went well. We shared pizza and salad, elevated the conversation past the cursory college talk, and genuinely had a good time. The only real negative was that I became the butt of ridicule as the other three gave me a hard time for not liking a certain pop culture filled animated television show.

We decided we were going to continue the evening and go out for drinks. Initially, the girls wanted to go somewhere "trendy and fun" but Omar and I reminded them that trendy and fun meant loud and noisy and that somewhere a little cozier might be better for first date conversation.

Selfishly I also wanted someplace that did not overcharge for watered down drinks.

We settled on a place that was sort of like two bars in one. The front half was like a sports bar, plenty of televisions, but it also had an oval-shaped bar smack dab in the middle of the room, giving 365-degree access to drinks. Something I found vitally important. Like most predators, I like to encircle my prey, even if said prey is an overworked bartender and the drinks he or she is about to pour.

The second room had a stage and large dance floor and was equally adept at hosting small concerts or housing a DJ and dancing. Tonight it was a combination of both as there was a disco cover band playing, which had more people dancing than watching the musicians.

Omar knew the doorman and we were able to get Rachel in without so much as a glance at her fake ID. We found a table and had a few rounds in the front portion of the place. I was a good boy and did not bet on any of the basketball games, so I hardly glanced at the scores.

The girls were actually hitting it off and decided we needed to go dance. Omar needed no coaxing, but I was less enthusiastic. Next thing I knew I was being pulled by the arm up the stairs to the second room and the disco cover band.

I am not a good dancer. I would not say I am bad per se, but no one would praise me for my moves on the dance floor. The same could not be said for Omar. Despite being 240 pounds of pure muscle, the guy could dance. Karina was a fairly good match in the moves department, while Rachel was clearly the superior dancer in our duo.

Whether it was his ability to dance that sealed the deal, or whether she was already sold earlier in the evening I will never know, but after only a few minutes it was clear that Jenna was into Omar. They danced close, the much smaller girl frequently melting into the big man. It was sometime during "Brickhouse" that they shared their first kiss and by the time "Get Down Tonight" finished, I was wondering if they were going to just go at it right there.

Jenna eventually pulled herself away, whispered something to Omar, then gathered up Rachel and went to the restroom. Omar and I went to the bar and quickly got a few drinks. Somehow being accompanied by a 6-3, 240-pound football player was a good way to get prompt service.

"We are going to get out of here," Omar said, guzzling down a third of his bottled beer. "I need a favor."

He turned to me and leaned in close. It was a bit awkward but I did not pull away. I realized he was pulling something out of his jacket.

"Be cool," he said as under his breath as he could with a live band playing. "I need you to take this, it is not something I care to explain right now."

He forced something into my hands and then made me press them to my chest. It took a moment, but I realized that he had slipped me his gun. I was shocked but tried not to let on. As smoothly as I could, which is to say not smooth at all, I slid the gun into my front waistband and hastily covered it up with my sweater.

My timing was good enough as the girls returned just as I was smoothing out my sweater. In my mind the bulge from the gun was gigantic, but no one seemed to notice.

"I am getting tired," Jenna said, utilizing a very fake yawn. "She turned to Omar, can you take me home."

She emphasized the word "take" and was not particularly subtle.

We walked to our cars, the temperature had dropped a bit and Rachel snuggled close. I was petrified she would find the gun, but she stayed to the side and all seemed well.

We got to a point of separation and said our goodbyes. Omar and I clenched fists and went in for a man-chest hug when we went shoulder to shoulder and a little pec to pec. It was like hugging a marble statue. The guy had not played football in a year but was still built like a Greek God.

"Thanks," Omar whispered in our man-hug. "I'll get it from you in a day or two."

Once we got into the car Rachel turned to me.

"She is going to screw his brains out," Rachel said. "She gave me a detailed preview in the bathroom."

She was laughing as she relayed the info.

"Maybe if you play your cards right I will demonstrate some of what she said."

Apparently, I played my cards right because we had a good time upon getting back to my room. I was fortunate that upon arriving at my dorm the three drinks she had hit her bladder and she desperately needed to use the bathroom. That allowed me to not only stash Omar's little gift to me but also ensure that Chuck was not returning to my room.

The gun was stashed in a drawer in my desk, buried under a ream of printer paper and a spare notebook. Despite the pleasant conclusion of the evening Rachel had in store, the firearm was never completely out of my thoughts. I was not particularly comfortable stashing it in my room, despite the fact I knew no one would find it.

I was not a "gun guy" and not real familiar with them, but that was soon to change.

34. Unexpected Expenses

March

Rachel and I woke up the next morning to the buzzing of my cell phone. At first, I was annoyed, but then I noticed it was after 10 AM. I was not happy to be woken up, but at least a call after 10 was reasonable.

I glanced down at the screen and noticed it was Harris. I kissed Rachel on the cheek and excused myself to the front room.

He skipped the pleasantries and was speaking a mile a minute.

"He made his move," he said, not pausing between syllables. "He wants money."

He proceeded to tell me that our suspect had sent an e-mail this morning and said he would leave Caitlin alone for $10,000.

"It looks like it was all a bluff," Harris explained. "He just wanted to scare us enough for a payday and does not have the balls to actually kidnap her and ask for a real ransom."

Ten thousand dollars sounded like real money to me, but I understood what he meant. When you are a multi-millionaire like Ed McCauley 10 grand is not all that steep a price to pay.

Harris told me that the drop was scheduled for tonight.

"Can you get the money that fast?"

"Yeah, that is no problem," Harris replied to my query. "We have some petty cash for, shall we say, unexpected expenses."

I almost laughed at calling ransom for the safety of your boss' daughter "unexpected expenses" but knowing how Harris has worked behind the scenes I could imagine what some of these expenses might be. I may not know tons about the unseemly side of politics, well the REALLY unseemly side of politics, but I imagine gathering information and preventing information from seeing the light of day did not come cheap and some petty cash might come in handy.

Harris said he would be driving down from Phoenix in just a bit and we made plans to meet and figure out our strategy for this evening in a few hours.

At 1:00 we sitting at a sandwich shop about a mile away from campus. It was a cheesesteak place, full of all the prerequisite Philadelphia signage and posters. There were maps of Philly, pictures of the Philadelphia skyline, and of course, plenty of Phillies, Flyers, and Eagles posters, pennants and pictures.

In addition to all the Philadelphia stuff on the walls, there were plenty of other sports and movie paraphernalia. Every room had dozens of Sports Illustrated covers and plenty of vintage posters. Add to that old vinyl album covers and it looked like a teenager in the 1980's room exploded and turned into a restaurant. My favorite part was the bathroom, which was wallpapered in baseball and football cards. Other than the floor, ceiling, and toilet, the entire bathroom was covered in collectible sports trading cards.

Harris was three bites into his cheesesteak when he started filling me in on the details. He had his suit jacket draped onto the chair next to him, his tie flipped over his shoulder and was careful to not get any cheese or grease on his light blue dress shirt. Considering his sandwich had Cheese Wiz, onions and mushrooms, that was no easy feat. Although his clothes remained impeccable, his hands paid the price and were covered with the contents of his sandwich that were not in his mouth or on the plate.

"He sent a text this morning," Harris explained. "All it said was that for $10,000 this would all be over tonight and to await further instructions."

I took a bite of my sandwich. While the cheesesteaks are great, they also make a great hot ham and cheese sub, grilled to perfection with a honey mustard sauce and thinly sliced onions.

"I gave him an e-mail address to send the details to and I am still waiting for more info," Harris added.

"Do you really think this is it? The end I mean."

He dabbed a French fry into some catsup before continuing. I could not blame him, the French fries are really good.

"I would say probably, though to be safe I would say 50-50," Harris said. "Although if we can resolve this for 10 grand, it is worth the risk."

Harris said that he expected the drop to be somewhere public, probably with a lot of people, though if it really was an amateur they would plan on something like the lockers at a bus station or the airport. The plan was to place a small tracking device and hope to catch the guy, but even if we didn't that the payoff might be enough to end this all.

I noticed he always referred to the person as a guy and I assumed that was either his own slight sexism or based on some kind of profiling of would-be kidnappers. I hoped later was the case because that meant Rachel and Karen were not involved.

We took our time eating, and I briefed Harris on what few new things I learned since our last talk, which was not much. We were both watching an NBA game when his smartphone pinged.

An e-mail came in.

It was from him.

Slowly over the course of 10 minutes, several e-mails came, spelling out the details of the drop. We were to get a black backpack and put the money into it. We were to go to the main administration building at 9:00 p.m. Out in front of the building is a large brick planter with benches built into it. We were to leave the money under the bench.

Of course, the police were not to be involved and the e-mails said if there was any evidence of the police or anyone else monitoring the drop that the deal was off and "we'd be sorry."

By 4:00 we had everything we needed and we went out to scout the location. The planter was in a fairly open location and that seemed to please Harris. He said we could monitor the planter from two separate locations without being seen.

Harris said he just needed to buy a few more items and that we would meet again at 7:00 to go over our final plan.

With a few hours to kill I shot Rachel a call. I had left a bit abruptly this morning, claiming my father needed me to do something. Although I had already canceled our plans, I thought I would be a good boyfriend and call her. She was going to go to the movies with some friends and I said if I got done early we would try to get together.

A few minutes before 7:00 I walked into the same pub I had lunch with Karen at a few weeks ago. I suggested the place because I thought the patio would be a good place to talk without being too conspicuous. There was a basketball game that night, and although most of the crowd would already be at the arena, game night would not be an unusual time to see two guys with such an age discrepancy having a meal close to campus.

I ordered a soda, and before it could be delivered Harris walked up. For the first time since I met him a few months back, Harris was not wearing a suit. He was still wearing black slacks but wore a black turtleneck and a lightweight black jacket. Since he instructed me to wear dark clothes, I had on the darkest pair of jeans I owned and a black hooded sweatshirt.

He mapped out the strategy. We would each set up on opposite sides of the administration building. He would be across the grass mall by the science and engineering building, while I would be at the student union, which was adjacent to the admin building. I would be the one to take the money to the planter and make the drop and then return to the union to continue the stakeout.

The hope was that one of us would be able to make a visual of our guy picking up the backpack, but even if we didn't, Harris would be able to follow with the tracker. Apparently, this one worked off of an app on his smartphone, but knowing his technical limitations, that might not be the most effective tracking method.

"Don't worry, I had a friend of mine who is an expert with these sorts of things give me a thorough lesson." He must have seen the look of doubt on my face.

I was still not convinced but did not let on that I was still skeptical he could make the tracker work. It did not help that he was also wearing a clunky Blue Tooth earpiece. We had decided we needed to keep in communication with each other and although he had some walkie-talkies, we both agreed that cell phones would less conspicuous and more efficient than trying to trade text messages.

I put my earphones in and headed off to my spot. If Harris called I could simply answer with a touch of the wireless earbuds and be in quick communication.

I asked if it was best if I made the drop, in case it really was one of the suspects I knew. Harris felt the baggy sweatshirt and a baseball cap pulled down low would do the trick. It turned out the area would be too crowded for anyone to really notice.

The plan was for me to set up shop in front of the student union, not far from the steps where I had spoken to Murph just a few weeks ago. As I got to the area I noticed a lot of commotion in front of the adjacent administration building. There had to be close to 100 people standing side by side, holding candles. It appeared to be some sort of vigil.

The phone rang and I answered.

"What are all those people doing there?" Harris said, a touch of panic in his voice.

"I don't know," I said, already trying to look it up on my phone. I quickly learned it was a protest of sorts in support of women's reproductive rights. A state senator was proposing a bill that many feared would make getting birth control tougher, and could lead to trying to limit abortions.

I relayed the information to Harris. "What should we do?" I added.

"Nothing," Harris said. "Continue on with the plan. I am sure he knew there would be people out here, making it tougher for us to see him grab the cash."

A few minutes before 9:00 I started walking over to the planter with the backpack full of money. With several spiny cacti jutting out, I wondered what the visibility might be. I sat down on one of the benches, set the backpack between my feet, and took out my phone. I texted Harris to make sure he could see me and he replied that he could. I spent another minute or two on the bench, then stood up, slid the backpack under the bench with the back of my foot, and then started to walk back to the front of the student union.

Once I got into the crowd I pulled off the cap and dropped it at my feet.

I kept my head on a swivel as I slowly walked away from the planter and noticed more than a few black backpacks among the protesters. A few more steps and I noticed something, or should I say, something else.

Karen.

She was standing in a pack of protesters, holding a candle, and listening to a speech from someone on the administration steps. She saw me and peeled away from the group. My stomach dropped seeing her so close to the cash drop, but she did not seem to have any of the same trepidation.

"Eric," she said, flashing me that great smile. "Are you here for the protest?"

I wanted to lie and impress her but also needed to get back to my stake out spot.

"Not really, I had a study group at the library," I lied. "But I was curious to see how many people were coming out."

It was a terrible lie. Anyone who knew me knew I would not agree to a Saturday night study group. Karen obviously did not know me because she took my deception at face value.

"You should come join us," she said. I had to admit I was tempted. Spending time with Karen, even if it was at a protest, seemed like a good idea. I would at least get to look at her some more.

"I wish I could, but I have other plans," I said. We said a brief goodbye and she rejoined the rest of those holding candles.

I returned to my spot in front of the union, making sure I could still see the planter. I also tried to keep an eye on Karen. Not from an aesthetic standpoint, I had to make sure she was not involved. While the protest was the most likely reason she was here, I could not rule out she was using the protest as a cover to take the money.

By the time I set up shop back at the planter I lost sight of Karen, but the planter was still in view, so I felt confident I would be able to see if Karen, or anyone else, attempted to take the backpack.

It did not take long for me to realize that was an erroneous idea. Two separate events proved to make staking out the backpack much tougher than it should have been.

First at a few minutes after 9:00 a huge crowd of people emerged from the student union. At first, I was confused, but as hundreds of people flooded out the side of the student union I looked up at the marquee, the was only a few dozen feet from me. Sure enough, the student union's movie theater was not only showing a movie, but it was a free sneak preview of a big comedy sequel that half of campus was anticipating.

While many of those film fans dispersed in opposite directions, several dozen steamed out into the area of the protest and, in turn, the area around the backpack full of cash.

Almost simultaneously, a second large group of people began filtering in from the opposite direction. At first, I was confused, but when I noticed most of them were wearing red and blue "Wildcat" t-shirts, I was able to figure out where they were coming from…the basketball game.

Basketball is a big deal at the University of Arizona with one of the most rabid fan bases in the nation. As such, every home game draws a capacity 14,545 fans.

Tonight's game was no exception. While the stadium was on the opposite end of campus, and most of the parking was over there, there were still several hundred fans who would have parked over at the parking garage behind the student union and the administration building.

I lost sight of the planter as it did not take long for the entire area to be filled with a combination of protestors, moviegoers, and basketball fans.

Apparently, our stalker turned extortionist also knew this, because my phone rang and Harris let me know the bag was on the move. He said the person was still in the area and so I sprinted over to the mob of people. I could not see the backpack, more specifically, I could not figure out which backpack was our backpack. There had to be at least a dozen people with dark backpacks on.

I went from person to person trying to determine if they had our backpack, but in the dark, with the orange glow from the area lighting, it was impossible.

The whole time I remained on the line with Harris, but he was not able to guide me with any kind of specificity. There were people everywhere. I was trying to navigate through people meandering in the same direction I was going, while also trying to avoid people walking my way. If that was not enough, I had a hundred other bodies standing still, with candles. I could hardly bump into them, for fear of burning myself or them.

After a few minutes of me scrambling around the area frantically, Harris chimed in that our guy was on the move. He said he was moving to the north, around the back side of the student union building.

I took off in pursuit. I wanted to run, but the area was too congested for me to really take off. I did my best running back impression, weaving through the people walking to the parking garage, but could not do much in the congested walk-way between the two buildings.

Eventually, I emerged from the walkway and was able to run. Harris said the tracker was now headed west, and I sprinted off that way. My knee was essentially healed, but in keeping up my charade the past few months, it did not take long for me to realize I was nowhere near in the shape I had been when I was still playing hockey. I was glad I had taken a few late night jogs, or I would have been in a heap of hurt.

My lung burned, my knee hurt, and I was quickly slowing down, but I kept running. Harris tried to guide me, but apparently, he was running as well because he was now struggling to speak.

As best as I could understand the tracker, and presumably the stalker, had again changed directions and seemed to be picking up speed.

"He's going faster," Harris gasped.

I kept following directions and soon I realized that the tracker was headed in the general direction of my dorm. I knew the area well and darted between a few different buildings that should shave some time off my journey if the person was indeed heading past my dorm.

I emerged from a small alleyway and was on the same street as my dorm when Harris piped back up.

"He's stopped," Harris said breathlessly. "He's not moving."

I was now barely jogging but kept my pursuit. I passed the all of the brick covered buildings. I jogged past the honors dorm, I passed the ROTC building and was so into my own head that I nearly tripped over the bike on the sidewalk.

Was that why the tracker sped up? Had our guy had jumped on a bike? If this was his bike, did that mean he was also around?

"Is he back on the move?" I asked.

"No," Harris shot back. "He's still stopped."

I did a full 360. There were not many places a person could hide. The bike, which was a beat-up, old 10-speed, had been discarded on the sidewalk in front of the concrete basketball court that served as the boundary between the ROTC building and my dorm.

The only hiding places were the bushes that ringed both buildings and that is where I began looking. I heard pounding footsteps and labored breathing and figured that Harris was just arriving. I did not turn around and kept looking in the bushes. It did not take long to realize our stalker was not hiding in the bushes but may have left something there.

Sitting under a bush was a black backpack. I picked it up and it was empty.

I turned around to show it to Harris. He started to speak, then it dawned on him that is was an empty backpack.

He extended his hand and I gave him the backpack.

He reached into it and unzipped a little side pocket concealed on the inside. He slowly drew out a small plastic circle that resembled a poker chip. As he pulled it out, his whole demeanor changed. He did not have to tell me we had our backpack.

He did not have to tell me we lost our $10,000.

35. Hard Times and Desperation

I always took Harris for a beer and a shot kind of guy, but apparently, I was quite wrong. We were at a downtown bar a few miles from campus licking our wounds and plotting our course after losing $10,000.

It was a bar that tried to give off the vibe of being a blue-collar bar, yet everything was brand new and shiny. The leather on the booths was shiny and just a little too colorful to be sat in by construction workers or longshoremen. The wood was too nice, too polished to have seen hard times and desperation.

It was as if a Hollywood set designer who had never stepped foot in a bar tried to construct one based on a verbal description of what a dive bar should be.

It lacked all the character, and the characters, that usually inhabit a dive bar. This was inhabited by young professionals and college kids. It was less than a year old and had never experienced cigarette smoke, tough times, or a good old-fashioned bar fight. The bartenders were young, recently tattooed, and meticulously put together their outfits in an effort to look like they threw something together. Their hair was messy on purpose, their flannel shirts too new, and they identified themselves as mixologists.

If I was going to a dive bar, I wanted a real dive bar. I wanted my bartenders to have missing teeth and faded green tattoos they got in the Navy, and that was the female bartenders. I wanted them to have learned their craft by living life, not by going to bartending school, or worse, culinary school.

I wanted them to have lived life, have been beaten down a bit by it, and have the stories to tell.

While it was a dive bar inspired, I could not help be impressed by the beer and whiskey lists, both of which covered the gamut from well-known big brands, to obscure small batch beverages with creative names and unique stories. The bar lacked character, the booze did not.

Harris was drinking a craft cocktail that I have never heard of. It had whiskey, but also had been smoked by the bartender and included a curl of orange peel that had been scorched by the bartender's lighter. It had an oversized, sphere ice cube to complete the look.

I went with a craft beer with a goofy name that had a few too many hops for my liking and was a tad too bitter, but I was not about to let on that I did not like it.

"I think this is the end of it," Harris said. He seemed to be resigned to losing the money and was now fairly even-keeled.

He was initially upset, but after changing his shirt (who knew he traveled with several perfectly pressed dress shirts?) and running some water on his face, he seemed mostly fine with how things progressed.

"My guess is that he will be happy with the 10 grand and won't want to risk getting caught," Harris explained. "In many ways, he has been very lucky and getting a quick, easy payday may be enough."

He held up his glass and played with it a bit before finally taking a small sip.

"You don't think this will give him just a taste?" I asked. "He has to be confident after pulling this off."

Harris continued to consider his drink another moment before speaking.

"He's very clever," Harris said. "He planned the money drop really well. To have the protest, the movie, and the basketball crowd all on the mall at the same time was smart. Lucky, but smart."

We drank in silence for a bit. Had this been a real dive bar there would have been nuts or pretzels to munch on, but there was nothing. Although we had dinner, all that running had made me hungry.

"So what do you want me to do?" I asked.

"Keep doing what you are doing," he answered. "While I think this is over, we really have no idea. Better to be safe than sorry."

I was relieved. First of all, I did not share Harris' view of the case. It seemed to me if getting $10,000 was so "easy" that he would soon try for more. And if this was about revenge, then the money was not the true goal, so getting the cash would not end things.

Secondly, when the case was over I would have to actually confront my feelings about Rachel. Clearly, I liked her, but was there enough to stay together without the Caitlin case keeping us together?

And in reality, I kind of liked the responsibility. Without hockey, I did not have much going on, so playing wannabe detective gave me a sense of purpose that school, friends and a mild gambling addiction did not.

"I'll see what we can learn from the bike," Harris said.

We had searched the area for a bit, hoping for some clue. Ideally, we hoped to find the culprit hiding somewhere, cash in hand, but at the very least we hoped for some kind of clue. Re-stating it now, I feel like I am on "Scooby Doo", but at the time it seemed appropriate.

After about 20 minutes of searching, we gave up. We returned to the area where we found the empty backpack and realized that the bike was still there. Again we had different ideas on what this meant. Harris was so impressed with our extortionist that he assumed there would be no fingerprints on the bike. I, however, was more optimistic. While I agreed that this person was smart, but would they be smart enough to know that they were dealing with people who had ties to law enforcement and could get prints run off the bike?

I did not know but was optimistic. Harris had me use my sleeves to cover my hands and then pick up the bike and then walk it over to his car. There he pulled out pairs of latex gloves for each of us to put the bike in the back of his SUV.

He saw the puzzled look on my face when he pulled the gloves out of a duffle bag in the back seat.

"You never know when you are going to have to retrieve evidence," he said. "Or plant it."

We put the bike in the back of the vehicle and that is when Harris suggested we get a drink or two, and de-brief.

A second beer was delivered when I got a text from Rachel. She was finally heading home and encouraged me to meet her. We went over some of the latest findings, I briefed him again on each of my suspects and was still very intrigued by the Volpe/Langdon/Karen trio and encouraged me to keep tabs on them.

He told me that he would be in touch if he learned anything from the bike or if he heard from our kidnapper again.

On the drive back to campus Rachel called, Caitlin and Tariq were there and she wondered if we could hang out at my place. We agreed to the venue change.

I was a few hundred feet from my dorm when I saw a familiar face. It was Murph. He and a few of his stoner friends were walking around, looking agitated. Murph and a skinny kid with long hair that covered his left eye, but was shaved on the right side, were verbally getting into it.

I debated whether or not to bypass the group, but realized that if Murph saw me avoiding him it might seem strange. I kept walking straight ahead. It wasn't until I was a few feet from the group that Murph saw me. I gave him a quick head nod of recognition.

"Oh, hey Slade," Murph said, a bit nervously.

"Everything okay?" I inquired.

"Uh, yeah, kinda," Murph said, still unsure. "Bobby here went to buy weed off a new guy and decided to 'sample' some of the shit before he left."

I did not understand, but I let Murph continue.

"It was some real potent stuff," Bobby interjected.

Murph shot him a dirty look.

"So dipshit here get so stoned that he can't remember where he parked his bike," Murph said.

"His bike?" I asked.

"Yeah, we're looking for his bike."

36. Playing Dumb, or Actually Dumb

Twelve hours and a full night's sleep did nothing to quench my curiosity. What was I supposed to make of my run-in with Murphy? While it was completely plausible that Murphy's buddy got so high that he lost his bike, it seemed like too much of a coincidence that he was looking for a bicycle in the exact same area that our extortionist ditched his.

Could Murph have had help trying to get the ransom? Would this Bobby character actually make the pick-up and race away on the bike? Could co-conspirators give Murphy an alibi?

I doubted that the Murph I had been dealing with was smart enough to concoct such an elaborate scheme, but I had been wrong before on this case. I did not know Murph well enough to know if he was actually dumb, or if a lot of it was just an act.

I had known Murph for years and always figured he was a little smarter than he led on, but that was not hard to do since he has acted like a doofus party boy since middle school. He was never good in school, and conversations with him rarely went beyond drinking and girls, but I did have the impression there was a little more going on in there than he allowed himself to reveal.

That being said, I just did not see him being a criminal mastermind, and if he was, it seemed like he would use his powers to rip off his pot dealer, not extort money from his ex-girlfriend's family.

That is what bothered me, the money. If Murph was really so heartbroken that he would stalk Caitlin, why ask for money? Murph certainly did not need the cash, and it was quite a risk to potentially expose yourself during the money drop.

It was apparent I might need to pay Murph another visit to get a better feel for the situation.

It was a lazy Sunday. Rachel and I had a late breakfast and then went our separate ways. She had to keep working on a group project, so I decided to try and study. I actually read for about an hour, but soon found myself watching a movie. I was 20 minutes into a bad American remake of a Hong Kong action movie when my phone rang.

It was Omar.

"Ike would like to see you," he said matter of factly.

I was suddenly worried. It was rarely a good thing when the enforcer for your bookie calls you in for a meeting. While I could not think of anything I did wrong, I was nervous nonetheless.

"Is everything cool?" I asked.

"I don't know," Omar answered. "He just asked me to have you come by."

I told him I could be by in less than an hour and he reminded me to bring the "package" I was holding for him. I quickly changed my clothes, grabbed a hooded sweatshirt, and fished the gun out of the back of my underwear drawer, where I had recently moved it.

I stuffed the handgun into the front pocket of my sweatshirt and was relieved to be getting rid of it. The campus had a zero-tolerance gun policy, and I did not want someone accidentally finding it. I figured I was safe stuffing it into my underwear drawer, I could not envision a scenario where someone would be fishing through my skivvies, but I would feel better when it was back in Omar's possession.

Fifteen minutes later I was parking my Jeep in a vacant lot down the street from Ike's. Omar was on the front porch and walked up to me. I had my hands jammed into my sweatshirt, and indicated with a brief downward head nod and a quick push of the gun against the outside of the sweatshirt to indicate that is where the gun was.

Omar pulled up close, and I slipped the gun to him. He could nearly fit the whole gun in his palm and slyly slid it into his waistband, and covered it up with his shirt.

"He's waiting," Omar said.

He did not indicate what it was about, but he also did not have a grave or worried look on his face. I hoped that meant I was not in trouble.

He was on the phone when I got there, jotting some things down on a piece of paper, and I had to wait a few minutes. He clicked off the cell phone and waved me over. He also held up the piece of paper he had been writing on and motioned for one of the Gupta's to grab the slip. He retrieved the paper and headed over to one of the laptops to enter what I assumed was a bet.

I sat down next to Ike, still unsure of why I was here.

Ike had several packages of Hostess Cupcakes in front of him.

"Your boy Tariq loves to bet the fights," Ike said. "I'm not sure you knew that."

I bristled when at the thought of Tariq being described as my friend. It also meant that Omar had not told him about our conversation two nights before.

Ike grabbed a package of orange cupcakes and slowly opened them. He deliberately opened it so as to not damage the cellophane wrapper other than breaking the seal across the side. Once open he slid a cupcake out. He was nearly surgical with how he handled the packaging, which was the exact opposite of how he ate the actual cupcake.

"I kind of gathered," I said, not wanting to sell Omar out. Since Omar had not said anything to him, I figured Ike would not be thrilled with his enforcer socializing with a client, and really wouldn't like him talking shop on a double date.

He picked up the cupcake and used his tongue to remove the disc of frosting from the cake. He snapped it in half, separating the two hemispheres so that the chain-like white frosting was on one half. He placed the side without the white frosting on his tongue and slurped it up like a frog eats a fly. He ate the other half before continuing.

"The boy knows his shit, knows a ton about fighters and fighting, but can't pick winners to save his life," he said. "In fact, he has been on a losing streak of late."

He picked up the cupcake and broke it in half. Once again the tongue was out and he licked the white frosting out of the middle of each half of the cupcake. He then shoved one half into his mouth and ate it quickly.

"He has not just been losing with me, but he has been spreading money out all over town," he said before stuffing the other half of the cupcake into his mouth.

"He owes me a couple grand, and I heard he may be in for even more with a couple of my competitors," he said, then wiped his mouth with the palm of his hand.

"What does this have to do with me?" I asked.

"Word is that he just gave one of these other odds makers a couple grand, sort of a goodwill gesture," Ike said, obviously pissed that he did not see any of that cash. "Were you aware of him suddenly having money?"

Then it hit me, could Tariq have been our extortionist? Could he have used some of that money to start to pay off his gambling debt? He had access, he has motive, and he surely would have known about the protest last night, it was his thing.

"I'm sorry, I don't know anything about him, save for he's an asshole who is dating my girlfriend's roommate," I said.

"Whose dad employs your dad," Ike said. "Let's not pretend there is not a connection there."

He removed the second cupcake.

"Just see what you can find out," Ike asked. "If he has some money, I want it. I can always send Omar to go collect."

I had to admit that I wanted to see that. I had half a mind to lie and say he had it just so Omar could teach that prick a lesson. Before I could do that, I had to figure out if Tariq could be our guy.

I assured Ike that I would look into it, apparently, my skills as a detective preceded me, and left before he could disassemble the second cupcake with his tongue. I did not need to see that again,

I left the house and Omar was still outside.

"Everything good?" he asked.

"Yeah, it doesn't really concern me per se," I replied. "Just need to check on something for the big man."

Omar seemed content with the answer and did not press anymore. He changed the subject.

"Hey thanks for escorting us the other night, as well as helping me out," he said, patting the gun. "I owe you one."

It was not the first time he had said that to me, but it was still comforting knowing that I was in good favor with a guy as dangerous as Omar.

When I got to my Jeep I dialed Harris.

"So Caitlin's boyfriend supposedly came into money over the past few days," I told him.

"Really?" he asked, sounding surprised. "How do you know?"

"Let's just say I heard he was paying down some debts," I said. "And other people may want their cut."

Harris congratulated me on the good work. He actually sounded impressed. I spelled out how he could have orchestrated things with the protest, and Harris admitted that it made a lot of sense.

I also added the information about Murph and the missing bike.

"This could be a big break, one way or another" Harris said, sounding very excited. "Let me look into some things on my end, but see what you can find out on your end."

Harris told me to expect a call in a day or two and told me to look into things, but to be careful as we did not want to tip off either Tariq or Murph that we might suspect them.

I was feeling good about myself after hanging up with Harris and decided in my good mood to pay Rachel a visit. If I ran into Tariq, it would be the first time I would actually be happy to see him.

37. Mo' Money, Mo' Problems

With mid-terms looming, I had picked the worst time to overextend myself, but that was exactly what was happening. Although Harris was unsure if our would-be kidnapper would even re-surface, I still felt compelled to keep an eye on all of my suspects.

I was still spending two nights a week helping out the campaign. At first, there was nothing unusual to report. It was the same routine the first two nights, but the third saw a few things that raised my attention.

First Landon arrived with beer. Not only did he buy the beer, which was a first, he bought good beer. In the scheme of things, dropping $50 on beer was not a huge deal, but Landon had made it well know that money was an issue. After his father's demise, the family was not left with a lot of money. His mother had remarried, but apparently, they paid for tuition and little else.

Several six-packs of microbrews was a nice enough gesture, but would not raise any real suspicions from anyone else. However, I was looking for any sign of something out of the ordinary, so this got my attention, but just a little bit. It was not like the guy was showing up with a new watch or sport coat.

That was Volpe.

On the same night that Landon brought beer from some of Oregon's finest breweries, Volpe showed up with a $250 watch, and brand new blue blazer. I was ashamed to know the cost of either, but my brothers were big fans of both brands. Needless to say, neither brand was cheap, though neither was outrageously expensive, just nicer than Volpe typically wore.

"Looking good professor," Karen said.

He looked a bit embarrassed, but simultaneously was enjoying the compliment.

"Thank you, I decided to splurge," Volpe said.

It was very possible that the watch was a knockoff, and the jacket was last year's fashion, now available at an outlet, but it was also possible that something was amiss considering two of my suspects were both showing off unusual purchases. I wondered if they were working together. I also wondered if Karen was also involved. Is that why she was at the protest? Could she have actually been the one to grab the bag? Or be a lookout? If she was either, did she see me before I took the hat off?

I grabbed a bottle of a particularly bitter IPA and sidled up to Landon.

"Thanks for getting the good stuff," I said, clinking my bottle to his.

He looked around sheepishly before leaning into me.

"It was on sale," he said quietly. "Buddy of mine works at a liquor store and said some of the microbrews were not selling and his boss was trying to unload them."

I did not know if I should believe him, as the IPA's were well regarded and seemed popular, but who was I to know the financial details of locally owned boutique liquor stores?

Volpe was less forthcoming. He was coy when I asked him about his newly acquired items. I poked and prodded a little bit, framing my inquiries in the form of compliments. The best I could gather is either the watch was a knockoff or that he got it on a steal via an online auction. Over the course of the night, he also told people that he "had his eye on it for a long time."

Suddenly we had two suspects acting out of the ordinary with expenditures, but they were not spending so much that they could not easily have come into the cash without fleecing a United States senator. That being said, I was still not ruling out the fact that Volpe and Landon were in this together.

Even worse, I could not rule out Karen as part of their crew.

Add to that Tariq supposedly paying down some gambling debt and I had a few possibilities. They would not be my last.

Next, I would run into Murph, and while he did not show a flash of cash, he did show me he had a reason to possibly need money, giving him a reason beyond being heartsick for keeping Caitlin McCauley.

Murph was in his usual place in front of the student union, holding the court with his usual crop of the unwashed.

"Your friend ever find his bike?" I asked Murph as I sauntered over.

He looked up at me confused for a moment. I could not be sure if he was confused by my query or by my identity. Suddenly, something clicked and he knew both who I was and what I was asking.

"The bike? The dumbass rode home, locked it up and then wandered off, forgetting he had ever gone to his house," Murph said.

Murph's friends certainly seemed stoned enough the other night to have forgotten things, but it could easily have been a story to cover up the fact that Murph and his friends had teamed up to pull a fast one on Harris and I. I did not want to live in a world where Murphy and his gang of stoner stooges could outwit me, but I had to put my ego aside and figure this out.

I tried to do some more digging.

"You doing anything cool for spring break?"

"Nah man," he said, no longer looking my way but staring off at something or someone across the way. "I was supposed to go down to Mexico, but my grades have gone to shit and my dad has cut me off. He's paying rent, food, and not much else unless I get my grades up."

Well, this was interesting. Murph had money problems, which would indeed give him that secondary motivation to extort the Senator. Of course, grabbing 10 grand would be a good way to pay for Mexico and other necessities, but maybe he was smart enough not to raise suspicions (the Senator's or his Dad's).

"That must cut into your, er, hobby," I said.

This caught his attention, and he again looked at me. He paused for a second, enough time to consider an answer (or recharge some brain cells).

"No shit, I had to sell one of my skateboards just to smoke last week," he said.

We said our goodbyes and I started to walk off when Murph hurried back over to me.

"Slade," he said, to get my attention. "I got some sweet Grateful Dead vinyl for sale if you are interested. Hell, I will part with nearly anything at this point."

I told him I would think about it and left. He truly seemed desperate for cash and I suddenly thought that there was no way he could be that good of an actor, especially not Murph. I wasn't ruling him out, but he was not at the top of my list.

A few hours later I could not say the same about my girlfriend.

Chuck and I were going to meet up with Rachel, "Kung-Fu" Tracey and a few more of their friends. Pretty much the same crew from out outing a few weeks ago where Chuck and Tracey first hooked up.

The four girls were already at the restaurant when we got there. We had decided to go to a local Mexican restaurant that had stellar tortillas, tasty frozen margaritas, and a manager who was inconsistent in checking ID's. By the looks of it, this was one of those off nights as the girls all had half-filled mugs of green and red frozen cocktails in front of them.

The girls were all giggling and I wondered if the drinks in front of them were not the first.

"What is so funny?" Chuck asked as we sat down at the table.

"We were just talking about spring break," Rachel said.

Rachel and her friends had been planning on going to Mexico for spring break since before we started dating, but those plans were on hold with some of the money problems her family was having. As a back-up, they considered driving to California, while she and I also discussed having a sort of spring break "staycation" in Arizona.

"Did you figure anything out?" I asked.

Rachel leaned into me.

"My dad's company has gotten a lot of new jobs, and he was able to send me some money to pay for the trip," she was happy, then looked at my face. "If that's okay."

My stomach dropped. While I was happy my girlfriend was able to go on her trip, the sudden influx of money meant she became another suspect I could not rule out. While it was perfectly conceivable that her father's plumbing company had a rush of new jobs, I could not rule out that she was somehow behind the missing $10,000.

"Of course," I said. "You guys have fun, just say away from any hard-bodied, local lifeguards."

She gave me a playful punch and then turned back to her friends.

I have to admit my attention to the group was lacking the rest of the evening. I tried my best to participate in the conversation, but I spent most of the night seriously considering whether or not the girl I cared for was responsible for the threats against Caitlin. While I had other suspects, including people I liked, none were someone I was intimately involved with.

At one point Chuck snapped his fingers in my face when I missed a question from Tracey. Apparently, she had asked me what I was doing for spring break.

"I am not sure yet," I finally said. "I am trying to avoid going home, so I might just hang out on campus and watch a lot of sports and play video games."

While I did keep zoning out, I managed to drink. Three margaritas, one of which I am not 100% sure I ordered. They are deceptively strong, and as we left I had that slight tinge of inebriation where I had to concentrate on my footsteps and words were not quite as easy to put out as they were an hour ago. I was not quite drunk, but I had quite the buzz.

Rachel did notice my distraction.

"Where were you tonight," she asked, cuddling up to me.

"Just worried about midterms," I lied, putting my arm around her.

We walked quietly behind the rest of the group, making the half-mile trek back to campus in the cool night air. Spring was upon us, and the days were getting warmer, but once the sun went down things were still cool enough at night to don a sweatshirt (or find an excuse to cuddle with your girlfriend).

Despite our mutual alcohol consumption, and the friskiness it caused, nothing could be done about it. Chuck had a huge test to study for and made it clear he was not keen about studying outside of our room. Likewise, Rachel said that Caitlin and Tariq were apparently binge watching documentaries and he was helping her with an English paper.

I dropped her off at her dorm, and we exchanged a long kiss, and I wondered if I was kissing the very person I had been hired to catch.

38. Cybernetically Enhanced Sentinel

D espite the distractions of a girlfriend and my investigation, I was cruising through mid-terms. Granted, being a junior taking a couple of freshman level classes did not hurt, but the bulk of my classes were either lower level courses or subjects I was actually interested in.

I can't claim that I was on my way to straight A's, but barring a collapse on my final mid-term I might find myself in serious contention for my highest GPA of my college career.

Because of my success, I was in no rush to study for that last exam, so I was wasting time playing a first person shooter video game. I was well on my way to leading my ragtag band of mercenaries past opposition forces when my phone buzzed to let me know I had a text message.

After a final head shot eliminated a cybernetically enhanced sentinel, allowing me to infiltrate opposition headquarters, I pushed pause on the game and checked my phone. It was Harris.

"He's back, can we meet?" he texted

I replied that I could and we agreed to meet later that night.

We met at a family bar and grill in one of the northern suburbs just off the freeway. This would save Harris nearly 20 minutes each way and was easier to park at than most of the bars near campus or downtown.

I got their early and ordered dinner and a beer and watched sports on several of the big screens. I was halfway through a mug of beer and my 12 medium-hot buffalo wings when Harris walked in. If this was a Saturday afternoon he would have looked very out of place with the college basketball fans, but since we were still at the fringes of the post work happy hour crowd, he blended in despite wearing a navy blue suit and a pink shirt.

He wasn't able to get a craft cocktail with an oversized ice cube but seemed impressed with their whiskey selection and ordered a glass of something I had never heard of that he assured me was a really good local craft whiskey.

He did not wait for his drink to begin.

"He's back," he said grimly. "He began texting the Senator this morning."

So much for the $10,000 being enough.

"He thinks he can get more money out of us," Harris continued. "Now we have to catch the son of a bitch."

He pulled out a sheet of paper and handed them to me. It was a print up of several text messages.

That was fun

"They started in this morning," Harris said. "It's a new number, most likely a prepaid."

Just because I have been silent, do not think I have not been around.

I have kept an eye on her, I know her every move

"They came in every 20 minutes, almost to the second," Harris added.

10K was a nice start, but I think you will pay more

Much more

I will be in touch.

"So what do we do?"

His drink arrived, causing a pause in our conversation. After the waitress walked off he took a sip and then replied.

"You need to be more vigilant than ever," he said, never setting his glass down. "Be around as much as you can. We need to really figure out who is doing this."

I filled him in on the sudden flashes of cash over the past week. I even told him about Rachel, though I probably downplayed it a bit. Much to my dismay, Harris took interest.

"That seems a bit unusual," he said. "If money has been so tight all semester, it seems weird that her dad would be so quick to fund a trip. If it was my kid, I would send them a little extra ramen money and not much else."

I was disheartened to hear he thought it could be Rachel, but oddly enough I also found myself realizing I knew very little about Harris. I had no idea if he had kids, or was married, or really anything about him.

"You think it could be her?" I asked.

"Probably not, but she has motive and proximity, so we can't rule it out," Harris replied. "She has no idea that you are working for us, right?"

"No, I haven't told anyone," I said.

We went over some strategies about keeping tabs on Caitlin, without being obvious. We also agreed on a more frequent reporting strategy. We agreed to touch base every 48 hours, and every 24 hours if there was something serious to report. He felt something was going to happen soon.

I turned the topic to spring break. The week away from school was rapidly approaching and I did not know how that would affect my keeping an eye on Caitlin.

"Little Miss Revolutionary cannot turn down a ski trip," Harris said chuckling.

He explained that she was going with her father to a ski resort and health spa in British Columbia.

"Apparently she is justifying it by saying she is going to see how Canada treats their indigenous people and maybe protest a logging company or two," Harris added. "In reality, she is going to hit the slopes and get a massage or two."

He assured me not only would Caitlin be safe, but this was likely the safest she would be until we caught the guy.

"So what are you going to do with a full week off?" Harris asked the closest he had really made to small talk.

"Not much," I answered. "My girlfriend is going to Mexico with her friends, and I have no plans. I am going to avoid going back to Phoenix, but that may not be possible if my father has his way."

"Should be an uneventful week," he said.

"Yeah, should be," I said, taking my final swallow of beer.

How foolish I was.

39. Deeper in Debt

Mid-terms were finally over for me, and I only had one day left of classes left before spring break began. I had a few Friday classes, and while I hoped they might be canceled since, as the day wore on. less and less students would be on campus, many skipping Friday classes to get a jump start on their vacations, but I knew I would not be so lucky.

I put the over/under on the number of students in my 1:00 literature class at 7.5 and wondered if Ike would take my bet. I would take the over, but it would be close.

With the tests done, no major projects due, and essentially no homework to hand in, I just had one short reading assignment for that lit class. I got the book out, popped in my earbuds, and found the motivation to read. I was several pages in when the song in my ears was replaced by ominous music indicating an incoming call.

For the most part, my phone just rings with a preset, electronic ringtone, but for a few people, I have special ringtones that act as a happy alert, as is the case for Rachel, or a warning (my father).

I let Rachel pick her own ringtone. It was some silly, terrible pop song she knew I hated, and that made it funny to her. When I first heard it I overreacted as to how much I disliked it. We were riding in my Jeep and she hijacked the stereo and began playing this awful song that featured terrible electronic beats and an over-processed voice.

"You actually like this song?" I asked, giving her a look as I would likely give someone eating insects.

She ignored me and danced in her seat, mouthing the words.

"It is literally one of the worst songs I have heard in my life," I said, "It sounds like music made by a tone-deaf android."

She gave me a half-mocking glare and continued to groove to the music.

"Well I like it," she said, sticking her tongue out at me. "I can dance to it."

I stared straight ahead and deadpanned, "I should break up with you."

Of course, she installed the song as a ringtone the minute I let my phone out of my sight. While I really did despise the song, it did make me think of her and that silly dance she did in my car and I couldn't help but laugh every time I heard it.

It made me think of her and how bad music will be after the imminent robot apocalypse.

For my father's frequent phone calls, the "Imperial Death March" from the Star Wars movies emanates from my phone. While my father is no Darth Vader, he is the type of man who can appreciate the stark, authoritarian aesthetic of the Galactic Empire from the science fiction franchise and the ominous tones of the John Williams score were a nice warning for me that my father was trying to reach me and a lecture or inquisition may be on the way.

Until my phone rang I forgot that he was not the only person on my contacts list with a warning for a ringtone. Beethoven's 5th, you know Dun Dun Da Duuuuun, took my attention away from my book and it took me a moment to realize that it was not only my phone but who it was.

It was Coach Kovalev.

I had not spoken to him since he kicked me off the hockey team. Needless to say, it was a one-way conversation with a lot of yelling.

I almost didn't answer, I was not in the mood to get yelled at, but if I did not answer he would just keep calling, and eventually, I would be curious as to what he wanted. So I could get yelled at now and have my curiosity quenched, or I could not worry about the tongue lashing for a while, but also have trouble concentrating until I knew exactly why my former coach, who kicked me off the team and probably wanted me dead for mistakenly thinking I slept with his niece.

"Hey coach," I said, assuming my voice was full of trepidation.

"Slade," he said as if he was doing several other things at once. "We need to talk about a number of things, including your scholarship."

I hadn't thought about my scholarship in some time. I was on an athletic scholarship, and even after kicking me off the team I remained on scholarship for the semester, probably more to avoid bad PR than to help aid my academic pursuits.

Now it was occurring to me that my days of having my tuition paid for by the hockey team were over. It was not that my family could not afford to pay for school, but one of the few things my father liked about my athletic career was that I was able to earn a full athletic scholarship. It was something my brothers could not do with their academics or their extracurricular activities.

We made plans to meet the next day and I hung up the phone feeling quite melancholy.

The hockey team does not play in the on-campus arena. The McKale center holds over 14,000 fans but was never designed to host hockey games. While it is primarily a basketball arena, the volleyball and gymnastics teams also compete there. The hockey team competes at the Tucson Convention Center, a building that hosts everything from concerts, to car shows, to Harlem Globetrotters' yearly appearance. Although the hockey team has an office on-campus, Coach Kovalev is rarely there. He prefers to work out of a closet-esque office at the arena, which also serves as a film room, a storage space, and a taping room.

I pulled into the underground parking adjacent to the arena and walked in through a doorway big enough to drive a semi through. Three steps into the doorway and the familiar chill from the ice surface hit me. I had felt that cold air so many times in my life and for the first time in months, I missed hockey. I had been so distracted by my amateur detective work and having a girlfriend that I forgot how much I loved this game.

I could not bear to walk by the ice and instead ventured into the bowels of the arena to meet with Coach Kovalev.

Players were not here yet, but I ran into a few support staffers who shook my hand and told me how nice it was to see me. After making a few seconds of small talk I ventured into the office. I was more nervous that I thought I would be, and had to steel myself for half a second.

I gave the door a quick knock and went in. Coach was at his desk, which was little more than a fold-out table with a lamp and a laptop. Coach paused some game film on the computer when I entered. Sitting across from him was one of the assistant coaches, who was taking some notes on a clipboard. Sitting on the medical table where players get taped up was Anna, who had her legs crossed and was leaning over her cell phone, probably updating the team's, or her own, social media accounts. As I walked in, she set the phone down and leaned back, giving me a nice view.

Kovalev instructed the pair to leave the room. The assistant coach gave me a pat on the shoulder, while Anna gave me a sexy smirk as she passed.

"Sit down Eric," Kovalev instructed and I took the open chair the assistant coach had been occupying.

Coach Kovalev was an intense guy. He was not particularly tall, maybe 5-8, but was still powerfully built now that he was in his 60's. He still hit the weights and had bulging forearms and biceps that he tended to show off with his snug polo shirts.

His hair was thinning and creeping up his forehead. He kept it trimmed short and slicked back, but with it receding, plus his beak-like nose, I always felt he looked like a cross between an eagle and an arrow.

He also had the eyes of a raptor. He had small, dark eyes that always seemed to be searching and analyzing. I always had trouble looking him into the eye and always felt like he saw every flaw, every mistake to my performance in net.

"As you know we are probably not going to make nationals," Kovalev said. Although I was paying little attention to the program, I knew they were scuffling down the stretch and needed to win their conference tournament to make the postseason. "So I am already looking towards next season."

He shuffled some papers, finding what he was looking for.

"As you know Duffy is graduating, and Jamison has told me he is leaving school at the end of the semester," he informed. Duffy was the junior college goalie who took my job, while Dylan Jamison was a freshman who was well on his way to bypassing me as the backup goalie when the knee injury occurred. "Jamison leaving caught me off guard. I have a freshman we really like from Chicago coming in, but right now he is our only goalie. I have a few offers out, but even if I land one of those players, we will still have just two rookies on the roster."

This seemed to be taking a different turn than I thought.

"I want you to come back," Kovalev said. "I can't promise you'll start, in fact, my hope is this freshman is the real deal, but I need a reliable, veteran player on the roster to mentor him and possibly lead this team."

Instead of losing my scholarship, it appeared I was getting reinstated. Not only that, I had a chance to actually play again. Apparently, whatever animosity Kovalev had for me was less than his desire to win hockey games.

"That sounds great, but you were pretty pissed with me that last time we spoke," I said, apparently not knowing when to shut my mouth and accept good fortune.

He glared at me for a moment, those piercing eyes making me uncomfortable.

"I won't pretend to approve of your actions with Anna, but she assures me that nothing physical happened," Kovalev said. "It took me awhile to believe her, and I just recently learned she had been seeing someone else on the team."

I did not have the heart to tell him she was probably "seeing" several someone elses on the team.

"When Jamison said he was leaving it was actually Anna who pled your case," Kovalev added.

We worked out a few details. They had filled my roster spot with a walk-on, so I was not able to re-join the team formally until after the season, but I did not really have time to practice with the team anyways. We worked out a schedule where I could get some limited ice time, but in reality, my return would not happen until the fall.

I left the office a few minutes later and Anna was sitting there at a table, working on a laptop of her own. She looked up when I emerged.

"Congrats Eric," she said. "It will be good to have you back around."

"Thanks," I said, trying to read her. "Coach said you put in a good word for me, I really appreciate it."

She flashed me another sexy smile. She was very good at that, maybe too good.

"I guess you owe me one," she practically purred.

Little did I know I would soon owe her lot more than a favor, I would owe her my life.

40. Girl Next Door Shtick

I made two phone calls after leaving the arena. First I left a message with my father that I had some good news, then called Rachel to let her know what had transpired. She seemed a little surprised, we had not really discussed hockey and she seemed a little shocked that I was going to play again. I could tell she was worried about the time commitment I would now be facing as I resumed my playing.

She seemed less worried when I explained that I would be abandoning my volunteer work with the local Democratic Party. She did not need to know that I was most likely going to do that the minute I figured out who was threatening Caitlin.

Rachel and her friends were leaving for Mexico first thing the next morning, so we only had a few hours left before our nine days apart. The plan was to have a nice dinner before she called it an early night, but Caitlin was nowhere to be found, so we partook in a quickie before we went out.

After we were done, Rachel went to take a shower and left me alone in her room. Our timing was pretty good because less than five minutes later Caitlin came home. She barely seemed to notice me as she plopped down on her bed. She fired off a few texts before she looked my way.

"You guys are getting serious, huh?"

"Yeah, I guess so," I answered, wondering where she was going with this.

It took her a few minutes to let me know.

"She's a sweet enough girl, I guess, but I just can't figure you guys out," she finally added. "She must be freakier in bed than she seems. That girl next door shtick must be an act."

She was not wrong, but I was uncomfortable with the direction of the conversation.

"Is everything still good between you guys?" she asked, which seemed strange as she was neither a gossip hound nor one to have my best interest in mind.

"Yeah, why?" I asked.

"Well her ex Vince came around a week ago, and then I saw her talking with a different guy two days ago."

Rachel never gave me any pause about Vince and I knew she had a few study groups with people from class, I could not help but feel that pang of jealousy. I had no reason to doubt Rachel's fidelity, I did not like what Caitlin was insinuating.

"Rachel told me about Vince," I lied. "And I know there were a couple of friendly guys in one of her study groups."

I had to admit I was a bit jealous at the thought of Rachel speaking to her ex, even if she did not initiate the conversation.

Caitlin seemed content with the answer, and she stood up and headed over to her closet. She began taking clothes out and tossing them over to her bed.

"Ok, but if you do break up with her can you either do it soon or wait until after the semester? I can't handle a bunch of tears and crying close to finals."

She grabbed a plastic grocery bag and walked back over to her bed. She began stuffing clothes into the bag and I realized she was packing. The girl had a $500 suitcase sitting at the bottom of her closet and here she was stuffing clothes into the free bag she received when she bought her snacks and toiletries.

She went to go grab another bag from the front of the room when she spotted something on the floor.

"Your phone is on the floor," she said, oblivious to the fact that I was actually holding my phone.

She pointed under Rachel's bed and I assumed she had seen Rachel's phone, so I leaned over the bed to retrieve it. It was indeed a phone, but it was not Rachel's. Rachel had a brightly colored phone case with some plastic jewels affixed to it. This was a cheap, black plastic no-name phone, the kind that you get at a discount store.

I'd like to tell you the only reason I kept looking at the phone was my duty to investigating this case, to make sure no clue was left unchecked, but if I am being honest, the mention of other guys had me a little jealous. I had no reason to doubt Rachel, in fact, she had given me her cell phone passcode, but I would not need it.

I hit the "home" button and the phone came to life and I was on the home screen. There were no apps downloaded, not even an e-mail. There was simply a phone icon, a text icon, and a system icon. It was as bare-boned as it gets.

Despite myself, I clicked on the little square with a picture of a landline handset.

There was nothing there. No calls, no contacts.

I looked up from the phone to see Caitlin continue to pack, oblivious that I was snooping through this phone.

I clicked on the text icon, there were two choices. The first was a phone number with a Phoenix area code.

I debated a moment before pressing the entry.

The text at the bottom of the screen, which was the last entry, simply read:

I will be in touch.

I had to read a few more entries before my brain processed what I was reading.

Much more

10K was a nice start, but I think you will pay more

In reality, I already knew what I was reading, but I had to make sure. I scrolled up to the top and there it was.

That was fun

Any last doubt I had was erased. This was the phone that texted the Senator. I doubled checked the phone number with the number I had for Senator McCauley in my phone.

It was the same.

I also checked the times of the texts. It was the same day Harris and I met, and the texts were 20 minutes apart.

Almost to the second.

Just like the texts Harris had printed up that were sent to McCauley.

I felt an odd combination of nausea and anger. I wanted to puke, I wanted to scream.

I even wanted to cry.

I again scanned the room and Caitlin was still doing her own thing, typing away at her laptop, possibly adding songs to her phone.

My gaze moved over to the door, knowing Rachel could walk in at any time. The door did not move, and I went back to the phone.

The second entry came from a blocked number that appeared as "No Caller ID." There was just one entry. It was from a few weeks ago.

Got money. It safe. Will get you some. Don't be flashy.

I let out a loud sigh, loud enough that Caitlin flashed me an annoyed look.

I stared back down at the phone and tried to process it all. There was no doubt that whoever had this phone was involved in the threats to Caitlin. There was also no doubt that they were not working alone. If this was indeed her phone, then there was also little doubt that Rachel was involved. I tried my best to figure out another alternative, but there really wasn't an explanation that sounded plausible.

The doorknob turned, and the door began to open. Panicked, I tossed the phone back under the bed. I hoped it was far enough under to conceal it.

The door opened to reveal Tariq. For once I was actually glad to see him.

"Katya," he said, giving her a peck on the cheek before heading over to her bed.

"Slade," he added, giving me a slight head nod. I waited for a snarky remark or an insult but it did not come.

I realized the phone was not where I found it and I debated whether to fish it out, or just leave it as it was still under the bed.

Before I could make a decision Rachel entered the room, she had changed into a new outfit but still had wet hair from her shower. I knew it would be at least a few minutes before she was ready to go. I had no idea how to treat her, how to act.

I excused myself and went to the restroom. For a moment I felt I was going to puke, but after a moment of staring the porcelain goddess in the eye, the feeling subsided. I sat down on the toilet to gather my thoughts.

Assuming the phone was hers, that meant Rachel was involved and she had a partner. The question was who was it, and was she the ringleader or caught up in something serious? I tried to figure out why else would the phone be there? Could the stalker have been back in the room and lost it there? It was a possibility.

Could it be Tariq's? I hoped so, but again, why would it be under Rachel's bed? Why would he, or anyone, be so cavalier with the phone to leave it on the floor? Of course, if it was Rachel's was she careless, or did she think it was hidden under her bed?

If it was Rachel, and that was the most logical answer, then I wanted to believe that she was being manipulated, that some horrible person was forcing her to help, but I knew that was silly. Rachel was a smart girl, and if she was involved in this she knew exactly what she was doing.

I stood up, intent to walk off and never speak to her again. I was just going to leave here and cut off all contact. Not answer calls, not respond when she showed up at my dorm. Just completely disappear from her life.

I would call Harris, and tell him what I found. Even if Rachel had an accomplice, Caitlin would likely be safe. The partner would have to disappear and quit, wouldn't he?

I was going to do that, but then it occurred to me that I was close to cracking the case. As betrayed as I felt, in reality, she hadn't lied to me. She had no idea I was trying to protect Caitlin. I was not the guy who had dated her in an effort to protect her roommate, I was that weird guy who showed up for Caitlin's notes and wound up with an awkward invitation to dinner.

Assuming she was not sleeping with her accomplice, she was not betraying me, she was just a criminal.

Assuming, of course, she was involved. I wanted to find an alternate theory, but the phone and the sudden infusion of cash before spring break was damning.

With that, my hurt dissipated, at least a tiny bit. My original reason for dating her was now more true than ever. I had asked her out in an effort to keep tabs of her roommate, and now I would continue to date her in an effort to keep tabs on her roommate and keep tabs on her. I could protect Caitlin and ensnare Rachel at the same time. I wanted to be the one to catch her and her accomplice.

If she was behind this, then I wanted to catch her, not just report on her to Harris and the authorities.

I ran some water over my face, took a deep breath and headed back to their room.

I walked into the room. Rachel was standing in front of the mirror, putting the final touches on her hair and make-up. I could smell her perfume, the one that drove me crazy from day one. Tariq and Caitlin were sitting on her bed engaged in a conversation. They did not bother to look up at me.

Half the resolve I had was lost as soon as I saw her. I could pretend that my sense of duty trumped by feelings for Rachel, but that was not true. I could keep up the charade, but it would not be easy. I cared for her, that was not changing overnight, but it sure seemed as if she was involved in this.

Dinner was tense, but I mostly faked my way through it.

"You don't feel well, do you?" she asked, full of concern.

"No, I guess not," I replied, not exactly lying.

We were at a little Italian place we both like. The plan was a quick dinner before she called it an early night. She and her friends were leaving for their trip early in the morning.

"Well, that is super sweet that you are spending time with me before I leave," she said, smiling.

"Yup, that's me, super sweet," I said, trying to mock enthusiasm.

Well, that is super deceptive that you are stalking me before I leave. I thought to myself.

As dinner wore on my anger subsided a bit more. Mentally, I was trying to justify things. She hadn't actually hurt anyone…well other than helping to extort money from a United States Senator. If she was not the mastermind, I wondered if there was some way to downplay her involvement or even "flip" her into helping me.

It was probably a silly thought, she was likely going to jail and I would have a hand in it.

I barely ate, which is rare for me, and she noticed. I had ordered manicotti with an extra meatball and ate less than half my food. Normally I would have finished mine and eaten a large part of her lasagna. Instead, I had two take-home containers to pick from the next few days.

We went back to her dorm. I considered just leaving her out front, but did not want to raise suspicion. If I was to figure out who her accomplice was, I could not let on that something was wrong. I had to play this cool, and even if I decided to back off, I could not do it unexpectedly.

She had some last-second packing to do so we put on a movie and I sat on the bed and stayed fairly quiet.

"I know you are not feeling good, why don't you go?" she asked, while folding some clothes and placing them into an already full suitcase.

"No, I'm good," I said. "I'll head out in a little bit."

She turned to collect her toiletries and I looked down at my phone. I had my text messages open to Harris' number and had started and deleted about 20 messages about the phone and Rachel to him.

"I've got to go to the bathroom," Rachel said and left the room.

I took that opportunity to retrieve the phone. I wanted to take one last look at the messages, so I could accurately relay them to Harris (and convince myself I did not 'misread' them), as well as make sure I put it back where I found it.

I reached my hand under the bed where I tossed the phone, but could not reach it. I leaned over the side and looked under the bed more closely. It still was not there.

I climbed down and laid down on the floor. I stuck my head underneath and used the flashlight on my phone to get a better look. I did not have a lot of time, but Rachel had enough plastic tubs and boxes underneath the bed to limit the space a phone could sit.

Despite my up close investigation, it was clear:

The phone was gone.

41. Fan of Stiff Free Drinks

I never left town for spring break. I considered going to Phoenix for a few days to get away from these familiar surroundings, but that would take too much effort. Although all I wanted to do was sleep and drink, I made sure I did more than that. I actually left the house on a few occasions to drink.

Rachel left town early Saturday morning and shot me a text to say she and her friends were on the road. I heard the ping of the text coming in, but could not be bothered to get out of bed to look at it. A few hours later I finally emerged from my slumber. It took me another half hour to actually bother to text back.

Passive aggressive, I know.

I considered a terse, one or two work text, but realize I had to be the bigger man.

Still feel crappy, I texted.

Have fun.

Spring break was coming at a perfect time. The time away from Rachel would let me take a long look at Rachel as the lead suspect, without having her around to sway me one way or another. The distance would be helpful in sorting through fact, suspicion and emotion.

With no classes for over a week, there was plenty of free time, and there was plenty of college basketball to watch. The beginning of spring break meant the end of the regular season of college basketball and most of the conference tournaments were being played this weekend. I could basically spend about 18 hours on Saturday watching basketball and that was what I was going to do.

I ran by Ike's to make a few wagers to spice up today's viewing. Omar gave me another half hug as I walked in and after a few minutes Ike waved me over.

"I hear you are rejoining the hockey team," Ike said. Word traveled fast in his circles. "I will understand if you will have to curtail your 'investments' but I would appreciate any, shall we say, under publicized gossip, you might hear."

I assured Ike that I would keep him informed, but I seriously doubted that I would get information that he was not already privy to. As I have learned, there is little going on around the school's athletic department, or with his clients, that Ike does not know.

After making a couple of bets I did not feel great about I departed the house. Omar was out on the porch on his phone and held up a finger that indicated he wanted me to hold on a minute and not leave.

He ended the call and turned his attention to me.

"That was Jenna, she went home for spring break and has already called me three times," Omar said with a chuckle.

"So I guess no double dating this week," I shot back.

"Nah," he replied. "You here all week?"

I nodded.

"If you go out, let me know," he added. "A lot of people are making bets, but most of them are out of town so I will not be making many collections or dealing with foot traffic."

I never really considered what the busy season was for a bookmaker and his staff. I assumed summer must be a slow time when there is not much more than baseball to wager on.

I told him if I bothered to venture out I would let him know, but as of now, my plan was to just chill.

That first night that was indeed my course of action. I bought a 12-pack of beer, filled up my trash can with ice, and plopped down in front of the television. My entire plan was to dull the memories of Rachel with beer and basketball and that is exactly what I did.

Sometime during the second half of the last ACC semi-final game, the number of empties outnumbered the number of beers on ice and I fell asleep. For a few hours, I hardly gave Rachel a second thought.

I woke up on my couch the next morning. Well, to be completely accurate, most of me woke up on the couch. I was about 2/3 on the sofa. My head and arm were dangling off the front, and one leg was splayed out as well. My shirt was off, and I lost one of my socks. The sun was up, television was still on, and I had missed three calls and six text messages.

Five of the text messages and all three calls were from numbers I had not heard from in awhile…my hockey teammates. A quick glance of the messages indicated they were aware that I was back on the team.

The final message was from Rachel. It had come in a few minutes after the others and I figured she had a similar evening as I did. Well, alcohol-wise, not college basketball-wise.

Her text was short and sweet.

Miss you

I really did not feel like texting back, but I knew I had to.

Miss you too

Short but sweet. I then turned my attention to my former, and soon to be current, teammates. A cursory glance at their texts and a follow up on social media, confirmed my suspicions. The team had lost in the conference tournament and their season was over. The end of the season traditionally means one thing, booze.

I won't insult your intelligence and say that college hockey players abstain from alcohol during the season, but with most games on the weekend, it cuts into your time to hit the bars and go to parties. The ceremonial end to the season is a pub crawl followed by a huge party the next Saturday. Since the team was eliminated on a Saturday afternoon, the pub crawl would occur on Sunday and the house party would have to wait a week.

I had no intention of going out that night. I wanted to be alone and sulk, but after answering texts and returning phone calls I succumbed to peer pressure and decided to join them on their tour of Tucson's bars.

The team was three bars in, well a few stalwarts had already hit three before that when I joined them on Fourth Avenue. They were at some dive that had a wall of frozen drink machines. The bar was far longer than it was wide and the hockey team was probably exceeding the fire code by themselves. It was still early, so there were not many others out and about.

I entered the bar and the team turned and gave me a standing ovation.

"The prodigal son returns," someone shouted, and I gave them a small bow. I walked to the closest group and got a number of hard pats on the back. While I wanted a beer, someone put a frozen drink in my hand that basically tasted like Tang and not the orange juice it was supposed to be. The oversized mug also had a test tube turned upside down and jammed into the frosty beverage, indicating that someone had not only bought me a drink but paid for an extra shot to be poured in.

It may not have been what I wanted, but it was potent, and more importantly, it was free. I must confess I am a fan of stiff free drinks. Over the course of the next two bars, I made the rounds, shaking hands, getting high fives and fist bumps, and best of all, getting a few more free drinks.

I may not have been the best goalie, but I was well liked.

At our third bar, I was cornered by Andy Knick. I was already well on my way to intoxication and by the look of his eyes, Knick was already closer than I was. His eyes were glassy and his footing unsure as he walked over to me.

"Is it true you got kicked off the team for sleeping with Coach's niece?"

"Yes, but no," I answered.

If Andy was 6' 2" and not 5' 8" he would probably play in the NHL, but with his lack of height, his chances of playing in the big leagues were doubtful. He was our best offensive player, and with his skills would probably play professionally overseas when most of us would be playing in beer leagues on weekends.

I looked around, I did not want people to hear this since coach was still saying I was out with injury.

"I was kicked off the team because Coach thought I slept with Anna," I confessed. "All I did was get drunk with her, which was probably bad enough."

I could tell by his expression that Andy did not believe me.

He was a tough kid from Long Island, or "Strong Island" as he called it, though it sounded more like "Strawng Island" with his thick accent.

"You're telling me you didn't hit that?" he asked.

"Why does everyone ask me that?" I asked innocently. "After I hurt my knee she came over with some booze and we got pretty drunk. That's it."

He still eyed me with suspicion.

"But you could have," he stated, more than asked.

"I don't know, maybe, it never came up," I explained. "She always flirted with me, but she never flat out hit on me."

Whatever I said, suddenly filled him with doubt.

"Dude, she had the biggest crush on you," he said.

Anna was a flirt, but she was a flirt with everyone. The fact that he could single me out as being the object of her affections seemed dubious to me.

"She has a crush on everyone," I stated.

"She's a flirt to be sure," he retorted. "But you could tell she was actually into you, not just being flirty."

I focused on my drink a bit to try and change the conversation, but Andy was having none of it. He just stared at me.

"What?" I finally said. "I never even flirted back, much less gave her any reason to think I was interested."

"I think that is exactly what she liked about you," he explained. "But I still think you slept with her."

I glared at him.

"Okay, okay," he said, putting his arms in the air like I had a gun on him. "but she totally had a crush on you."

I shook my head and focused my attention to a television. Again, Andy was not dropping it.

He shouted for Ricky Wayne, a defenseman from Chicago to join us. Wayne was a tall, skinny kid with a mop of wavy hair that fell into his eyes. He had a sparse, wispy goatee and wore his Chicago Blackhawks jersey over khaki cargo shorts.

Like Andy and I, Ricky was well on his way to complete drunkenness. He ambled over, working hard to focus on the two of us.

"Why did Grady break up with Anna?" Andy asked, jabbing his brown beer bottle at the much taller player's chest.

"Because she had a crush on the goalie," Ricky said, apparently not realizing who I was. "He was totally into her, and he felt like she could never quite commit like she always had one foot on the door."

"Out the door?" I asked.

"Yeah, one hand out the door," Ricky said, drunkenly botching his figure of speech for the second time.

Ricky seemed confused if he should stay or go, so he stayed. Andy turned to me.

"See? I told you," he said triumphantly.

He then leaned in and asked, "So why didn't you hit that?"

Before I could answer, he scurried off. Had I been soberer I would have let it go, but I was drunk enough not to have a filter.

"She's 17," I yelled across the bar, drawing looks from half the patrons.

42. Neon Green Monstrosity

Twenty-four hours later I was drunk again. Needless to say, I was not taking Rachel's involvement in the Caitlin fiasco very well. If the night before was a testosterone-fueled Neanderthal bro-down, this was a high brow excuse to drink. I was back at a local Democratic Party think-tank session, and once again their poor excuse for a bar was causing me to get creative. There were seven good bottles of wine, but like the meeting I attended when they were recruiting me, I was having to experiment with the limited resources I had.

We were at Volpe's house, which was within walking distance of the university. Well, it was walking distance for those who really like to spend 45 minutes walking to work. His house was an all brick shoebox that used to be a duplex. At some point a wall was knocked out, a kitchen was converted into a dining room and two tiny houses were made into one moderately sized house.

I was still in the kitchen drinking a neon green monstrosity that had vodka, mountain dew, and Gatorade. I won't lie to you, it was a sugary mess, but it went down smooth and was a good way to achieve intoxication in a hurry.

My father would have a coronary if he saw me drinking this crap, and in a few minutes, a potential state senator would as well.

Jessie Griffin entered the kitchen with a mostly empty glass of wine. She grabbed one of the bottles and re-filled her glass. She took a hearty swig, then replaced the amount of she drank in her glass before re-installing the cork into the bottle.

Tonight she had her curly hair tied into a ponytail, but a number of tendrils spilled forward into her face. She replaced the oddly attractive, unflattering red glasses from our last meeting with subtler square black frames, but still had big, dangly earrings. She wore a denim jacket with intricate southwestern beadwork over a light sweater and a long denim skirt.

The state senator eyed my drink and wrinkled her nose in displeasure.

"That looks awful," she said, subtly shaking her head.

"It's an Ovechkin," I said proudly holding up my glass, realizing I probably looked like a little kid who proudly showed off his "artwork" that was drawn in crayon on the family room wall.

And yes, if my first drink was named after hockey great Wayne Gretzky, this one was named after Russian hockey great Alex Ovechkin.

She grabbed a small glass and plopped a few ice cubes in there. She then took the bottle of tequila, added about three fingers worth to the glass. She then added a healthy dose of lime juice and then after fishing a bottle out of the cabinet behind us, put just a tiny bit of agave syrup into the mix and stirred it up.

"Here," she said handing me the glass. She took the bright green cocktail out of my hands and poured it in the sink. "It looks better and I will respect you more."

I took a sip and nodded my approval. The tequila was too overpowering for my liking, but I could make it work in an effort to impress the "grown-ups" at the meeting.

"You are saying my Ovechkin won't convince people of my maturity?"

She chuckled. I'd like to think I was winning her over with my roguish charm but knew she was probably laughing at my overall lack of sophistication.

"That shade of green is not found in nature," she said laughing.

I realized in our first meeting I had not seen her smile. It suited her, she had a really nice smile.

We shared an oddly comfortable silence as she looked out at the gathering, silently sipping her wine. I got the feeling she was just trying to soak up some slice before having to go be "on" in front of everyone.

"I can leave," I said, nearly falling as I started to turn. She reached out and steadied me.

"You are very drunk, maybe you should stay here with me for a minute," she said, with some pity in her voice.

"Girl problems," I said, vaguely speaking the truth.

We drank in silence for a few more moments. I tried not to wince when I took a sip. The silence did not seem to bother her, but it did me. I did not know where to look. If I looked at her I would seem creepy, but I did not want to bury myself in my phone because that would seem rude (and a tad childish).

I did steal some glances. She was pretty, in that 'I am a really smart woman who takes good care of herself' kind of way. She was embracing her age, not fighting it, but I suppose it is easier to embrace your age when it does not bring an extra 25 pounds and saggy skin. She didn't have those poofy, fake lips, and did not hide behind too much make-up or clothes that were designed for a 25-year old. She looked and dressed like a woman in her mid-40's, but a very good version of a woman her age.

"Are you really going to run?" I blurted out when the silence got too uncomfortable.

The way she looked at me I realized I said it a little bit too loud, and maybe with a tad too much enthusiasm.

"I can't win," she finally replied, a tone of resignation in her voice. "The only reason to run is to get my name out there. I would be better off running for the House, that race is wide open, but they don't want to hear that. They think I am their great hope, but the fact is McCauley is far too popular to unseat."

She took another sip.

"Unless there is a scandal, we'll probably have to wait until he retires to even have a chance to win the seat," she continued.

"Well I'd vote for you," I blurted out, a little too loud once again.

"That's nice of you to say, but you have to say that," she said, again giving me that look that was slightly condescending, yet concerned. "You would probably vote for any Democrat."

The booze was making my me talk more than I should. I knew I should shut up, but I wasn't going to.

"I'm not a Democrat," I said. "Well not totally. Technically I am an independent, but I generally prefer the democratic platform. I know you and I know McCauley, and I can say that I would definitely vote for you."

"Why?" she asked. "What would make you cast your vote for me and not your family friend?"

I took another small sip, caught myself wincing, and then answered her.

"You seem genuine like you really want to help people," I said. "McCauley is a nice guy on the surface but does not have a genuine bone in his body."

"You're smart, capable, engaging, sexy..."

The words were out of my mouth before I realized what I was saying. She gave me a look that was one-part surprise, one-part intrigue, and about five parts amusement. I assumed she regarded me as a drunken simpleton.

She sipped her wine and gave me an embarrassed smile. Whether I had embarrassed her, or she was embarrassed for me I could not tell.

"When my husband finally leaves me for a younger woman I will come and look you up."

No sooner than the words came out of her mouth, she was gone. If I had been more sober I would have been mortified, but as drunk as I was, I was only mildly embarrassed and within moments I was over it.

I knew I was too drunk to interact with most of these people, I was about half a drink from total buffoonery, so I decided to search for Volpe and Landon, who were not in the main part of the house with the rest of the party bigwigs.

The house was not so big that it took me very long to find them. They were in Volpe's makeshift study. I started to say something but could see they were in an intense conversation.

"That's the best part," Volpe was saying as I picked up the conversation mid-sentence. "McCauley will actually help fund the campaign without ever knowing it."

Landon saw me and his eyes widened a bit. Volpe picked up on it and looked my way, a startled look on his face.

"Eric," he said with a little bit too much enthusiasm, stressing the "I" in my name. "We were just talking a little shop."

I fully entered the room.

"Anything interesting?" I asked.

Volpe looked over at Landon and then back to me.

"Not really, just some fundraising ideas," he said. "There are some creative ideas on how to fund Jessie's primary run."

I knew I shouldn't say anything, but I was trying to glean more from their conversation...plus I was drunk and not editing myself very well.

"She doesn't think she can beat him," I said

"It will be tough," Volpe conceded. "But I think he is ripe for the picking. I think there are skeletons in his closet, and you never know what could distract him."

Knowing what I knew about Caitlin and the Senator, that sounded a bit ominous. The question was whether I was picking up on something or if my three-day booze binge was impacting my cognitive ability?

It wouldn't take too long for me to find out.

43. Booze and Self-Pity

After three days of booze and self-pity, it was time to get to work. Rachel was involved but I had to figure out who her accomplice was. My hope was she was more of a victim in this than a mastermind, but I realized the chances of that were slim.

I did not want her to be guilty, but it did not look good. I kept going over everything in my mind. I had no proof that the phone was hers but who else could it belong to? Add the suspicious money to go on the spring break trip, and I was not coming up with any conclusions.

At the very least I could not trust her.

My first goal was to see if she could be working with any of my other suspects.

There did not seem to be any connection between her and most of those that I identified. There was nothing to indicate that she knew Murph. Unless he was the stalker, there was no evidence that he had even spoken to Caitlin, much less her roommate.

I also could not think of a connection between Rachel and Volpe or Karen. As a freshman she would not have had a class with Volpe and other than the make-over for Landon, she had no ties to Karen. Although we discussed double dating at some point, it hadn't happened.

That left two. She had met Landon, but they met well after the stalker made contact. I guess they could have been working together before I came on the scene, but wouldn't they have been tipped off in my involvement when I "coincidentally" met both of them? It seemed implausible that I could have accidentally sniffed out both of them, and then brought them together. Even if I had, wouldn't they become suspicious? Even if they kept me around to keep tabs on me (like I was going to do to Rachel) would they really think I was investigating Caitlin's situation?

That left Tariq.

The thought of Rachel being friends with Tariq was enough to make me livid, but what if there was more? What if they were in this together? What if they were more than just co-conspirators?

The thought of Rachel and Tariq being romantically involved was more than I could stand. I am not normally a jealous person, but I literally wanted to punch something and eventually hit the wall harder than I should have.

I needed to clear my head, so I cracked open a beer and drank half with one sip. I finished the beer while pacing the room and shaking my now sore hand out. I finally settled down a bit. I opened a second beer and sat back down.

Tariq might be my best hope of clearing Rachel. I realized my own bias against the guy was coming to play, but Tariq seemed just as likely to blackmail her into helping him as he did talking her into it.

Of course, that was assuming she was not the mastermind.

I also had to realize that there was a greater possibility that I had not suspected her accomplice. The problem is I really did not know much about her. I knew her dorm friends, but could one of them be helping her? I suppose it was possible, but it seemed unlikely. Tracey was always with Chuck, but maybe that was her cover. The others did not strike me as criminal masterminds, but maybe that was the point.

Then there was Vince? Could the breakup be the cover? Could she be working with her ex-boyfriend? Much like Tariq, I did not want to consider that she could be involved with someone else.

Of course, it could be someone I did not consider and did not know about. Maybe one of these "mystery guys" Caitlin was referring to.

It was clear, I might be mad at her, I might eventually be responsible for her going to jail, but I still cared for her.

A lot.

My jealousy subsided enough for me to get to work. While we followed each other on social media, I had never taken a deep dive into her life.

First I did a Google search. Not much came up, and certainly nothing incriminating. Her Little League Softball team won a county title when she was in seventh grade. Her local hometown newspaper mentioned her a few times. The first was her involvement in a science fair, the second was when she and her family helped raise money for a family who had their food truck destroyed in a fire.

That was it.

I turned to social media, and that is where things got interesting. I knew about her family. Her mother and father were still married and she had a sister who was a senior at Rutgers and a younger brother who was still in high school.

I figured the younger brother would be the quickest to investigate, and I was right. Robbie was not exactly full of depth, but how many of us were at 15? He runs cross country and loves to skateboard. He posted a lot of videos of he and his friends performing tricks and also liked to post skating blooper videos. He must have posted 75 videos of people falling on their faces, skidding across the asphalt, and plenty of videos of guys hitting their crotches on railings, trees, and other objects.

He liked hip hop, anime and gross-out comedies and not much else.

Her sister Rebecca was far more well-rounded. She was studying to be a teacher and had decent taste in music and movies. She posted a lot of articles on educational funding and seemed to really disagree with a lot of New Jersey politicians who supported charter schools.

There were plenty of pictures of her at school, she went to a lot of parties and sporting events, and she took a lot of selfies. She also had several pictures with her family, and there was the one that made me take notice. It was a picture of a much younger Rachel and her siblings. It was from Christmas from three years ago. The three siblings were in front of the tree. Rachel had a Santa hat on, her brother had his flat-brimmed baseball cap on at an odd angle, and Rebecca was there with a gray sweatshirt that said "Wahoos."

Wahoos is the unofficial nickname for sports teams of the University of Virginia. They are officially referred to as the Cavalier, but the fans have embraced the term "Wahoos" and even have a school yell of "wa hoo wa."

It turns out Rebecca attended Virginia before transferring closer to home to Rutgers. Virginia is also the school where Karen did her undergrad. Suddenly I had a connection, no matter how tenuous.

I then spent the next hour looking for a concrete connection between Karen and Rebecca. I had one window open on Rebecca's profile and another on Karen's.

Rebecca and Rachel actually looked a lot alike. Rebecca was a little curvier, and had lighter hair, though I assumed she dyed it. So for the next hour, I felt a little like a stalker, checking out the profiles of two very pretty girls.

In the end, it was for naught. I found one party that they were both at, but from the looks of the pictures so were 1,000 other people.

Eventually, I gave up trying to find any further connections between Rebecca and Karen, and in turn Rachel and Karen. I next turned my attention to her father and that is where things got even more interesting.

It did not take long to realize that her father was very involved with the Plumbers and Pipefitters Union. He did not post often but was tagged by a lot of his fellow union members. There were a lot of pro-union articles and memes, as well as pictures of him and his guys at various union events.

It was one of these events that I was drawn to. When Wisconsin was trying to pass anti-organized labor legislation, Rachel's father and a number of the local unions made the trip to Madison to share their support. Unions from all over the nation made the pilgrimage to Wisconsin to protest the legislation. Joining them were politicians and other pro-union supporters. And there it was, on the cover of the Wisconsin State Journal, a picture of pro-union protesters. Although they are on opposite sides of the photo, it was undeniable. In the back, arms crossed and glaring was Rachel's father, and up front smiling for the camera, was Volpe.

44. Poultry Excursion

I had no evidence that Volpe and Rachel's father ever spoke, much less form a friendship that could lead to becoming co-conspirators, but they did share a cause. In fact, not one, but two of Rachel's family members had ties to Volpe and Karen, and suddenly there was a real chance that three people, and maybe four if Landon was also involved, that I genuinely liked could all be behind the threats to Caitlin.

All I had right now were some coincidences, but they seemed like pretty major coincidences and it had me concerned.

It took me some time, but I finally got the courage to call Harris. I did not want to call him and let him know what I learned. The minute I said it out loud, it became real, but it was my duty to keep Caitlin safe.

Harris answered. He decided we did not need to meet, and I filled him in on what I had found. I did downplay things a bit, hoping he'd somehow come to the conclusion that Rachel was a bit player or a pawn in someone else's game.

He didn't.

"That's pretty damning," he said. "Too bad you could not have taken the phone so we could learn more, but you did the right thing. We do not want to tip her off."

The more he seemed to think she was involved, the more I wanted her to be innocent. I wanted him to be wrong. I wanted to be wrong.

"You never told her your role?" he asked. "She does not know about you? About your role in this?"

"No, I didn't tell her anything," I said, a defensive tone to my voice. "I don't think I have tipped my hand at all."

"I am sure you didn't," he said. "Just making sure. If she is our girl, then keeping you close is the best thing for us."

We talked a little bit more about how she fit into all of this. He could see my skepticism.

"You are going to have to face the facts that she is probably involved," he scolded. "Put the emotions aside and look at the evidence."

"Look, she has motive, the need for money," he said, pointing to an extended finger. He then extended a second finger and pointed at that one. "Opportunity, and there is some evidence, some damning evidence if the phone really said what you said it did."

He held the three fingers up for a moment, before returning to his drink.

"If you think about it, I am sure you'll find more suspicious actions or events," he added.

I racked my brain for a moment and recalled the "borrowed" cell phone with the blocked number and even the jokes about Caitlin having a stalker. By themselves, it was not overwhelming evidence, but when added to the text messages and money, it painted a damning picture.

"If we are going to be successful and protect Caitlin, I am going to need you focused," he said. "I need you to get your emotions in check and do your job."

That was the kick in the ass I needed. I wanted to do a good job. I had something to prove to Harris, and the senator, and my father.

And myself.

"I'll get someone to delve deeper into her family's background," Harris said. "See if there is a legit connection between her father and Volpe or the sister and Karen."

Not only was he thinking my girlfriend was guilty, but possibly other people I considered friends. While I thought Volpe was a blowhard and someone desperately trying to remain in the spotlight, I think he actually wanted to do good. Karen was also an idealist. An incredibly attractive idealist, which I admit was possibly clouding my judgment.

He said he could probably get in contact with some people in New Jersey and Virginia who could do the digging thoroughly, yet discretely and we might know something in a few days.

He let me know that Caitlin and her father were having a good vacation, but that when she got back it was imperative I keep close tabs, especially if "The Roommate" was involved.

Harris made a little small talk, inquiring about my spring break. I told him I went out a few times early in the week, but my plan for the next few days was to stay home and watch college basketball.

I thought about what I knew and what Harris had said and decided I had to proceed as if Rachel was guilty. I realized there was no playing both sides. By not letting sympathy or emotions get in the way, there would be no surprises. I could not let my guard down, I could not let my feelings lead me astray, even if I wanted her to be not guilty. I could still consider other possibilities and keep my eyes open. Keeping Caitlin safe was the most important thing, and that could best be accomplished by staying close to Rachel. She did not know my real role in all of this, but I knew hers, and that gave me an edge.

The first weekend of the NCAA Tournament is my favorite sporting event, and truth be told my favorite event period. As much as I loved Christmas as a kid, as an adult, I love the NCAA Basketball Tournament more. I love watching basketball all day, filling out brackets, and betting on a game or 30.

After talking to Harris I did more research on the teams in the NCAA Tournament than I did my last term paper. If I studied as much for midterms as I did the Syracuse/Dayton match-up I might have a 4.0. I placed my bets, filled out several brackets, then went to stock up on beer and snacks. If I had my way the next 48 hours would be filled with basketball, beer, and bad food.

I also checked in on Rachel. We had exchanged a few text messages, but fortunately, she was too busy having fun in Mexico to know that I had no interest in chatting. Because I was now a suspicious son of a bitch, I scanned her social media to confirm she was still indeed in Mexico.

During my investigation into her family I saw tons of pictures of her on the beach and in cantinas South of the Border. Now I not only checked her various social media accounts but those of her friends. Unless they were masters of photo manipulation and could manipulate where the images were being uploaded from, then Rachel and her friends were indeed partying in Mexico.

After two days of clarity, it was time to drink again. After delving into Rachel's family I needed to numb the pain. I cracked open a beer, cracked open a book and read until I fell asleep.

With only a trace amount of a hangover, I woke up in time to start watching the early basketball games. By noon my bracket was already looking wrecked, but I was up $50.

By midafternoon there was a break in the games. I finally left the house to go get some wings. I had already downed a breakfast burrito, frozen pizza and a bag of pretzels, but some hot wings sounded like a perfect addition to the menu.

While on my poultry excursion I got a couple texts from some guys on the team. They invited me out to watch games and grab drinks, not in that order, but I wanted to continue my one-man pity party.

Around 6:00 I was watching Michigan State pulling away from a small southern school when the phone rang. It was Harris.

"Where are you?" he said frantically.

I let him know I was home, at my dorm.

"We just got a call, it came from the call box at Caitlin's dorm," Harris said.

Every dorm has a metal call box with a speakerphone that allows someone to call up to a room, thus avoiding the front desk. What many do not know is that it is a real phone that can make local calls, regardless of whether it is an on-campus number or not.

I sprinted out the door and raced to Caitlin's dorm. It is less than a five-minute walk from my dorm, and you can see the front of the dorm from the street that runs in front of my dorm. It took me less than two minutes to reach the call box.

There was no one there. I did not pass anybody and there was no one on the street. I called Harris back and let him know what I saw, or specifically, what I did not see. He filled me in and let me know that they got a call on the McCauley house phone that Harris had forwarded to his.

"All they said was 'how is the ski trip?'" Harris said. "They know where she is."

Harris explained that the call came a few minutes before he called me and he had to look up the number. He asked me to keep an eye out and I roamed around the front and side of the dorm for a few minutes. I assumed since I did not pass anybody on the way over, that the caller probably hid in the parking garage 100-feet away from the front of the dorm.

I was about to call it quits when Harris called again.

"Another call, this time from your dorm," he said breathlessly.

I raced back over to my dorm. Again there was no one there, but the call box was open and I could hear a voice yelling, it sounded like Harris.

"Reveal yourself," Harris said.

I spoke into the metal speaker.

"It's me, Eric," I said, trying to catch my breath. "There's no one here."

Again I agreed to look out, but was not optimistic,

Fifteen minutes later I returned to my room and Harris called me back 20 minutes after that.

"He called from three more dorms," Harris said. "Each time he said something specific about Caitlin's spring break trip."

"You sure it was a guy?" I asked.

"If it wasn't, then it is a woman who does a hell of an impersonation," Harris said. "It did sound like he was disguising his voice."

I took some solace that it probably wasn't Karen but then realized Rachel's partner was a guy and the pangs of jealousy returned.

"Are you going to be around tonight?" Harris asked. "If so, keep an eye out."

"I'm not going anywhere," I answered. "I'll be here alone all night."

I told him that I would keep an eye out for anything fishy, that I had no plans. And I didn't. What I didn't realize is by night's end I would not be alone anymore.

45. Acceptance of My Slovenly Ways

What happened next I am not proud of, but my mistakes proved to be lifesaving.

I try to be a good guy and genuinely do the right thing, but in the course of my investigation, I had become a good liar and manipulator. The majority of my interactions, including my relationship, were at the core dishonest, even if my intentions were good.

What I was learning was that each successive lie got easier, and it each misdeed weighed less on my conscious.

I had crossed lines and was about to cross more.

The basketball games ended around 10:30. I had plowed through 24 hot wings, a few more beers, and plenty of salty snacks. Despite my best attempts at being careful, I was still getting peanut and sunflower seed shells on the floor and the old steamer trunk that served as our coffee table. Between the shells, the beer bottles, and empty chip bags, I was going to have to clean up this area or invoke the wrath of Chuck.

His acceptance of my slovenly ways only went so far.

I made a weak attempt at cleaning up, but after filling up a small wastebasket my motivation was gone and I turned my attention to video games. For the next hour and a half, I nursed a beer and played games, spending most of my time playing first-person shooters against online foes around the world. Video games: bringing dudes together across the globe.

A knock at my door startled me out of my pixelated meditation. There were maybe 20 people in the dorm during spring break, so the knocking startled me enough to allow a sniper to get in a clean head shot, killing my digital warrior. Somewhere an anonymous 10-year old had bragging rights over me.

I staggered over to the door and threw it open. I had assumed it was the RA or one of the other hapless dorm denizens looking to borrow a beer, or just bored enough to search out human contact.

I expected to see a fellow disheveled dude, but instead, I saw a five-foot-two bombshell.

It was Anna Kovalev.

I was having flashbacks to that fateful night when she showed up with the two six packs that led to my demise as a hockey player.

"I hear you are having girl trouble," she said, as she brushed past me and entered the room. She carried a small Arizona Hockey duffle bag.

I stood there stunned. So many questions ran through my slightly inebriated brain. She made herself at home, plopping down on my sofa and clearing a spot on my makeshift coffee table.

I began to walk over and caught a glimpse of myself in the mirror. I wore baggy basketball shorts and a gray t-shirt with more than a few wing sauce stains. My hair was a mess and I had about four-days growth on my face, which was about two day's worth for most men.

While I was underdressed for a soup kitchen, she looked great. She wore leggings that showed off her legs, and an oversized turtleneck sweater that went past her hips and with the belt she had on, it acted as a default dress. As usual, the sweater was tight in all the right places, gripping her hips just right, and accenting her chest.

I am pretty sure I stared a little too long, and I am pretty sure she did not care. She had pulled a bottle of tequila out of the bag, as well as a couple of limes and a knife.

"What are you doing here?" I asked.

"Today is my birthday, and you are going to drink with me," she said as she began slicing the limes into quarters.

"We both know what happened last time I drank with you," I said referring to the incident that got me kicked off the hockey team.

She looked up at me and smiled.

"Yes, but I got you reinstated and I said you owed me one," she said. "So what I want is to celebrate my 18th birthday by having some drinks with you."

She pulled out more items from the bag, including a couple of shot glasses and a salt shaker.

I didn't have the strength or willpower to debate her. I was already pretty tipsy and just too depressed about Rachel to do anything about getting Anna to leave. Plus, she looked great…and had booze.

If Rachel was the hot girl next door, and Karen the stunning nature girl, then Anna was the sexbomb athlete. She was not tall and had a lot of feminine curves, but she was also powerfully built. Having spent her entire life on ice skates she had powerful legs, that were still shapely as hell. Her arms had just enough muscle to show off the effort she put in the gym, but they remained perfectly feminine.

I pulled up a chair near the steamer trunk/coffee table, refusing to sit next to her on the sofa. I felt it best to keep my distance.

She poured two shots of tequila, handed me one and then gave me a lime. She licked the back of her hand, dumped some salt on the wet spot. Then she licked the salt, slammed the drink and plopped the lime into her mouth, sucking the juice out.

I wish I could tell you that she looked ridiculous doing the shot, but she looked hot as hell. She held out her salty hand to me, in effect offer me a lick. I passed on her offer and slammed down the liquor, minus the salt or the citrus. Despite her providing a high-quality tequila, I was not prepared for the straight booze and made a face as the burning liquid slid down my throat.

"Lightweight," she said with a giggle, as she refilled both shot glasses.

I wanted to defend my drunken honor but asked a question instead.

"How did you know I had girl trouble?"

She did another three-step shot, slamming the little shot glass down as she finished and gave off a little "whooo" sound.

"Because you don't shut up when you drink," she said. "The other night you told half the team your girlfriend betrayed you and it was probably over."

I barely remembered any conversation as that night wore on, but knowing how upset I was that night, it would not surprise me if a few drinks, or 20, would cause me to air my dirty laundry to the world.

I followed suit with a shot of my own, this time I partook of the salt and lime, but still winced a bit. My hard liquor credibility was shot.

I told myself that the next shot would be my last, then told myself that a few more times. The last one was my fifth of the night and that spelled the end of the bottle. I slumped in my seat and assumed that was the end of the evening. I was going to ask her if I could call her a ride but never got the chance.

She got up and headed to the mini-fridge. She pulled out a pair of beers and used the bottle opener to remove the bottle caps. She strolled over to where I was sitting and looked down at me. I realized halfway through that I slowly looked her up and down. She handed me one of the beers and I accepted it. I brought the bottle to my lips and almost choked on its content. After handing off the beverage she plopped down on top of me, straddling me as I sat in the chair.

I did not know what to do but tried to play it cool. I took a second sip of my beer and she mirrored my moves, while never taking her eyes off me. She stared at me and it made me a little uncomfortable.

I tried to think of something clever to say but failed.

She took the beer from my hand, then set hers and mine down on the floor. Still straddling me she put both hands on my face and stared for just a second. Just when I thought that was the extent of things, she pulled in and gave me a firm, passionate kiss. It was sexy, but tender at the same time. I did not want to halt it, but I did. I grabbed both of her wrists gently and pulled her away.

"Stop," I said.

"Why?" she asked.

I pulled her off of me and stood her up. I guided her to the couch and sat her down, then joined her.

"We can't," I said.

"Why?" she repeated, smiling, but with a deadly seriousness to her eyes.

"I have a girlfriend…"

"Who you claim you are breaking up with," she interrupted.

"But I haven't," I shot back.

"It's just semantics at this point," she retorted.

She leaned in again, and this time I was prepared and avoided her kiss.

"Look, I'm not going to sleep with a high school girl," I spat.

I expected her to be hurt, but instead, she laughed hysterically. Not just a chuckle or giggle, but full-on laughter. I have to admit, I did not get it.

"High school?" she said between guffaws. "I am a freshman…in college."

I was confused and I am sure my face did nothing to hide it. I wanted to say something but was speechless. I am 64.7% sure it was the alcohol, but maybe I am just dense.

"But you just turned 18?"

"Yes, I graduated at 17," she said, slowly as if I was a small child. "I started school early. I am the exact same age as the girl you are dating."

"My girlfriend," I corrected.

"The girl you are dating and about to break up with," she said dismissively.

She leaned over me to grab the beers, making sure she rubbed up against me. She smirked as she handed me the beer.

We drank in silence for a few seconds.

"So why me?" I asked. "Of all the guys on the team, why are you here, tonight?"

"Because off and on over the past three years I have had a massive crush on you," she said.

"So why me?" I asked again. "Of all the guys on the team I am not the best looking, not the best player, and certainly not the most fun."

"But you were the nicest," she said. "Guys on the team have either been hitting on me since I was 13 or treating me like a child. Not you. From the time I met you three years ago, you treated me as an equal. Sure you flirted, but it was innocent. You could have crossed the line, but never did."

"But other guys did," I half asked and half exclaimed.

"I have been getting hit on by hockey players since I was 13," she said. "But, despite my flirting, you never put the moves on. You talked about movies and music, and hockey. Too much hockey, but you talked to me. At first I thought you could not take a hint, or thought I was ugly, but eventually, I realized you were a good guy."

"I am not a good guy," I shot back.

We drank in silence a few more minutes.

"So if you had this crush on me why did you date all those players?"

She started laughing again.

"All those players?" she spit out. "I am no angel, but I am not the devil either. I have dated two players. You can't believe everything you hear. You should know not to believe locker room talk."

I wish I could tell you I did the right thing. I wish I was as good a guy as Anna believed, but I am not. I had every intention of escorting her to the door and wishing her a good night. I took her to the bedroom instead.

46. Lies and Half-Truths

I t was hard to get up the next morning, for a number of reasons. First, I was feeling the effects of all the booze. I had managed a bottle of water before falling asleep, but it was clearly not enough. It would not be a bad hangover, but I was feeling all of the beer and tequila.

Secondly, Anna was draped all over me. After our evening's activities, she donned one of my t-shirts and fell asleep in my arms. Now, several hours later she was still there, having hardly moved over the course of the night.

My phone rang several times before I was able to untangle myself. I was able to locate my phone in the other room before the call ended. It was Harris.

"Our guy made calls from four more dorm call boxes last night," said Harris. "He also sent a couple e-mails, all from different accounts, and sent a text from a new number."

"What did he want?" I managed to ask, my mouth quite dry and my balance unsteady.

"He didn't say anything on the calls," Harris said. "The texts and e-mails all said the same thing 'be ready.'"

"What does that mean?" I asked, fishing a bottle of water out of the mini-fridge.

"I don't know, but my guess is they are about to act," Harris replied. "Were you in all night? Did you see anything out of the ordinary?"

"No," other than the beautiful girl, who is not my girlfriend, sleeping in my bed. "It was pretty quiet."

He told me he would keep me up to date if there was anything else to report. As the call concluded Anna emerged sleepily from the bedroom, clad only in my t-shirt.

"Who was that?" she asked, taking my water bottle and helping herself to a swig.

"A friend of my dad's" I half lied. "I did some work for him over the break and he was just updating me on the project."

I was getting too good at lies and half-truths.

Anna slid up to me and gave me my water back. I took the bottle with one hand and drew her near with the other. We kissed again, which led to us "breaking in" another room.

The rest of the day was mostly uneventful, but also a lot of fun. We watched basketball and drank beer the rest of the day. The day was not much different from how I would have spent my day alone, save for having sex during a 20-minute break between games.

Being around hockey her whole life Anna was a sports fan. Although she did not look or dress like it, she was a bit of a tomboy and was perfectly fine indulging me in my basketball obsessions. She was also more than willing to indulge me in another, more carnal obsession.

I was feeling bad, after all, I was still with Rachel, but she had not so much as texted me in two days…and was extorting the McCauley's. Despite that, I felt like I owed her something and did not feel right going out in public with Anna, though admittedly, what we were doing staying in was a lot worse.

We had just ordered a pizza when Harris called back. He asked me what I was doing and I replied truthfully.

"Waiting for a pizza to be delivered," I said.

As I slipped out into the hall to avoid prying ears, I explained that I was having a lazy day to myself before Rachel and the rest of the suspects returned.

"So no plans?" he asked.

"No why?" I replied.

"Our guy has been e-mailing and calling all day," Harris said. "If he slips up I just want to make sure you'll be available to go on a moment's notice."

He explained that he did not want me to confront the culprit, but if I could identify them, or better yet, photograph them, it would go a long way to proving our case and ending this fiasco for good.

Harris let me know that they had gotten five more e-mails, a few more texts, but no more phone calls. He assumed our guy was not going to get caught making too many cell phone calls, in case we were actually tracing calls. E-mails were much harder to track.

"I have a guy who thinks he may be able to figure out where the e-mails are coming from" he revealed. "He usually works with apprehending scammers, but things he might be able to help us figure out where some of these computers he is using are."

I assured him I would be around and could drop everything if need be.

Then I turned my attention back to Anna. We had one last night before things got even more complicated. In 24 hours Rachel would return.

47. Duke of Duplicity

I had begun to master my life of duplicity, and now I was making it even more complex. It began as I pretended to be severely injured so I could cover for the fact that I was instead a disgraced hockey player who had been dismissed from the team. That enhanced injury led to my role keeping an eye on Caitlin, and in turn, dating Rachel and befriending my suspects.

At times even I forgot what was real and what was fake. Of course, there was a natural blur. I started dating Rachel to keep better tabs on Caitlin but soon found myself falling for Rachel for real. Now that I knew she was behind this, I had to again put on my façade and stay involved long enough to ensure Caitlin was safe.

If all of that was not tough enough, now I had to factor Anna into the equation. I did not know how I felt about Anna. I mean, there was a lot to like, she was smart, funny, hot, liked sports, liked me, and was hot, but I did not know how I felt. I could fall for her, I knew that, but I had to be honest, my actions were far more motivated by lust than anything else at this point. She made no secret that she had feelings for me, but also knew that I was not just the type of guy to jump girl to girl, leaving a wake of broken hearts in my dust.

I still cared for Rachel but felt betrayed, even if her actions had nothing to do with me. Plus, this thing with Anna, whatever it was, was new and exciting. I had only been with Rachel a few months, but we had already settled into a routine. It was a good routine, but one that was starting to veer off in an uncharted direction with my latest discovery.

While Rachel was great, it did not begin organically. I did not ask her out because of attraction or chemistry, but because of proximity. It was not hard to become attracted, because she was indeed pretty and we had things in common, but I had no choice but to make it work. It was manufactured chemistry, I took a few small things I liked, even loved about her and latched onto them. Some might say this is how most relationships work, but in this case, I actively worked to make sure the relationship lasted to suit the needs of the case.

I often wondered if Rachel and I would work out if we had met, and dated in different circumstances.

It was hard to say what was going on with Anna and me. While she had previously felt obvious chemistry, I had not, but was that because I would not allow myself? There was no doubt now that there was great chemistry between us, but was there a foundation between us or would we burn up upon re-entry?

I was semi-honest and told her that I had to sort through my feelings and do the right thing by her and Rachel. While not entirely happy with it, she accepted this decision. We texted frequently over the next few days and spoke at least once a day. In an odd way, it felt like high school.

I also made the decision to keep my transgression with Anna a secret from Chuck. While my roommate made it perfectly clear that he believed I should have made the moves on her previously, he was not real fond of infidelity and would have shamed me already more than he had.

Chuck was many things, but mostly he was loyal. His father left his mother for someone else when he was very young and was never in his life from that point on, so Chuck had a very negative view on those who cheat. Even though I was not married and there were no kids involved, I knew he would still be disappointed in me and he was one of the people whose opinion I most valued. At the end of this, it would be his friendship I did not want to risk losing.

Rachel returned to town on Sunday night but got in late enough that I did not have time to see her. I remained extra busy over the next few days, some legitimately, some by choice. I stopped by Monday night, and much to my relief Caitlin was there.

Oddly enough, she engaged me in conversation.

"How was your break?" she asked and seemed at least mildly interested.

"Uneventful," I answered. "I stayed here, drank a lot, watched a lot of basketball, went out a few times. Nothing special."

I inquired about her trip and she gave me a lengthier answer than I expected.

"To be honest, it was just what I needed," she said. "I needed to just get away, clear my head, and be one with the mountain. I know it seems like something for the rich, and there were plenty of unsavory patrons I had to interact with, but the actual time spent skiing is such a great way to embrace nature and center yourself."

While the irony of going to an elite ski resort in British Columbia to get back to nature was not lost on me, but at least it did not seem to be lost on her either.

She looked a little different. She was wearing make-up again. Not much, and if I had not seen her the week before I might not have noticed, but it was there. She also wore a simple silver chain. Previously all her jewelry had been made of rope and shells and beads and rocks. She still wore a braided bracelet on her wrist and a similar one on her ankle. She was also sporting the subtle little hoop nose ring.

Rachel and I went out to dinner. After a small game of "I don't know what do you want?" we settled on Chinese. I was apprehensive, even angry, but I did my best to hide it. I could not return to the "I don't feel good defense" again.

By the time our food came, I was faring better. While hearing about her vacation I almost forgot what she was up to.

Almost.

We were settling into familiar roles, and I may have cracked a joke or two. She gave me a hard time about the second of the jokes being a "dad joke." I felt like I could keep this up for a bit, but not a whole lot longer. Regardless of the presence of Anna, knowing what she was up to meant the end of us unless I found out she was somehow coerced or threatened.

Or we were just wrong about her. Harris was convinced and was working on setting a trap. He believed the accomplice was the key to all of this. Like me, he was not convinced that Rachel was the brains behind the operation and was instead drafted into the scheme.

While I was swayed by my own emotions and my closeness to Rachel, Harris was swayed by hard data, as well as a touch of sexism. He said traditionally these plots were carried out by men, and that even when women were involved that more often than not they did not do the heavy lifting. They either came up with the idea and then found someone to carry it out, or they were enlisted by a man into helping.

Harris believed that Rachel was the key to finding the accomplice and keeping Caitlin safe, and that meant I had to stay close to Rachel.

Much like the early stages of our relationship, I was having real reservations about being intimate. Not only had I cheated on her, but I was no longer sure I really liked her. For a few days, it did not matter. That first night Caitlin was still at their place and I lied and said that Chuck was at my dorm. The next night saw me working late with Volpe and the crew.

It was the middle of the week and we were again at her place. She tried to initiate and we were in the process of kissing when the door unlocked and Caitlin strolled in. She threw her bag on her bed and promptly followed suit. She kicked off her sandals and pulled out a textbook. It was marine biology, a class that had not previously been on the schedule I received when I began my investigation.

"Marine Biology, huh?" I asked. I already knew she was taking the class but was just making small talk. When she was coherent and away from Tariq, we actually got along fairly well.

She turned the book around so she could see the cover, confirmed to herself that it was indeed the subject I was referring to, then turned the book back around.

"Yeah, I picked up the class a week into the semester," she explained. "I was on the wait list, but a few people either dropped the class or failed to pay their tuition. Either way, score for me."

"Are you interested in marine biology?" I asked.

"Yeah," she said unconvincingly. "I am worried about our impact on the oceans…plus there is a field trip to Mexico in a few weeks."

Ah, yes, the famous field trip. Marine Biology courses were among the most popular because of the trip to see the tide pools in Puerto Penasco (aka Rocky Pointe). More often than not students think they are going to learn about dolphins and sharks, and then get a trip to play in Mexico. The course is actually much tougher than that, and the trip is dedicated to actually study of the marine ecosystem than it is whale-watching and margaritas.

I was actually impressed that she had stuck it out this long.

A little while longer Tariq dropped by. I was anxious to see the interaction between him and Rachel. What I wanted to see was him drop subtle physical clues and her react with a slight trace of fear. While I did not get that wish, I also did not get my great fear of seeing some previously hidden chemistry. In fact, they completely ignored each other.

What I could not ignore is how Caitlin and Tariq interacted. Normally she seemed to almost revere him but I saw her roll her eyes when he went on one of his anti-establishment diatribes. When he first arrived he noticed her chain, and lifted it briefly with two fingertips, then snorted and let it fall. In the past, she probably would have taken it off. Instead a few days later she specifically put it on after he called to tell her he was on the way.

Was there trouble in paradise or was Caitlin carving out just a little more individuality after a week with her family, a ski slope, and a world-class resort?

Tariq actually gave me a head nod as he entered the room, and no snarky remark of criticism accompanied it. This was now a common occurrence. While he was never overtly friendly, we had gotten to the point where the two of us could be in the same room without getting into a debate or raising our voices. It did not happen every time, in fact, the majority of the time I still wanted to punch him, but there were more than a few instances of civility. We would never break bread, or become friends, but we just might be able to coexist until I was able to finish this.

While my relationship with Tariq was slightly improving, he and Caitlin's was not. As bad as theirs was, mine was worse.

There was clearly trouble in my relationship, but Rachel did not seem to notice. She remained ever the attentive, affectionate girlfriend. Eventually, we found ourselves alone and there was no escaping the inevitable. I admit I was tormented and was afraid it might show in my performance.

"Wow, you really did miss me?" she said when we were done.

"Why do you say that?"

"That was more, um, aggressive than normal," she said, blushing a bit.

"I'm sorry," I replied.

"Oh, don't, it was different, but a good different," she said.

And for another 48 hours, the routine would continue. I would continue to play loyal boyfriend while sneaking texts to Anna and keep tabs on Caitlin. I did my best to determine who her accomplice was.

Things would remain that way, until a phone call, and subsequent discovery would change everything.

48. Excuse Me, I Am Dumb, Puppy Dog Eyes

Nothing seemed out of the ordinary on Monday, until Harris called. I had gone to classes in the morning and was eating lunch at the student union when my phone buzzed.

"My tech guy had a breakthrough," Harris said, trying to conceal his excitement. "He identified three of the locations of the computers that sent e-mails last weekend. They were all public computers near campus."

He said he would e-mail me the locations and wanted me to check out each location.

"I am not sure if there is anything we can use, but it can't hurt to look," he requested.

He wanted me to look for cameras or any other way to identify someone who may have used one the computers.

The first stop on the list was a public library about a mile and a half from campus. The library was one of the older, and smaller ones in town. It was one of the few that actually shared space with a small neighborhood park.

The library had a small group of six older computers for public use. I looked around, three of them were in use, and I did not notice anything that I thought I could use.

I ventured over to the help desk. After a moment a woman in her early 40's came over. From the neck up she looked like what you might expect from a librarian. She had a graying hair cut into a bob and wore thick glasses that were resting in her nose.

From the neck down it was something else. She wore a t-shirt that read "skip the movie, read the book", which she tucked into black jeans, with a metal studded belt. The most noticeable things were her tattoos. Each arm was covered in a full sleeve of tattoos. At a quick glance, one arm seemed to be covered with characters from Shakespeare's "A Mid-Summer Night's Dream." The other with characters from the Wizard of Oz. They were not the movie versions of the characters, but the more grotesque versions from the books by L. Frank Baum.

"Can I help you?" asked the punk rock librarian. I pictured her getting violent in a mosh pit, while also reading a book.

"I'm not sure," I said. "I had someone steal my identity and use my credit card to purchase some items. They tracked the transactions here and I was wondering if you had any kind of sign-in sheet."

"That is strange," she said. "Most commerce sites are blocked on our computers, though there are some workarounds I suppose."

I was afraid she was going to see through my charade.

"Unfortunately, we don't have a sign in sheet," she said. "You don't even have to have a library card to use the computers. It is just first come first serve,"

I asked a few more questions but soon realized identifying anyone at this location would be a dead end.

The next location was a hotel on the outskirts of campus. According to Harris, one e-mail was sent from their business center. Ten minutes after I left the library I was walking through the automatic doors of the hotel. The hotel had undergone a few different ownerships and was currently a boutique hotel without a national franchise attached. Over the past few years, it had undergone a renovation and was now decorated in a stark, minimalist style that was a huge contrast from the newer Sheraton built within the past decade on the other side of the campus.

This hotel was painted white, with a few chrome accents, but looked like some kind of futuristic spaceship or a comfortable hospital, as much as a hotel.

I walked in and went to the lounge. I sat in a seat where I could see most of the lobby. I ordered a beer and surveyed the scene. The hotel lobby was not very busy and it took about 15 minutes before I saw anyone use the elevators. I quickly discovered that you had to have a key card to get anywhere within the building.

Now that it was clear that I would not be able to just visit the business center on my own, I had to formulate a new plan. What better way to gain some inspiration than to chug half a beer?

Once finished, I had the rough idea of a plan. It was not a great plan and would be completely reliant upon my ability to bullshit, but I figured I was getting pretty good at it.

I went up to the front desk. There was an African American woman in her late 30's working. She had her thin braids pulled into a ponytail and sported a gray blazer. She was typing something into the computer when I approached. She instantly looked up and asked how she could help me.

"I am looking for a hotel for my mom and dad to stay at when they visit me next month," I said. "They are pretty particular, so I was wondering if I could ask a few questions."

"Sure," she replied. "What do you need to know?"

I pulled out my phone and looked as if I was consulting a list.

"Do you have a workout room?"

She nodded in the affirmative. I then went on to ask her what kind of equipment was in the workout room and nodded my head as if I was impressed, though, by the sound of it, it was actually somewhat crappy.

Next, I inquired about the business center. She informed me that it had Wi-Fi, six computers, a few phones, and a fax machine.

"Is there any way I could see it?" I asked. "My dad is really particular about where he does his work.

She said she was not really supposed to give tours, but since they were not busy she could take me up there for a moment. She came out from behind the desk, inserted the keycard, and a moment later we boarded the elevator.

She pushed the button for the eighth floor.

"So where are your parents coming in from?" she asked.

"Chicago," I said without hesitation.

We got off on the eighth floor and we rounded a corner, and there was a frosted glass wall and door with a sign clearly marking it as the "business center." She scanned the keycard to gain access to the room. Inside were three computers against one wall, and two more empty spaces that I assumed could be used if one had a laptop. There was also a fax machine and a small table with a telephone.

"What are the hours?" I asked, even though I could see them posted on a small card behind her.

"8 a.m. until 8 p.m.," she said.

I purposefully frowned. Unless the person who sent the e-mails was a guest of the hotel, then there was no way they could have sent the e-mail. I needed to see if there was another computer.

"What's wrong?" she asked.

"My father has a number of overseas clients and needs to interact with them at all hours," I misinformed her. "Is there any other computers available?"

"Well there is one next to the concierge desk," she said. "It's an even older computer than these, but it is available as long as the concierge is not using it."

We went back towards the elevators again, but went past them and rounded the opposite corner. There instead of the frosted glass walls was a small alcove with a small desk facing two chairs and a side table with an older computer. There was no card access needed to get to this computer, as long as one could get up on the elevators.

There were no noticeable cameras and no sign-in sheet that I could see.

I thanked her for her help after we returned to the lobby and left.

My final stop was an on-campus computer lab. At one time there were computer labs all over campus. Half the dorms had their own, but now in this era of affordable laptops and even smartphones that could do many of the same jobs as a computer, the number of computer labs on campus had dwindled. Most were used for specific majors that either needed very high powered machines or required very expensive software packages, and these were generally located within the buildings that housed their majors.

This particular lab was housed in the basement of a building that served a number of different majors. It was a multi-use lab, that served as a sort of back-up for other labs, and kept longer hours, which explained why it was open over spring break. It had a handful of PCs which were mostly used for word processing, though they also had access to the internet, spreadsheets, and servers of specific colleges. There were a couple of big-screened Macs that could be used for graphic design, photo editing, or video editing. There were also some other powerful machines that could handle the extensive programs that were required for various engineering and architecture programs.

I walked down a short flight of stairs and entered the lab. Despite it being mid-day, the room was very dark. Since it was mostly underground, the windows were small and at the top of each wall. If you stood on a table and were able to look out of them, you would see the feet of those walking by.

There were just a few students working, all had their ears plugged with their devices. The attendant, a bored looking Asian girl, did not look up from her book. She sat in the corner, behind two desks that met in a 90-degree angle, basically keeping her separated from the riff-raff working on their various assignments. On the desk in front of her was exactly what I was looking for.

The sign in sheet.

It was a clipboard with several sheets of well-worn paper. It looked as if no one had changed the pages in quite a while and that served my purposes just fine. Considering the attendant did not give me a second notice, I figured I could just rifle through the pages and not draw a second look, but I did not want to risk it.

"I'm sorry," I said, distracting her from the book. "I think I left my I.D. here last week, is there a lost and found?"

She looked at me annoyed, grabbed a little plastic box in front of her and asked my name.

"Slade, Eric Slade," I said.

She flipped through the box, going through the cards which should have been organized alphabetically. I started flipping through the pages.

"It was…uh…March…"

She stopped on what I assumed was the "S" section.

"No Slade," she said tersely.

"Could they have put it under 'E' for Eric?" I asked, trying to give her my best "excuse me I am dumb" puppy dog eyes.

She rolled her eyes, so much for customer service, and looked back into the box. I went back to the pages. And found the right date. I slid a pen onto the page so as not to lose my place.

"It would have been on March…"

"It does not matter what day it was," she shot back. "There is nothing in 'E' either."

"Really," said acting very confused. "Could it be in an envelope or folder?"

As I said that I reached toward a folder on the desk.

"Like that one," I said, and as I did I purposely stumbled, and knocked a bunch of papers, and folders on the floor.

"What the crap," she questioned, before kneeling down to pick up the items. She picked them up without looking at what I was doing, slamming each one onto the desk in annoyance.

I went back to the page from the day the e-mail was sent. There were about 10 names and I scanned them quickly to see if there were any names I recognized and sure enough there was indeed one name I recognized.

Eric Slade

It was me.

49. Stalk The Stalker

I stared at my name for what seemed like hours but was actually seconds before my brain processed what I was seeing. At first, I recognized the words as being a name I knew, but I did not instantly realize I was reading my own name.

When it finally clicked, I was confused.

When did I come here?

Only after another second did it finally come full circle and I realized what was happening.

Someone forged my name.

I was about to tear the page out of the log when the attendant slammed the final piece of paper onto the desk and then emerged from under the desk. She glared at me with what looked like real hatred.

"Your…identification…is not here," she spit out, speaking slowly so as to not yell.

"Ok," I said weakly.

I turned around and left the computer lab. My legs were actually wobbly as I traversed the stairs and once I emerged from the building I sat on a concrete bench to regain my bearings. I mentally went down a list of questions.

How did my name get there?

Who wrote my name?

Why did they write my name?

Then it dawned on me, I was being framed.

After another moment I realized Rachel was framing me.

While I was not 100% sure she was involved before, this seemed damning. Of my suspects, who else would think enough about me to write my name down? Most of the people I was looking into would not know my connection to Caitlin, but Rachel would.

I went from being confused and nervous to being irate. I was already feeling betrayed because I thought my girlfriend was extorting Caitlin's family, but at that time that was not a personal betrayal. Now she was not only an extortionist, but she was attempting to pin the blame on me in case someone tracked down the e-mail to this location.

I pulled out my phone to fire off a call to Harris, to finally give him further details on Rachel and her plan, but I halted. I wanted to prove to Harris that I could do this and to do that I needed more information. I could not go running to him the first time something went wrong.

I put the phone away. I needed to figure all of this out.

I thought about my name in the book. It was very blocky print handwriting that did not betray the gender of the author. In trying to visualize the page it dawned on me that Rachel was not the one who wrote it. She was in Mexico at the time.

I pulled my phone back out and checked both her and her friends' social media accounts. There were multiple pictures of Rachel partying on the beaches of Mexico. Unless she and all her friends had a coordinated effort to post fraudulent pictures, then Rachel was indeed south of the border when my name was written down.

So who was it and did Rachel know he or she was framing me?

At first, I assumed it had to be a he, how else would they get to use a computer with my name? Then I realized that not only did the attendants usually not check the sign in sheet against the ID but half the time they failed to look up from whatever they are doing. While the odds are that it was a man who forged my name, it was not a sure thing.

What was a sure thing was that someone wanted my name associated with the damning e-mail.

Someone wanted to frame me.

While I did not want to believe that Rachel was behind framing me, I had nothing else to go on. I still had fantasies of someone blackmailing her into helping them, but I realized that was like most of my fantasies…highly unlikely

What I really needed to figure out is who she was working with and what their endgame was. Personally, I wanted to know at what point was I selected to be her patsy. Was I chosen from the beginning or was this a late decision?

I eventually realized the irony of my situation. I started dating Rachel in an effort to keep Caitlin safe, and there was a chance Rachel started dating me in an effort to do Caitlin harm.

I went home to stew. I knew I needed to formulate a plan, but was so upset I needed a bit to just be mad and sad.

Harris called me shortly after I got home. He wanted to know the results of my expedition.

"No luck," I lied. "The library and hotel do not keep records of those who use the computers, and the hotel would not let me know who was staying there that night, just in case they were registered as a guest."

I explained to him the need for a keycard to access the elevators and the business center, though he mentioned how one could sneak in the elevator if need be.

"I may float some cash to see if I can get us a guest list," he said more to himself than to me.

"What about the computer lab?" he asked.

"They have a sign-in sheet," I said, sticking to the truth up to a point. "But the page for that day was already gone."

"Really? That's too bad. I had hoped we might get lucky."

I don't know why I didn't tell him. Part of me was worried it would get me into trouble, or at least taken off the case and I was determined to see it through. If someone was trying to frame me, I wanted to bring them down.

He said he was still working on concrete proof that connected Rachel's family to Volpe or Karen, but so far there was nothing more than we already had.

After we hung up I tried to concentrate on school, then video games, and eventually on sleep but I wasn't able to focus on anything, nor could I shut my brain off.

Sometime around 2:00 a.m. it occurred to me. I was doing this wrong. Instead of keeping tabs on Caitlin to keep her safe, I needed to instead focus my attention on Rachel and keep tabs on her to keep Caitlin (and possibly myself) safe.

Although the last thing I wanted to do was spend more time with Rachel, that is exactly what I did. I gave her very little free time to herself, and when I was not with her, whenever possible, I followed her. I was not proud of essentially being a stalker, but I owed it to Caitlin and myself to keep us safe. Someone wanted to possibly kidnap her, and frame me, but I was determined not to let that happen.

My new plan was to stalk the stalker.

50. Imperfect Plan

I realized it was an imperfect plan, but it was all I had. I could not wait for Rachel and her accomplice to make a move. I realized I had been several steps behind this whole time. I had thought I was so clever when in reality I was setting myself up. Dating Rachel seemed like a great plan, but I got too close. I let my feelings override my common sense. Even when faced with evidence against her, I downplayed it or overlooked it completely.

I felt like a sucker.

I had felt so bad about potentially toying with her feelings, that I allowed her to play me. I wanted to believe that it was not her intention to involve me, I wanted to believe her accomplice went behind her back to frame me, but that kind of sentimentalism is exactly what got me into this trouble in the first place.

I had to be cold, calculating.

Originally I was going to try to spend less time with her, lie and say I had commitments with Volpe and the Democrats, only to use that time to spy on her. I soon realized that if she was in cahoots with Volpe or Karen, she would know that I was lying.

So I went the opposite direction and spent as much time with her as I could. I was at her place every time she was. I encouraged her to come to my place. Who needed alone time? I was going to smother her with attention.

If I was putting a crimp in her plans, she sure did not show it. She seemed thrilled that we were spending so much time together.

All was not perfect. She picked up early on that I was upset, and I had to create a cover story. I was only partially lying when I said I had barely spoken to my mother since Christmas. The truth was we had spoken only twice, but it had not bothered me as much as it might have.

"It sucks when someone you love betrays you," I spat.

While I clearly meant her, Rachel, fortunately, did not pick up on it and tried to console me.

"I am so sorry," she said, giving me a big hug. "Maybe she just has a lot going on. You could try to call her."

I had to find a balance between being a suffocating boyfriend, tailing Rachel, and living my own life. I attended most of my classes, still made my weekly meeting with Volpe, but other than that I was with Rachel one way or another.

Following her proved to be uneventful. On the first day, she went to class, got a lot of coffee, and went to her dorm. Day two was essentially the same routine, except she had lunch with some friends. Unless they were her co-conspirators, and the amount of laughing did not seem much like the meeting of a secret cabal bent on extorting a United States Senator.

Things changed on day three of my mostly ineffective stakeout. On day three Rachel went to her morning classes, then grabbed a pre-made wrap and a bottle of tea and headed out, presumably to return to her dorm.

I went out a side door where I could keep an eye on her, but still not be seen. Seconds later she came bounding out of the Student Union, pink earbuds in place. She traipsed down the stairs and almost ran right into a taller man. He was skinny, with messy blonde hair that I instantly recognized.

It was Murph.

It looked like a spontaneous encounter. He held out his hands to ensure she did not fall when they collided and she did not appear to instantly recognize him, but when she did the earbuds came out, and her face brightened.

It was clear they knew each other.

Pangs of jealousy and anger returned, despite the fact that it really did look like a chance encounter and not a clandestine meeting of criminal minds.

Was I just supposed to believe they just happened to meet? Was it a coincidence that the woman who was not only my prime suspect but likely framing me was also friends with one of my other top suspects. It could be a coincidence, but I was starting to not to believe in coincidences when it came to Rachel.

I ended my stakeout and engaged. I strolled up and acted like I just happened to see Rachel standing there.

"Hey pretty," I said wrapping an arm around Rachel's waist, ignoring Murph for the time being.

I startled her at first, but once she realized it was me and not some creepy, handsy stranger she relaxed and slightly leaned into me.

"Eric," she said, sounding genuinely happy to see me. "What are you doing here?"

"I was craving a bagel, and needed to buy some pens," I lied. Normally at this time I had a break between classes and was likely napping or playing video games.

"Hey Slade," Murph said, confused.

I pretended I just noticed Murph.

"Murphy," I said as if it was the most interesting thing to see Patrick Murphy standing in front of the Student Union.

"You know Patrick?" asked a seemingly confused Rachel.

"Yeah, we've known each other since high school," I replied, trying to hide my anger. "How do you know each other?"

Rachel said she always saw him around the dorm and that he looked sort of familiar. She finally realized he was in one of her classes.

"One day we sat near each other and I said 'I think I've seen you around' and we started chatting," she added.

"So you didn't know Murph and Caitlin's used to date?" I asked.

He looked pale, she looked confused.

"I had no idea," she said. I almost wanted to believe her. If she was acting, then she was better than she let on. She had an academy award in her future.

"You know Caitlin?" Murph asked, regaining his composure.

"She's my roommate," Rachel said.

"Weird," Murph said.

"Yeah, weird," I said, slightly mimicking Murph's tone and inflection.

We all said an awkward goodbye and Rachel offered to accompany me to buy a bagel I did not really want and some pens I did not need. We ended up eating outside, enjoying a beautiful Arizona spring day.

"You didn't know Murph used to date Caitlin?" I asked.

"I didn't know he was Murph," she said. "I just knew him as Patrick from Sociology."

She paused and eyed me.

"Why are you jealous," she said, in a playful way stressing the second syllable in 'jealous.'

"Kind of," I said. "He may not look like it now, but Murph really had a way with the ladies back in high school."

She reflected on it for a minute.

"Really?" she asked. "I mean I guess if you gave him a shower, and a shirt that did not reek of weed he might be cute."

She paused and looked around.

"But between you and me, he's a total moron."

51. Make Their Move

I was confused what to make of Rachel's statements. In fact, I was just confused in general by Rachel. She gave me absolutely no indication she was involved, which I assumed made her perfect for this role.

After a few days, I felt my bitterness subsiding and I was starting to remember what it was I liked so much about her. She continued to be the super sweet girl, who was not afraid to flash a little east coast attitude from time to time. We were still finding classic films to watch together and analyze. That did not prevent me from sneaking off to spend an evening with Anna.

Anna was exciting, while Rachel was comfortable. She was smart and had a saucy attitude that was a nice departure from the sweeter Rachel. Anna was flirtier and more self-confident. Rachel was nice to be around, Anna was thrilling.

There was also the whole part about where she was not trying to frame me for extortion. That scored her a lot of points in my book.

I would have said she was no pushover, but she was sleeping with me, while I was still dating Rachel.

I was still at Anna's when my father called. It was early, even by my father's standards. I slipped out of her bed and ventured into the family room, trying not to wake Anna or her roommates up.

I mumbled a hello into the phone.

"Eric, I am surprised you are awake," bleary-eyed, I realized it was 6:30 in the morning. "I just wanted to let you know that I might be hard to reach over the next few days."

I was so tired I had trouble focusing and standing seemed like too much of a chore, so I sat on the couch.

"The Senator has a trip to the South Pacific and just found out some donors are going to be there," he said. "He wants me to go along and make sure we are maximizing the donation potential while staying within the rules."

"Uh huh," was all I could manage to reply.

"If you need me, it might be best to just send an e-mail, I am told the cell service could be unreliable," he said.

I would not say my father and I were speaking more of late, I did find myself initiating phone calls to bounce ideas about the case off of him, although I had not mentioned my recent findings about Rachel, nor did I tell him about my name being placed in the log book. Frankly, I was afraid he'd make me resign and I was going to see this through.

While I was still sort of enjoying Rachel's company, I was not letting my guard down. I may like spending time with her, but I did not trust her and was expecting her eventual betrayal. It made every encounter odd, though strangely thrilling Imagine trying to be yourself and having feelings for someone, but at the same time analyzing their every word and action.

18 hours after I hung up the phone with my father, Rachel and I were sitting on her bed watching a movie when Tariq burst in.

"Have you seen Caitlin?" he asked, quite annoyed.

"Not since yesterday," Rachel replied. "I assumed she was with you."

He looked agitated.

"No, we were supposed to meet an hour ago, but she did not show up," he said.

I pretended to watch the movie but was keenly aware of what they were saying.

"Did you try her cell?" Rachel asked innocently.

"Don't you think I would have tried that already?" Tariq said in the most condescending way.

"Well…" Rachel was now flustered after being spoken to that way. I stepped in.

"You don't have to be a dick about it," I stood up and glared at him. "She was just trying to help."

He took a step towards me and started to smirk.

"Stupid questions are not going to help," he said, half annoyed, half worried.

"And neither is being an asshole," I spat back. "Take 10 minutes off from being a condescending douche bag to be civil so we can figure this out."

Tariq did not like being spoken to this way, and I got the impression he was not used to being stood up to. He frequently had insults hurled to him during his protests, but those trolls were just as cowardly as Tariq, choosing to insult him from across the street, or staying in their pick-up trucks. He was not accustomed to someone challenging up close.

Rachel attempted to play peacemaker.

"Guys, calm down, we aren't going to do any good by fighting," she said this before turning to Tariq. "When did you last see her?"

He glared at for a moment, then seemed to calm down.

"Yesterday, at lunch."

"She was not with you last night?" Rachel asked, and I would swear she was genuinely puzzled.

"No."

"She was not here last night," she added.

I was already worried, but now I was in panic mode. If Rachel was missing, that might mean a move was made.

"Should we call her dad?" Rachel asked me.

I explained he might be hard to reach, but I had the number of one of his staffers. Rachel and Tariq looked at me quizzically, but I did not have time to explain.

I asked Rachel to look around the room and see if anything seemed unusual. I asked Tariq if he knew any of her other friends she might be spending time with. He said he would make some calls and departed.

I told Rachel I would be right back and I went outside to call Harris. He did not pick-up and I texted him.

We might have a problem

I went back into the dorm room. Rachel seemed mostly calm. She was on her phone and explained she was trying to call Caitlin but it was going straight to voicemail. She said nothing looked too out of place, but that her backpack and laptop were gone.

My phone buzzed and it was Harris, I took it outside.

"They made their move," he said hurriedly. "I got an e-mail 10 minutes ago. They claim they have her and will make their demands known."

"Do we know when?" I asked.

"No, why?"

"I have been with Rachel for most of the day, but I was not with her last night," I explained.

There was a pause on the line.

"Okay, keep an eye on her," Harris said. "I cannot get ahold of the Senator, I am waiting to make a full blown report until I see what they want, but I did tip off a friend of mine at the University Police, Sergeant Steel and tell him what was going on."

For a split second, I thought that was an awesome name, and pictured a police officer with metal skin like Colossus from the X-Men. I pictured a police officer in his blue uniform bursting out of a police car, sunlight glinting off of his metallic skin. Criminals from central casting, complete with pencil-thin mustaches were firing their revolvers at him, but their bullets just deflected off his steel exterior.

I probably should quit watching cartoons and then wondered why I imagined an investigator wearing a patrol uniform.

"I am making some preparations up here, then I will be down," he added.

I went back inside. Rachel was looking worried. I had to give her credit, she was one hell of an actress.

"Anything?" she asked.

"No, but they are looking into some things," I said. "I guess they have ways of keeping tabs on her because of the Senator."

I lied about that, I was the thing keeping tabs on her, but I wanted to see her reaction. If she was troubled by the news, she did not show it. Maybe she could spot bullshit better than I could.

"I checked her social media accounts, but she hardly ever posts," Rachel said. "I did not see anything that indicated where she was."

An hour later Tariq came back and indicated that none of her friends knew where she was. The last anyone had heard from her was yesterday afternoon. I felt like a fool, while I was at Anna's, Rachel and her partner could have been taking Caitlin. If I had just stuck around, I could have possibly put a crimp in their plans.

Harris called again. He said they sent a follow-up that they indeed wanted money, and he better be prepared to gather a lot of it. He assured me that we would get to the bottom of this quickly.

He was right, sort of, and that is where the trouble began.

52. Fugitive Lifestyle

I had been on the run for about 30 minutes before I had actually formulated a plan. I had never been a fugitive from the law before, so everything I knew about avoiding the law came from movies and detective paperbacks. Not exactly the best reference material.

I assumed there were probably some good online resources on how to avoid capture, probably a really good "on the lam" YouTube Channel, but I did not have time to do a deep dive into the fugitive lifestyle, I had to keep moving.

I was still at Rachel's place when the phone rang. It was Harris, and I sprang into action.

"You son of a bitch," he screamed. "It was you."

I did not know what he was talking about.

"I came down to circle the wagons, but had a nagging suspicion, so I went to check out that computer lab," he said. I now knew where this was going. "You've been behind this the whole time."

I tried to protest, but he cut me off.

"Don't go anywhere," he commanded. "Tell me where Caitlin is and McCauley might go easy on you."

I hung up the phone, Rachel could tell that something was wrong. She started to say something, but I cut her off.

"I have to go," I said, not giving her any explanation, although she may have already known since she was behind this. I wondered if Harris' "nagging suspicion" was somehow tipped off by Rachel or her partner.

I bolted out of the dorm and went straight to my Jeep. I did not bother to stop by the dorm. I shot off a text to Harris that said "I am being framed" and another to Chuck that said, "In big trouble, reach out soon.

I tried to call my dad, but his phone was out of service, as he had warned. I then turned off my phone. I did not know if they could track me if it was merely powered off, but I knew they could if I left it on.

I hit a bank near campus and took out $200. I headed south, towards Mexico and filled up with gas, and took out another $200. I kept south, and stopped in Green Valley, a retirement community 25 miles south of Tucson, on the freeway towards the border. I used a credit card to take out another cash advance at one bank and then went across the street to do the same at another bank. I also stopped in a drug store and bought a roll of medical tape, which I used to slightly alter my license plate. It would not pass a close inspection but might make it harder to tell what had happened.

Now that I had clearly made it seem if I was headed south to the border, I stopped at a payphone and called Anna. I felt lucky that I could still find a payphone, but I suppose a community with a large number of retirees was the perfect place for this increasingly antiquated technology.

I needed someone I could trust, or at the very least someone, no one affiliated with the case knew I was involved with. My shame of cheating on Rachel would now pay dividends. If they question Chuck, my father, or any of my friends, they would not know about Anna.

I also assumed Rachel did not know about Anna and could not sell me out.

She picked up immediately.

"Hello?" she said, obviously not recognizing the payphone's number.

"It's me," I said, hoping she recognized my voice.

"Eric," she said in a sing-songy voice.

"Just listen, I am in huge trouble and I need to borrow your car. I will explain when I see you if you will help me."

"Of course, are you okay?"

"I am for now," I shot back.

I gave her the location to meet and then headed back north. My hope was that the police, or FBI, or secret service would not think I was actually headed back to Tucson.

I then turned on the radio to an a.m. news station. I figured the kidnapping of a Senator's daughter would make the headlines, but after 10 minutes it was clear the media had not gotten wind of it. I saw that as a good sign.

I was to meet Anna at a Walmart just off the freeway. My plan was to leave my Jeep there. I figured it would be several days before someone noticed it. This Walmart was one of the bigger ones in the area and attracted shoppers from Mexico, as well as rural parts of Eastern Arizona. There was a lot of traffic at all hours of the night.

Anna was waiting when I got there. She drove a sporty Toyota and emerged as soon as I parked next to her.

She threw her arms around me and asked if I was alright. I assured her I was and then filled her in on what was going on.

"I know it sounds far-fetched," I said when I was done. "But I swear I am telling the truth and I did not do anything to her."

She gave me one of her seductive smiles, which I thought odd.

"So that is why you did not break up with Rachel," she cooed. "My feelings were getting hurt."

I shook my head; I was not in the mood to discuss our relationship at this point. I needed her car and her help.

"Let me have your keys and I'll give you cash for a ride," I said. "After I get clear of town I will let you know where I left your car."

"No," she said sternly. "I am coming with you."

"Uh-uh, no," I said. "I can't put you in danger. Just let me go."

She glared at me. For someone so short, she sure could be fierce.

"Either I go with you, or you find another mode of transportation," she said, in finality.

I did not have time to argue, so I relented. We went into the store to get me some new clothes and toiletries, as well as some food and drinks for the road. 20 minutes after I pulled into the parking lot we were back on the road.

She insisted on driving and we headed east on the interstate towards New Mexico. I had hoped I left enough breadcrumbs south toward Mexico, that no one would think to look for me heading in a completely different direction. I had cash, I had food, and, unexpectedly, I had company.

I had no intention of getting Anna, or anyone else, this involved, but it was too late. Now I had an accomplice.

53. Saloons and Brothels

Bisbee, Arizona is a former mining town located 90 miles southeast of Tucson and nestled among the Mule Mountains. Much of the city is built into the side of the mountain, with homes nestled within the rock, winding roads, and stairways carved into the mountain itself, give the town a very unique feel

Once a booming mining town, today it is a draw for tourists due to its extraordinarily well-preserved early-twentieth century downtown. It draws visitors from around the world, who appreciate its historic architecture, it's welcoming, creative spirit and its cool climate. It has become a haven of artists and latent day hippies. In 10 years Caitlin and Tariq would feel right at home.

To get there Anna and I headed east on the interstate as if we were going to New Mexico, but after about an hour we cut south. The final portion of the drive sees one slowly drive up the Mule Mountains, pass through a darkened tunnel within the mountain and then emerge into another world.

After passing through the tunnel, the roadway starts a rapid descent. Small cottages populate the hillside, surrounded by the rich, red soil that is a product of the minerals from the mine. We switched drivers halfway there, and as I drove Anna had found a small bed and breakfast in the Brewery Gulch portion of town and she made us a reservation.

We finally came down the mountain and found a public parking lot right by town hall and the Copper Queen, a large, historical hotel that was once one of the gems of the west back when Bisbee was the largest city between San Francisco and St. Louis. Although a tour bus now sat outside, you could still picture old prospectors and saloon girls roaming the area.

The area now contained trendy microbrews and antique shops, it was once the home to saloons and brothels. In its heyday, the Gulch boasted nearly 50 saloons and was considered one of the liveliest spots in the west.

Although distinctly western, the town also felt very European to me. With small, windy roads, many paved in brick and cobblestones, and houses built into the mountain, it did not seem like America.

The small streets, many of which were one-way, made parking tricky, so we left the car in a public lot at the entrance to the Gulch and made the short walk to the Bed and Breakfast that we were staying.

I figured no one would think to look for a fugitive in a romantic bed and breakfast, assuming they knew I was in Bisbee and not headed toward Mexico.

The entire ride in I monitored the radio, but there was no word of Caitlin being missing. I assumed this was some kind of strategy, but I did not know what the play was. You would assume I would be easier to catch if m picture was plastered everywhere, but they were the professionals.

Part of me hoped that this meant they had figured out I was innocent, but I could not take the chance to turn on my phone.

We found the address, it was a two-story house that was probably 50 years old, but was in very good shape. It had a new coat of white paint over its stucco exterior, and the dark wood has almost zero signs of weathering. There was no yard to speak of, save for about a 20 square foot patch of grass that was well maintained and several planter boxes with a multitude of bright colored flowers.

The sun was setting as we entered the house. It was just as well maintained inside as the outside but had an old feel to it. It did not look like it had been redecorated in years. The front door entered into a small sitting room, that had a large plush sofa and a matching chair, both covered in the same floral print. The paintings ion the wall had large wooden frames, not the small metal or plastic frames you would find at a big box store.

A pleasant woman in her early 50's emerged from within the house and greeted us. She brought us into the kitchen to check in. I paid cash and although she had us sign the guestbook, but she never looked at my ID.

"What brings you two here?" she asked.

"It is our first date," she said, pulling me close.

The old lady looked confused, and I am pretty sure I did too.

Anna leaned in.

"His divorce just became final," she lied. "Poor thing was married to a horrible woman who had been cheating on him."

The owner of the bed and breakfast suddenly looked very interested.

"I am a paralegal in his law firm and always had a bit of a crush on him, but he would never so much as give me a second look while he was married no matter how much I flirted with him," Anna continued to weave her tall tale. "I told him as soon as his divorce was final I was going to whisk him away for a romantic vacation."

"Well, isn't that sweet," the owner said, not entirely convinced.

She showed us up to our room. Pointed out the communal bathroom, then showed us where to find towels and extra linens, then left us to go finish dinner.

"What the hell was that?" I asked. "Divorce? Lawyer? Paralegal?"

She slinked up to me, gave me a lingering kiss, then sat down on the bed.

"She barely looked at you," Anna explained. "She was fully interested in my story. By the time we leave, she will not remember some 22-year old college kid, but swear she played host to a 30-something lawyer and his very young looking secretary."

"I do not look like I am in my 30's," I said.

"No, but I tried to keep the attention on me," she said. "You'll make yourself scarce, but I will keep running into her, so by the time we leave she'll remember every detail about me, but mostly forget about you."

"Am I that forgettable?" I asked, feigning insult.

"Hopefully," she said.

I sat next to her on the bed, with every intention of making myself unforgettable, but made the mistake of laying down. I don't remember falling asleep, but the stress of the day must have taken its toll because I did not wake up for 16 hours.

54. A Walk Wasted

I woke up alone and a bit confused. It took me a few seconds to gain my bearings. The room was small, probably just 10 feet wide, and most of it was filled with a very fluffy bed. I was still wearing my clothes from the day before, though my shoes and socks had been taken off and I was straightened out a bit.

I assumed I had Anna to thank for that.

There were two ornate stuffed chairs and a small table at the foot of the bed, under a window that still had its heavy curtains drawn. The table was also ornate, with fancy carved feet. A similarly carved nightstand sat next to the bed and a small dresser was on the opposite wall.

Like the rest of the house, the walls were covered in wallpaper, though this was a very subtle design, an off-white ivy pattern on top of white background.

I was still afraid to turn on my phone, so I ventured downstairs to see if I could find her. She was in the kitchen, regaling the homeowner, and another man I assumed was her husband with a story I could not hear. The lady's eyes focused on me a bit, and Anna figured out I was behind her and turned around.

"Hi, sweetie, did you sleep well?" she said, a little extra cheer sprinkled on her words. I was not quite ready for extra cheer to be honest.

"Yeah," I said, my grogginess still apparent.

"I had Mrs. Page save you a sweet roll in case you're hungry," Anna added. "Why don't you take it and the paper upstairs and I will meet you in a bit."

She handed me a small plate with a really big frosted sweet roll on it and then gave me a stack of newspapers to read. I took the clue that I should make myself scarce.

I sat at one of the tables and dug into the papers. Anna had picked up both a local Tucson newspaper as well as the USA Today. Normally I go right to the sports page and then entertainment, but today I went right to the news to see if there was anything on Caitlin.

There wasn't.

I was trying to figure out what this meant. I had taken a few nibbles of the sweet roll when Anna came in.

"There's nothing on Caitlin in the papers," I said as she sat in the chair next to me.

"I know," she said. "They don't have Wi-Fi here, so I went down to a little coffee shop down the road. There is nothing online, nor is there anything on the news channels."

"I wonder if they found her?" I queried. "Or is this some kind of strategy to catch me."

"I don't know, but it seems really weird," she added.

I decided I needed a hot shower, and after I was done we decided to risk it and head to the coffee shop so I could check things on her laptop.

Feeling more human, I put on my newly purchased Walmart clothes. A hooded sweatshirt and a ball cap might help conceal my identity. We walked hand in hand down the street and I thought another time, another situation this would make a great romantic weekend. As for today, the walk was wasted.

The coffee shop was one part small town diner, and one part modern coffee shop. There was the typical lunch counter on one wall, with a waitress tending to customers behind and an open window that looked into the kitchen. On the opposite wall were red pleather booths that sat next to wide windows.

The big difference was in the corner opposite the door, where several booths were removed and instead two couches and a pair of small desks were sitting. It seemed like someone figured they needed to cater to the Starbucks crowd, but could not alienate the typical diner crowd.

We chose one of the couches and Anna ordered a coffee drink. I just wanted a water. Both came while I was logging into my e-mail. There was nothing out of the ordinary. I debated whether to check social media, as I was not sure if I could be tracked that way. I figured I could, but it might not be a quick process. I logged into my Facebook account and had several private messages from Rachel.

Where are you?

Pick up your phone

Is everything okay?

What's going on

Other than that, nothing unusual.

Before I could log off Rachel sent me another direct message.

What is going on, are you okay?

I debated whether I should answer her at all. After all, she was directly behind my predicament.

Family emergency, left in a hurry, left phone and computer on plane

I typed the message and then logged off of the account. I did not know if she was trying to find me to turn me in, or was she unaware that I knew she was framing me and genuinely did not know where I was. Either way, I probably gave her too much information.

We walked around town for a little bit as I further tried to clear my head, but it didn't work. I was still distracted. We risked being seen and had a quiet early dinner at one of the small breweries, but again the conversation was limited.

We retired early to our room and Anna did her best to take my mind off of my problems. This time I was not distracted and gave her my full attention.

The next morning Anna woke up earlier than me again. She had gone downstairs to get some coffee and was sitting in one of the plush chairs when I finally stirred from my slumber. I sat up in bed and saw her sipping her beverage and perusing the paper.

"There is still nothing in the paper about a kidnapping," Anna said. "It seems very strange that they could keep this a secret for four days."

She put the paper down and walked over to the bed. She sat down across from me and took my hands.

"Let's go over this again, and don't leave everything out," she said.

I told her the story again, but this time I went into far more detail than I did in the Wal-Mart parking lot. I started from that fateful meeting over Christmas vacation and went right through the events of the past few days.

When I was done she was smiling.

"Is that it?" she asked.

"What do you mean 'is that it?'" I asked her.

"If your story is accurate the only thing they have on you is your name in the computer lab logbook," Anna said. "That is circumstantial at best. Even with your name in the book, that does nothing to prove you sent the e-mail."

She took a sip of her coffee then looked down into the cup.

"When was that e-mail from the computer lab sent?" she asked.

"That last Saturday of spring break," I answered.

She started laughing and did not quit for half a minute.

"Not only is it all circumstantial, but you have an alibi."

"What's my alibi?" I asked.

"Me," she said. "I hope you did not forget, but I spent all day and all night with you on Saturday. In fact, it was technically Saturday morning when I first came over."

I tried to be optimistic, but I had not told anyone about us and told her as much.

"It is just your word against theirs," I said. "There is no proof you were with me."

She laughed again, then got up and went to her purse. She fished out her phone and swiped and pushed a few buttons until she found what she was looking for. It was a photo that filled her screen. It was a selfie, with Anna filling up the bulk of the picture. She was clearly in bed, with a blanket pulled up above her breasts. In the background was me, fast asleep.

"But that does not prove I did not send the e-mail," I said.

"No, but it does prove we were together that day," Anna replied. "It is more evidence than just your name in the logbook. Not only is there a timestamp from when I shot the photo, but I may have, 'accidentally', sent it to a few friends."

She tapped the screen a few more times and went to her text messages. She held it up again, this time it was the same photo within a text message. By the looks of it, she had sent it to a few friends with the tag "Happy Birthday to me!"

I may have been her birthday present, but she was the one giving me a gift. Suddenly I had at least a partial alibi.

It was time to clear my name.

55. Surrender

The trip back to Tucson would take about two hours. Half an hour into the drive I turned my phone on. It beeped for nearly a full minute announcing all of the missed calls, texts, e-mails, and social media notifications.

The majority of the calls were from Harris and Rachel, while Rachel also flooded my phone with text messages.

After figuring out I had Anna as a semi-alibi we stayed in the room and brainstormed how I could best use this information. Part of me wanted to confront Rachel directly. Anna thought it best to go right to Harris and give him my evidence. I also thought about sneaking back into town and trying to solve the case but realized I was pretty much an abject failure at this whole detective thing, so that was out.

Then it occurred to me.

I would turn myself in. I would just go to the police and explain everything that happened. It might take a few days, but soon they would see that all the evidence was circumstantial and when they got Caitlin back if they got Caitlin back, they would discover I had nothing to do with it.

Anna pointed out that Rachel and her partner were probably not trying to get me arrested, but likely framed me as a backup plan in case something went wrong. Her hypothesis was that they were trying to get more money out of the senator and would be happy disappearing into the night, but if something went wrong, they could leak the clues about me.

I would turn the plan on its head and turn myself in, give up Rachel and spell out some other candidates to be her accomplice. I am sure Harris had already done much of this, but I would do it as well and, in turn, help myself.

Hopefully.

The first thing I did was fire off an e-mail to my dad spelling out everything. I knew he might not get it for some time, but it was further evidence of my alibi. He would also be able to help me until this got sorted out. At the very least he could send a lawyer my way. As you could guess, many of his friends were lawyers. I just hoped at least one was a top-notch defense attorney.

Once the beeps subsided I placed a call to the University of Arizona police department.

Since the University has nearly 50,000 people on campus at one time they have a pretty sizeable police department. As an organization, they have over 60 people, with just over 30 officers including public information officers, traffic, and investigations. It did not take long for me to track down Sgt. Steel and I placed the call.

It took a few minutes to get connected, but eventually, he picked up announcing who he was.

"It's me, Eric Slade, I am innocent, but I am willing to turn myself in to prove it," I spit out rapid fire.

"Who is this?" he asked.

"Eric Slade, I am being framed for the kidnapping of Caitlin McCauley, the Senator's daughter," I added.

"Look, if this is a prank..."

"What are you talking about?" I yelled. "This is serious."

Anna looked over at me, taking her eyes off the road.

"Look, kid, I have no idea what you are talking about," he said, clearly annoyed. "I do not have time for practical jokes."

"This is Sgt. Steel, the investigator for UAPD?" I asked and he confirmed his identity.

"I was told by Martin Harris, who works for Senator Ed McCauley, that he called you to report the disappearance of the Senator's daughter Caitlin," I exhaled. "He said he was friends with you. Later he mistakenly believed I was involved, but I am not."

It seemed to take forever for him to replay.

"Who did you say reported it?" Steel finally asked.

"Martin Harris, he does investigations and security for Senator McCauley," I said, a mix of desperation and annoyance in my voice. "He said he was your friend."

"Harris," he said more to himself than to me. "Yeah, I know who he is but we aren't friends. We both worked for Phoenix PD, and then I saw him over the summer to set up some security protocols for the Senator's Daughter, but I have not heard from him since last August."

I was perplexed. Was this a trick. Were they trying to keep me on the line? Was he trying to trap me?

"He did not report her missing three days ago, or at least tip you off that something was wrong?"

He sounded less annoyed but was still frustrated.

"No, he did not call me," he said, I could hear the tapping of a computer keyboard behind me. "and he did not report anything to the department. We have nothing in the computer about a missing girl."

I could hear some more tapping.

"Let me check with some other departments, hang on," he added.

I was worried this was a trick to keep me on the line and track me.

"I'll call you back," I said and instantly shut my phone off.

I looked over at Anna who looked as confused as I felt. I filled her in on my conversation with Steel.

"I feel like it is a trap," I said.

"I don't know," she said, clearly thinking. "If they thought you had Caitlin, wouldn't they ask about her wellbeing? Sure, they'd try to keep you on the line, but they would also be trying to get you to tip your hand, or make sure she was safe?"

What she said made sense. I was glad that she was thinking things through much better than I was. Apparently, her insistence in coming with me was going to pay dividends.

Fifteen minutes later I powered up my phone and called Steel back. This time I was able to get him much quicker.

"I checked every database I have access to and she has not had a missing persons report filed with any law enforcement agency in the state," Steel said. "Just in case I called some people I know in both Tucson and the Valley and they said the same thing."

He said he not only called the Tucson Police Department but also called a few different agencies in the Phoenix area.

"I don't know what to tell you, but if the girl is missing, no one has reported it," he said.

"Could they have reported it to the FBI or Secret Service or something?" I asked.

"Sure, but it would be really unusual for them not to provide local law enforcement the information," Steel said. "At the very least if anyone was running a formal investigation on campus, we would know about it. Even if the FBI and Secret Service wanted to shut us out, we would know if they were on campus."

I apologized for wasting his time and thanked him for his time. He offered to take my number in case he heard anything more and gave me his cell number in case I needed anything.

We were halfway home, racing through the Sonoran Desert. I was unsure of what was going on. Anna continued to come up with theories, but none of them fully made sense.

I started combing through my missed calls and text messages. Rachel called me 35 times, while Harris called 28. Rachel sent as many, if not more text messages. At first, they were just questions about what I was doing or when were we going to meet. They then took on a worried tone, and eventually, I could read her frustration and anger.

Was she worried about me, or worried she did not know where her patsy was?

The last few text messages came after our brief internet chat.

Hope everything is okay

Call me when you can, I'm thinking of you

I was about to put my phone away when a new text message from Rachel appeared.

Caitlin says you need to call me ☺

56. Adrift on a Sea of Confusion

I looked down at the text message for a moment to make sure I was reading it correctly.

Caitlin says you need to call me ☺

Was Rachel really this brazen or had I completely missed something? Obviously, Caitlin's disappearance had not been called in to local law enforcement. Was this a plan by Harris? Was he directed no to do so by someone higher up? If so, why did he lie to me about reporting it to the University police?

Or did Rachel do something to force him not to rely on the police? Was she threatening Harris with Caitlin's life, and if so, did he still believe I was involved?

I held the phone out to Anna to show her the latest message. She took her eyes off the road and read it.

"You have to call," she said.

"I do?"

"Absolutely," Anna replied. "You have to see what this is about."

Did this mean she had Caitlin with her? Was this just bait to get me to call or was I going to get some confirmation that Caitlin was indeed okay? And what the hell was the smiley face?

I took a deep breath dialed the number. To say I was nervous was an understatement. I felt dread as I hit her name on the screen of my phone. Rachel wasted no time picking up.

"Eric!" she squealed. "Is everything okay?"

She sounded happy and relieved to hear from me.

"No," I said.

"Is there anything I can do to help?" she asked.

What I heard next was a game changer.

"Hi, Eric," a familiar voice said in a sing-song tone.

It was Caitlin.

"So you have Caitlin," I said, matter of factly.

"What?" she sounded confused. "Caitlin is here. She got back a little while ago."

Anna must have read the confusion on my face as she mouthed "what?" I held up one finger to tell her that I needed a few minutes.

"What do you mean she got back?"

"It turned out she went to Mexico a few days early for the marine biology field trip and apparently didn't tell anyone," Rachel said. "She just got home a little bit ago."

"So she is fine?" I asked.

"Yeah, just a misunderstanding," Rachel said.

Caitlin was not missing? She was not kidnapped? What was going on? I was apparently adrift on a sea of confusion because nothing made sense.

"She wants to talk to you?" Rachel said.

"Hello, Eric," Caitlin said in a bored voice. "I told you I could not handle any drama the rest of the semester and I come home to Rachel freaking out because you take off."

"And where were you?" I asked, anger rising in my voice.

Anna looked over at me, more confused than ever. I cupped the bottom of my phone in an effort to prevent Caitlin from hearing.

"It's Caitlin," I whispered loudly. "She's back."

"What the fuck?" Anna mouthed. At least I am 90% sure that is what she was mouthing.

"I was in Mexico for marine biology," Caitlin said as if it was the most obvious thing in the world.

"It was supposed to be a weekend trip and you disappeared mid-week," I shot back.

"I went early," Caitlin said. "Some people from my class wanted to go and party a few days before the field trip started so I went."

I raised my eyebrows and shook my head in disbelief. I was on the run because Caitlin wanted to party.

"Tariq was worried, did he not know you left early?" I asked.

"Um, I guess not," she said. "I am not sure I told him, we have not been talking as much lately."

I still had a laundry list of questions. Some for Caitlin, some for Harris, a few for Rachel. I had to sort things out mentally.

"Did Rachel know you left early?"

"No," Caitlin replied. "Why would she?"

At least I knew Rachel was not playing me when she acted like she had no idea where Caitlin was. Suddenly I wondered if Rachel was not involved at all. If that was the case, where did the cell phone with the text messages come from? More importantly, where did it go?

I needed a few more answers from Caitlin but knew from past experiences that keeping her focused could be a challenge. I needed to get my answers fast.

I was able to gather that after a few days of partying in Mexico she got bored of "marine biology-ing" and wanted to go home. Apparently, she did not think a marine biology field trip would involve so much actual learning.

Next, I asked her who knew she was back.

"Just the girl I rode back with," she said.

"So no one else knows your back?" I asked.

"No, I don't think so," she said.

Things were starting to click into place. I was not able to put it all together, but I knew if I could keep her return a secret I would have an upper hand. Against who, I was still not entirely sure, but the more information I had, that no one else had, the better.

"This may sound weird, but can you not tell anyone you are home?" I asked. "I can't explain everything right now, but things would be better for all of us if everyone believed you were still in Mexico."

She started to protest, I needed a reason for her to keep quiet.

"I mean, your dad would freak if he thought you bailed on a school trip," I said, hoping her new "commitment" to education would help keep her from revealing her location.

After a little more coaxing I got her to commit to keeping her location a secret for 24 hours.

Before the call ended Rachel got back on the line. I assured her I would be home soon and I would fill her in on all the details.

I was pretty sure she was innocent, that someone wanted me to distrust her, but after almost two weeks of feeling betrayed by her, I was suddenly filled with guilt. Not only did I believe she betrayed me, but I had cheated on her.

I did not have time to wallow in self-pity and remorse. I had to formulate a plan and finish this once and for all.

57. Leaps in Logic

had a decent idea of what was going on. At least part of what was going on, but it would require at least one more phone call to make sure.

I called Harris.

Like Rachel before him, he answered quickly.

"Where the hell have you been," Harris yelled. "If you hurt her…"

"I don't have her," I said.

"Just turn yourself in and we can work this out," he said, suddenly calmed. "If you are indeed innocent, turning yourself in will be the best way to clear your name."

"That's a good idea," I said. "I will meet you at the police station."

We were now about a half hour outside of town, on the main interstate. I could be back at my dorm in 45 minutes. After hanging up with Rachel and Caitlin I plotted with Anna. While I had all but cleared Rachel. I had a pretty good idea who was behind this.

"No, no, don't do that," Harris replied. "The police are on high alert looking for you. They know me. Let's meet first and I will call them to let them know I am bringing you in."

And there it was. Another lie. I had already caught Harris in a few lies. How many more had he told me?

"That sounds like a good idea," I said. "You're the expert, I trust you."

Harris asked me where I was. I lied, telling him I had just crossed the New Mexico border and was coming back to Tucson. That lie bought me at least a couple hours.

"I can come get you," Harris suggested.

Despite his insistence, I declined his offer to chauffeur me to the police. I suggested we meet somewhere private so that the police did not find me before I could get him to grease the skids. We settled on a time and location, a private place on campus where I could safely enter into his custody.

I hung up the phone and told Anna the plan.

I had just agreed to meet the man who was framing me.

58. Isolation

There are a number of parking garages on campus, and most of them are by places of interest. There is one next to several dorms as well as one of the main retail areas. Another sits right behind the student union and the administration building. Another is situated adjacent to the basketball arena.

One is a little more isolated. While it sits on the southern edge of campus, the road that runs next to it is not very busy late at night. Although several other buildings surround it, two belong to the University maintenance staff, and two more are offices that do not host classes. After 10 p.m. the area is pretty empty.

That is what we were both counting on.

A little after 11:00 I arrived at the parking garage. I drove up to the third level and parked my Jeep in an isolated corner. Harris' black sedan was already waiting for me.

I did not walk into this completely blind. Anna and I hatched a rough plan. It was hardly foolproof, but we knew what we wanted to accomplish and had a rough idea how to make that work. On my way into town, I made a few more calls and lined a few things up.

I got out of the Jeep, clad in a hooded sweatshirt and baggy cargo shorts. I moved around the vehicle and stood by my back bumper. Harris's car was parked across from mine and when he got out we were about 20 feet apart.

"Where is she, Eric?" Harris asked.

"You can give up the act, we both know I didn't take her," I spat back. "She's in Mexico on her field trip."

He laughed and shook his head, giving me a smirk.

"There never was a kidnapping plot, it was you all along."

He pulled a handgun out of a shoulder holster and trained it on me.

"I don't know what you are talking about," he said, maintaining his innocence. "I am just here to take you into the authorities."

"Cut the crap," I growled. "I called Steel, he barely knew who you were, much less knew what the hell I was talking about when I offered to turn myself in."

A confused look spread over his face. He had not figured I'd try to turn myself in.

"The funny thing about forging my name in the computer lab logbook is that I had an alibi," I laughed nervously, though I hoped he thought I sounded confident.

"Bullshit," he said. "You said it yourself that you were alone."

"I lied," I said. "Forgive me if I did not want to advertise the fact I was cheating on my girlfriend."

I felt horrible saying it, but I knew I had to buy time. He had not anticipated this. I did not know what his intentions were, but I had seemingly thrown a small wrench in them.

"I highly doubt that," he finally said.

"I have the sex tape to prove it," I exaggerated but gave him a knowing leer.

He fidgeted before jamming out his hand and demanding my phone. I reached into my front pocket and he jabbed the gun at me.

"Slowly," he commanded.

I pulled the phone out of my shorts, wincing at this order. The voice recorder was running, as it had been the entire conversation.

He gave me a little wave, indicating he wanted me to give him the phone right now.

"Toss it at my feet," he said.

I grabbed the edge of the phone and flipped the phone over there as if I was dealing a playing card. It helicoptered over to him and landed by his perfectly shined shoes. He stomped on the phone…and nothing happened. I had a pretty solid case on the phone and a quick stomp was not enough to do damage. He tried his heel, with little more in the way of success.

Finally, he bent at the knees, squatting down to pick up the phone. He kept his eyes and his gun on me. He rose back up and spiked my phone hard into the concrete floor. That was enough to do the damage and my phone's glass screen shattered, small pieces of plastic flew off, and it looked like pieces of the internal electronic components were damaged.

The phone was ruined, and my recording was stopped.

"Did you really think I was stupid enough to confess to something while you still had your phone?"

I shrugged my shoulders as if to say "maybe."

"Now what?" I asked.

"Now I kill the man who tried to harm Senator McCauley's daughter and become a hero," he confessed.

I reached behind me and pulled out my gun to ensure that did not happen.

59. Verbal Foreplay

Shortly after hanging up with Harris and setting up the meeting I called Omar. While I did not know exactly what Harris had planned, I knew that he could not be trusted and I needed protection.

While I had won my share of hockey fights, fighting a former police officer was another thing altogether. I figured he was armed, as I had seen the gun under his jacket before.

I needed to even the odds.

Omar picked up and I heard a door shut behind him. I figured he was at Ike's and ventured outside.

"Slade," he said, seemingly happy to hear from me.

"You know that favor you owe me?" I asked. "I am cashing it in."

"No 'hi, Omar, how are you?'" he mocked. "No 'how is your day?' You just jump right in to 'I need a favor?'"

"I am in a shitload of trouble and don't have time for verbal foreplay," I said. "I am sorry if I am being a dick, but this is quite literally life and death."

"Oh, shit, you serious?" he asked.

"Yeah, I am serious," I replied. "Ironically enough, I need a gun."

Omar balked for a moment, but when I reminded him of how much trouble I could have gotten if I had gotten caught holding his gun a few weeks back. Before he agreed he wanted to know what it was for. I figured he did not want the full story, but I gave him vague re-cap, stressing I probably just needed it to bluff, but that I was in a lot of trouble.

I did not know if Harris was working alone or when he planned on getting to the parking garage. I could not risk being seen too early, and I did not know if Harris knew my usual haunts. For all I know he knew my every move for months and may have been fully aware of my visitations to Ike's.

I gave Omar the instructions on where to leave the gun and hoped he followed them.

Twenty minutes before I was to meet Harris I pulled my jeep up in front of the Modern Languages Building on campus. In the daytime, there was no way I could leave my Jeep here, but at 10:30 at night it was no problem. I hit the hazard lights and left the car on. I jogged up to the building and went up to the metal newspaper dispenser. It was one of those that opened by pulling on the front window, like an oven.

On the front was a hastily written "out of service" sign, which I had instructed Omar to craft. At least I knew he had been here. I placed the coins into the machine and pulled. For a brief moment, the door seemed to stick, and my heart leaped. Finally, it came loose and I was able to pull it free.

Inside were two copies of the daily paper, I reached underneath and I felt the handgun. I wrapped it up in one of the papers, and carefully took the weapon back to my car. I passed a couple walking together, they were engaged in conversation and never gave me a second look, though my heart was pounding as they walked past.

I got into the car and ejected the clip. It was full. I inspected the gun closer. I was not a "gun-guy" though I had gone to the gun range with my dad and brothers when I was younger and knew the basics. Despite that, on the drive in I watched a few online videos to make sure I knew what I was doing.

The gun Omar kept on him was a Glock 9mm, but this was not the same gun he had me keep during his date. This one was a little heavier, despite being a tad bit smaller. I had assumed he'd just leave me that gun, but apparently, he left me a different firearm. I had to familiarize myself with the differences, the main one being that this one had a traditional safety that had to be on the "off" position in order to fire.

With the clip out I also ejected the shell in the chamber. I knew enough about guns that you always treat them as if they were loaded, but I also had to make sure I knew what the hell I was doing. I pulled the trigger a few times to familiarize myself with what it took to get a shot off. I could not afford to experiment on the fly.

I put the clip back into the gun, I chambered a bullet and I set the gun on the seat next to me.

I drove to the parking garage. I drove up to the third level and parked my Jeep in an isolated corner. Harris' black sedan was already waiting for me. I grabbed the pistol and as I got out of the Jeep I tucked it into the back of my waistband. I hoped that Harris did not see me do it.

I would learn in less than five minutes that he didn't.

50. Belying Bravado

I could tell Harris had not anticipated me pulling a gun on him. He tried to shrug it off, bu his eyes belied his bravado. As I pulled the gun out from behind me his eyes widened and they lingered on the barrel a little too long.

Had my intention been to kill him, he would be dead. Well, he would be dead assuming I hi the target.

"Is that supposed to scare me?" he asked, reverting back to the tough guy routine. "All you did is make it so I don't have to plant a weapon on you. Face it, you are in over your head."

He was right on that point.

"You are not going to do anything with that," he continued, selling the concept to himsel as much as he was taunting me. "What are you going to do, shoot me?"

"If I have to," I said calmly. Two of us could portray a false sense of confidence.

"You don't have the stones," he said with a laugh.

"Are you willing to take that chance?" I replied.

I had played a hunch about Harris and I was right. He specifically told me the kidnappers had sent him word that they had taken Caitlin, but that was obviously not true as she was in Mexico the whole time. That alone was not enough to make me think it was Harris. After all, he could have been duped just as easily as I had been and been tricked into thinking Caitlin was taken.

When you add that to the lie he told me about reporting me to Sgt. Steel, then the evidence pointed to him. Now I had him confirming it.

Since my goal was not to shoot him, I knew I had to keep him talking. The gun gave me leverage, but only for so long.

"So was that the plan, kill me and take the credit for rescuing Caitlin," I asked.

"That is the plan," he said and raised his gun.

I raised mine just as fast. Again, his eyes widened.

"There is a big flaw to your plan," I said. "All you have is my name in a log book, and I have an alibi. Even without the alibi, the evidence is flimsy at best."

He laughed. Hard.

What had I missed?

"You really think I am stupid," he said, this time the bravado was real. "I have you dead to rights. I have a cell phone with threatening texts, as well as texts to a co-conspirator with your fingerprints all over it."

It took me a moment to figure out what he was talking about. In that instant, his hand twitched, but I saw it and I extended my arm to tell him I too could easily shoot.

He was talking about Rachel's phone, or at least the phone I thought was Rachel's. In all my nosiness I had practically fondled it. He was right, my fingerprints would be all over it.

The bigger question was how did he get it? Was Rachel really involved? Was he able to sneak in the room and retrieve it?

Now I really knew I had to keep him talking. I had every instinct to run. I was only about 25 feet from him, not an easy shot, but hardly a shot a capable shooter couldn't make. I considered pacing, but I was worried the movement would spook him or cause me to drop my guard for just a second.

I noticed we both had lowered our gun hands ever so slightly. They don't tell you on television that they are not the lightest thing in the world, they have a little heft, and keeping your arm parallel to the ground is not the easiest thing. Both of us now had our elbows bent, but neither allowed the barrel to leave the other's chest.

"Was that always to plan, to frame me?" I asked, praying he'd want to show off his brilliant plan.

"No that was a happy accident," Harris said.

Some of what follows he told me directly and some I would learn later. I filled in a lot of blanks after that night. Harris was falling out of favor with McCauley. He was analog in a digital age. After missing the scandalous photos about the staffer, he was on thin ice. Thorough, cheaper, more discrete inquiries could be made with a few keystrokes. The need for a bag man and someone who reverted to old school intimidation tactics was less necessary.

Harris had to make himself useful. So he invented the threats to Caitlin.

"My plan was to string it along as long as I could," Harris said. Later McCauley told me although Harris was on retainer, he charged on top of that. The longer the case went, the more he stood to make.

"Soon I realized I had to prove my worth solve the case," Harris said. "I needed a perp."

"So you hired me," I added.

"No, I realized that after you came on board," he said. "Originally I was going to have you find me the perfect candidate to frame, but then you did all the work for me. You're the one who changed your schedule and started dating the roommate. You inserted yourself into her life. I didn't have to frame anyone. You framed yourself."

I knew the end of this was coming soon. I still had a few trump cards to play, but could not play them too early, and definitely could not play them too late. What good is a trump card to a dead man?

"So you'll say I was stalking her," I said. "The only problem is that McCauley knows how involved I am in the case."

"Does he?" Harris asked, giving me the smirk and turning his head ever so slightly. "As far as McCauley knows all you are doing is dropping by to see your old friend every few days and helping me come up with a list of her friends and associates."

He had undersold my "official" involvement in the case so all of my actual legwork would seem to be the act of a stalker, not a plucky young investigator. His smile widened, but I was still mostly focused on the end of his gun.

"He does not know you were stalking his precious daughter," Harris said in a mocking tone, a look of exaggerated shock on his face. "Once I paint the picture of you being a depraved stalker, he won't care that I put a bullet or two into you. He wields a lot of power, even if all the evidence does not point to self-defense."

While he was talking, I ever so slowly took a few steps back. I went from the back rear bumper to the edge of the door. It was still open, where I purposely left it. My back was probably still three-feet from the front of the car, but a lot closer than when we began the dialogue.

"The only problem is that I never actually kidnapped Caitlin," I pointed out. One of my only hopes was to continue to poke holes in his plan, but I had to admit he had covered most of the bases.

"Even as we speak a Policia friend of mine in Mexico is stopping your 'associate' in Mexico," he replied, making air quotes around associate with his empty hand. "They will find him with a phone with messages from you, some of the $10,000 we failed to recover, and one of the guns registered in your name."

Now it was my turn to laugh, but it would be short-lived.

"I don't have any guns registered in my name," I shot back.

"Yes you do," said a familiar voice.

Tariq stepped from the shadows, and suddenly I had two guns trained on me.

61. Welcome to the Gun Show

I would learn most of this later. Tariq was no dummy, and despite a few missteps, he and Harris were several steps ahead of me. Our little verbal jousting matches were often his way of gleaning information from me without my knowledge.

No more so than when we had our little debate on the merits of Thomas "The Hitman" Hearns. While we had a nice little debate about boxing, Tariq could not end the conversation on a civil note. Specifically, he made some gross generalizations about me as a young, white male. While I thought I was just a victim of Tariq's somewhat ironic limited worldview, he was actually digging for information.

He said to me, "You probably like to watch MMA with your bros, while you pound Budweisers, energy drinks and make plans to go to the gun show this weekend."

This was not a random list of insults. He was trying to find out one specific thing…was I going to the gun show?

So when I shot back "and wouldn't know where to find a gun show even if I wanted to go, which I do not" I opened the door for Tariq to further frame me.

Normally Tariq de La Rocca would not be caught dead at a gun show, or anywhere else near guns. Publically he was about as anti-gun as you could get. He did not even want the police armed, and was quick to protest any police incident that even remotely had a whiff of impropriety.

I almost have to laugh at the thought of the wannabe leftist revolutionary milling around a gun show. I am sure that Tariq did not wear his Mao or Che Guevara T-shirt, but that is the only way I can picture him. In my mind's eye, he is roaming the halls of the fairgrounds event center with the face of a communist leader emblazoned on his shirt, amongst the camouflage and Confederate flags.

Apparently, he was able to find a dealer who could not tell the difference between the identity of a 5-foot-8 brown skin man and a 5-foot-11 white guy

Either that or one that did not care.

Tariq borrowed my wallet without my knowledge on at least one occasion and used my ID to purchase a pair of handguns. One was in Harris' car, which he was going to presumably plant on my body after he shot me. The other had already been planted on a former crooked Mexican police officer who had run afoul of a rival drug cartel and was murdered by an even more crooked cop during a dramatic "raid" that prevented the "kidnapping" of Caitlin. Of course, they found this disgraced police officer in a dilapidated apartment next to a cell phone with incriminating text messages from "me", and some of the $10,000.

The phone was a burner, one of two pre-paid cell phones that Tariq bought at a liquor store with my credit card. Again, any identification that was requested was basically ignored. The second was the phone that I found under Rachel's bed.

I did not know any of this at the time. All I knew standing there in the parking garage was that not only did I have to avoid getting shot by Harris, but now I had to avoid getting shot by Tariq.

62. World Conquering Super Villain

The only reason I was still alive was that Harris was almost as startled by Tariq's appearance as I was. He took his eyes off me for a split second to confirm it was Tariq and not a witness, and I used that instant to slip in front of my Jeep, using my vehicle to shield myself from the two men with guns.

Harris tried to take his shot but had not anticipated my sudden movement. His gun did not have a silencer, so he would only get one shot at stopping me. An errant shot would raise an alarm.

I considered firing a round myself to bring witnesses but realized that before anyone could get there to help me he would put me down. Not only would I be dead, but my once fired handgun would give him further credence that it was a matter of self-defense.

My best chance for survival was to keep these guys talking. Hopefully, they did not figure that out.

While I was now a much tougher target to hit, my vision was also lessened. I could see where both men were at, but their subtle movements were now obscured.

"So you guys have been working together the whole time?" I asked.

"I had investigated Tariq when he and Caitlin first started dating," Harris said. "McCauley did not like his baby girl dating someone so politically opposite to his base. He wanted me to get rid of Tariq. Instead, I found an ally."

I turned to Tariq, who had not moved.

"So you are just a pawn," I said. "Let this guy call the shots, and take whatever scraps he gives you."

My plan had shifted again. Now I was not going to only keep them talking long enough to escape, but maybe, just maybe, get them to turn on each other.

"Those 'scraps' will be worth a quarter mil," Harris said.

Since Harris is not a world-conquering supervillain in a movie, he did not actually tell me the final step of the plan. It would come out through the investigation. Harris would kill me but a third member of my crew would get away with the ransom money. Harris really did have e-mails and texts about the kidnapping, including a doctored photo of Caitlin that looked valid enough to warrant believing she had been taken and ransom should be paid. He had access to a large chunk of cash and accessed it in an effort to assure Caitlin's fictitious safe return.

In reality, Tariq and Harris would divvy up some of it. Six figures each, and Harris would be able to continue the investigation looking for the mysterious third kidnapper. It could take months, maybe even years to find this mystery man. Eventually, his police friend in Mexico would need to eliminate another enemy of the cartel and a small amount of the ransom money would be found with a body and the final chapter of the Caitlin Saga would finally be written.

Now I just needed to stay alive and screw up that plan. I would try again to drive the wedge between the two unlikely partners.

"You seem to have everything pinned on be but motive," I said. "Tariq has motive, plus he leaves a better corpse for the media and cops. He's a cop hating revolutionary with a history of causing trouble, while I am just some fresh-faced rich white kid with a clean past."

Harris did not say anything, but I noticed Tariq scowl. Scowl and touch his pocket. It looked like he was canceling a cell phone call. I took that as a sign that I should keep making my case to the detective.

"He has the gambling debt," I said. "He had the access before I came into the picture and best of all advances McCauley's platform and rallies his base. Of course, I'll give you all the credit and tell McCauley what a wonderful mentor you are."

I looked at Tariq. He was not happy. I also noticed he and Harris were creeping ever so slightly apart. They were flanking me and I was running out of time.

After taking a few more steps, Tariq appeared to shut off another call.

"It is tempting," Harris said. "But I already have all of this great evidence planted against you. That, and I know where his skeletons are buried."

They were still moving slowly to get in position, though I noticed that Tariq kept glancing at his front pocket. Harris noticed as well.

"What is it?" Harris growled.

"I don't know, but my phone is blowing up," Tariq answered.

"Shut the damn thing off," Harris said to Tariq.

Tariq pulled his phone out and after glancing at the screen, looked like he had seen a ghost. Harris did not notice, his attention on me.

"Eric, I am tired of this chit-chat, your time is up," he said calmly. "Tariq let's go."

Harris started to move towards me, but Tariq did not.

"Stop," yelled a panicked Tariq. "We're on the Internet. He's broadcasting us all over the Internet."

63. Going Viral

Anna held a wide variety of roles with the hockey team. When she was 12 years old she sold souvenirs and programs. The older she got the more responsibilities she was given. She began helping with marketing and promotions when she was 15. Last year she was given control of the team's social media accounts.

She gave the accounts a snarkiness and sarcasm that attracted a loyal following and began doing short videos that became quite popular. Some of the videos were informative behind the scenes mini-documentaries, some were commercials, and some were Anna reveling in her sexuality, essentially flirting with the viewers (which her uncle hated). The videos led her to start helping with the team's coach's show, and she slowly upgraded the team's audio and video technology.

This season she and two of her really attractive friends began serving as rink girls. Clad in tights and half shirts, they would skate between periods cleaning the ice and throwing out t-shirts to the crowd. Considering that a high percentage of the fans were drunken male college students, you can imagine their popularity. Anna created social media accounts for the rink girls and within weeks they began rivaling the popularity of the team itself.

Not to be outdone, Anna also began utilizing her personal accounts, blurring the line between her personal life and her life as a part of the hockey organization. I had only begun to learn that in real life her flirtatiousness, and apparent promiscuity, was mostly an act, but you would not know it from her social media account. She posted a number of pictures of herself clad only in oversized hockey jerseys and nothing else (though she claims she had plenty of clothes on underneath), but it was the picture of her wearing ice skates, hockey gloves and a bikini that set the local hockey internet community ablaze.

Now that we were spending time together I understood this was not just her craving attention, but she was marketing herself. She talked about "creating her brand" and looked at ways to expand her reach. While I was a tad jealous that everyone could see these photos, I saw the genius in what she was doing.

Needless to say, she had plenty of admirers, including one local television sports anchor, and several athletes at the school. She always said she was exploiting these fans to bolster her reach and influence, and tonight I was hoping to exploit them to save my life and trap Harris.

We discussed how we would finish this on the drive into town. My original plan was to try and record Harris on my cell phone and subtly send the file to the police. Anna said it was too risky, that it could take way too long for Steel or someone else to even notice the e-mail, much less act on it.

She had the idea to broadcast the confrontation live, but I wondered if anyone would watch it. She assured me they would. As we drove into town she sent out messages to tune into both the official hockey team accounts and her personal accounts about a major announcement. We stopped at a rest stop and took a few suggestive pictures as well as a flirty video publicizing the announcement. She ended it by leaning into the camera, showing off a little cleavage, and blowing a kiss to the world.

"I'll see you tonight," she said giggling and giving a little wave. I did not know if it was going to work, but I knew I would tune in if I was watching at home.

We stopped at the rink and got all the equipment we would need. We mounted a small internet camera on the back of my Jeep. It was black and blended pretty well with the top of the tail light. She attached a small microphone to it and I taped it down so it was almost invisible as the wire ran down the side of the square light, under the tire mounted to the back and down to the bumper.

We tested it out and voices were reasonably clear up to 40 feet away. If I could hear it with my ears, I could hear it with the microphone.

We realized we had one shot at this, so we had to be sure we captured the encounter. We could not risk having the sound cut out, or not being able to park in a space that could capture Harris with the camera. I did not like the idea of Anna being there, but I had no choice.

At the rink, I donned a wireless mic. We put the small battery pack in my back pocket and it essentially looked like my wallet, save for the small wire emanating from it. We ran the wire up the inside of my shirt, over my shoulder and clipped it to the hood of my sweatshirt. It would have been noticeable with good lighting, but the parking garage would be dark with the occasional very bright, harsh orange floodlights.

Anna would find a vantage point and shoot the encounter with a second camera, this one linked to the wireless mic clipped to my sweatshirt. This camera would be streaming the proceedings to a second internet account.

I tried my best to talk her out of coming with me, but she was not having any of it. She was not going to allow me to go it alone.

We could not turn the camera mounted to the car on too early, nor did we want Harris to see us. I had no idea what his plan was, but I would not have been surprised if he was watching my entry into the garage. We had to use a little subterfuge, so Anna drove ahead early, parked in relative close proximity to where I would meet Harris and then grabbed her backpack and took off in the direction of the library.

As I approached the garage she was ready. At the exact moment I prepared to turn into the garage, she stepped off of the curb, forcing me to slam on my breaks. I honked at her and she pounded my hood. I had to admit her performance was good because I was worried she dented it.

"Watch where the fuck you are going," she screamed at me, as she extended both middle fingers. She continued to flip me off as she walked along the side of the Jeep. She kept yelling at me and kicked the rear tire for effect. As she worked her way to the back, she pressed the button on the mounted camera, turning it on. Once the green power light came on, she slapped the ack window, my cue that the camera was on and we were broadcasting. If you were not paying ttention, it looked like she was furious at me almost hitting her.

With the camera on and her signal to me, she walked to the stairs on the opposite side of the arage from our meeting spot.

Prior to leaving for the garage, she reminded all of her followers, and all of the team's ollowers to tune in. She also called the sports anchor personally to invite him to tune in and uggested his news editor might want to watch.

I sent out a group text to all of my friends, as well as a text and e-mail to my father and AcCauley himself. I tried Steel, but he did not pick up. We sent him an e-mail with a link to the roadcast, as well as several other members of the University Police Department.

We went live as soon as I got out of the vehicle. I reached behind to flip on the mic, with lso let me check to make sure the gun was in place. We went live with 7 people watching and hree dropped off as soon as they saw that Anna was not on the screen.

When the guns finally came out there were 50 people watching. At that point, the television tation decided to link to the feed. One of their news reporters called the police to ask for their eaction, another called the network.

Three people watching called 911, while 120 either liked or forwarded the video feed. While should be glad the video spread, I am still concerned that 117 more people felt it as prudent to nake sure their friends saw it than to alert the authorities about multiple gunmen on a college ampus.

Thirty seconds after Tariq said, "We're on the Internet. He's broadcasting us all over the nternet" the sirens began to become audible.

That's when I knew I had a pretty good chance of making it out of this alive.

64. Fueled by Animal Protein and Rage

I had two men with guns pointed at me with only my Jeep serving as a barrier between me and their bullets. Harris and Tariq were moving into position and soon I would have to turn my back to one to face the other and that is when I was probably dead.

During this maneuvering, Tariq's phone appeared to keep ringing. Eventually, at the behest of Harris he pulled it out to shut the device off, that is when he not only learned my plan but learned it was working.

"Stop," yelled a panicked Tariq. "We're on the Internet. He's broadcasting us all over the Internet."

"What do you mean?" Harris shouted, confusion creeping into his cadence.

"Three of my friends said they are watching us on the internet," Tariq said. "They can see and hear us."

The panic increased in Tariq's voice.

"He's fucking playing everything for everyone to hear," Tariq screamed, his voice breaking. "They are going to know what we did."

That is when I first heard the faint sounds of the sirens.

"How is he doing it?" Harris screamed. "I smashed his cell phone."

"How the fuck should I know?" Tariq answered.

The sirens grew louder, and now I could hear some voices "whooing." It turned out students were not only watching, but some in nearby dorms were coming to the area. They were making loud noises in an attempt to get the microphone to pick it up. They wanted to hear themselves on the broadcast, never mind lives might be at stake.

I could also hear Harris' phone ringing. The noise seemed to surprise him until he realized it was his own phone.

The sirens were very loud now and I could see the faint glow of red and blue lights. Harris pulled out his phone, glanced at the screen and spiked it into the ground.

For the first time, his gun was no longer trained on me and he put it up to his head. He then shook his head "no" and pointed it back at me and fired. My mind did not process what was happening until after it was done. There was a booming noise, and then a second sound about two feet over where my head had been. I was now sprawled out on the ground, a maneuver I made without a conscious thought.

I looked up and there was a hole in the wall behind me. I was fortunate that Harris had panicked and missed so poorly because there was no way I was dodging that bullet.

After missing me, Harris turned around and started to run. He was almost to the edge of the parking lot aisle when a black pickup truck rounded the corner going a little too fast and collided with Harris who never saw it coming. There was an awful noise, that was louder than you would think a human body and a metal truck should make, and Harris let out an awful scream.

It was at that point I realized Tariq was running away in the opposite direction. The police cars were almost here and I considered staying put, but the thought of Tariq getting away was too much and I gave chase.

He was already to the stairwell before I was fully on my feet and I nearly tripped before I took my first step.

I hit the stairs and took them two at a time, somehow I avoided falling, and actually felt like I had made up a bit of distance when I emerged from the parking garage. He was sprinting across the street towards some storefronts and I followed without hesitation. If there had been any traffic I would have met the same fate as Harris, as I did not look to see if the coast was clear.

Tariq rounded the businesses and headed down an alleyway. My knee was fully healed and despite my recent lack of participation in organized sports, I was still a somewhat well-conditioned athlete. I was pretty sure Tariq had not stepped foot in a gym. I am sure they were racist or sexist or promoted unhealthy body images and the sexualization of the female form, or some other horrible offense.

Tariq liked to smoke a lot of weed and was one of those ultra-thin vegans. He was lean and healthy, but hardly in-shape for a long run. Fueled by animal protein and rage, I had easily made up half the distance on him. I may not have been in the shape I was before the injury, but I was still faster than he was.

I could hear him breathing, practically wheezing, and I knew that he was tiring. My adrenalin had fully kicked in and I felt like I could run forever.

He turned onto a residential side street and I guessed I was now about 40 feet behind. Without warning, he changed directions and bolted down another alley. His deceptive move did not impact me and I was able to navigate the shift in his movement and proceed down the alley as well.

As I rounded the building I saw that he had stopped. He had the gun drawn, but his chest was heaving so hard that he could not keep it steady.

I slid to a stop and realized that I still had my gun in my hand. While I was winded, I was not gasping for air like he was. I trained the gun on him and we stood for a few seconds in silence.

He straightened up, and it looked like he wanted to say something, but he could still not form words. Instead, he tried to smile, though it looked more like a grimace.

"Fuck…"

We both fired before he could say "you."

65. With Little Remorse or Pity

Apparently, I was a better shot than Tariq as mine hit, while his just missed. To be fair, his was closer to where he was probably aiming, but I was still standing.

He was not.

His shot passed to the right of me. It actually got a pretty good piece of my sleeve, putting a big hole in my sweatshirt, but failed to connect with any part of my body. The sweatshirt was toast, but that was a small price to pay.

Although I was aiming at his chest I hit him in the thigh. Since he did not have a lot of meat on him, it did a ton of damage to his leg. One of the paramedics would tell me later on that the bullet shattered his femur and caused a lot of vascular damage. He would need multiple surgeries.

"He'll likely walk with a limp the rest of his life," I was told.

I looked down at Tariq with little remorse or pity. He was screaming, a high pitch whine convinced he was dying. There was a ton of blood, and it seemed to me the leg was at an odd angle, though it was hard to be sure since he spun a bit before he crumpled to the ground.

"Don't let me bleed out," he screeched. He reached up his hand so that I could console him, but I ignored it and just looked down at him, probably taking a little too much pleasure from his misery.

Sirens drew louder and I could see their lights reflecting off of the walls and fences of the alley. I heard two police cars screech to a halt.

I threw the gun down and dropped to my knees before I was instructed. I then put my hands on my head and waited. One of the officers shoved me to the dirt and cuffed me.

"He's in bad shape," I said calmly, trying not to wince at the knee in my back.

I heard one of the police officers call for an ambulance, while I was being dragged to my feet and shoved towards a squad car. One of them read me my rights, then put me in the back of the car.

"My name is Eric Slade, I am the one being threatened in the video," I said, hoping they knew what I was talking about. Considering the blank stares I was getting, they did not.

For the most part, my face was obscured on the video. The video camera mounted to my car was next to me and did not have me in the frame. The camera Anna held was mostly behind me, so other than the side of my face, there was not much you could discern from the video about my identity.

They drove me back to the parking garage. We rounded the corner and I noticed the crowd in the area had grown to several hundred, most with their phones out recording. Police officers were keeping them across the street from the parking structure, but that did not seem to numb their enthusiasm. They seemed to be having a lot of fun and making a party out of it.

They pulled up to the curb and one officer hopped out. The other one turned to me.

"What the hell happened?" he asked. "We just got a call about multiple gunmen."

I tried to figure out where to start.

"I decided to broadcast my potential murder on the internet," I said.

I could feel the adrenaline rush waning. Suddenly I was exhausted. All I wanted to do is slump down in the back seat and sleep.

The police officer was probably in his early 30's. He was lean, with short, shaved blonde hair. If I had to guess he had a military background.

He just stared at me, confused.

"They were trying to frame me for something, and were going to kill me," I said. "This was the only way I could think to stop them."

The other police officer returned to the car. He was a bit older and stockier but still looked like he could handle himself. It was pretty obvious he hit the gym several times a week. The entire perimeter of the parking garage was already wrapped in yellow police tape. We ducked under the tape and then ventured up the stairs to the level where my encounter with Harris had occurred.

Climbing stairs while your arms are handcuffed behind you is not the easiest thing. I don't recommend it. It is hard to balance when your arms are stuck behind your back, doubly hard climbing the stairs.

We emerged from the stairwell and everything was just like I left it, except there were now three police cars and an ambulance parked up there. Red and blue lights now illuminated the building, drowning out the harsh yellow lights.

Harris was still down in front of the black truck, only now there were several paramedics tending to him. He was already strapped to a yellow plastic spine board, with his head and neck immobilized. There was a larger gurney next to him, on which he would be loaded when it was time to take him to the hospital.

Steel saw me and waved for the officers to bring me over.

"Take the cuffs off," he indicated and the skinny officer did just that.

I tried hard not to rub my wrists like they do in the movies, but I wound up doing just that. I felt so cliché.

"I guess you were telling the truth," Steel said. He was wearing a white dress shirt, but no longer had a tie. An older man walked up behind him. He wore a golf shirt, tucked into khakis.

"Eric, this is Chief Eslinger," Steel said.

The chief shook my hand.

"Are you alright son?" the Chief asked.

"Yeah, I think so," I replied. "I am still trying to process everything."

"We'll take you down to the station in a little bit to sort through all of this," Steel said. "But someone wants to see you."

I was not sure where she had been up until that moment, but a female officer walked up with Anna. She jogged over and gave me a huge kiss. Had I been a little more self-aware at this moment I would have been embarrassed, but I had no time to consider who was watching. I was just glad she was there.

I saw Harris loaded into the ambulance and had no pity for him. I was disappointed he was not dead. I wanted to shake the hand of the driver of the black truck, but he was being interviewed by the police.

After the ambulance drove off, I was escorted back down to the police car and driven the quarter mile to the on-campus police station. I assumed I would give a statement and leave, but I was about to learn that my night was just beginning.

66. Admiration and Concern

Y ou don't know how reliant you are on your cellular phone until it is destroyed by a would-be assailant who was in the act of framing you for the kidnapping of someone who was not even missing. I did not have any phone numbers. I could call my dad's house phone, but he was still out of the country.

Luckily they let me log onto the internet and I was able to look up my contacts and phone my father and leave him a voicemail to let him know what was happening. I also shot an e-mail to McCauley, explaining what happened and to let him know Caitlin was safe.

I gave an initial statement to an officer and they explained to me that I was not free to go just yet. They still had to sort through what happened and see if any charges would be filed. I was a little surprised that there was even a chance I could be charged with something, but I was not overly worried about it. I assumed once Steel got back, he could clear things up.

I was sitting on a bench facing several desks. A few officers were there, despite the fact it was the middle of the night. At some point, I could tell they had started to watch the video. The same officer who came to Rachel's dorm to take the report of the stolen laptops came up to me and gave me a look that was a mix of admiration and concern.

"You just don't know when to stop," he said giving me a fist bump. "You are either stupid or one crazy."

"Probably both," I said and "Officer McHotty" laughed.

A second older officer slowly shook his head and said: "that took balls."

I guess I had their seal of approval.

Eventually, they led me into an office and after a few minutes, Anna came in. She gave me a big kiss and explained that she had also given a statement and was told to stick around. She had planned on just going home, but the officers stressed that she should call her parents, and eventually she called her mother and stepdad and they were on their way.

We sat next to each other and she held my hand and put her head on my shoulder. She was looking at her phone and I saw her perk up.

"The video has blown up," she said, excitedly. "Thousands of people have viewed it and several news agencies are asking for permission to air it."

I could tell she was happy, but the last thing I wanted was to deal with this anymore. I just wanted this to be over and to get on with my life. I had fences to mend, and relationships to repair. For the first time, I just wanted to be a normal student at school and little else for a few weeks.

I must have drifted off because what seemed like just a few minutes later there was a knock on the door. It was a new police officer that we had not seen. He informed us that Anna's family was here. The officer let Anna's mother and stepfather into the room.

Anna and her mother looked a lot alike. Her mother was a stunning woman in her early 50's. She was wearing a very nice warm-up suit, that clung to her fit body, though she was leaner and less athletically built than her daughter. Her hair was lighter and shorter than Anna's, a more conservative, yet modern hairstyle.

I had seen her around the rink a few times, her real estate business was a sponsor of the team, but we had never formally met.

Her stepdad was a good looking guy. He was tall and fit, very tan, with short slightly graying hair, and a goatee to match.

Anna stood up.

"Uh, mom, James, this is my boyfriend Eric," she said, sheepishly.

Her mother just glared at me and I gave her a half-hearted smirk. Meeting a parent of someone you are sleeping with is never easy, add the drama of a gunfight and potential criminal charges, and it was nearly impossible to make a good impression.

Finally, her stepfather stepped forward and extended his hand.

"James, Anna's stepfather," he said as we shook hands. "Thanks for keeping her safe."

Anna's mother gave her husband a dirty look, then regained her composure and offered her hands.

"I am Anna's mother Catherine," she said coldly. "I am glad you two are okay."

Anna gave me a peck on the cheek, then left with her family. After the door closed I heard her mother exclaim "what were you thinking?"

They said it would be a few hours until the crime scene was fully processed and that I would need to stick around a while longer. I had been here a few hours already and that seemed like a long time just to give a few statements, but I did not know what else to do. I tried my father again but got the voicemail.

I fell asleep in one of the chairs, pulling a second one over to put my feet on. At some point in my slumber, I put the hood of my sweatshirt on and pulled it over my eyes. It was not the most comfortable way to sleep, but I was too tired to care.

The sun was up when Steel woke me up.

"Your lawyer is here."

My first instinct was to say that I did not have a lawyer, but I knew better. Of course, my father would send a lawyer, whether I needed one or not. Turns out I did.

Steel walked me to a small meeting room and motioned for me to sit down. A few minutes later my lawyer walked in and extended a hand.

"Miranda Lacy-Collins," she said. "Your father called me."

She was in her mid 40's, dressed in a navy suit with a skirt, a white shirt underneath. She wore black heels, nothing too tall but enough to give her some extra height, and carried a black leather briefcase. She had an auburn bob haircut, that ended just before it hit her shoulders. She had a serious look on her face, which I gathered was her default setting. She had some deep frown lines, probably from near constant scowling, but was otherwise pleasant to look at.

She wasted no time getting to work. Before I could sit back down she had a legal pad and pen out.

"Fill me in on everything from your perspective," she demanded.

I proceeded to tell her everything that happened. She took copious notes, asking just a few questions along the way.

"What have you told them?" she asked.

"Pretty much everything I just told you," I replied, she winced when I said that.

"That was not smart," she countered.

"I didn't think I was in trouble," I said. "I thought I was the victim."

"Even the victims can be charged with a crime," she said.

She asked about whether I was read my rights, and I said I was, but that was before they knew who I was.

"It does not matter," she said. "You were made aware of your rights."

She asked me a few more questions, then departed. Twenty minutes later she returned.

"Initially they are going to charge you with several crimes, but I am not overly worried," she said. "In the end, you are the victim here and you were trying to protect a United States Senator's daughter. The optics would not be good if they threw the book at you."

"Then why charge me at all?" I asked.

"Leverage," she said. "They will use this to ensure your full cooperation in all phases of their case. They also have to make sure you are telling the truth. If they find your motives are less than pure, then they can say they have done their due diligence."

Out in the hall, I could hear a small commotion, less than a minute later my father barged in. To my surprise, he gave me a big hug. Then grabbed me by the shoulders.

"Are you okay?" he said.

"I'm fine," I said, the weariness returning.

We reviewed everything once again. He was angry that I was in the position. I think he was angrier with Harris first, and me second, but focused all his anger on the police and prosecutors.

Shortly after I was processed McCauley showed up. He tried to throw his weight around a bit, but initially, it did no good. Later his influence would prove to be more valuable.

Around lunchtime, McCauley pulled me aside.

"I am so sorry this happened to you," he said. "But thank God you were there. You saved Caitlin."

"I am not sure they were actually going to do anything," I said.

"Well now they won't get a chance to, will they?" he added. "I am in your debt. Whatever you need, let me know."

The last favor I called in got me in this mess, to begin with, but it likely also kept me alive.

"We will get this taken care of I promise," he said.

Eventually, he did. It took a few weeks, but eventually, I was charged with a misdemeanor weapons charge and had to pay a fine of $500, which McCauley paid for me.

Even when we left the jail that day, several of the charges had been dropped or lessened. Walking to the car my father got a call, which he took and looked displeased the entire duration.

"It is the University," he said. "They are trying to expel you."

67. Goodbye Eric Slade

The University of Arizona had a zero-tolerance policy when it comes to firearms and that is what I had to answer for. Although I would have my time in court, so to speak, due process did not work the same way it did in the judicial system. I was not yet expelled, or even suspended, but I was kicked out of the dorms.

McCauley vowed to fight the eviction, but I did not want to rock the boat and decided to abide by that decision. My father offered to put me up in a hotel, but Omar insisted I stay at his place and that small bit of near-normalcy appealed to me.

I put most of my stuff in storage and brought a couple of bags over to Omar's apartment, which was a few blocks away from Ike's house. Omar told me that it was less than five minutes door to door.

Omar's place was a pretty typical University area apartment. It was in good repair, but showing its age. The building was probably built during the enrollment boom of the 1970's and refurbished in the late 90's.

It was sparsely furnished, as Omar spent most of his time at Ike's. He had an old couch and a mismatched recliner. His 55" television and multiple gaming systems sat on a particle board entertainment center that would probably get left behind if he ever chose to move. On the wall, he had framed posters of "Scarface", "Enter the Dragon" and the Wu-Tang Clan, and the eyes of Al Pacino, Bruce Lee and eight rappers seemed to always be on me.

His kitchen was visible from the living room. The top of his fridge was full of cereal boxes, and his kitchen counter was covered in bottles of bodybuilding and sports supplements.

I made myself home, rolling out a brand new sleeping bag on the couch and laying down a pillow and comforter. I hoped I would be back in the dorm in a week, but knew I may also be looking at my last days of being a college student.

I wasn't there long before Jenna came over. According to Omar, they were now a serious couple. She was wearing short shorts and a top, both showing off her curves that Omar seemed to really appreciate. She brought a tray of brownies as a housewarming gift of sorts and Omar broke out some beers.

"Who knew you were such a bad boy?" Jenna queried a few beers and a few brownies in. "I guess for once I am dating one of the nice ones. I never had you pegged for trouble."

Apparently, Omar failed to tell Jenna about his job as a bodyguard/enforcer, or the fact that it was his gun that I used to get into so much trouble. She apparently did not know or did not care that just a few years ago he was considered the dirtiest player in the Pac-12.

McCauley pledged his support and wanted to get out in front of the story. While he certainly had a political motivation for wanting to create a pro-Eric narrative, he also thought it might help my case. The lawyer disagreed, and when he finally held a press conference I stood in the background as he thanked myself, as well as local law enforcement. Caitlin and Anna were front and center, two pretty, heroic girls flanking the Senator. It was a good photo op, but other than putting a positive spin on a negative story, he really did not politicize it. That impressed me a bit.

Since I wanted to be in the shadows, we pushed Anna to the forefront and she loved it. We spun the narrative to make her the real hero of the story. We correctly said it was her idea to broadcast the encounter, and played up the danger she was in while trying to protect her boyfriend.

She went on a few cable news shows but had her big break out on a comedy news show. She was her typical flirty, engaging self. She showed off her brains and her quick wit. The host ate it up, though her pretty face had to help.

"I assume you can't major in conspiracy thwarting, so what do you want to do after college?" the host asked.

"I want your job," she said laughing, her ever charming laugh.

This summer she will intern on the show and I would not be shocked if big things did not come her way. After her television appearance, a professional photographer offered to do a photo shoot, and the photos of her with a video camera seemed to fit nicely on her social media pages, though they were not as steamy as her bikini photos.

I met with the lawyer a few times. At this stage I was still facing charges, though more and more it was becoming apparent they would get reduced. Since the proceedings with the University were not of the legal variety, she could not represent me, but she could advise me how to present my case and coached me on what to say and what not to say.

She told me that both Tariq and Harris were expected to make recoveries, but neither would be the same. Tariq's leg was severely damaged, and Harris suffered some grave internal injuries.

Lacy-Collins told me that they were going to throw the book at Harris. Since he threatened a United States Senator and did things over state boundaries, as well as international borders, he would be facing a mix of state and federal charges.

They probably did not need Tariq's help, but she cautioned me that he would most likely be offered a deal to testify against Harris. His testimony would be the final nails in the case's coffin. He would likely see prison time, but it would not be a long stint.

Two days after being released from jail Volpe called. He was surprisingly cheery. I assumed he would hate me, but apparently, I was still seen as something as an asset by the Democrats. They felt this whole incident reflected poorly on McCauley and the type of person he would hire.

Volpe offered to keep my spot on the campaign, even though there was no real tangible evidence the Caitlin Incident impacted his public perception at all. Two weeks after and his approval rating had only dropped 0.5%. In the scheme of things, it was a minuscule drop, but to the Democrats, it was a shot across the bow. To the Republicans, it was a best-case scenario considering how bad things could have been since one of his own employees not only tried to fake a kidnapping and extort money but was seen all over the internet trying to kill me.

Karen and Landon were not as forgiving. Karen's hatred of Caitlin and Landon's hatred for McCauley could not reconcile my working for the family and the few times we ran into each other they were cold.

A few hours after Volpe called, Jessie Griffin called. She told me she would not be running against McCauley but would look at returning to the state legislature or even making a House run.

"Your taste in booze may be terrible, but I get a good vibe from you," she said. "I looked into what you did for McCauley and I am impressed. As I delve deeper into this political quagmire I may need your help, if you are interested that is."

I told her I was. Despite the outcome, I had actually enjoyed the investigation part of all of this and thought it could be interesting to help someone I felt I could admire.

"I'll be in touch," she concluded.

Although I was calling Omar's place home, I was trying not to spend too much time there. I did not want to disrupt his life too much. I was also trying to avoid stirring up too much trouble by being seen on campus. I would go to class, then depart quickly. I did a lot of studying at area restaurants.

I had lunch a few days a week with Chuck. That might have been the toughest part of all of this, no longer living with my best friend. I still managed to see a lot of Anna, though her roommates seemed to be wary of me and it was awkward when I visited her.

My father and McCauley had spent a lot of time in Tucson since the incident in the parking garage, but as my hearing drew nearer, they set up shop in town. I met them a few times at their hotel, a luxury resort with a world-class golf course, but today we met near campus because of my class schedule. We had lunch at the same faux-British pub I originally met Karen at for lunch and I decided to stay behind and do some reading before my next class. Somehow I decided it would be a good idea to consume a pitcher of beer while doing my reading.

I was well into my second glass of beer when Caitlin arrived. She sat down across from me on one of the outdoor benches.

She was continuing her evolution of de-hippie-fying that had begun at the conclusion of spring break. Her make-up was a little more noticeable, nothing outlandish, but considering she went make-up free the past few months, the difference was now striking.

Her hair was brushed, pulled back in the ponytail that showed off her features. She wore denim shorts that displayed her long legs and a plain t-shirt that was also flattering.

"My dad said you would be here," she said, taking a long swallow of my beer.

McCauley had dropped by the dorm to check in on her and told her that I might be at the bar. A waitress came by and brought her a glass to share my pitcher. She never checked Caitlin's ID.

"Thanks for risking your life for me," she said. "I am sorry that all of this is happening to you."

She told me that she was unhappy that her father kept her in the dark, though she appreciated my role in trying to keep her safe.

"It was oddly fun," I explained. "Well, the amateur detective part, not the being framed and almost killed part."

She laughed and poured herself a beer.

"I also didn't like having to deal with Tariq, and that was before he tried to shoot me," I said.

Caitlin laughed again, something I am not sure I had seen her do a whole lot over the past few months.

"He was kind of an asshole," she admitted.

She explained that she was first attracted to him because she admired his conviction, and liked the idea of dating someone who was the polar opposite of her father. She had added that she had begun to have more and more doubts about him the past few weeks. He seemed to enjoy material things more and more. While he had no money, he was more than willing to suggest expensive meals or outings and have Caitlin pay for it.

"If he did not piss off my dad so much, I probably would have broken up with him," she said. "After spring break I almost did it a few times, but never pulled the trigger."

She winced at her choice of words.

"He did," I joked. She groaned more than laughed, but mixed in a little of both.

"And to think I was starting to like having you around," Caitlin said.

We sat in silence a moment, watching people walk past. I had a class in 20 minutes but had already decided not to go.

"How's Rachel?" I finally asked.

"Not good," Caitlin answered. "She spends a lot of time at her other friends' room. I hardly see her. I think she blames me, at least partially."

She took another long swallow and refilled her glass.

"She really liked you, and this blindsided her," Caitlin said.

"I really liked her, but when I thought she was trying to frame me, I…" I paused. "I messed up."

It was my turn for a big sip and a refill.

"I was so mad, so hurt, that I…I just did not care if I hurt her."

After my night in jail, I tried to call Rachel, but she would not reply. Tracey let Chuck know that she had learned of Anna's involvement in the recording of the confrontation in the garage, and had correctly deduced that we were involved. She incorrectly surmised that we had been together for some time.

"I guess she hates me," I said.

"I think she hates both of us," Caitlin corrected.

She told me that Rachel was going to move back to New Jersey at the end of the semester. Caitlin finished her second beer.

"Don't be too hard on yourself," she said. "You may not realize it, but you are a good guy."

She stood up and walked over to me.

"Thanks again," she said, giving me a peck on the cheek.

She walked down the small set of stairs from the patio seat we were at. She paused at the exit of the restaurant, a small gate that led to the sidewalk, but never turned around. She simply raised her arm, turned her palm towards me and waved.

"Goodbye Eric Slade," she said. "Don't be a stranger."

And with that, she walked off. I returned to my beer but lost all interest in studying. I had an expulsion hearing to worry about.

68. The Verdict

Now

And with that, I finished telling my story to the tribunal. The room was in utter silence, hanging on my every word. In reality, my story pretty much ended with the incidents at the parking garage, and I did not go into as much detail about my personal life and left a lot of details pretty sparse in an effort to protect people.

The tribunal really pressed to learn where I got the gun, but I was able to keep any mention of Omar, or Ike's operation a secret, except to say I learned that Tariq had a lot of gambling debt.

Following my story, the tribunal asked a few questions, then excused me. I found a seat in the crowd and then had to watch as several other people had to also give statements including Chuck, Anna, Caitlin, and Rachel.

Most of their testimony was centered around whether or not I had a gun previous to that day. Anna had to give a more detailed account of what went down in the garage.

After they testified and answered questions, they asked for character witnesses and this is where Senator McCauley finally used his influence, though he used his powers of persuasion and excellent verbal abilities more than his status as a United States Senator to make his point. He was trying to tug heartstrings more than he was trying to pull strings.

After everyone was done, one of the professors spoke up.

"We will take a break to discuss the facts you all presented and the come back to render our verdict,"

The recess began and several people left the room, but the rest of us did not know what to do. I had no idea how long it might take. For all I know they could come back in five minutes, or we could be here for hours.

Chuck came up to me and gave me and gave me a half hug, half chest bump. It really wasn't his style, it was a little bit too much of a "bro move" but a full hug or a handshake did not seem quite appropriate.

His testimony was brief. He made a quick statement to my character, then answered a handful of questions, most of them involving whether he had seen me in possession of a weapon, or whether he had ever seen me behave in a violent manner.

One of the professors asked him if he had ever seen me in a hockey fight. This was funny for a pair of reasons. First, was the fact that despite being my best friend, he had never seen one of my hockey games. Chuck was not a sports fan and had no real reason to come see me play. In theory, he would have come out to a game if a girl was interested, but Chuck's romantic interests were more poetry reading and wine types, rather than hockey and beer types.

The second reason it was funny was I was a goalie, and goalies rarely fight, though as I mentioned once before I did get into a scrum with another goalie back in juniors, but it just does not happen at the collegiate level unless all hell is breaking loose.

Anna was keeping her distance. While we were together, we thought it best not to flaunt things since a lot of this decision would come down to how the three judges felt about me. They already knew I had dated Rachel, and wound up with Anna, they did not need to see me flaunting my infidelity.

Anna and her family did sit near mine. Twenty-four hours before the hearing we had a last strategy session, and afterwards, her mother and stepfather, my father and mother, and the two of us all had dinner. While Anna's mother was still not a fan, her stepfather and my father found a common interest in fine dining, travel, and golf. It seemed as if they both had played the same little-known course in North Carolina, that was a "hidden gem."

Before he had landed back in the United States my father had reached out to my mother. She was in Montana, learning about nature photography from a world famous photojournalist. It took her two days to get the message, but she was touching down in Tucson eight hours after finally talking to my father.

At first, my mother was livid, blaming my father for getting me in the mess. I assured her that this mess was my own doing. I did not have a lot of time to spend with her, and frankly, I was still a little bitter at our lack of contact the past few months.

Dinner was awkward at first between her and my father, but he started asking her about the photography. They were not only civil the rest of the night, but almost friendly.

Standing there talking to Chuck and my family, Anna walked by, she reached out and touched my hand. Her touch lingered and she slid her hand down mine until just our pinkies were touching. We linked pinkies for just a second before she walked off.

Anna had to speak for longer than Chuck. Without getting into the details of our hooking up, she told the story about how she accompanied me to Bisbee and then helped with the recording of the incident.

They grilled her on the gun. She had to explain multiple times that I did not have the gun to begin with. She was asked to describe my call to Omar several times, but like me, she did not give up his name. While I just avoided the subject, Anna simply said she did not know who I got the gun from, only that I called someone to arrange the drop.

Rachel's testimony was strange. She gave a very brief statement. Nothing she said was incorrect, and she actually said some good things about me, but her delivery was very cold and detached. I could not blame her, and in fact, I almost expected her to say something negative, but to her credit, she did not let her scorn distort the facts.

Where the testimony got very strange is how the members of the tribunal treated her. They spent several minutes grilling her in her involvement. They really wanted to make sure that she was not involved. Even though I had cleared her of wrongdoing, and the police never considered her a suspect, the tribunal was not as sure. They asked her if she knew Harris, what her relationship was with Tariq, even if she had any reason to suspect my involvement in the investigation.

While I realized that it was Tariq who planted the cell phone under Rachel's bed and later took it back, they did not seem to make that connection and asked her three different ways about the phone. Her testimony, which should have taken 15 minutes, became a 45-minute inquisition.

I felt horrible for her and came very close to saying something. I whispered to my father whether I should intervene, and he said it could only hurt me.

Rachel did not return to the room after speaking to the tribunal.

I was back inside talking to my family when the three judges came out and took their seats.

"If there is anyone left outside, could we please let them know we are ready to proceed?"

Less than five minutes later we were ready. The crowd had thinned a bit, apparently more people were interested in my story than my fate.

Finally, they began.

The Vice President for Student Affairs began.

"We have reviewed the facts of the case and although there are some truly unique circumstances, we cannot ignore that you put yourself and others in harm's way," he said. "It is our jobs as educators to keep the students on our campus safe, which is why we have a zero tolerance policy regarding firearms."

I did not like what I was hearing.

"Though your intentions were noble, and maybe even necessary, we cannot overlook the fact that you not only brought a gun onto campus but discharged said weapon," he continued. "In addition, you knew there were dangerous parties on our campus, also armed, and did not immediately alert the authorities.

"Therefore it is the finding of this panel, that Eric L. Slade is to be expelled from the University of Arizona, effectively immediately, and will not be allowed on the campus, or any University property, for one calendar year," he concluded. "At that time you may apply for reinstatement."

And like that, I was no longer a student at the University of Arizona.

69. Sunset

The proceeding had taken the bulk of the day, so when we emerged from the building the sun was setting, treating us to one of the patented Arizona sunsets. I was in no mood to enjoy the pink, orange, and yellow watercolor sky.

I should have been upset, but was mostly numb.

My father was livid, and Senator McCauley was equally irate.

"We'll fight this," my father said. "We'll get the best lawyers money can buy to overturn this decision."

"My entire legal team is at your disposal," McCauley said. "I'll put pressure on the Board of Regents. Hell, I will get the governor involved."

I turned to these two men who wanted nothing but to help me.

"It's okay," I said. "Maybe this is for the best."

My father and McCauley heard me but were still creating a plan of attack. My mother was chiming in, wondering if we could use the media to put pressure on the school to let me back in.

"Seriously," I said with more force. "It's okay. After all of this, maybe the best thing for me is to take a break from school."

I had their attention now.

"I've never been the most motivated of students and maybe I need to take this time off to get my priorities straight and figure out what I want to do with my life," I said.

My mother and father started to protest, but I stopped them.

"I will take this time off to explore things, discover my real passions other than hockey," I added. "Maybe I will discover what I really want to do and return to school. Maybe my calling lies away from education. Who knows?"

My father did not look happy, but he did not say anything. My mother seemed to understand what I was saying, and in a way, she could relate.

Things were quiet and tense for a moment. It was McCauley who broke the silence.

"Eric, my family is in your debt," he said. "If you need a job, or a reference, or even someone to open up some doors and make some calls, you don't hesitate to ask."

I shook his hand.

"Thank you, sir," I said. "I will probably take you up on it."

I could see that my father was still not convinced.

"It's not like I am just going to sit around the house and play video games," I said. "I really intend to figure things out. I will get a job, I will get a place. I screwed up and I will make it right."

He seemed to accept it and reached out his hand. As I went to return the handshake, he grabbed me and gave me a big hug. Other than at the police station, I could not remember the last time we shared such an embrace.

After he let go my mother gave me a hug, and a big kiss on the cheek.

"I am sure you will figure it out," she said, tears welling in her eyes.

McCauley excused himself, he was going to get dinner with Caitlin before returning to Phoenix. My father asked if I was hungry, and I said I would be, but I was not right now.

"I just need a little time to myself," I said.

We made plans to meet up later. I watched them walk, thinking it was strange to see my parents together. When they were out of view I sat on the stairs and watched the shadows creep over the campus.

Anna sat down next to me and took my hand. We sat in silence for a second and when I turned to her she gave me a deep, hard kiss.

"I'm not going anywhere," I said. "I'm going to stay here in town."

I really liked this girl. She was the total package, but I could not help but think that there was an expiration date on this relationship. Eventually, she would realize I could not live up to the image she had created of me when she was a lovestruck teenager. Or maybe she would take that internship and wind up with a talk show of her own. She had brains and beauty and drive, and I was an unemployed, former mediocre college hockey player who had just been expelled from college.

But for now things were good and I could not dwell on the future and events that may or may not happen.

After a few minutes, we both stood up and walked hand-in-hand to our cars. Her car was on the first floor of the parking garage and we slowly made our way to it. I did not want to let her go, but while my educational career was over, she had a study group to attend. She gave me another kiss.

"I'll see you later tonight," she said, forcing a smile. "Maybe we can figure out a way to make you forget your problems for a while."

I waited for her to drive off before heading to my car. I made the slow climb up to the second floor of the parking garage. As I had been the past week or so, I was tired and was in no rush to go anywhere. I rounded the corner and saw someone standing by my car.

It was Rachel. She had her back to me and had her arms wrapped around her body. She must have heard my footsteps as she turned around as I approached. I could see the hurt in her eyes, but there was also anger. She looked like she had been crying recently, but there were no more tears.

I took another step towards and did not see the punch coming. I have to think she was aiming for my jaw but caught a large portion of my shoulder before grazing my cheek. Frustrated, she gave me a shove for good measure.

"You are such an asshole," she said.

I could not argue.

"Rach…" I started, but she held up a finger at me and shook her head "no." I knew not to continue

"Did you ever really care about me?" she finally asked.

"Yeah," I said, softly, barely above a whisper. "More than you know."

That made tears well up again in her eyes.

"Then how could you?" She cut herself off.

"I thought you were guilty," I said.

"How?" she asked. "How could you think I was behind all of this?"

I tried to explain about the phone and Harris, and all of the so-called evidence, that was obviously circumstantial. The words seemed weak when they were coming out of my mouth.

We stood in silence for a bit. I could not tell you how long it really was, probably less than a minute, but it seemed like an hour. She did not look at me, staring down at the concrete, chewing on her lip.

She finally raised her head, and manage a weak smile. She took a small step in my direction, and for a split second, I thought she wanted a hug. Instead, she threw another punch. This one connected with my nose. It rocked my head back and I dropped my phone and keys. There was a good chance it was broken, but at the very least my eyes filled with tears and it was with obscured vision I watched her march off.

I was bending over to collect my items when my phone rang. It was Ike.

"What's up super sleuth?" he asked. "I hear you may have some time on your hands. How would you like a job?"

Acknowledgments

T wenty years ago I started writing a book with a basic idea and one scene in mind. It wasn't the first book I started to write, and it certainly wasn't the last, but it was the project I kept coming back to. It was the story I kept having to make work.

The original concept was pretty simple, "how come there are not any Gen X detectives?" At the time I was working a job that afforded me a lot of downtime and I was doing a lot of reading, with mysteries and detective novels being a particular favorite. The one thing I noticed is that most of these characters were in their 30's and 40's. The standard was to skew older, not younger. The same thing seemed true on television (this was before Veronica Mars).

So I set about trying to write a Gen X detective novel. Of course, I had to figure out how someone in their early 20's would become a detective and who would hire a college-age kid to solve a mystery. It did not take long to come up with the basic plot, map out how it ended and begin writing. The first five or six chapters were written quickly, on yellow legal pads. Within a few months, I had the first 10-12 chapters done.

Then life happened. After spending a few years toiling in bad post-graduation jobs, I got my dream job and became a sportswriter. Suddenly writing wasn't what I did in my spare time, it is what I did all the time. I was writing for a weekly magazine, a website and had to update a message board. Eventually, that turned into writing for newspapers, websites, message boards, and social media. Along the line, I began co-hosting a radio show, doing spots on television, and got married and had kids.

I would work on the book when I had a chance, but those chances were few and far between. In the 20 years since I first started this project, I have written upwards of 10 million words, hosted a few thousand hours of radio, drawn over 400 webcomics, and made several dozen television appearances.

Last year I changed careers. I left journalism full time, and although I still write for a living, the demands are not as great. The 60-70 hour weeks were a thing of the past and I was able to spend more of my free time writing. My co-workers challenged me to come up with a passion project, and this book became that renewed obsession.

Over 20 years my Gen X detective novel has aged into a Gen Y detective novel, a millennial detective novel, and now he is either a post-millennial or a part of Gen Z, or both. When I first started writing the book I did not have a cell phone and the internet was accessed through the phone line. Over 20 years I have had to update the technology, the pop culture references, and a number of the local landmarks.

Over 20 years a lot of the details have changed, but the core story has not. The book I stated 20 years ago, is still pretty much the book you are reading now, the characters just have smartphones and no longer reference music of the 1990's. The ending has not changed, but some of the ways we get there have.

There are many I need to thank on this journey. First, I need to thank my parents for giving me the love of reading. They set the example by not only reading in front of me but encouraging me to read the same books they were and by rarely telling me "no" when I found something new to read at the grocery store newsstand or the bookstore.

It was my mom and dad who introduced me to characters like Dirk Pitt, Archie McNally, and Jake Lassiter, and a host of others who would all influence Eric Slade one way or another.

I have to thank my brother Canyon, who is more like Slade than I ever was or ever will be, who challenged me to follow my dream, though he was talking more about writing comic books than mysteries, but the principal was the same.

My Aunt Linda showed me it was possible to actually write, finish, and publish a book. She shared her love of good stories and good music, both of which are key to my process. She also served as an editor and was invaluable to the final product.

My Aunt Connie inspired me to think outside the box and never be afraid of a crazy idea. Her scary stories she told me as a kid challenged my notion of what could be, and taught me how to evoke emotions from people.

To my current co-workers at the Town of Marana who pushed me to finish the project. To Kim Bauer who was the first to read the thing from start to finish and would not let me stop until she knew what happened.

To John Schuster, my occasional writing partner, longtime radio host, and the guy I tasked with cleaning up my atrocious grammar and spelling. I owe you one (or many).

To my wife and kids, who were kind enough to go to bed at a decent hour so I could write way to late in the night. Finally, to my friends, some of whom will recognize themselves in these characters, and some I pray that don't.

About the Author

B rad Allis has been an award-winning newspaper reporter, a magazine editor, a college basketball and football recruiting analyst, illustrator, and a sports talk radio show host. He currently works in the communications division for a small municipality.

He is the author of Rebound, a webcomic with over 400 strips, and two unsold screenplays.

He is the father of twins- a boy and a girl- who sometimes let him write in between soccer practices, arguments over what shows to watch, and debates on whether chips are a healthy breakfast. He currently lives in Tucson, Arizona.

91602556R00156

Made in the USA
San Bernardino, CA
22 October 2018